Victoria Brown

Stealing Athena

DOUBLEDAY

New York   London   Toronto   Sydney   Auckland

Stealing Athena

A NOVEL

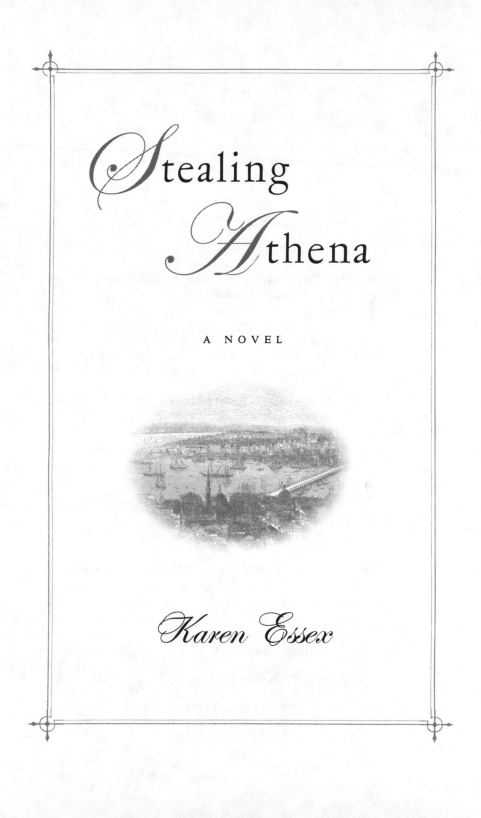

Karen Essex

DD
DOUBLEDAY

Copyright © 2008 by Karen Essex

All Rights Reserved

Published in the United States by Doubleday, an imprint of
The Doubleday Publishing Group,
a division of Random House, Inc., New York.
www.doubleday.com

DOUBLEDAY is a registered trademark and the DD colophon is a
trademark of Random House, Inc.

Book design by Nicola Ferguson

Library of Congress Cataloging-in-Publication Data
Essex, Karen.
Stealing Athena : a novel / by Karen Essex. — 1st ed.
p. cm.
1. Ferguson, Mary Nisbet, 1777–1855—Fiction. 2. Hamilton, Emma, Lady,
1761?–1815—Fiction. 3. Aspasia—Fiction. 4. Elgin marbles—Fiction. 5. Greece—
History—Athenian supremacy, 479–431 B.C.—Fiction. I. Title.
PS3555.S682S74 2008
813'.54—dc22
2007043859

ISBN 978-0-385-51971-7

PRINTED IN THE UNITED STATES OF AMERICA

1 3 5 7 9 10 8 6 4 2

First Edition

For Amy Williams

King Priam of Troy: Who put up this huge thing, this horse? What do they want with it? Is it religious or a means of war?

Sinon, the captive Greek: The whole hope of the Greeks in this war rested in help from Athena. But Diomedes and that criminal Odysseus dared to defile her holy shrine. After that, the goddess was against them. Her apparition rose three times in a flash of lightning, with shield and spear trembling. They built this horse to dispel the curse of stealing the image of Athena.

—Virgil, *The Aeneid*

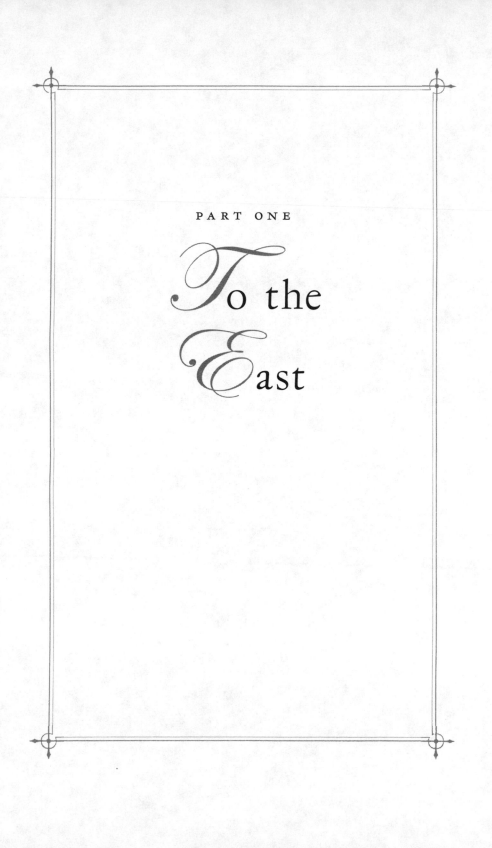

PART ONE

To the East

Aboard the Phaeton,

1799

MARY HIT THE FLOOR of the ship's squalid cabin with a dull thud, jolting her awake and sending a pain so sharp up her spine that Zeus might as well have hurtled a thunderbolt into her backside. She tried to breathe, but the fetid odors— dank wood; stale, trapped air; foul clothing; and the urine and excrement of humans and animals—were unbearable partners with the sickness that went along with the early stages of pregnancy. The stench she'd briefly escaped during her nap came rushing back in to claim space in her nostrils, and she gagged. Her head spun like scum swirling under a bridge, but that was nothing compared to the sick feeling in her stomach. On this voyage, sleep—when one could come by it through a good dose of laudanum mixed with iron salts, all dissolved with strong liquor in a syrupy elixir—was her only respite from the miseries of sea travel.

She reached up for the glass in which the good doctor had mixed the medicine, drained it, then stuck her tongue in deep enough that her face formed a suction as she licked up the last of the metallic-tasting liquid.

Her illness had been so relentless that Dr. MacLean—sober when on call during the day—had insisted that the captain dock at ports along the way to Constantinople. But the few times they had gone ashore, Mary had to walk through the cities with ammonia-soaked rags covering her nose and mouth, her only protection from the plague that raged through Europe's ports. The disease had been carried into the towns, the radical doctors of the day now professed (and Dr. MacLean concurred), on little rat feet. Apparently, as human passengers disembarked, so did the rodents, whose fur housed the fleas that transmitted the pestilence. These risky shore excursions were not even worth the temporary relief from the discomforts of the ship. The flea-and-lice-infested inns, replete with greasy, rancid food and the most inhospitable hosts, in which Mary and her party slept made conditions on board seem almost luxurious. Mary told herself daily (hourly, truth be known) that retaining her good cheer despite the horrible conditions boded well for her ability to meet the challenges she would undoubtedly face as a diplomat's wife in the strange and exotic land of the Turks.

These inconveniences were a small price to pay for the glorious life that awaited her. She was married to Thomas Bruce, Lord Elgin, the handsomest aristocrat ever to emerge from Scotland, who at the early age of two and thirty had been appointed Ambassador Extraordinary and Minister Plenipotentiary of His Britannic Majesty to the Sublime Porte of Selim III, Sultan of Turkey. At this crucial juncture of history, when England's alliance with the Ottomans against Napoleon and the French was in its infancy, her Elgin had been charged with nurturing the delicate relationship with the Sultan. Elgin's mission was to reassure the Sultan that the alliance with England would hasten Napoleon's defeat in the Ottoman territories, particularly Egypt. Everyone knew that Napoleon had invaded Egypt to gain a stronghold from which to take India away from the English. And that, His Majesty King George III had told Elgin, simply would not do.

Oh yes, Mary reiterated to herself for the hundredth time, it was the king himself who had suggested to Elgin that he apply for the ambassadorship to Constantinople. Which was why Mary now found herself—pregnant, dizzy, and nauseous—lying on the hard floor of the malodorous compartment of the *Phaeton*. She was there by the express and direct wish of the king. Surely the rewards would be worth the temporary agony.

Mary was leaning over on her elbow so that she could massage the pain shooting through her backside, when she heard Masterman approach. It could only be Masterman, her lady's maid, for the footsteps were not heavy like Mary's husband's or those of any of the members of his staff or of the ship's crew. Mary stared up at the horrid green curtain—her only means of privacy these many weeks—waiting for her maid to push it aside. "If it isn't the color of vomit!" Mary had exclaimed the first time she saw the curtain, for she had just performed that very act, riding out the first of many violent storms she was to face at sea. Now, the putrid green thing was swept aside, and Masterman peeked in, her eyes quickly moving from the empty cot to Mary struggling on the floor.

"I was thrown quite out of my cot," Mary said, answering the older woman's unspoken question. "Is there a storm?"

"The captain is taking advantage of a brisk gale to give chase. The earl wishes you to remain below."

"Give chase?" Mary bolted upright, shaking off the dizziness. "To French gunboats?"

"It appears thus," Masterman said dryly, standing aside and making way for her mistress. Masterman had been with her since Mary's girlhood and had long ceased to argue for practical measures. Why shouldn't the young, newly married, pregnant countess put herself and her fetus—firstborn heir to all manner of money, land, and titles—at risk of being struck by one of Napoleon's cannons? To mention the obvious would do no good. Masterman picked up Mary's robe and followed the younger woman out of the hole. When Mary recovered from her moment of excitement, she was sure to notice that she was wearing only a nightgown.

On deck, Mary felt none of the queasiness that had troubled her every moment during the voyage. It was as if the sea air, cooler than it had been for days as it moved across her face, blew away all her ailments—the asthmatic choking disease that she shared with her husband (which was how they knew that they were inalienably meant for each other); the morning sickness, which despite its moniker knew no time of day in her body; the unrelieved seasickness; and, most incurable of all, the loneliness she'd felt for her home and for her parents since the day she told them goodbye.

But all that be dashed at the moment as she balanced herself against a taut rope, making her way along the undulating deck as the *Phaeton* raced through choppy waters. She tried to ignore that the wind was hardening her nipples into uncomfortable little cones. She looked down to see them making a tent in the linen sheath and realized that she was rushing toward her husband and the ship's crew in a state of undress. She turned around to ask Masterman to fetch an appropriate garment when she saw the woman, not two paces behind, holding her dressing gown at the ready. Slipping into it, Mary turned toward the helm and nearly collided with two sailors, their arms full of shot brought from below, who were rushing toward the cannons.

On deck, the crew manned ten of the frigate's thirty-eight guns. Mary could see the American vessel that sailed with them for protection taking the lead. Nothing annoyed Captain Morris more than the fact that the American ship was faster than the *Phaeton*, but Mary was grateful that the swifter vessel could buffer their ship against the early rounds of fire.

They'd been fired upon before. Napoleon's gunboats dogged any English vessel on the Mediterranean, civilian or otherwise. Some weeks ago, off the sunburnt coast of Africa, a gunboat had taken them by surprise, its cannon fire rocking the sea. Mary had begged to stay on deck to observe, but Elgin virtually carried her below and held her on the cot while the explosions created chaos in the waters around them. The *Phaeton* was not hit directly, but Mary could feel the impact as the shot exploded just yards away, tilting the boat so far to one side that she ended up on the floor on top of her husband. Shaken, the two turned away from each other and regurgitated their barely digested lunches.

This time, she would not miss the action. She had just written to her mother that though the voyage was spent in sickness and fear, she was developing quite a new and wonderful character, a mature one that would serve her well in her future as ambassadress and beyond. She was unafraid; the excitement completely obfuscated the queasiness and dizziness, she could not help but notice. She was determined to witness firsthand whatever exchange of fire was about to happen. The sky was gray and foreboding, but the fresh air cleared her lungs, and she ran up behind her husband, threw her arms around him, and hugged him. He turned abruptly.

She loved looking at her husband. She had fallen in love with him the first time she saw him, what with his tall figure; his thick blond hair; his deep, intimidating brow; and his fine, aristocratic nose—not one of those thin little parcels that sat so unceremoniously upon the face, but a feature that bespoke of elegance and nobility. Not to mention his stately carriage that belied the more passionate elements of his character with which he'd been acquainting his young bride—his sexual appetites and expertise.

"What the devil, Mary? Get below before you're knocked into something."

"Not a chance, Your Lordship," she replied. She could tell by the look on his face that he loved, but wrestled with, the fact that his wife was the disobedient sort. She imagined that admiration and indignity were waging a battle behind those gorgeous blue eyes. She knew that he did not want to be seen by his staff, the crew, or the officers in their blue and white—all of whom were staring at the disheveled countess in her dressing gown—as a husband whose authority could be questioned. But he also adored having a wife who had courage.

The ship lunged forward, throwing her into his chest. "Oh, all right," he said. "But if fire is returned, you will go below. That is an order from your lord and commander."

"Yes, Your Lordship and Commandership," she said, with a touch of the saucy inflection she knew aroused him. "But if the gunboat is a danger, then why is it running from us and not attacking us as the last one did so unabashedly?"

"Because Captain Morris has taken this one by surprise and has gone on the offensive."

"But we are so far away!"

"That is the point of the American vessel, Mary. Protection. They will fire first, and take the first rounds. At least that is the present strategy."

"Are we to remain passive?"

"May I remind you that there are on board an ambassador on an urgent mission, his entire staff, and his beautiful wife, all of whom must be protected? May I remind you that you are a civilian? And a pregnant one? Will you please behave as the latter, and not as a boatswain or a gunnery officer?"

"What I should like to be at sea is my own master at arms, for then I would never confine myself below when there is action to be seen above."

Elgin shook his head, suppressing a smile before the ship lurched forward, sending the two of them into a pile of rope on the deck floor. Except for the guns, the ammunition, and basic supplies, the deck had been cleared in anticipation of attacks. Elgin grabbed the rope and held on to Mary so that she would not crash against the wet planks. He was opening his mouth to command her to return below, Mary was sure, when one of the officers lowered his lookstick.

"Messenger approaching the ship," the officer called out. Elgin rose, balancing himself with one hand on the rocking deck as he helped Mary to her feet. A gust of air hit her face as she stood, and she worked hard to regain steady breathing. If one of her choking fits took hold, Elgin would surely send her back to the miserable hole of a cabin, even if he had to carry her himself. For one brief moment she fantasized that that might not be so objectionable, given what usually happened whenever Elgin carried her into a bedroom, but she did not think that she could suppress her disgust at the cabin—or guarantee their privacy behind the flimsy curtain—long enough to make love. At any rate, Elgin's attention had already returned to the sea, where he directed Mary's gaze to a rower in a dinghy carrying what appeared to be an American officer toward them.

The crew waited impatiently as the officer made his way up the ladder and onto the boat; the men were certain that he carried with him orders for firing the guns. He conferred briefly with Captain Morris and his officers, and then approached Elgin. "Sorry for the alarm, Lord Elgin," he said. "The vessel we've been chasing is not a French gunboat at all but one belonging to the American navy. We shall have a peaceful afternoon after all." He bowed to Mary. "So sorry for the fright, Lady Elgin."

"Oh no, sir," Lord Elgin said. "No need to apologize to Lady Elgin. She adores a good round of cannon fire, do you not, my dear?"

"Yes, quite," Mary said. "I shall try to recover from the disappointment."

When the officer left them, Elgin turned to his wife. "Are you so disappointed to have averted danger? You did not like being fired upon the last time."

"That was the young Mary Nisbet," she said. "The one who grew up on solid and secure Scottish soil. Now that I am grown and a woman and a wife and the Countess of Elgin, I wished to try out my new bold character. I could face Napoleon himself if need be."

Elgin's face suddenly turned serious. "Then I shall enlist you in helping me to face my staff. They are very unhappy with the conditions on the ship—as are we all—and each, in his own insinuating way, has begun to ask that certain luxuries be afforded him once we are ensconced at the Porte. I must sit them down and make it clear that except for the salaries negotiated before we set sail, they are entirely on their own."

AS THE WINDS BEGAN to pick up and the skies darkened in anticipation of a storm, Elgin called his staff to a meeting on the deck, announcing that he wished to elucidate certain facts about the terms of their employment. "It must be stated clearly. Each of you is responsible for his own expenses while in my employ," Elgin said. "Which are to be paid either from your salaries or from your private funds, whichever is more agreeable to you."

Mary looked at the men's faces; each man seemed to be fighting to repress his shock at this news.

"But Lord Elgin—" began Mr. Joseph Dacre Carlyle, an earnest man somewhere in his thirties or early forties, Mary guessed. Carlyle was an orientalist from Cambridge who spoke and read Arabic. Elgin had hired the scholar as a linguist and communicator, and as a decipherer of the rare and ancient texts Elgin hoped to collect while in the East. But Carlyle had made it known that his true purpose was to distribute Arabic versions of the Bible to convert the Muslim heathens to Christianity. His idealism would now be tested, Mary thought as she watched him absorb Elgin's news.

Lord Elgin did not allow Carlyle to carry on with his protest. "You are undoubtedly aware of the very limited budget given to an ambassador of the Crown to outfit and run a foreign embassy," he said, "and I am afraid that neither Mr. Pitt nor Lord Grenville has seen fit to make an exception in my case." Elgin managed a forced little smile, but none of the men responded in kind.

Flanking Mr. Carlyle, and grimacing as severely, were Elgin's two secretaries, John Morier and William Richard Hamilton, both twenty-two years of age. Morier would be useful, having been born in Smyrna, but Mary knew that he did not admire her husband. She had overheard him complaining to Hamilton in hushed tones that Lord Elgin was parsimonious, "even for a Scot." Young Hamilton suffered aboard the ship more than the others owing to a limp resulting from an accident at Harrow where he was educated before moving on to Oxford and Cambridge. Now he revealed another cause for suffering. "But I brought only a few coins with me. I thought all expenses were to be paid. What am I to do?"

Morier looked pointedly at Hamilton, as if to confirm his prior assertion about Elgin.

"You must write to your families or to your bankers or to whomever you look to for your private funds," Elgin said.

Mary heard a groan rumble from the Reverend Philip Hunt, who sat to her left. Elgin had assured Mary that Hunt's excellent knowledge of spoken and written Greek and thorough familiarity with the classics would compensate for his uninspired sermons.

"He will know the history of the ruins we encounter," Elgin had said in London at their Portman Square home, where he and Mary had interviewed the men. He'd called Hunt "a crucial component of the mission."

After he was hired, Hunt had confided to Mary that he believed that his position with Lord Elgin in the prosperous and extravagant East would help him lay the foundation of a splendid fortune. Mary had thought this a naïve and unlikely ambition for a scholarly man of God. She could not imagine how he thought he might fulfill this ambition by giving sermons and examining ancient artifacts for Elgin. She pitied Hunt, who had embarked upon the mission with an enthusiasm that one would have thought more appropriate to the young puppies Hamilton and Morier. Now the proud Reverend Hunt had to not only adjust his grand ambitions but also ask his family for additional support.

Elgin's words inspired nothing in the room but a universal grimace, which sent his own little smile back into a fastidious pursing of lips with which he delivered the rest of his speech. Mary listened to her husband, thinking that while he did speak with conviction, his words were entirely too predictable: that representing His Majesty on foreign shores was not a mission for personal glory but an act of patriotism, and that one mustn't complain about one's sacrifices but must endure them in the spirit that had made their small nation a great presence in the world. "We few," Elgin said, "we happy few, we band of brothers assembled for foreign service, must agree to shed our blood *together*. Or so to speak."

The newlyweds had just seen a vigorous London production of *Henry V* and Elgin had been particularly impressed by the passion with which Mr. Charles Kemble had delivered Henry's St. Crispin's Day speech. But her husband was no performer. Poor Elgin continued, trying to rally his troops to go into the breech. He spoke of the sacrifices that he and Lady Elgin, two patriotic Scots, were making in the service of the united kingdoms of England and Scotland, a union barely a century old. He proclaimed his young wife's fortitude and commitment in making this dangerous voyage while in the family way. Of course he, being a gentleman and concerned only for her welfare, had offered to allow her to remain in the comfort of family while he sailed to Constantinople, or to refuse the post if that were her wish.

"But this valiant lady would hear of neither. Forgoing all that is familiar and dear, she would not send her husband off to distant lands without her by his side. I suggest that we emulate her graciousness and her spirit of sacrifice."

The men nodded in Mary's direction, but she felt no surrender from them. Elgin continued, elaborating on the urgency of their mission in the East. But he did not possess that quality of camaraderie that had made King Henry's vow that "he today that sheds his blood with me shall be my brother" convincing. These men knew that in Elgin's eyes they would never be his brothers. There was nothing in his words to give this away, but rather something in the demeanor that Mary knew made his staff regard him as stingy and cold. Besides, the reality was undeniable; given Elgin's title and his position and his wife's money, neither his physical person nor his pocketbook would feel the "sacrifices."

"I suggest you contemplate the extraordinary opportunity this mission brings you. That, and the number of men who would be most anxious to replace you should you find it impossible to continue in my service," he concluded.

Having said all that he was going to say upon the matter, Elgin stared frostily at his staff. His look and demeanor forbade any further comment from the men. Mary had seen this prickly side of her husband's disposition before. Perhaps this was the way that men must manage those in their service. She was grateful and flattered that Elgin was the sort of husband who wished to include his wife in these affairs, for her curiosity about his work was boundless and she wanted to be a full partner in his every endeavor.

Finally, Reverend Hunt looked up at the skies and declared in a sulky voice, "The rain begins." Then the staff went below to compose frantic requests for funds to their families that they might get into the post at the next port.

Hamilton took Mary aside. "Lady Elgin, I do not know if

my family will be able to compensate for Lord Elgin's thrifty economics."

Mary patted him on the arm. "I assure you that I will not allow you to starve in our service," she said, and this at least put a smile on the poor youth's face. "You shall be very comfortable."

"It's beginning to rain, Lady Elgin," her husband said. "You must go below."

Mary turned to her husband, who still wore on his face the stern expression that he used with his staff. She wished that the private face that she saw in their moments of happy familiarity would return.

"These are obviously not men of means," she whispered to him. "Can we not be more generous?"

"You are aware of the small and inflexible budget of six thousand pounds out of which we are to manage the entire embassy and ambassadorial staff? I suppose I should never have accepted this post. Diplomacy is notoriously a rich man's game."

"That is nonsense. You are perfectly suited to this post. The king himself thinks it so."

"That is true. And yet His Majesty did not see fit to augment the funds. No, Mary, I'm afraid that if you feel sorry for the men, you shall have to find it in your heart to be more generous on their behalf, what with your greater purse." His sweet expression returned, and he kissed her delicately on the forehead.

"I shall try, my darling," she replied, happy to have returned to the place of affection in which they held one another. She found it intolerable when the sweet bond of their intimacy was broken. She could be playful to the point of insolence in their private life, but in public life he was the superior one, and she, as his helpmeet, wished to please him.

As she went below, she overheard Reverend Hunt speaking to Captain Morris about the injustice of the situation. "Lady Elgin's father holds most of the land in Scotland; it's a well-known fact. And we are being asked to deplete the meager resources of our families to subsidize His Lordship's post!"

"Aye. The rich rarely give a black dog for a white monkey, my friend. It's the way of the world." Captain Morris sighed. "We all suffer the circumstances."

Apparently neither the captain nor the men believed that they were getting a fair exchange from her husband. It occurred to her, perhaps for the first time in her life, that this was the notion that prevailed among all subordinates, and she made up her mind to do what she could to mollify the disgruntled, and to help her husband succeed in his mission.

MARY HAMILTON NISBET HAD set her sights on Elgin the first time he came to tea. She had heard about him all of her life, of course, since their families were practically neighbors, two prominent families living on opposite sides of the Firth of Forth— the Nisbets in the green, seaside village of Dirleton at their expansive estate, Archerfield, and Elgin on the Fife side at Broomhall, the mansion he was building in place of the more modest residence he had recently torn down. He was known to all simply as Elgin. Thomas Bruce, 7th Earl of Elgin and 11th Earl of Kincardine, had not been called Thomas since the nursery, not since the day when, at five years old, he inherited the title.

Though she was already well acquainted with many of the details of his life, the two had never met. By the time Mary was born, in 1778, Elgin was away pursuing his education at Harrow, Westminster, and St. Andrews. As she entered Edinburgh society, attending the events that would naturally have thrown them together, he was reading law in Paris. They might also have met at court; Mary spent a great deal of time in London at Grosvenor Square with her grandmother, Lady Robert Manners, where she participated in all the festivities and rituals of the Season. Elgin's mother, Lady Martha, was governess to King George's granddaughter Princess Charlotte, and Elgin was no stranger either to London society or to the royal family. But Elgin was rarely in the city. After his studies in Paris, his mother was able to procure for him a military commission; he quickly advanced from the lower ranks and found himself in command of his own regiment, the Elgin Highland Fencibles. He had been elected one of the sixteen representative peers to the House of Lords at only twenty-four years of age, and by twenty-nine he held the rank of lieutenant colonel in His Majesty's army. While managing these precocious accomplishments, he was in service in diplomacy in foreign lands. Thus, it was a well-known, if heretofore unseen, entity who, on a brisk December 8, as the year 1798 was dying down into a cold, brown winter, suddenly invited himself to tea.

The Nisbets were not mystified by his appearance. Mary was just twenty years of age, the sole heiress to their various estates, and a beauty. Her curly raven hair, her pale hazel eyes, and her slim but curvaceous figure attracted every man who set eyes upon those assets. Mary's was not a rarified beauty, nor an ethereal one. She had the wholesome and unobjectionable healthy good looks of a pretty milkmaid, wrapped nicely in the body of the heiress to the largest privately held landmass in Scotland. More than physical beauty, she also had what her parents referred to as sparkle. They were a little afraid of this quality; they did not approve of any sign of flightiness in a young woman. Their daughter was confident, but for the most part she remained modest in the way she behaved in front of others. She did not have airs of conceit; however, she could be unapologetically alluring in the company of men.

Mrs. Nisbet had coached her daughter to converse with Lord Elgin upon light topics that could not be found offensive on the tongue of a young lady, but Mary ignored her advice. There was something about Elgin that called up Mary's flirtatiousness right from the start. While formal words were being exchanged and his hat and coat given to the footman, the two young people circled each other like beautiful, hungry animals at the same prey. But in this case, the prey was the other. Mary saw the alarm and disapproval in her mother's eyes, but she did not care. She'd been courted by many men in the last eighteen months—all eligible and all predictable. None had excited her in the way that she knew was possible, not from experience, but from her reading of literature and love poetry. She knew that she was not being foolishly romantic, only demanding. How could one spend a lifetime reading about the great passions without desiring to experience them in one's life? She knew that she was destined for marriage—respectable, conventional marriage. But why could not a respectable marriage be tinged with the kind of passion described by her favorite writers?

Here was Elgin, who looked at her with mirth in his eyes, which swept over the length of her body as he introduced himself. She felt herself shiver when his eyes returned to meet hers. Taking her hand and staring intently, he replied to their introduction with a single word: "Delighted." That solitary word and the way that he uttered it told her everything she needed to know about the impression she'd made upon him.

"How was it that you entered diplomatic service?" Mrs. Nisbet asked as tea was poured, though all of Scotland already knew the story. Mary's mother was a firm believer in giving a man as many opportunities as possible to brag upon himself.

"After I gave my first speech to the House of Lords, Mr. Pitt invited me to dinner."

"Dinner with the prime minister. Oh my. And you were such a young man. Isn't that exciting, Mary?"

"However did you cope, Lord Elgin?" Mary asked slyly, ignoring her mother's shocked look.

Elgin smiled at Mary's comment, but addressed her mother. "I was the right man at the right moment, Mrs. Nisbet. Mr. Pitt was rather desperately looking for someone to go to Vienna to make an alliance with Emperor Leopold II. Within twenty-four hours, I was appointed Envoy Extraordinary and on my way. I traveled for one year through Italy with the emperor until he died, but I'm afraid that I never convinced him to love Britannia."

"Perhaps in the future you will be more successful in convincing others to love," Mary said. She was engaging in risky behavior, she knew, but if Elgin was a man to reject a saucy woman, he was not the man for her. She also risked annoying her parents, but as she was their only child, she was sure that they would forgive her, and continue to love her. What did she really have to lose?

"She is joking with you, Lord Elgin," Mrs. Nisbet said. "Mary is known throughout Scotland for her sense of play."

"A charming quality, Mrs. Nisbet, and one that I appreciate." He did not look at Mary as he spoke. Perhaps he was seducing her parents, one at a time, before he returned to completing the deed with the daughter. Or perhaps he sensed that the daughter was already won.

"You are very gracious, my lord," Mrs. Nisbet replied, straightening her spine to sit even more erect than usual, which Mary knew was an indirect order to her to cease her insolence and emulate her mother's correctness. Mr. Nisbet, on the other hand, was not one to endure foolish wordplay when there were serious matters to be seen to. He stood, ostensibly to adjust the fire, which he did, before turning to confront Elgin. "After the unsuccessful mission in Vienna, you were sent to Brussels and Berlin, am I correct, Lord Elgin?"

Mary wished that her parents would strike a balance between her mother's solicitousness and her father's inhospitableness, but she also knew that it was a mother's duty to charm a suitable marriage prospect, and a father's duty to put that prospect through the rigors of interrogation, no matter how illustrious his title. Mr. Nisbet would never allow his daughter—and her fortune—to go to a frivolous man, no matter how many titles the man had inherited. And Mrs. Nisbet would never allow her daughter's impudence to ruin her chances with a good prospect for a husband.

"I was sent to Brussels to serve as liaison to the Austrian army. I chose it over Berlin so that I might return home from time to time to attend to my duties in the House of Lords. Eventually I was sent to Berlin anyway as British Minister Plenipotentiary to the Court of Prussia. I remained there three years. The mission, Mr. Nisbet, was successful for the English government, but the climate was less than satisfactory for my health, I'm afraid. I spent too much time in German spas taking the waters for rheumatism."

Mrs. Nisbet took the opportunity to turn the conversation once again in Elgin's favor. "I do not doubt your suffering, Lord Elgin, but despite your troubles, we heard from travelers that your German home provided shelter and entertainment for many an English and Scottish guest. You have a reputation as a generous and amiable host."

Particularly to the ladies, Mary thought. Elgin's conquests of foreign women were well known in Scottish circles. Rumors circulated that he had honed his ambassadorial skills on the nobility and the politicians, and his other skills on their wives and mistresses. Mary hoped that her parents were not privy to those rumors; Mr. Nisbet would never allow his daughter to marry a sexually profligate man. But she imagined that, at their advanced ages, her parents were too dignified to participate in such tawdry gossip.

"You are too generous in your compliments, Mrs. Nisbet," Elgin said. "I merely did my social duty, as would any gentleman."

From what Mary had heard, Elgin's duties were indeed of a broad range. Elgin had been friends with another envoy who eventually married one of Mary's dearest friends. The two girls spent many an hour gossiping over Elgin's foreign exploits, as delivered in vivid detail by the young husband, who had used the prurient details to titillate his reluctant bride in the bedroom. "He told my Harold that he discovered in Paris that he had a natural talent in the erotic arts," Mary's friend had confided. "Which he refined in the company of that city's wicked women!" But she added: "I could never repeat what I heard, Mary. You would never hold a good opinion of me again if you knew some of the things I allowed Harold to whisper in my ear!" Nothing Mary said could persuade her friend to reveal the specifics of Elgin's exploits with French women of ill repute. But her friend did continue: "In the Prussian territories, he turned his interests to married women and widows. Imagine!" This much Harold did divulge: Elgin grew to love the company of older women because, in his words, they did not swell, they did not tell, and they were grateful as all hell. Mary's friend had to explain the joke to her, much as Harold had had to explain it to his young wife, but once Mary understood the meaning, the two girls giggled until they were sick in the stomach and had to call for seltzer water.

"He sounds deplorable," Mary had said insincerely, for to her eighteen-year-old ears he sounded most intoxicating.

"Oh no. Elgin is a gentleman. Harold assured me that he would never, never ruin a proper lady."

Mary mused on these delicious tidbits of information as she watched the formidable Elgin attempt simultaneously to impress her father and to appear as modest as a gentleman must appear. Her amusement must have shown on her face.

"You find diplomacy amusing, Miss Nisbet?" Elgin asked.

"I am smiling because I am certain that in your more recent assignments, your ability to convince our foreign allies to love the English were improved. At least that is your reputation."

"She is joking again, Lord Elgin," Mrs. Nisbet said, this time, more sternly. But Mary did not care. She knew the cards she was holding, and it was a winning hand. She was as desirable a bride as Elgin might hope for. Though this was their first encounter, she felt already as if she knew the man, and knew that their liaison was meant to be. She was prone to presentiment and had been since girlhood. She knew in advance when grim news was to arrive with the post. She could predict with fair precision when a favorite mare would give birth to a colt. And she could predict at this moment that Lord Elgin was making up his mind to ask her to be his wife.

"Indeed, Mrs. Nisbet, I hope she is not joking at all," Elgin said, this time looking directly at Mary. "I should like to be thought *very* convincing in these matters, both now and in the future. But particularly in the present."

After passing this preliminary interview with her parents, Elgin called upon Mary several more times, arranging to be alone with her on various walks through the gardens of Archerfield, and taking her hand at opportune moments, helping her across rocky terrain by putting his arm around her waist and caressing her side as thrills coursed through her body. This fast courtship culminated in a visit to his home, which was under construction—and was the talk of Edinburgh and its surrounding countryside.

"I am working with the architect Thomas Harrison," Elgin said. "He has made his considerable reputation designing in the Greek Revival style, inspired by classical values and proportions, which he and I agree embody perfection in all aspects of art, architecture, and design."

In the carriage ride on the way to Broomhall, Elgin announced his plans. King George himself had suggested that Elgin apply for the position of ambassador to Constantinople, and it seemed that Elgin had received the appointment. Mary did not know how to react. Had Elgin been courting her for his own amusement, only to abandon her, leaving her embarrassed and disappointed when he went off to his new post? Elgin quickly allayed her fears.

"I intend to speak with your father, Mary, but I wish to know in advance whether you would be willing to leave the comforts of family and home to accompany me to the East."

He would not allow her to answer until he had elaborated on the importance of the post. Napoleon's ambitions were no secret. He intended to wrest India from the British, and to seize and control all trade routes to the East—the lifeblood of the English economy—and dismantle the Ottoman Empire, thus capturing a significant portion of the globe's resources in the name of France. The English economy would be in shambles, and the Crown would no longer be able to guarantee the safety and welfare of its people.

"The English must have an alliance with the Turkish sultan to rid the world of the Napoleonic menace," Elgin said. "It is my patriotic duty to do my small part in preserving the nation's security. I cannot envision any woman by my side in this historic endeavor but you, Mary Nisbet."

"But sir, it is so very far to go for a Scottish girl who loves her family."

She adored him, it was true. And she had craved romantic adventure since she was a young girl. Here was this glorious man offering it to her, replete with a proposal of marriage. Still, having to make a home for her husband, herself, and possibly their children in the Ottoman realm did seem a rather extreme road to take in life.

Elgin let Mary have her private thoughts. When they arrived at Broomhall, he helped her from the carriage, not speaking until they had walked through the grand entrance. As he guided her through the wide corridors of the mansion, he spoke confidently of their future, and of the brood of healthy, chubby children that would thrive in this home, with Mary and himself to guide them, and with their adoring grandparents nearby. All of these dreams would become reality as soon as he completed his foreign service.

"Mr. Harrison, my architect, has given me a passion for a secondary mission in the East, Mary, one that I believe is crucial to our country's future. The Ottomans occupy Greece, of course. Athens, that glorious beacon of democracy, the city of Pericles, is under the rule of the Sultan and governed by those who report to him. With the Sultan's permission, and with a team of scholars, artists, and craftsmen, I will be able to have first-rate casts made of Greece's most spectacular architectural ruins. Think of it, Mary. Every element of design, from the superb columns, cornices, and pediments of the temples to the great statues of the gods, and even ordinary household goods, can be copied in molds and drawings and brought back to England for our artists, architects, and craftsmen to study and to emulate. My embassy shall be known throughout history for its benefits to the Fine Arts in Great Britain. You and I together shall be responsible for elevating the taste of the nation."

Elgin's eyes were vibrant as he revealed his ambitions to his prospective bride. Here was the man whose romantic notions seemed to exceed her own. Hers were girlish and selfish, she knew, whereas his were designed less to bring joy to himself than to change the very world in which they lived. Elgin was striving to improve an important aspect of the British national character, infusing its already superior nature with a heightened appreciation of the highest level of art achieved thus far by man.

Yet it was almost impossible to think of leaving her family and all that was familiar and living in Constantinople. Mary was an only child, and her parents would be inconsolable at the loss. Her beloved grandmother was quite aged and might die while she was away. And to have children in such a strange land, known for its arcane medical practices and its uncontrollable smallpox outbreaks, seemed an adventure that even she was not prepared to undertake.

She voiced these concerns to Elgin, who listened carefully, taking the liberty of stroking her gloved hand with great concern as she spoke.

"We shall take the most esteemed physician in England with us in the event that you require his care," he answered. "I would never put you in danger, Mary."

He must have seen from her expression that she still harbored doubts, because he took a deep breath and continued: "When I was in Paris, I made the acquaintance of the American Benjamin Franklin. He was on a diplomatic mission for his country and he was a great inspiration to me, a young man aspiring to a career in diplomacy. His keenest interest, however, was the study of electricity. He contrived a device called the lightning bell, which chimes whenever lightning is in the air. He demonstrated this for me, and I believed the invention quite magical at the time. But he explained to me that lightning is naught but electrical current, that invisible and mysterious thing that is a conductor of energy."

Mary waited patiently while Elgin explained his interest, but she could not imagine what the element of lightning had to do with their future.

"When I am near you, Mary Nisbet, I feel as if there is lightning in the air. I feel a bell chime inside me, as if I am more alive than I was before you entered my experience. I feel the sort of current Mr. Franklin described make its way up and down my spine whenever we are close. You cause my heart to pound, Mary. I do not believe the days of my life shall be tolerable if you do not marry me."

He took her hand and put it directly over his heart so that she could feel its rhythm, which was rapid and strong. She squeezed his hand and said that he should speak to Mr. Nisbet as soon as possible, before her good Scottish sense overtook her passion for him.

But Mr. Nisbet proved to be unimpressed by Elgin's proposal, his ambitions, and his prospects. "He is in debt up to his brows fancifying that estate of his," Mr. Nisbet said, his tone threatening to crush Mary's hopes. "I do not care to think of my daughter's dowry going to pay a man's debts on an extravagance that is beyond his means. Elgin is just like his father, an impractical man with grand ideas and no head for business."

Indeed, it was well known that the late earl, after borrowing heavily to finance an ill-fated quarry business, had died leaving his wife and six children with little more than a celebrated lineage.

"Father, you are overlooking every one of Lord Elgin's most excellent qualities and focusing on the singular aspect not in his favor. Do you forget that it was King George who suggested that His Lordship apply as ambassador to the Porte? What might a man so regarded by the king not achieve? His mother, Lady Elgin, is beloved of the king and queen, and governess to little Princess Charlotte. He is titled. He is a favorite of His Majesty and Mr. Pitt. His ancestry traces directly to William the Bruce. How much more illustrious need a man be to be my husband?"

"He needn't be *illustrious*, Mary, but he should at least be *solvent*. Why is he throwing all of his money—no, the money given by lenders—away on turning out an estate fit for a king when he himself has no money?"

"Will Broomhall not be my home too? And the home of my children, and your grandchildren? Why must we consider his income at all? Is my father not one of the wealthiest men in Scotland, and am I, a brotherless child, not his only heir? The income from our lands exceeds eighteen thousand pounds a year. Why, that is three times the annual amount Elgin tells me has been allotted by the government for his embassy. Given the ways in which we are blessed, and the seriousness and excellence of the man who is asking for my hand, and the feelings I have developed for him in recent weeks, why should money be a consideration at all? What is money in the face of love? I would have thought that my happiness meant more to you than mere money. We Nisbets will never be without money, but oh how easy it would be to spend a lifetime without ever finding the kind of love—yes, love—that I have begun to feel for Lord Elgin."

"Such a gift for speech-making, Mary," her father replied. "Pity there are no *lady* ambassadors." Then he adjourned to his study.

Within a fortnight, however, and with her mother on her side, Mary easily won the day. Mr. Nisbet, ever the dutiful father and skeptical Scot, arranged to give the newlyweds a bond, the interest of which Elgin was free to spend as he liked. But Elgin could not touch the principal of Mary's fortune without Mr. Nisbet's permission. "A little insurance against his habits," Mary's father explained to her, and to Elgin privately, which mortified the bride.

A modest wedding was hastily prepared so that the bride and groom might take up residence in London, where Elgin would hire a staff to accompany him to Constantinople. Mary spent the weeks before the wedding in a fusion of anxiety and ecstasy over the enormous changes her life was soon to undergo. She felt both her happiness and her nervousness grow, finally reaching a crescendo as she stood before the altar. But during the wedding ceremony, her head started to spin and she fainted. Neither Elgin nor any of the attendants could reach her in time to prevent her from hitting the floor. As she regained consciousness, she wondered if she was having another of her premonitions. She feigned unconsciousness a moment longer so that she might have time to think. Was her spell some kind of warning? Should she reconsider this marriage, with its drastic move to a foreign land? But Elgin's deep voice, filled with concern, calling for a physician, and insisting that they must not continue until Mary had been examined by a doctor, dispelled her fears. Of course she would marry this man, who sounded as if his own life would end if any harm came to his bride. Besides, did she not experience portents of good events as well as evil? This was indeed a premonition, she told herself, but one of the exciting, love-drenched life she was to lead as the wife of her beloved. She heard her mother whispering about "a young girl's nerves on the brink of this great event," and Elgin saying that they must make certain that the cause was not something grave. Mary sat up and smiled, dismissing their fears. Nothing would stop her from marrying Elgin, who on his wedding day cut a gorgeous figure in his dress coat— a figure commensurate with his titles and aspirations. She stood slowly as her mother rushed forward to straighten her gown and veil. Bishop Sandford looked her dead in the eye, asking if there was anything she might have to confide in him. But she shook off her dizziness, stood upright, and became who she'd been destined to become: Mary Hamilton Nisbet Bruce, Countess of Elgin. No daughter of an untitled Scottish landowner, no matter how wealthy, could have made a better match for herself.

BY DINNERTIME ON THE *Phaeton,* following an after-noon of riding the endless lolling waves of the unsettled sea, Mary's ailments and miseries reclaimed residence in her body. She sat down with Captain Morris, Lord Elgin, and his still-morose staff to the nightly meal of salt beef, sauerkraut, peas, dried anchovies, and hard biscuits. The strong smell of the ship's timbers, swollen with salt water and mildew, hid any scent of the food. She could not judge whether this was good or bad because her appetite was low, as was the quality of the food before her, along with her energy on this rainy evening. She had spent her entire twenty-one years ac-customed to boundless vigor, but now, after another entire day of the "morning" sickness, she was so listless that it was difficult for her to cut her meat. The old fork with its flattened prongs was a perfect match for the dull knife. She would have liked to ask her husband to help her but did not wish to appear like a baby in front of the others. Elgin had fed her once before—honey-coated straw-berries and sweet bits of melon—but that had been in the privacy of their bedroom at home. She felt a stir in her body just from the memory of it. After he had put a few bites of fruit into her mouth, he sliced a berry in half, placing a piece upon each of her nipples, and eating them slowly away, licking the "plate" clean, as if devour-ing her very flesh. That would not do at this moment, of course, but it was nice to think about, even if it made her blush inexplicably. For one brief moment, a little thrill supplanted the nausea. Recall-ing those moments of ecstasy, Mary looked at her husband, but she saw no evidence of the lover he had been on that morning just two months ago.

He sat in perturbed silence, methodically sawing his meat with his knife, bringing the pieces stiffly to his mouth, and washing each mouthful down with a generous swig of wine—not the swill Elgin had feared would be aboard, but one of the fine selections from his own cellar. His staff, too, was silent. Mary thought that the sound of their jaws working the food, combined with the clink and clank of silverware, would drive her mad. She supposed that the men had the right to remain upset after Elgin's announcement that afternoon, but what good was it doing them or anyone else to remain in a sour mood?

She took stock of the sullen collection of men seated at the table. Despite her delicate and irksome physical condition, she speculated that it was her job to elevate the level of cheer, save the evening, and repair her husband's relations with his staff. Otherwise it would be not only a long evening, but a long two years in a foreign land. It was important to start off on the right footing with these men. Elgin was staking his reputation on the success of his mission, and after all, Elgin's success was now also linked to the happiness and welfare of herself and their yet-to-be-born children.

A guid word is as easy sayed as an ill ane. Mary's old nanny used to say it, and Mary had always believed it. She was one to bring up the spirits of her companions, not one to be brought down by them. She had inherited a combination of the Scottish pragmatism of her father and the English resolve of her mother. She was keen on the idea that a strong mind, enforced with a strong will, could overcome any difficulty. One could utterly control one's moods and feelings, even one in her miserable condition, living under the dreadful circumstances of this voyage. She also believed that if one were clever enough, beautiful enough, and *woman* enough, one *should* be able to control the moods and feelings of men.

"I see that we have all survived the afternoon's storms in our cozy quarters and are no worse for the wear," she said cheerfully, not knowing what she was about to unleash. Reverend Hunt, when he was not reading Greek or writing dull sermons, demonstrated his scholastic abilities in another way—by measuring and cataloguing any and all spaces that he inhabited. He decided to break the silence of the meal by sharing his recent discoveries.

"Given the weather and the lack of privacy, which precludes the sort of serious study I would have preferred to engage in, I measured the space below, Lady Elgin," he began. "The ship's cabin is composed of six compartments. The compartment we staffers share measures exactly twelve feet in length by six feet in width by another six feet in height, barely the height of a man, the average of which I am certain is no less than five feet and nine inches, or perhaps eight."

Mary looked to Elgin for a response. Normally the earl would have shivered with impatience during Hunt's mathematical homilies, but this evening he stared ahead and continued to drink, perhaps grateful that his wife had initiated any conversation at all, thereby relieving him of the duty.

"You must be speaking of Englishmen, my dear Reverend," Mary said. "Italians and Frenchmen are surely much smaller."

"Indubitably true, madam," Hunt replied politely. He was not to be deterred. "The space in question holds thirteen trunks—each with three locks—five beds coinciding with the five of us gentlemen who must sleep in them, three basins, three small nightstands, six hats, six great cloaks, five foul clothing bags, two pewter bottles, two umbrellas, cabin boys in and out preparing one's shaving necessities, and one ladder, tied to the wall with four knots, rendering it potentially useless in any emergency."

"A miracle of physical science that it all fits," said Morier.

"Indeed. But that would be admitting that it, and we, do fit, Mr. Morier."

"We tried to arrange for you to travel on Cleopatra's barge, Reverend, but it was confiscated by Napoleon in Egypt and unavailable," Mary said lightly, hoping to ignite any sense of humor the preacher might have. But he did not indulge her, though Morier and Hamilton did chuckle.

"The quarters are crowded because the deck must be kept clear in the event of attack," Captain Morris said, defending the conditions on his ship. Mary thought he must be weary of hearing the men complain about their quarters. "Isn't that correct, Lord Elgin?"

Elgin responded with a tilt of one eyebrow. It seemed that no one would be able to lure her husband into conversation this evening. Why was he still sulking? Mary wondered. The staff was not happy, but no one had shown signs of mutiny.

"The smallness is made even smaller when shared with the odors of chamber pots and filthy clothing," Morier said.

"That is why ladies carry perfumed handkerchiefs, Mr. Morier," Mary said, cajoling him. Morier was one year older than she, but she had no problem talking to him as if he were a boy. "I do wish gentlemen would try the remedy. They would find it ever so useful."

Elgin's eyes—narrow slits all during the meal—were now wide and glimmering with the wine he had been steadily ingesting. "Very amusing," he said to his wife, but without any conviction.

"What is a dinner without amiable conversation?" Mary continued. "We are all sharing the same cramped quarters. Let us be comrades-in-arms in the woes."

"Here, here," said Dr. MacLean, raising his glass, happy to have another excuse to keep drinking. The physician was joining them in a rare appearance. When he was not tending to Mary's needs, he spent all of his time in his compartment with a bottle of whiskey. Mary raised her glass and the others followed begrudgingly. Soon, however, they were lost in convivial talk, speculating on what lay ahead in Constantinople—the gorgeousness of the Golden Horn, the magnificent Hagia Sophia built by Emperor Justinian I, and the mysteries of the Sultan's seraglio, with its veiled beauties and multiple wives.

Mary seized the opportunity to build on the fellowship. After dinner, she insisted that Captain Morris play his harmonica. With the men clapping in time with the music, Mary sang old Scottish folk songs, none of which they knew. She invited the two young lady's maids she had brought as her personal attendants to accompany her in song. Their high, unsure voices became steadier as they sang the second and third tunes, harmonizing nicely with Mary, who had been developing her singing voice since she was a child. No one wanted the evening's entertainment to end, except Elgin, who had sat quietly as if no one else were in the room as he drank his brandy. He did smile from time to time, which made Mary think that he was enjoying the entertainment as much as his staff was but may have thought it unsuitable for an ambassador to join in the fun. By the time he was on his third glass of brandy, Mary noticed that her husband was no longer either distracted or amused, but was watching the men watch her. She could not read the expression on his face, but it was one that she had not yet been acquainted with. Finally, Elgin stood up in the middle of a song and announced that the evening must come to an end. Whether the men were genuinely touched by Lady Elgin's desire to make them happy, or whether they did not wish to return to their horrid sleeping quarters, Mary did not know, but it was past midnight when Elgin spoke up, and his words were greeted with some protestation.

"Lady Elgin is in a delicate way, and I do not wish her health to be taxed any more than it has been on this wretched voyage," Elgin said, whereupon everyone knew that no argument could or should be made against him.

As the staff and crew retired below, Elgin held Mary's arm, pulling her toward him.

"A word, Mistress Poll." It was not a question, and it was the first time he had used the affectionate name he invented for her without a trace of playfulness.

"Whatever my Eggy wishes," she said, using the name she had invented for her husband. She always had a secret thrill using such a silly name for such a formidable person as Elgin, and at present she was in an inflated mood for having so visibly raised the spirits of Elgin's staff. She turned her face to her husband's waiting to accept his praise, but none was forthcoming. She continued: "I had no idea that our sourpusses could transform into such jovial fellows. And all over the songs Nanny sang to me in the nursery. Are you not proud of your Poll?"

"Did you not think your behavior with my subordinates a bit festive?"

"It did not occur to me that singing songs meant to soothe babies to whining, grown men was unseemly."

"Then we must revise your concept of appropriate behavior for the wife of an ambassador in His Majesty's service."

Mary felt herself shrinking from within. "But I only tried to raise their spirits for your sake."

"My sake? What do their spirits have to do with me?"

"Do you not think that a contented staff will work more efficiently and with greater enthusiasm and loyalty than a disgruntled one? You must believe that my motivations were entirely on your behalf and for the sake of the mission."

Elgin took a deep breath and looked up at the sky. "I do not like the way that men look at you."

"And how do they look at me, my lord?"

"As if they are hungry."

"That is the way you look at me, Lord Elgin," she said, willing her own spirits to rise. It would not do to submit to this silly jealousy. Elgin had courted and married a spirited girl. The longer she knew him, the more intimidating he became. She must recover the saucy lass he had won. "That is why I married you. Because you looked at me as if you were the hungriest of them all."

He laughed, pulling her toward him. Thank God he laughed, because she was afraid that she might have angered him further.

"You are correct, Mistress Poll, and I am hungry still. I am hungry for so many things."

"What might I feed my lord that shall satiate him?" Mary asked coyly, nuzzling against him.

Elgin sighed. "An artist for the Greek project," he said flatly. She had hoped that he would ask for a taste of her lips or tongue or more. The nausea and choking during the voyage—in addition to the lack of privacy—had caused a state of disgust in her whenever she thought about sex, but now the sea was calm and the darkness enveloping them gave the illusion that the two of them were the only people in the world. She wished he would take her into his arms and kiss her while they had the chance, not begin another discussion of replicating the artifacts of Greece.

"My mind will not rest until we have hired an artist to make the illustrations we need. Damnation to Bonaparte. He not only raped Italy of all its treasures, but of its artists as well. He courted them. The ones who did not leave Italy with him had to flee the country because they had cooperated with him. No one is left! A good illustrator is nowhere to be found."

"Is it absolutely necessary? Why can we not make use of the craftsmen who will make the molds? An artist is going to be a great expense."

"We might have had Mr. Turner. He is the only English artist worthy of the mission."

"Mr. Turner holds an opinion of himself worthy of Mr. Romney or Sir Joshua Reynolds. His price was absurd." Mary thought Mr. J. M. W. Turner an insolent young puppy. They had interviewed him in London, but he'd demanded twice the salary that Elgin had offered, and then balked when he understood that he was also to give Mary painting lessons. He had behaved in a very conceited manner, Mary thought, for a man just twenty-four years of age. She was delighted when Elgin informed him that he would not be hired. "We are better off without Mr. Turner."

Elgin backed away from his wife, one hand on his hip and another on his brow. He looked like an actor, she thought. He was certainly handsome enough to appear on the stage.

"Napoleon took a staff of one hundred sixty-seven artists and scholars to Egypt, and I must make do with these few grumbling men. I cannot abide the lack of foresight that Lord Grenville has shown. He refused even the most meager sum to help pay for the art campaign. The state of the arts in Britain will be an embarrassment compared to that of France."

"I did not realize that we were in competition with Napoleon himself," Mary said.

"Not we, Mary, but our nation. A great empire must produce great artists in order to build great monuments. The Greeks knew that, as you will see."

Sometimes Mary thought that her husband believed his campaign to improve the arts of Great Britain more important than the ambassadorship, which seemed to her an overwhelming task in itself. Elgin was charged with persuading the Sultan to open trade routes and to establish a postal station at the Red Sea, and with a thousand small things, in addition to keeping the Ottoman

Empire on good terms with Great Britain. She had complained to her mother, allowing herself to wonder aloud if Elgin's judgment was correct in further burdening his ambassadorship with these grandiose plans to have all of ancient Greece copied for the benefit of the English arts. She had been excited about these ambitions until she realized that once the government had refused to fund them, Elgin thought it was up to her to provide the money. The costs would be enormous. They would have to pay the salaries of a crew of artists to live and travel throughout Greece to paint, draw, and cast the colossal monuments of that country. Transportation alone for the men and the materials would cost a fortune.

"I may have a wealthy father, but I do not have the resources of Napoleon!"

Mary had shared her concerns with her mother, who delivered a surprising perspective. Mary had thought that her mother would bring Mary's concerns to Mr. Nisbet, who would have a sobering talk with his son-in-law. Instead, Mrs. Nisbet told Mary that it was now her job to help her husband become the great man he aspired to be. She owed it not only to Elgin, but to herself and to her children.

"A smart wife completes her husband's ambitions," Mrs. Nisbet had said. "His fortune, his reputation, and his legacy are now yours."

Those words loomed large in Mary's mind. Her mother knew what a woman's duties were. Mr. Nisbet had thrived inside his marriage, and as a result, Mrs. Nisbet and Mary had too. She must remember at all times to be the good and supportive wife her mother had groomed her to be.

"We must dock at Palermo, Poll," Elgin said. "I would like to consult with Sir William Hamilton, one of the world's great antiquarian scholars and collectors. He will advise us correctly, I am sure."

Mary recoiled from Elgin. "Are you suggesting that we stay in the home of a *courtesan?*" It was the most polite word she could conjure in the moment. Sir William's notorious wife, Emma Hamilton, was simultaneously Admiral Lord Nelson's mistress, and the three of them were living under some strange arrangement in Sir William's Sicilian palazzo, where the lovers were known to cavort under the aging husband's nose. "Unthinkable! What would my parents say? And your mother?"

"We are married now and we must be our own persons and not bother so much about what the previous and more conservative generations think of our behavior, Mary. I have a mission to fulfill, and you are my wife and must assist me."

"I do not think it wise or proper to associate with that class of female," Mary said, feeling the indignation rise.

"Sir William is a gentleman and England's long-standing envoy to Naples, and Admiral Lord Nelson the premier hero of Britain. I do not think it unseemly that we visit with men of that caliber. Sir William and his wife are exiled from Naples at the moment, along with the Neapolitan king and queen whom the French chased away."

"But that woman!"

Elgin laughed at Mary. It was almost a sneer, she thought, his look mocking her protestations. He took her chin into his hand and with his other arm crushed her against his chest, holding her tight so that she could feel his arousal. "Mrs. Hamilton merely enjoys in the open that which you only acknowledge in the dark," he whispered into her ear. She wanted to rebuke him, to repeat the rumors that Emma Hamilton had worked her way up from a scullery maid and a streetwalker to marry into the aristocracy and take as a lover a war hero who was regarded as a national treasure.

Gossip held that Emma's first rich lover, the playboy Sir Harry Fetherstonhaugh, sloughed her off on the more stern Sir Charles Greville, who got tired of her expenditures and traded her to his wealthy uncle, Sir William Hamilton, in exchange for debt relief. How could Mary possibly agree to be in such company? But she knew that what Elgin was saying had a certain spirit of truth, at least in this moment, so she gave in to his embrace, letting him lift her face so that she could kiss him, taking his wet, brandy-laced tongue deep into her mouth, and abandoning any concern of being seen. Perhaps she had a bit of Emma Hamilton in her, as Elgin was suggesting.

He let her lick and suck on his tongue, which he knew she liked, and then took her by the hand, leading her to where the night sky met with the darkness around them in the shadow of the sail, sheltering them from the sight of the ship's lookout. He pushed her against something hard and cold, which she quickly realized was one of the ship's cannons. He pulled her dress and chemise high above her hips, and she felt the clammy sea air hit her thighs. The unfamiliar feeling of the wet night air made her tremble.

"Will we be seen?" She thought that she should at least, in the name of decency, raise the possibility, but Elgin answered by slipping himself inside her so quickly that she gasped. He covered her mouth with his hand, pushing himself deeper and deeper into her, but slowly now, patiently, waiting for her to rise to his level of excitement, rocking in perfect rhythm with the ship as it lolled over the sea. She was losing herself in the motion when she began to worry if the force of his thrust would harm the tiny unborn creature growing inside her. But she remembered that one of the old cooks at Archerfield used to joke that all ten of her babies had been born with sperm on their heads. Surely the babe would be safe, she thought, as she wrapped one leg around her husband and slid into that empty space where nothing else existed but her pleasure.

The town of Palermo,
on the island of Sicily

FOR THREE HOT AND seemingly airless days, they sailed toward Palermo without sight of shore. The morning after the erotic interlude, Mary, mortified by the lustful act in the ship's shadows, clothed herself most primly and attended Sunday services on deck. The sailors, dressed in their best, showed no sign of having witnessed the nocturnal antics of the ambassadorial couple, but listened with great decency and attention to Reverend Hunt's sermon. Mary, too, listened, with feigned concentration. She was ill again, reduced pitifully from the glory of the previous evening, having spent the morning gasping in her quarters, nauseous and dizzy, while Masterman bathed her face with vinegar water. Mary did not know if she could survive the service, but felt that she had to make amends to God for last night's brazenness.

After two more punishing days spent in her quarters, the ship finally docked, but into weather yet more stifling than what they had experienced at sea. The thermometer read ninety degrees at seven o'clock in the morning, and when Mary emerged on deck, the heat hit her face as if she'd stepped into an oven. Captain Morris complained that Sicily was the only place where he ever was plagued by rheumatism. In her condition, would she be able to tolerate a climate that defeated a rugged sea captain accustomed to every discomfort? Why had she insisted upon accompanying Elgin? She should have stayed at Archerfield and spent her pregnancy being cared for, and then joined him when the baby was old enough to travel. She was imagining herself at Archerfield, sitting under her favorite sycamore's dome of shade in the fresh air wafting in from the Firth, sipping tea with her mother, when she was brought a message from "Her Ladyship, Emma Hamilton."

As she read the note, Mary felt her ire rise. " 'Her Ladyship,' " Mary began, waving the letter and inflecting her speech with as much sarcasm as her diminished spirits allowed her to conjure, "sends her respects, with regret that she cannot greet us today for she is 'sent for by the king.' "

Mary lowered her voice so that only her husband might hear her. "I wonder, is she *his* mistress too?"

Elgin shrugged.

"She will do us the honor of calling tomorrow morning on the ship." Mary fumed. "How dare she? It is against all protocol to neglect to meet the ambassador and his family. It is rude and inhospitable."

Elgin's look made her conscious that she was overreacting. Rather than concede, she decided to defend. "They say that 'Her Ladyship's father was a blacksmith in the coal mines. I would not be surprised. Ill breeding always demonstrates itself in the end."

"I do not disagree with you, my dear, but a message has also come from Sir William offering us his home for lodging," Elgin said. He looked to Mary as if he were about to accept the invitation. "In your pitiable condition, you would be better on steady ground in a comfortable palazzo, no matter how wicked the hostess."

Did her husband think that because she made daring love with him in the darkness she would stoop so low? He had implied last night that she and Emma Hamilton were of the same nature—one overt and one covert in her desires. Because Mary was anxious for his love and to please him, she had not protested. She must reorient his thinking now.

"This good Christian girl will not stay in the home of a strumpet. Character must prevail over comfort, Elgin."

"As you wish. I will send Duff out to search for more suitable lodgings. But if he is unable to find them, be prepared for another long night in Hades."

"I would prefer to spend one night in Hades rather than the eternity to which I would be sentenced for sharing a roof with that woman."

Mary fired off a curt reply telling Lady Hamilton that Lady Elgin would not be receiving any guests on the ship, but might encounter her this evening, as she intended to disembark. "And do not shrink from demonstrating my peevishness when the missive is delivered," she told Duff.

The next day, when Mary was introduced to her quarters in Palermo, she wondered if God was seeking further retribution, either for her nocturnal indiscretion with her husband on deck or for her reluctance to imitate Christ's charity toward prostitutes. The ancient, dilapidated palazzo was to be shared with their entire staff. The grand salon, though spacious, was home to dirty plaster, broken-down chairs, and tables with no tops. Upon entry, Reverend Hunt began to pace off its dimensions, hands behind his back, taking deliberate, measured steps. "The room is seventy-six feet long and twenty-five feet wide," he said. "I estimate the ceiling height at twenty-two, perhaps twenty-four feet." He stared at the winged, painted putti hovering above as if they held the answer to his speculation.

Mary sighed. "Reverend, please go measure the kitchen, for that is where I am afraid you shall sleep this evening."

They had carried their traveling beds from the boat because the palazzo, despite its lavish dimensions, had none. Once magnificent, with finely painted ceilings and great gilded mirrors on the walls, the home seemed long abandoned by its owners. Dust covered every surface, gathering on Mary's skirts as she swept along the tile floor, trying to set up a comfortable room for herself and Elgin. She watched the particles of age-old dirt fly into the air, illuminated by the sun shining through the tall windows; she feared that the dust would bring on her chokings, which inevitably brought on vomiting, which brought on headaches. She made a quick promise to God to be more charitable in the future if He would spare her for a few evenings so that she might get some much-needed rest.

Which was how she found herself—having accepted an invitation to dinner from Emma Hamilton—standing at the door of Sir William Hamilton's bizarre Sicilian home, Palazzo Palagonia, a vast, rambling mansion decorated with a jumble of grimacing gargoyles and unidentifiable monsters that Mary was sure anticipated the iniquitous happenings inside.

"Conspicuous indication that the devil resides within," she whispered to Elgin, as an elderly woman in a faded bonnet and what looked to be little better than an old white bed gown over a black petticoat slowly opened the heavy wooden door. Her hunched shoulders were draped in a tatty black shawl. Mary was stunned when the woman announced herself as Lady Hamilton's mother.

"She employs her mother as a servant?" Mary asked Elgin.

"They say she uses Admiral Lord Nelson as a servant. Why not her own mother?" Elgin whispered back.

They were ushered into a candlelit parlor where several guests had already been seated, and informed that they were to be treated to a performance of the "Attitudes," the dramatic enactment that had made Emma Hamilton famous throughout Europe. "This is more than we bargained for," Mary said to Elgin, afraid now that she was going to be forced to witness something that no amount of prayers or Sunday services might amend. But Elgin was smiling, nodding at Lord Nelson as if the two were old friends. Did he really expect her to sit through one of Lady Hamilton's erotic performances?

Apparently he did, because he ushered her past a group of musicians to a seat and sat next to her, putting a firm hand on her arm. "I am in the Foreign Service, Mary," he said to her. "I must submit to whatever entertainments are provided. And you are my wife and you must do the same. You will see stranger things than this in the land of the Turks, and I will not allow you to run away like a skittish girl."

"As you wish," she replied, and focused her attention upon Lord Nelson.

Strange to think that the diminutive, one-armed, and apparently one-eyed creature before her was the same hero who had inspired the admiration of a nation and ignited the romantic imagination of virtually every woman in England. His hair was unruly and of a strange color, somewhere between carrot and ginger, with coarse gray strands running through it. He was unreasonably short, so short that he looked like a child in his chair.

"Why, I believe he is even shorter than his adversary, Napoleon," Mary said to Elgin. "And I cannot tell whether he has one eye or two."

The visible eye was cloudy and rheumy, and the other was shut, whether by infection or the absence of an eyeball she could not tell. Nelson was missing a few crucial upper teeth as well. He looked particularly horrid in comparison to the handsome Elgin, but Mary was not even certain that she would have chosen him over the elderly but elegant Sir William, who sat next to him. Sir William was tall and lean and had a pleasant face that still held a shadow of his younger self despite the fact that he was in his mid-seventies.

His hands were rather crippled and craggy, but at least he still had both of them.

The chatter in the room came to an abrupt halt. Everyone's eyes turned to the drapes made of swirls of scarlet and violet silk, flanked by two antique-looking columns. Upon the shorter column sat an ancient Roman urn. Suddenly a tall woman with ebony skin and a turban piled high upon her head and a cuff of gold around her neck dashed into the room with long gliding strides and whisked the curtain aside, revealing a voluptuous figure draped in purple, huge eyes turned upward, arms flung dramatically to the sides. The woman was even taller than her dark-skinned accomplice. Her lush raven hair rippled in waves over an abundant white bosom, but was purposely positioned, it seemed to Mary, to cascade along the sides of her breasts so as to not interfere with the overflow of cleavage. She stood still as a statue. A violinist picked up his instrument and sounded a mournful note, but all eyes remained riveted upon Emma Hamilton.

She was not young, Mary thought with satisfaction, and was perhaps a little fat. But as Emma began to move, taking from the accomplice a sheer cloth and draping it over her face, Mary found herself rapt, following each fluid movement. Emma picked up the funerary urn from the column. Two small girls appeared, and with each grasping Emma's flowing robe as if clinging to a mother, the three began a solemn procession through the seated audience, the children cowering as Emma moved them along, and she staring into the faces of her spectators with a mixture of ferocity and fear.

"Agrippina!" shouted one man. Emma raised an approving brow at him, but did not break her stern countenance. She moved soundlessly, but her lips looked as if she were miming a hiss.

"She is returning the ashes of Germanicus to Rome!" exclaimed another.

It was not mere performance, but parlor game. "Look at her face," a woman whispered. "She knows her husband has been poisoned."

Some people gasped as Emma confronted them with her eyes.

"Upon seeing Agrippina with her children and her husband's ashes, a single groan arose from the multitude," someone intoned.

"So wrote the historian Tacitus," added Sir William.

Satisfied that her character had been identified, Emma whirled around and made the return voyage through her audience. She placed the urn back on the column and the children disappeared behind the curtain. Sinking low into a pile of fabric and props, she emerged wrapped in a white outer drape, her hair crowned with a wreath of fresh ivy. She stood slowly as if in a state of delirium, though her movements were graceful and seamless. The dark-skinned woman appeared, placing in Emma's hands a coiling snake. A few of the ladies made audible noises, apparently thinking the creature real, but Mary, from her vantage point, saw that it was a replica, though lifelike.

Emma raised the thing above her head and began to sway, first slowly, and then faster, not to any music but to some internal rhythm. Her hips rolled in slow, mesmerizing circles, which Elgin, Mary could not help but notice, followed with his eyes. One of the musicians picked up a flute and began to play a slow, low tune that slithered into higher and more frantic reaches as Emma twirled in a circle, her dazzling hair floating behind as she whipped around.

"A bacchante!" "A maenad!" Several people guessed the panto-mime at the same time, pleased to display their knowledge.

An ingenious parlor game, Mary thought. No wonder the woman was so popular. She entertained the audience and made them feel not only intelligent but involved in the performance.

And no wonder all the great portraitists of England and France had vied for this muse. The gossips would have one believe that a woman like Emma traded on providing easy sexual services that a more respectable woman would not offer. But Mary saw now that it was more than that. Emma embodied an authentic classical grace, but unlike the statues from which modern man had formed his appreciation for the ancient arts, Emma was flesh and blood, alive and sensual. Here was a modern woman bringing the qualities for which the ancient statues were praised into living form, and doing so with graceful ease. Mary now made sense out of the rumors that poor Mr. Romney, after having painted Emma so many times in the poses of the most beautiful and memorable women of history, was half out of his mind with lust for her. Emma represented not merely one woman but—to a man, and especially to an artist—all women.

Emma's body seemed to unravel from its core as she twirled and flailed, giving in to the frenzy of the Dionysian ritual. As she succumbed to the thrall of the pagan god, she captivated every man in the room, holding them all in the spell of her erotic offerings. Sexuality is its own witchcraft, Mary thought. Why must highborn women be confined in their behavior when what men truly seem to desire is sensuality unleashed? She could not resolve the contradiction, but she understood the power that Emma Hamilton held over these powerful men.

All eyes followed Emma as she finished the dance of the maenad, shedding the white robe and slithering into a sort of cocoon on the floor. The black woman draped a cloth of shimmering gold over one of Emma's shoulders, and in what seemed like only a few seconds, Emma stood again, completely transformed, wearing a crown in the shape of an asp. The rosy cheeks of her bacchanalian celebrant had gone stark white. Now she was entirely solemn. She still held the snake, which she turned toward her breast.

"Cleopatra!" Several people guessed it at once.

" 'Age cannot wither her, nor custom stale her infinite variety.' "

The same might be said of Emma, Mary thought. Infinite variety, indeed. What would it be like to be unshackled from the conventions of society with its strict customs and manners, free to play the muse to men?

The black assistant fell upon her knees, begging with outstretched arms, while Emma stoically looked away. With her accomplice clutching at her feet, Emma put the snake to her breast, throwing her head back, feigning great, searing pain, and then falling slowly, like silk itself, to the floor. The other woman took the snake from her mistress, put it to her own neck, and fell promptly as if dead upon Emma's prone figure.

Silence. Then applause.

"*Brava! Brava!*" shouted the Italian guests, who were soon joined by Admiral Lord Nelson, who leapt to his feet. Sir William slowly struggled to stand, rubbing his hip with one hand as he tried to clap with his other.

Emma rose majestically, like Aphrodite being born out of the waves. She stood tall, taking in the applause and shouts of approval before sinking into a low curtsey, so low that her luxuriant hair almost touched the floor. Then she disappeared behind the curtain before the clapping stopped.

"There's a fine woman for you," Elgin said, still clapping his hands. "Excellent flesh and bones."

"Yes indeed!" Mary whispered for Elgin's ears alone. "A real whapper!" She was not sure she had ever before said out loud the nasty slang word for a loose woman. Was Emma Hamilton's transgressive behavior influencing her?

Elgin smiled. "Did you find her performance vulgar?"

"Of course," Mary replied, sounding to her own ears a bit too haughty. The performance *was* vulgar. But it was many other things as well, which Mary could not quite put words to at this moment. She realized that she found the notorious Mrs. Hamilton as fascinating as she found her repugnant.

Emma reappeared at dinner, wearing what all the ladies' fashion magazines were calling Dress à la Nile. Her earrings were big gold anchors. Not unlike one of her costumes, her dress was a loose, white satin gown, draped and flowing, bound just above the waist with a ribbon. She appeared to wear no stays. Loose flesh, loose woman, Mary thought. She did not know whether she could walk about in decent company with her body unbound. And yet Emma did not seem to have a problem with her freedom. She wore flat-heeled slippers, but she was still taller than any woman in the room. A gold and white triangular shawl embroidered with the words *Nelson* in one corner and *Victory* in the other was draped loosely about her shoulders, and she was graciously soaking in her guests' compliments for her performance.

She was pleasant, Mary had to admit, aware that Emma was refraining from suggestive eye contact with Elgin—though Mary thought it was causing the seductress much pain to have such a hand-some and highborn man in her presence without being able to cast her spell. Emma begged Mary to take an apartment in the couple's palazzo, where Her Ladyship and Sir William would see to it that she had complete privacy and every comfort and service that they could provide "in these strange circumstances in which we find our-selves, exiled from our Neapolitan home." Determined that she would honor her vow not to share a roof with "That Hamilton Woman," as the gossip magazines called Emma, Mary politely declined.

"The queen and king desire your presence tomorrow at the rowing matches. The royals are quite anxious to make your acquain-tance, Lady Elgin," Emma said. "But please do not bother about your dress. We are very casual here away from the formalities of the court at Naples. I shall wear the simplest of morning dresses."

"Will the queen not take it as a sign of disrespect?" Mary asked. She would be relieved to wear a light dress in the horrible Sicilian heat, but for the sake of Elgin's prestige, she did not wish to make an unfavorable impression. She particularly did not wish to be pre-sented to the royals by Emma, but Lady Hamilton was the wife of the envoy to their court. Mary hoped that the king and queen would not confuse obedience to protocol with approval of Emma Hamilton.

"Oh, no!" exclaimed Lady Hamilton. "I shall hardly bother to do my hair."

Soon after dinner, Mary and Elgin departed, leaving Sir Wil-liam asleep in a chair by the fire, and Lord Nelson hanging on his mistress's every word and gesture. An uxorious, lovesick puppy, Mary laughed to herself, and hardly befitting the role he carried in the public eye.

DUPED. TRICKED. Deceived by that Jezebel. Why did low-class females always, no matter what opportunities and indulgences they were granted, inevitably live up to the wickedness that the highborn assign to them?

The casual rowing match to which Mary was invited by Emma

was, in fact, a formal occasion, attended by every grandee on the island of Sicily. The queen had welcomed Mary and Elgin, giving them places of honor in her private stand. Mary was also presented, with every dignity and honor, to the three princesses and the king. It should have been a festive and triumphant occasion.

Except that while Mary was in a simple cotton day dress, Emma Hamilton showed up in a fine gold and colored silk gown worked over with diamonds and every type of jewel. The queen and the princesses were turned out in fine dresses sewn through with thousands of pearls. Mary, horrified, apologized to the queen, who would not allow her to speak of the indiscretion.

"Mrs. Hamilton advised me to dress simply," Mary said to the queen, perhaps indiscreetly. But she would not allow herself to be thought so provincial that she did not know what costume was proper for such an event. "I must be allowed to return to my quarters to change clothes."

"We will not hear of it," replied the queen. "We are delighted with your presence and we will not hear you speak of it! Is that not correct?" she asked the king, who agreed that Mary should not bother about her clothes but enjoy the day.

They seemed genuine enough. Mary now understood how Emma Hamilton garnered so much attention; she designed every event to be a theatrical presentation starring herself. Mary despised Emma, to be sure, but she understood that there might be a lesson worth learning from her. Emma certainly knew how to captivate men, though Mary chose to undercut Emma's powers when she spoke of her with Elgin.

"Her lovers are Sir Old Body and Sir Maimed-A-Lot," Mary whispered in Elgin's ear.

"Why Mary, 'tis a pity you were born a good Scottish girl and not someone who could contribute to *Town & Country* or *Bon Ton Magazine*," Elgin laughed. "For I do believe that you can sneer with the best of them when you wish to."

All day long, Mary noticed that the queen and king made a great fuss over Emma if she was in the presence of Lord Nelson.

Elgin explained that her influence with the great man earned her the attention.

"Even so. Sir William and Lord Nelson and that woman are the three biggest dupes I have ever laid eyes on," Mary said, not about to give voice to her own growing fascination with Emma Hamilton. "They think they're duping the world, but they are fooling no one but themselves. She flaunts her intimacy with the queen with even more transparency than she flaunts her affair with the admiral. And the queen, I have heard through the infallible gossip of servants, laughs very much at her to all the Neapolitans. The woman deserves nothing better."

Mary was furious enough to refuse to accompany Elgin to a final meeting with Sir William, but after being assured that Emma Hamilton had gone to the country—which Mary guessed was a euphemism for running off somewhere with Nelson—she agreed to "take a turn in Sir William's library," as Elgin had put it.

"Is not your home a lonely one when the lady of the house is away?" Mary asked Sir William provocatively as he ushered her and Elgin into his "much-reduced collection of books." The majority of his manuscripts were either still in Naples or, with a great many of his vases, statues, and other antiquities, had sunk to the bottom of the sea in the transport. Mary could not tell whether it was the loss of so many of his treasures, the loss of his health, or the loss of his wife to Lord Nelson that caused him to seem so melancholy.

"My dear, I am seventy-four years of age. Lady Hamilton has recently passed her thirty-fourth birthday. I was sensible of the fact and said so when I married that I should be superannuated when my wife would be in the full beauty and vigor of youth. Now that time has arrived, and we must make the best of it."

"A man of your stature deserves naught but comfort in his later years," Mary replied. She did not care if Sir William detected her disapproval of his situation.

"I shall remind you of that in years to come," Elgin said.

"My dear young Lady Elgin," Sir William said, "I am an elderly man, plagued with gout and stomach disorders. I can no longer retain the king's confidence by hunting the day long with him as I used to. I am dependent upon the talents of a young wife to fulfill many of my ambassadorial duties."

According to Sir William, it was Emma who organized the escape of themselves and the royal family from Naples to Sicily when the French were marching on the city. "If she had not used her influence with Admiral Lord Nelson, who evacuated us, surely we would have been torn apart by the antimonarchists who welcomed a French-style revolution in Naples. If you wonder why Queen Maria Carolina is so very fond of my wife, it is because Emma saved her from the fate of her sister Marie Antoinette in France. The masses were calling for her head, you see."

Sir William listed Emma's services to himself and to the government as if he were telling a well-rehearsed tale. Mary felt awful; she was undoubtedly just another visitor to whom he had to defend his wife. According to Sir William, Emma had acted as a spy, passing secret letters written to Maria Carolina by the king of Spain to British intelligence, who considered the information contained within very valuable. Emma's service as a spy to the British government was instrumental in securing an alliance between Naples and England, preventing Naples from going to the French. She was responsible in part for Nelson's victory in Egypt because she single-handedly convinced the queen to provide victuals for the British navy after the Sicilian government had refused him.

No wonder Nelson had fallen in love with her!

"Her beauty is naught compared to her selfless courage and the breadth of her heart," Sir William concluded.

Mary tried to contain her astonishment as well as her dismay that Sir William was extolling Emma in Elgin's presence. She'd had no idea that a diplomat's wife could or should be so influential. She intended to be a great partner and fierce helpmeet to her husband, but she wondered now if she would be able to be as effective as Emma Hamilton. But surely a woman of Mary's birth, connections, and stature should have no difficulty in comparison to a former prostitute and the daughter of a blacksmith. Surely.

Mary had been lost in her thoughts about Emma—for how long,

she did not know, but it had been long enough for Elgin and Sir William to have segued into the subject that Elgin had intended to raise. Apparently Elgin had found a way of bringing up his Athens mission, because Sir William was at this moment extolling the superiority of Greek art over the Roman. "Greece was the great mistress of the arts. In Rome, all but the most admired buildings were merely imitations of the Grecian originals. What an opportunity you have before you, Elgin," Sir William said. "The great works of Pericles and Pheidias lay for ages buried in its ruins, but from those ruins they may, Phoenix-like, receive a second birth. And through your efforts."

"I have been trying to explain the urgency of the mission to Lady Elgin," her husband said.

"My dear Lady Elgin," Sir William began patiently, "Cicero himself said that nothing more perfect in kind exists than the statues made by the hands of Pheidias. And as for the Parthenon, which houses them, no pen has adequately described nor pencil faithfully depicted its beauty. It was dedicated in the year four hundred thirty-eight in the era before the birth of Our Lord, and still has no architectural rival."

"Imagine!" Mary replied, trying to muster an amount of enthusiasm to match that of the men.

"But now it is in a ruinous state. When the Romans subdued Greece they became enamored of its architecture and arts. Not so the Turks. They call the ruins old stones and don't care a fig for their preservation. Lord Elgin, if he proceeds with his ambition to make casts of what is left of the masterpieces atop the Acropolis, will be a national hero for his contribution to British arts. Indeed, he will be performing a service to Art itself, and to History!"

"I intend to support my husband's every ambition and decision, Sir William," she said.

"Sir William has a splendid suggestion, Mary," Elgin said.

"Yes, you must make a trip to Messina to meet with Giovanni Battista Lusieri. He is a superb artist, one of the finest in Italy. He served for many years as court painter in Naples. He is the perfect man to head your Athens project."

"It is a rigorous journey, is it not?" Mary asked. How many days could she, in her condition, endure the crawl over Sicily's sweltering hills? "And would it not be expensive to hire so illustrious a painter for the two years in which we will require his services?"

"Lady Hamilton and I will be delighted to host you if you do not wish to accompany Lord Elgin to Messina."

Elgin knew how Mary felt about staying under Lady Hamilton's roof, but his eyes were twinkling with enthusiasm. If he thought he would be able to hire a competent artist to head his Athenian project, he would happily leave Mary in the hands of the whapper.

"My place is with my husband, Sir William, though I do appreciate your kind offer."

"My dear, have you studied *Life of Pericles*?"

"Plutarch's version?" Mary asked. "I have not."

"Then I entreat you to accept my copy of the translation by Mr. Dryden. I think you will find it most illuminating. You must do all that you can to apprehend the meaning of the monuments built by Athens's great statesman Pericles and his friend, the genius Pheidias."

Mary took the book from Sir William. It appeared to be more than one hundred years old, though he assured her that it was a more recent copy of the original edition. He must have read and reread it a thousand times. The leather cover was crackled and worn. Mary flipped through the pages, turning her nose away at the musty smell they released.

"I shall read it with great enthusiasm and great care," she said. After Sir William had listed with pride Emma Hamilton's contributions to his career as an envoy, it would not do for him to think that Mary Elgin would be any less enthusiastic or deft in supporting her husband's every endeavor.

"You might find the stories of Pericles and his mistress Aspasia quite interesting."

"Aspasia? I am not familiar with the lady."

"Lady!" Elgin exclaimed. "She was his courtesan." Mary could see that Elgin regretted his words and wished that he could retract the faux pas. They were, after all, in the home of a courtesan, or a former courtesan, before Sir William had made her his wife.

"What was her relation to the man who presided over Athens's Golden Age?" Mary asked.

"Plutarch says that Aspasia was courted by Pericles because of her knowledge of politics and rhetoric. Socrates was her friend, and a frequent guest at her dinner soirées."

"Then why have I not heard of her?"

"She sounds like one of the characters in a lady's romance, Mary," said Elgin. "That she was Pericles' adviser and Socrates' friend is probably the invention of some ancient gossipmonger or weaver of romantic tales—an ancient Greek version of our Mrs. Burney or Mrs. Radcliffe. For I am sure that there have always been women to craft stories that appeal to the darker regions of ladies' imaginations. You would do well to overlook the more gossipy elements of Plutarch's stories and stay the course of proper history."

But Elgin's admonition did not deter Mary's curiosity. Later that evening, when they had returned to their makeshift bedroom in the crumbling palazzo, while Elgin reviewed maps that showed the roads to the city of Messina, Mary opened Sir William's copy of Plutarch's *Lives* and began to read. She sped through the stories of Pericles' younger days, searching for the name of Aspasia. Was the political efficacy of courtesans some theme in history that had escaped Mary's attention? Did one have to be a fallen woman to participate openly in the civic world of men, from which women were traditionally barred? She would find out. She searched the pages for a mention of Aspasia, finally settling on her name. It was said, according to Plutarch, that she was from Miletus, a Greek city in Asia Minor, and that she modeled herself after the courtesan Thargelia, a beauty who influenced men of power in olden Ionian times. Another courtesan still!

And there it was: Pericles fell in love with Aspasia because she was astute. And Socrates, the great philosopher and the wisest of all men, would sometimes spend time in her company. And yet Mary had never heard of the lady! How could that be?

Mary turned the lamp key, carefully raising the flame, hoping the extra light would not attract Elgin's attention. She did not wish to be disturbed, nor questioned about what she was reading.

*In the city of Athens,
in the fourth year of the
Thirty-Year Truce with Sparta*

I WANT YOU TO BEHAVE meekly, and not at all like yourself," Alkibiades said, dragging me by the arm at a pace faster than my tall platform shoes would allow me to walk. "If Perikles sees what you are truly like, he will promptly rescind any offer to help us."

"Slow down! You are bringing me to him like a slave to market!" I protested.

Though it was very early in the day, the marketplace was crowded. The vendors had already set up their stalls, and the slave women were negotiating loudly with them for fish, cheese, olives, and oil, disturbing the tranquility of the morning. One of the women smelled a length of sausage, throwing it back in the vendor's face.

"Everybody knows that you mix the offal of the cow with dog meat and try to pass it off as first-class sausage!" she cried. "My master demands high quality!" The man saw that I was an amused witness to this exchange, and he shook his head helplessly.

Nearby, a black-robed sophist walked with alacrity, posing questions to the young boys who raced to keep up with him; they were shouting "Yes, master" and "No, master" to the questions he asked while flailing his arms about like an angry bat. I slowed down to listen to the lesson, but Alkibiades jerked me away, dodging the peripatetic classroom and crossing the square, where moneylenders sat under colorful tents doing their daily business amid other sellers of goods.

For a hefty man, Alkibiades walked quickly, driven by his meanness and his desire to get me out of his household. How my sister tolerated him on top of her at night was beyond me. I knew that she complied; sleeping in the room next to theirs, I often heard his heavy grunting, followed by the sigh of release that brought blessed silence. Now, his belly shook from side to side as we trudged along, crossing the western side of the agora, where the Council House and many of the government buildings were organized. Hundreds of men were lined up in the shade of the buildings' colonnades.

"Alkibiades! What are you doing with that tasty morsel? She's not your wife."

I heard a bunch of my brother-in-law's cronies cackling even before I turned around to see the smug faces and ever-present paunches of men his age. They were standing in the jury lines—the favorite daily pastime of interfering old men who had nothing better to do than pass judgment on their fellow Athenians. Perikles had passed a law that jurors had to be paid, and now the elders of the city fought for the privilege.

"This is my sister-in-law, if you must know," Alkibiades answered. "I am taking her to meet Perikles to see if he will take her off my hands."

"I'll take her off your hands," one of the men said. I looked down, not because I was shy, but because I had to prevent myself from cursing him.

"I'd like to see a pretty little thing like that in my hands," said another. "I need a young wife. The old one wore out and died on me!"

This brought even more laughter.

"She is an orphan with no dowry," he said.

"In that case, she is not so pretty," the man replied.

"And she is a metic—a foreigner—so you can't marry her anyway," Alkibiades snapped, rushing past them. "Good day, gentlemen. Can't keep the 'great man' waiting." He said it grudgingly, so that they would know that any groveling he was about to do before Perikles was a ruse. All the old men snickered, as if they shared his sentiment, and we sped away.

We were to meet Perikles under the Painted Stoa, one of the many colonnades in the agora that protected the Athenians from the fierce July sun. I looked across the plateau to the Temple of Hephaestus, sun bouncing from its strong marble pillars, and then up to the Akropolis, where I could see men at work on the exterior of a temple to Athena Parthenos, at the moment a skeleton of marble columns that was supposed to become the most majestic building in Athens. I trembled to think that I was waiting to be introduced to the very man who was responsible for commissioning this grand monument.

Kalliope, my sister, had braided ribbons into the crown of my long, light brown hair. I powdered my face to appear fairer, and I wore our mother's hammered gold necklace and matching earrings with little pearlescent tortoises. I borrowed my sister's platform sandals, since I knew that Perikles was tall and I wanted to appear statuesque rather than petite, with its implication of submissiveness. I had no aspiration of having him fall in love with me—far from it. My highest ambition for the meeting was to be seen as a woman who was too respectable to serve in a brothel.

"Keep your head tilted nicely to the side and your eyes cast downward," my brother-in-law instructed me. "Do not look Perikles straight in the face. That's a clear sign of insubordination in a woman, and I don't want you showing him your brazen ways."

My sister had met Alkibiades when he came to Miletus, where we were born; it was a coastal city in Ionia situated south of the great city of Ephesus, which had been fought over many times by Greeks and Persians. He had been exiled from Athens on a political charge and could not wait to return, Athens being the center of the world, as he liked to say, and the rest of it, her appendages. He always complained of my big appetite—for food and for conversation and could not wait to "unload" me on a husband, some Attic farmer "who could keep my mouth full." While we traveled on the boat, leaving behind Miletus and everything we knew, he cautioned me to be quiet and soft-spoken while he shopped for a husband for me. He was worried that I would let on about my "knowing," which would render me an unsuitable wife.

"No man," he explained to me, "wants the responsibility of maintaining a female relative, especially one such as you who is lousy at housework and who considers herself above drudgery. You're useless in my household. In my opinion, you'd make a sorry wife, and an even sorrier slave. Pity the man I trick into marrying the likes of you."

No amount of cajoling by Kalliope would cause him to treat me nicely. He did not like women such as myself. After our mother died, my sister, named after a Muse, but having none of the characteristics of one, had assumed most of the domestic responsibilities, and I grew up with the freedom of a motherless child. My father was amused by my verbal abilities and allowed me to go to the marketplace and listen to the lectures of Thales the Sage, who was first in wisdom among all astronomers. He had studied the stars in Egypt with the priests of higher learning, who taught him how to predict solar eclipses, making him seem more magician than scientist, until he wrote down the formulas by which such things could be foretold. From Thales, I learned the equations of geometry, for he said that it was important to understand space because all was contained within it. He taught us how to know the height of things by measuring shadow. He believed that the gods were in everything, an inexplicable intelligence that animated all living things as well as the natural forces. He spent hours explaining that there was no difference between life and death—an argument that, at thirteen years old, I could not apprehend, and still cannot in any reasonable or practical way. It was my privilege to listen to his last lectures, as he was a very old man in those days. He died when I was fourteen, in the year of the fifty-eighth Olympiad, sitting in his chair watching an athletic competition. From him, I learned how to lay out an argument; how to reason my way through an incomprehensible, abstract thought with careful and persistent inquiry, allowing it to reveal itself to me slowly like a flower opening to the sun.

"Your father let you run wild in the marketplace," Alkibiades had said as we were crossing the sea to Athens. "He nearly ruined you for any man. Fortunately, you are pretty. That will go a long way toward getting someone to take you off my hands. And it shan't be a moment too soon for either my pleasure or my pocketbook."

But when we arrived in Athens, we discovered that Perikles, in an effort to limit citizenship, had just passed a law making marriage between an Athenian citizen and a metic illegal. Alkibiades was furious, thinking he was stuck with me.

"It doesn't matter," he said. "I can always sell you into prostitution or concubinage."

My sister pleaded with him, shedding many tears over this threat. "Please, dear husband, I could not live if my sister was forced to submit to such a fate."

"If you can convince her to keep quiet and be a good girl, I will try to help her," he said to Kalliope. But privately, he continued to threaten me with a life of prostitution. If he could prove that I had lost my virginity—he said he could establish this by raping me—under Athenian law he could sell me to a brothel and obtain a good sum of money.

My sister continued to beseech him to seek a respectable situation for me, so he decided to take his complaint directly to Perikles, whose law had spoiled any plans to marry me off, and who had just divorced his wife. Perikles assured Alkibiades that he would not change a new law for the sake of one girl's fate, but agreed to "take a look" at me to see if he had any ideas as to what might be done with or for me.

"Just remember, Aspasia, you have no father and no dowry. Worse, you're a glutton for food, and your education has made you a glutton for conversation. You are the very opposite of all that is desirable in a woman," Alkibiades said as the Painted Stoa came into sight. "When you meet Perikles, you must act very sweetly to make up for your shortcomings."

Thales believed that men were better than women, and Greeks better than all barbarians. Athenians carried the philosophy one step further, believing that citizens of Athens were better than all other Greeks. Perikles, though a member of the democratic faction, had been born an aristocrat and was said to be more imperious than any of his conservative opponents. I was terrified to meet him. Busts and statues of him appeared in public parks and buildings all over the city. He controlled the government, it was said, by the force of his personality, the breadth of his vision, and the power of his oratory, though the only office he held was that of general. Born into the nobility, he had changed the laws of governance so that common men might hold high offices. He was described as both grand and egalitarian. In his private life, he was parsimonious to the extent that the comic playwrights mocked his cheapness, but he spent public funds extravagantly. He was a paradoxical, enigmatic, and totally incomprehensible man. And I was to be at his mercy.

Under the Painted Stoa, a gigantic pavilion with murals of the historical battles between the Greek people and their foreign enemies, I saw a head of dark, curly hair rising above a crowd of men. The owner of this hair stood quite still before the colossal painting of the Battle of Marathon, almost as if he belonged to the scene on the wall rather than with the men who vied for his attention. He was composed, appearing to listen to them, but with an air of detachment. The men were interrupting one another, gesticulating, laying out some sort of argument or perhaps issuing a request, but he merely shifted his eyes from one speaker to the next. Alkibiades waved at him, and he looked past his petitioners and met my eyes, staring at me for several moments. His face was inscrutable. He waved off the men who were making their appeal and walked toward us. He was a full head taller than me, even with my platform shoes. He had a long face, deep-set intense brown eyes, and a nose so straight it might have been drawn with a mathematician's ruler. He walked with purpose. His beard was short, dark, and curly. The comic playwrights who called him Onion Head, making fun of his long face and big head, had exaggerated. I thought he was solemn and handsome.

He did not smile and he barely looked at Alkibiades.

"So this is the lady in question."

"Yes. My wife's sister, Aspasia of Miletus. Out of the goodness of my heart, I brought her with us to Athens when I was able to return from exile. She is under my guardianship."

It pained Alkibiades to pretend that he cared for me at all, but he was afraid that if he revealed to Perikles how awful he thought I was, it would foil his plans for getting rid of me. Perikles said nothing, but stared at me, and I, against my brother-in-law's instructions, stared back.

Nervous, Alkibiades continued. "I had hoped to find her a respectable husband, but thanks to the law you passed while I was away, no citizen can marry her."

"Well, then. There it is," Perikles said, as calmly as if he were commenting on the weather. Barely looking at Alkibiades, he took me by the arm and ferreted me away. I did not look back, but smiled to myself, imagining the look of shock on Alkibiades' face. It took me a few moments to realize that the most powerful man in Athens was taking me away and that I should consider being afraid of what he would do with me. But I could not fear him. I felt—and without any reason—that I was under his protection.

We walked a short distance, saying nothing. Somehow, the quiet was not uncomfortable. Then he turned to me and said, "I almost lost a great friend yesterday."

"Did he malign you in some way?" I asked, surprising myself with how natural my tone sounded, as if talking to a great statesman was something I did every day. I cannot explain it, but I felt that I had immediately connected with some essential thing inside this man.

"No. He is a great man, a great friend, and a great mentor. He might have died in my neglect. I should have been sending him money. By the time I remembered to look in on him, he was very ill."

"Was he elderly?"

"Yes, quite so." Now he was looking at me with his great chestnut eyes.

"Then perhaps he was merely sick with old age and not because you were not there to tend to him."

"But he blamed me. I went to his bedside and begged him not to die, for I could not continue without his wise counsel. He answered, 'Perikles, even those who use a lamp must put oil in it so that it gives light.' "

"Are you his only resource for sustenance?" I asked, for it seemed impossible that a man held in esteem by Perikles would not be taken care of by other men too.

"He was a great teacher. Unlike the sophists, he prefers not to take money for his labors. He is dependent upon me now. His neglect is a stain upon my character."

"Why is he so special to you? Is he an elder in your tribe?"

"His name is Anaxagoras. He taught me to reason and to inquire. He showed me—and many others—that the mysteries of the world had solid explanations that one might decipher with enough investigation. The world needs minds such as his. I do not want to be responsible for the loss of him."

"Oh? I am interested in pursuing these sorts of inquiries myself," I said. "Might you give an example of some of his ideas?"

He looked down at me from his position of greater height, skepticism on his face.

"He has demonstrated that the sun is not a god but a very hot rock that is larger than the Peloponnese. He taught that the universe is not ordered by the whims of the gods, but by a pure intelligence that suffuses all things."

"I believe that he must have been under the influence of my teacher, Thales of Miletus," I replied. "I am certain that he devised this theorem first."

"Are you trying to make me believe that you studied with Thales?"

"I am not trying to make you believe anything. The sophist tries to convince. The philosopher merely inquires. I am rather stating a fact, which you may believe or not according to your desire. Whether you believe me, sir, does not make what I say either true or false."

He did not answer me, but walked with me in silence. I had no idea where he was taking me, and I did not think I should ask. We walked up a hill to a dwelling not much larger than the one I had grown up in.

"This is my home," he said. I was surprised. I thought that the leader of the Athenian people would live in a grand mansion. "I'll have the slaves bring us a tray of food and some wine. Come with me."

We walked through the courtyard and up the stairs to a bedchamber, and I, all the while, noticed the plain décor. "This is your room," he said. "I am sure you'll be comfortable. Ask for whatever you like."

He shared a bowl of dates with me, and some cheese and bread, asking me various questions about Thales and my early life in Miletus. Then he left the house, and I wondered what I was supposed to do. The slaves were reluctant to speak with me. I explored the house in search of the women's quarters where I might find a grandmother or aunt or sister to indoc-trinate me in the ways of the household, but there seemed to be no other women living on the premises. I remembered that Perikles had recently divorced his wife. Perhaps she had taken all of the women of the house with her back to her family's home. I resigned myself to confinement in the room he had said was mine and waited to see what was going to become of me. Perhaps he would offer me to one of his friends, or marry me off to some lesser man in his service. Finally, dark-ness settled over the household. All was quiet, so I lay on the bed and went to sleep.

Late into the night, I heard Perikles come into the room. "Why is a lamp not lit?" he asked, standing over me in the dark.

"Because I do not sleep with a light," I answered.

"Why are you not prepared for me?"

"Because you did not share with me your plans for the evening."

He pulled the sheet from my body. I was not wearing any clothing. He looked at me dispassionately, sliding his hand up my leg. I pulled away, grabbing the sheet and hiding my nakedness.

I braced myself, waiting for an outburst of ire, but he looked more baffled than insulted. "You are not honoring the terms of my agreement with Alkibiades."

"What terms?"

"We had agreed that if I was pleased with the sight of you in the marketplace I would take you for my concubine."

"Your concubine?" I pulled the sheet tighter against my body and looked around the room for a means of escape. It was not a rational reaction, but all I wanted to do was run away.

"Alkibiades assured me that you are highly experienced in the ways of the courtesan. He said that you had pleased him many times."

"My own sister's husband? That would be depraved!"

Perikles shrugged. "I have heard of such things."

"Sir, I am as virginal as Athena herself. I've never been touched by any man, much less engaged in a sexual act."

"Surely you are lying," he said, pulling away from me but scanning my face for a sign of dishonesty. "I must tell you that money has changed hands, compensation for all the food you've eaten since your father died, and for the two dresses that your sister made for you—one out of linen and one out of wool of good quality."

He certainly had all the facts. Kalliope had squeezed the money for the fabric out of her meager household budget so that I would look nice.

Perikles looked bewildered, a sentiment that I both appreciated and welcomed as I let this information wash over me. After all, he could have done with me whatever he liked— taken me against my will; returned me in a fury to my brother-in-law, who would surely have punished me severely for not pleasing the mighty Perikles; sent me to a brothel; or beaten me in anger and thrown me out into the darkness.

"He said you were an expert in the sexual arts," Perikles insisted, trying to make sense of it all. "I believe that is the precise word that he used."

I quickly assessed my options. Here was a man who was not, at least at this moment, using the supreme power that he held over me to bully me. With the exception of my father, I had not had the acquaintance of such an individual. Even the wise Thales lorded his superior status over me, always making me grateful for being allowed to listen to his words. I looked at Perikles' hands, which were surprisingly slender, with long tapered fingers and clean square nails. They were altogether delicate for a man who had distinguished himself as a general. I decided that I could imagine, in fact would invite, those hands laying themselves on my body.

"I am not lying. I have never done this before. But I am willing to learn."

. . .

AFTER WE FINISHED, I began to cry. "I've hurt you," he said. But he had not. I had gasped at the moment of entry, but less because of the startling pain than because I realized that along with his thrust, he was delivering a definitive outcome to my life.

"I am crying because my virginity is lost and my fate is sealed. Never will I be a bride. Never will my groom lift the veil from my face, and never will I raise my eyes to show that I have accepted him."

My mind continued: Never would I offer him my left hand to take at the wrist as a sign that I submitted to him. Never would I receive the bridal gifts from my community of women. I had never consciously wanted these things, but something deep inside me must have longed for them. Entrance into the traditional female world, with its rituals and quotidian chores that I had abhorred, was barred to me. Moreover, I was also forbidden membership in respectable Athenian society. If that door was forever closed, what was left for me?

"Never will my father—may the gods keep him safe in the realm of the shades—give me to another man for the sake of having legitimate children," I said, crying premature tears over my unborn children.

"I suppose that is true," he said. "But you are a woman unique among women. You have just given yourself away of your own volition."

And so our arrangement began. At first, all I could manage in bed was the art of compliance. As time passed, and he came to me more regularly in the evenings, I asked him to show me the ways in which I might better please him. He did this, and also shared with me the ways in which I might please myself. He showed me how pleasure is enhanced by the use of oils and ointments, and encouraged me to tell him the ways that would bring me to the most intense climaxes. I soon came to take as much pleasure in our carnal desires as in our conversations, and he, I believe, came to take as much pleasure in our conversations as in our carnal delights. With every passing evening, he further unburdened himself to me after we made love.

But as soon as I left the sanctuary of the bedroom, the insults began. I could hear them muttered by the slaves under their breath, though Perikles was never around at these times, and I could not prove a thing. Concubine. Whore. Slut. Courtesan was the nicest among them. At first, the balm of his affection could not salve the insults and hurts. Later, as I grew in power both in the home and outside of it because of his attachment to me, the derogatory words stopped—that is, until much later, when they escalated again in a more public fashion.

But soon enough I realized that these slurs constituted my freedom. Now I was free to traipse about the marketplace— a freedom denied to me since I was fourteen years old. I was free from the sequestered life of a respectable woman, locked within a shadowy existence in the female quarters of a house. I was free of the tyranny of Alkibiades, and under the protection of a man who seemed to want me in his household because of, rather than in spite of, those very attributes that my brother-in-law had promised that other men would consider my flaws.

ONLY A FEW WEEKS after coming to the house of Perikles, I learned that one of the primary duties of a courtesan, which set her apart from a wife, was entertaining the men at dinner and drinking parties. When Perikles announced that he had invited some of his close associates for one such event, I knew that it was to be a test of my worth in my new position. I had no idea how to begin to organize the evening. I knew that I would probably be one of the only women present. Women were rarely, if ever, invited to dinner or drinking parties. Even if they were, a married female, or a female otherwise on the inside of the social realm of "decency," would never agree to attend, much less attend one being hosted by a concubine—even if the concubine was being kept by the most powerful man in the state. I tried not to worry over these things. Though my sister was as blind on the subject of being a hostess as I was, fortunately Alkibiades was a picky eater and a gastronome, and Kalliope was well trained in ordering and presenting fine cuisine. I insisted that she come to the markets with me to select premium ingredients for the meal. She agreed, though she would have to keep the adventure a secret from her husband, for respectable women always sent their slaves to market. But I would not give the sneaky slaves in our home an opportunity to sabotage me on this important occasion.

Perikles had been on a campaign to invite wealthy foreign investors to move their businesses—and their money—to Athens, and the guest of honor on this evening was a rich manufacturer of weaponry, newly arrived from Cyprus with thirty slaves, who was setting up a factory in the city.

"Who else is to come?" I had asked so that I might send the slaves into the market to gossip with the slaves of the guests and discern their tastes.

"Oh, various wits, fops, and politicians," he said. "Speak to the steward and make sure he hires enough whores and entertainers. The men will want to have their fun."

He was clearly not in the mood to give me specific directives, and I had wondered if he wanted me to fail so that he could get rid of me. I asked no more questions of him and prepared as best I could. As the guests poured into the courtyard, I pretended that I was a sophisticated and gracious hostess, but I had no idea what to expect. The slaves had filled me in on the protocol at Perikles' gatherings, but I did not trust them to tell me the truth. Though I was dressed and perfumed and smiling broadly, my stomach and my mind were in a turbulent state.

The dinner itself went very well, with everyone complimenting me on the expensive ostrich eggs imported from Africa, the eels wrapped in beet leaves, and the spiced, roasted

tuna belly. I must admit that never had I eaten so well. In the
house of Alkibiades, the women did not eat the same quality
of food that was served to the men, but subsisted on simpler
fare.

Some of the men brought professional courtesans—daughters and granddaughters of the educated class of women kept
by the wealthiest and most demanding men—who wore fine
silks and too-big jewelry. They sipped their wine most delicately while they asked studied questions of the men. The men
loved this because the courtesans made it easier for them to
expound on the subject at hand, helping them feel more intelligent than they actually were. We women did not speak to
one another as women who live in the same household would
do. Rather, we smiled at the men's humor, occasionally commenting on their observations. One of the women recited a
poem while the flute girl played her instrument, and another
did a dance. I had none of these sorts of skills, and I wondered
if I was supposed to be developing them. The prostitutes were
kept in a separate room through the dinner, were fed lesser-
quality food and wine, and were invited into the dining room
only as the dishes were being taken from the tables.

I was terribly embarrassed as they brazenly entered and
plopped themselves into the men's laps, as their breasts spilled
out of their dresses and their legs went wide open so that one
could see all the way up to their thighs. Would they have intercourse right here in front of us? I did not think I could watch
such a spectacle. I did not know whether Perikles would select
one of the women and couple with her while I sat watching,
or, indeed, whether I was expected either to straddle him as
these women were doing to his guests or, worse, to service his
guests. What would happen if I refused to do it? I could not
believe that the tender man under whose roof I lived would
throw me to his associates, but life in Athens was full of sur-
prises. I was relieved that the men who had brought courtesans remained with them, while the others coupled with the

whores and began to disappear from the tables to attend to their iniquitous business in private. Perikles seemed to have no interest in such diversions. He ignored me and settled in with Kephalos, the manufacturer, to discuss business.

The night wore on. I was sitting alone, trying to maintain the smile that had been frozen on my face all night like an icy half-moon, when an older man sat next to me, dramatically throwing the flow of his robe of expensive white linen over the back of the couch. "Are you as bored as I am?" he asked. He did not wait for me to respond. "I do not know why Perikles insists on wasting my time at these boorish events when I should be working. Do I look like a man who cares to entertain merchants?"

"Not at all," I said. He was most grand. His head was bald at the top, with light brown waves at the sides, falling well below his ears. His brow was very fine and deeply furrowed, and he had a full, well-manicured beard, though his eyes dominated his face. He possessed a certainty that would make it very difficult to contradict him.

"We are having enough trouble with our funding for the buildings, and if momentum is not kept up on the construction, we will have to answer to the Assembly. Those idiots already think we are doing all of this to get rich!"

From this I discerned that the speaker was Pheidias, the architect and designer of Perikles' ambitious plan to rebuild the Akropolis, and by all accounts the greatest sculptor in the world. I continued to smile, assuming that he would carry on the entire conversation by himself, as the other men had done throughout the evening.

"Do you even know what I am talking about?" he asked impatiently.

I took a deep breath, trying to compose myself before I opened my mouth. "The building project is much discussed in Athens and beyond, sir, where city-states dependent on Athens for their security are not so gleeful about being forced to contribute funds. I am from Miletus and heard talk of it in the marketplace. But as to details of the plan and its funding, I must confess my ignorance."

"You are a well-spoken girl. And you have a most interesting face."

I knew that I was pretty, but I had never thought of my face as interesting. My features were well formed and well defined, but nothing out of the ordinary. I had wider eyes than the average woman, and my lips were pink and full. I suppose that when my father was alive, he used to tell me I was a lovely girl who would steal hearts. But after he died, all I heard from my new guardian, Alkibiades, was how unfeminine I was.

"I appreciate the compliment coming from one so illustrious," I said. "Before I came to Athens, I was studying rhetoric and philosophy."

"Were you? A woman and a philosopher?"

"Yes, two entities that mingle uneasily in the same body," I replied, which made him smile.

"I imagine so," he said. "But perhaps your skills will serve you at these interminable dinner parties—not that these boors will ever let you get a word in."

"Perhaps," I said.

"As you are so well spoken, tell me, do you approve of our plans to transform the Akropolis?"

I could not tell whether he was challenging me or mocking me, but I answered as if I assumed that he was asking me a question to which he expected a serious answer. "As a philosopher, I form an opinion only after serious inquiry into a subject. I have not made a serious inquiry into the building project."

Pheidias threw his head back and laughed. He called out to Perikles, who was draining the last of his bowl of wine. "Perikles, are you training this young lady to be a politician?"

Whereupon Perikles burst into laughter, not because of what Pheidias had said but because when he looked into the empty wine bowl, he saw attached to the bottom the little ceramic fly that I'd been waiting all night for him to see. I had found it in the marketplace among other novelties and hoped to entertain him with the surprise of it.

It was the first time I had made him laugh. For all the extraordinary things for which Perikles was known, laughter was the least among them, and I felt joyous that I was able to accomplish this simple thing. He had a reputation for never allowing cracks in the surface of his public face. It seemed to me that he had constructed a self that lived to serve the state, and he believed that any fissures in that veneer could harm not just him, but the state as a whole.

"Perikles, our young philosopher here wishes to make an inquiry into the merits of our building project."

Perikles looked at me, surprised.

"I never said such a thing!" I protested.

"As a philosopher, she cannot dispute the charges of our critics nor answer the question of whether we are just in our desire to carry out our plans without an inquiry. Why have you not told her of our reasoning?"

Was the sculptor mocking me after all? Still carrying the bowl and still smiling, Perikles left his inebriated merchant and came to sit with us. "You see, Aspasia, our critics do not understand. The temple to Athena Parthenos and the surrounding buildings will be the ultimate expression of all that is great in the city of Athens."

"It will demonstrate to the world the artistic potential of mankind," Pheidias added.

"And the collective will of the Greek people in conquering our enemies and in advancing our superior ideals and way of life," Perikles said. "It will be an expression of Greek values."

"And of what a human being can achieve if he strives for greatness in all aspects of his life," Pheidias added.

"And of what things are possible when one honors the gods," Perikles said.

"Or at least negotiates well with them," countered Pheidias, who was not a politician but an artist and could therefore
say—and believe—irreverent things with impunity.

"Shall I call for more wine?" I asked. Their bowls were
empty, and I wanted to keep both of them talking to me in this
way. I had not had a decent conversation since I left Miletus,
and I felt myself come alive.

"No, don't," Perikles said. "If you do, these people will
never leave, and I am exhausted with them. Aspasia, tell the
slaves to pass the word that we're out of wine. They'll be gone
within minutes."

"Yes, thanks be to the gods, get rid of them," Pheidias said.
"And when they are gone, we shall take this pretty girl with us
and go to look at our creations."

IT WAS A STARLESS night, and the air was cool and
damp. I was not accustomed to being out of doors at this hour,
and I drew my shawl tight around me. Even in the darkness,
we could see the bronze helmet of Pheidias' sculptural masterpiece, the statue of Athena Promachos—a celebration of the
goddess in all her magnificence as a fighter and champion. In
the gleaming light of day, sunshine reflected off the goddess's
bronze helmet. It could be seen all the way out to sea, heralding sailors as they approached the harbor of Athens at Piraeus.
The goddess was sheltered from behind by a wall that was said
to be a thousand years old, constructed by the mythical creatures of Homer's tales.

A north wind blew across the plateau as we climbed to the
top of the steps to enter the citadel. Guards were stationed at
the entrance, but when they saw Perikles and Pheidias, they
promptly stood aside, allowing us to enter. The men walked
briskly ahead, but I stopped to look around me. Deep into
the darkness the pillars of the white marble buildings under
construction seemed to be springing up like some miracu-
lous and immense stone garden. The old gates to the Akropolis

still stood, though I had heard that a newer, grander entrance would soon be constructed. Everywhere, dozens of carts filled with rubble sat incongruously beside fluted white columns and stacks of tiles and other new materials.

Perikles turned to see that I had lagged behind. He noticed that I was shivering. "What is the matter? You are cold?" he asked.

"Yes," I replied, though it was the eerie feeling of being atop the Akropolis, where the great gods were worshipped, in the silent stillness of the night. "I feel as if the gods are here, watching us, as if we might be disturbing their peace."

Perikles held out his arms for me, and I went to him. He put his arm around me, and I was grateful for the warmth and the protection. Surely the formidable Athena would not harm me if I was in the company of one who was building these mighty structures to honor her.

Pheidias took a torch from one of the slaves. "I shall show you what we intend, Aspasia, and you will decide for yourself if our endeavor is worthy." He pointed out the locations of the four great structures around which the new Akropolis was designed: the Propylaea, or Great Gateway, which he was designing with the architect Mnesikles; the temple to Athena Parthenos, which was under way but far from completion; the temple to Erechtheus and Pandrosos, which would encompass and replace many of the old temples and sanctuaries on the Akropolis; and the temple to Athena Nike, which was still in the planning stage.

Pheidias explained his governing theory for the buildings. "Cities are always developments in progress. We build the new atop the old, but here I have integrated the ruins of the Akropolis into the new construction as much as possible so that our history—and the sacredness that lives in the very stones of the old temples—will be preserved." Some of the old shrines that were still standing would not be toppled, he explained, but rather encased in new surroundings. "We have already used many of the stones of the old in the foundations of the new," he said. Long remnants of the old citadel wall were to be preserved and integrated into the more fortified encasement. Pheidias had instructed Mnesikles not to destroy the walls adjacent to the Propylaea, but to bevel them so that they would fit seamlessly against the corners of the gleaming new building.

"Some say that the old walls date from the time of the Trojan War," he said. "It seems a paradox to create something bold and new by incorporating ancient ruins. But you shall see by my results that I know what I am doing."

We walked down the footpath toward the Parthenon, with great piles of stone flanking us all the way. The framework of Athena's temple shone through the black night. The columns and colonnades were constructed, but the rooftop was still open and the walls had not yet been enclosed.

"The temple will be the most majestic ever built to the goddess and will commemorate her assistance in Athens's ultimate victory over the wretched Persians," Perikles said.

"Yes, those bastards who menaced Greek shores for so many generations, trying to sabotage our advanced way of life and suppress us back into the same dark past in which they live. If Athena had not fought with us at the Battle of Marathon, we would not be standing here today," Pheidias said.

"It was there, almost fifty years ago, that we demonstrated our superiority over the Persians once and for all," Perikles said. "At the end of that long and grim day of fighting, six thousand four hundred Persians lay dead, while we had lost only one hundred ninety-two warriors."

"It seems inconceivable," I said. I wondered if the numbers of the Persian dead had been inflated to make the Athenian victory more glorious.

"It is inconceivable," Pheidias said. "Only through the goddess's intervention could it have been done."

"I know what you are thinking, Aspasia," Perikles said. "But if you visit the site of the battle, as I and other patriotic Athenians often do, you will see that the great mounds of mass

graves can prove the outrageous numbers. Our fathers and
grandfathers fought the battle, and were witness to the deaths.

"Ten years after the Battle of Marathon, the Persians
returned to Greece and made their way to Athens," he continued, staring first at Pheidias and then at me, his two captive
listeners, making sure that he had our full attention. "Everyone
had evacuated the city save the priests, priestesses, and those
patriots guarding the sacred monuments on the Akropolis and
what was left of the treasury. It was right here, Aspasia, that
those noble Athenians made their stand."

A cold night wind blew across my face, making me shudder,
as if we were suddenly in the presence of the ghosts of those
last Athenian heroes.

"The Persians camped out on the Hill of Ares and shot
flaming arrows into the temples. Though the Athenians were
but a few—and none of them warriors by trade—they put up a
valiant defense. They held them off long enough, but they had
left the eastern ascent to the citadel unguarded, thinking that
it was too steep to climb. When they saw that some Persians
had made their way up the sheer cliff and were coming toward
them with swords, they threw themselves off the Akropolis and
died. The barbarians murdered the other suppliants and then
plundered and destroyed every building, temple, sacred object,
and work of art."

"They even wrecked the sacred temple to Athena and every
holy statue and relic within it," Pheidias said. "Can you imagine the outrage? The bastards massacred the people, then they
massacred the art."

It was hard to tell which sin Pheidias considered more
grievous. Nothing was more precious to an Athenian than the
sacred images of the goddess who presided over the city that
bore her name.

"But the goddess cursed them," Perikles said. "Anyone who
destroys a holy image of Athena or dares to plunder her temples
will come to a very bad end. That is her promise. The Persians
believed that they had destroyed us, but in fact, in destroying

our monuments, they were merely laying the foundation for their own destruction."

I wished that the Athenians could see him in his present state, full of wine and patriotism, drunk on his love of the city more than on Dionysus' grape, for then they would know that his ambitions sprang from these sentiments rather than from self-interest.

"After the sacking of the Akropolis, Themistocles crushed the Persian fleet at Salamis, and then later, in the battle at Plataia, we drove the menace from Greece once and for all," Pheidias said.

"The new temples will honor the memory of all the heroes of Marathon and the other battles against the Persians," Perikles said.

"Let us toast to that," Pheidias said. The Syrian slave boy who had carried the last of the wine on our journey gave the goatskin flask to Perikles, who took a long drink from it and then passed it to Pheidias, who passed it to me. Was I now one of them?

"At the time of the victory at Plataea, the Athenian leaders vowed to leave the Akropolis in ruins as a reminder, a memorial of ruination for men hereafter to witness," Pheidias said. "But after twenty years of looking at the devastation, our friend here made the observation that colossal monuments of grandeur and beauty would do more to remind our people of their greatness than a mountaintop of rubble."

"And so it shall be," Perikles said. "It will also be a reminder to the rest of the world."

"Still they doubt us, Perikles," Pheidias said. "After all we have shown them, and in a few short years, they still want to cut off our funding. Typical Greeks. They want all of the glory at no cost."

"Do not say that, my friend," Perikles said, suddenly sober. "The price was already paid in blood at Marathon, at Thermopylae, and at Plataea. There has never been a lack of willingness among Greeks to shed our own blood for gods, state, and freedom."

"Only a lack of willingness to shed coins," Pheidias said.

The sky was slowly lightening to a dark gray. Soon the city would come to life again, breaking the spell of night.

"It doesn't matter what they think," Perikles said. "We are the victors, and victors must live in glory, not in rubble."

SEVERAL DAYS LATER, PERIKLES came home at twilight, overwrought with either anger or anxiety, I could not tell which. The slaves alerted me to his arrival as usual, and I rushed down the stairs to greet him, only to see him knock a vase off its pedestal as he tore through the reception hall, and curse it as it crashed to the ground and shattered into little pieces. I had never seen such a display from him.

I called for wine, taking his hand and leading him into the courtyard, where we often enjoyed the evening breezes. I already knew from marketplace gossip that he had been in a severe struggle all day with Athens's conservative faction over money for the building project. We sat down on our usual chairs, and after a short silence, he began to talk to me.

"I grow weary of their hand-wringing and woe over how much money the project is costing the Athenian Alliance and how long it will take to complete."

I never would suggest it to Perikles, but I often wondered at his lack of doubt over the costs. "Do you never worry on these matters?" I asked cautiously.

"No," he said with finality. Truly, he did not seem like a man who was ever aware that he was taking a risk, but rather like a mystic who has heard the word of the gods and will suffer no opposition.

"The leader of the conservatives has accused me of misappropriating public funds in an attempt to 'deck out the great city of Athens like some vain woman.'"

"That seems a foolish accusation. Do they not know how you abhor ostentation?" I asked, understating the matter. Perikles spent very little money on himself or his pleasure. Why would the Assembly doubt such a frugal man, who demonstrated no need for extravagance in his own life?

"Why is Athens great?" he asked, not waiting for me to answer. "It is great because it is protected by Athena. Why does she offer us protection?"

Again, my response was not called for.

"Because Athena and Athens are one," he continued. "This is what I said today in my speech: 'The goddess chose this spot on earth to found her city because she saw that the happy temperament of the seasons might produce a race of men of supreme wisdom. She taught us to develop a system of law out of divine elements, showing us every sort of knowledge essential for human life. She instructed us to model ourselves from her very qualities—valor, boldness, love of beauty, respect for the arts and crafts, moderation, and wisdom.' "

He paused to look at me, an assembly of one. I was rapt. He continued, " 'The Persians came at us, slinging their arrows by the millions, but with Athena's help, we vanquished them. Two generations ago, they sacked Athena's temple and every other sacred structure on the Akropolis. It is imperative that it be rebuilt more grandly than men's imaginations allow. The new Temple of Athena Parthenos commemorates the victory at Marathon, where Greek blood runs deep into the soil. Have you given your imagination over to scenes of Greek life if our warriors had not been victorious? All of history would have changed its course. Today, we would be enslaved by a decadent and tyrannical despot, rather than thriving as the greatest and most freedom-seeking civilization upon the earth.' "

"I cannot believe that the Assembly could question you after that speech," I said. It sounded blithe as it came out of my mouth, but Perikles had enchanted me with his passionate words as much as he enchanted me with his skills in the bedroom or with his power in the public arena.

"Oh, they have heard this same speech many times," he answered. "Why do they not realize that if Athens is to remain what she is, we must continue, man for man, to emulate the qualities of the goddess? The monuments honor her, as well as remind us to hold to our standards. We are not just building temples, Aspasia, we are sending a message to the world. If we wish to remain supreme, we must make visible our superiority. That is not my unique idea, but the way of the world."

"And if your enemies manage to cut the funds for your projects before completion, what will you do?" I asked.

"I suppose I will pay for it myself," he said in his matter-of-fact way, astonishing me. Did the man actually possess such wealth? Since he was not prone to exaggeration, I assumed that he spoke the truth.

"Why don't you offer to do so?" I suggested.

"Because I do not wish to do so, but desire the Assembly to arrive at the wisdom of my point of view."

"It seems to me that it is you, and not this city, who have the greatest passion for achievement," I said, not unaware that I was appealing to his vanity. Yet I meant what I was saying. "Why share the glory with those who do not share your vision? Build it in your own name. Immortalize yourself, and not this civilization, which does not share in your ambitions or your virtue."

"The monuments need to belong to the citizenry if they are to be effective. They are symbols of our achievements as a people, not of one man's efforts. That is antithetical to our way of life. However, you have given me a splendid idea."

The next day, Perikles went to the Assembly and vowed to reimburse the city for the entire project from his private funds, adding that he would be happy to do this, but that he would also make the dedications in his own name rather than in the name of the city. It was a calculated risk, but it paid off.

The opposition, applauded only moments before, was silenced. By the end of the session everyone had agreed that these great monuments must be made in the name of all Athenians, all of whom enjoyed the protection of Athena, and not just one great man, Perikles.

In the evening he came to me as usual, but brought into the bedroom a white linen shawl shimmering with gold threads.

"Stand up, Aspasia," he said. He draped it over my face like a veil and then lifted it. "In the eyes of the gods, I take you as my wife. Will you accept me as a husband?"

"What has brought you to this?" I asked, stunned that he had, on that first night, actually listened to and taken to heart the sorrows of a pitiable woman, and now sought to assuage my grief. For nowhere in the stories that women tell of the fate of other women had I ever heard of such generosity and tenderness on the part of a man.

"You and I are like Athens itself, which is strong only when its citizens are united. I will be more if I stand with you than if I stand alone."

I turned my face upward and looked at him, hoping that he did not see how surprised I was. I was afraid that I might do or say something to make him withdraw whatever love he had miraculously and mysteriously mustered for me in our short months together.

"Will you stand with me?" he asked.

"Forever," I said. I had started to shake. He produced a necklace of gold with garnet jewels made to look like little pomegranate seeds, Persephone's symbol of fertility.

"This is my wedding gift to you," he said, placing it around my neck. "May it bring us sons and daughters."

I offered him my left hand, as I would have done in a true marriage ceremony. He took it and, kissing it, he led me to the bed. I had given him my body on that first night, but at this moment, I gave him my heart.

In the realm of the Turks,

1799

MARY PUT ONE HIGH-HEELED shoe on the accommodation ladder, hoping that she would not slip and fall backwards into the sea in front of the delegations of several nations. That would not be too fine an introduction to the high Turkish official and his staff who waited on the deck of the *Selim III*, watching in astonishment as an unveiled female—head bare, face raised to catch the fresh sea air and warm afternoon sun—put one prettily-turned-out foot and then the next on the rungs of taut rope, climbing up to her first official duty as ambassadress to the Ottomans.

The official who had come to greet Mary on the *Phaeton*, a handsome prince, Isaac Bey, had spoken perfect English and French, and explained to her, as he presented her with sumptuous golden pillows, that Lord Elgin would be dining aboard the Turkish barge. He'd tried in a diplomatic way, eyes downcast, voice low and solicitous, to explain that Mary would not care to dine with the gentlemen, since, in Turkish life, women were sequestered out of respect. But Mary had assured him in her own diplomatic way—eyes wide open and seeking to engage his—that she did care to dine with the gentlemen, for, in English life, ladies were terribly upset when they were left out. Once she had him in her gaze, she saw that she would prevail. The prince, as polite a man as ever lived, did not wish Lady Elgin to feel left out.

"I will not be responsible for your unhappiness," he'd said. So he had waited patiently while she dressed to meet her husband and Hussein Bey, the Capitan Pasha, aboard the latter's luxurious barge.

Now the seas were calm again after the Capitan Pasha had fired nineteen cannon rounds to welcome the Elgins into Turkish waters. Mary had wished that Emma Hamilton had been there to see how an ambassadorial couple should be received, remembering the snub of that woman's early-morning note of regret. No matter. Those days were behind her now, and she was ready to bask in the notorious lavishness of Turkish hospitality.

Mary took a moment to look about at the Dardanelles, the narrow strait the ancient Greeks had crossed to conquer the Trojans, as had Alexander the Great and so many other generals with their armies since time out of mind, in search of the riches of the East. And here she was, Mary Elgin, taking her own place in history, she could not help but think, as her eyes scanned the mere mile, the troublesome fissure between Greece and Turkey that separated the East from the West. The two lands looked substantially the same to her eyes, yet for centuries, crossing from one to the other always seemed to signify entering an exotic land. Often, the crossers were doomed, she thought, like poor Leander who swam from shore to shore every night to see his lover, Hero, high priestess of Aphrodite, before the light she used to guide him burned out and the two drowned in the sea.

Enough, Lady Pining, she said to herself, quoting her husband, who laughed at what he called a woman's tendency to wallow in the romantic. She turned her attention to this important ascent, trying to protect her small pregnant belly by holding her body farther from the ladder than she would have liked. She tried not to think of the precariousness of her position, moving as gracefully as possible in the awkward circumstances, when a large brown masculine hand reached out to take hers.

She had heard that there were twelve hundred men and one hundred thirty-two guns aboard the Capitan Pasha's vessel, and now she believed it because all—men and cannons alike—were lined up on deck to greet her. Elgin must have prepared his host for the fact that it was unlikely that his wife would remain on her own ship, because as soon as she stepped a foot onto the deck of the grand barge, a band of pipes and drums began to play what sounded like a Turkish interpretation of a ceremonial English tune. The turbaned officers, swarthy and unsmiling, drew gleaming swords to salute her, while similarly dressed but unarmed youths played their instruments. Most eyes were straight ahead, perhaps in respect or embarrassment, though no one seemed discomfited by her presence. Soon Elgin and a tall man in a red turban crowned with a peacock feather came rushing to meet her. She was glad that she had taken her time and dressed for the occasion. The grandeur of the Capitan Pasha was apparent in the bright colors of his silken robe and the elaborate carving in the handle of the weapon sheathed at his side. His beard was as black as onyx and shaped so finely that it appeared that each bristle had been individually groomed. Everything about him was crisp, except his eyes, which were a soft amber color. He was not old, but not as young as Elgin, and he walked at a stately but brisk pace commensurate with his position as military commander of the Ottoman Empire. He had a strong, beaklike nose of a kind that Mary had also seen on men of her own country, and she marveled at how a characteristic could repeat itself on individuals existing in lands so far apart, with so little else in common in coloring and appearance. He had the demeanor of a military man, which made sense. She knew that he had spent many years fighting with the Russians and had been engaged in the conflict with the French in Egypt.

"Welcome, Lady Elgin," he said with a slight bow before whisking her into his cabin, where she was met with a taste of the Turkish magnificence that had previously been only a rumor. The room was large and the walls were lined with lush sofas made of bright yellow silks embroidered through with gold. Above in ornate cabins sat an extensive collection of weapons old and new—guns, pistols, swords, knives, and scimitars.

"I did not know that ships' quarters could equal the most elegant drawing rooms of England," Mary said to him, thinking of the squalid conditions she had just endured for months at sea.

"I have never seen anything equal to the sharpness of these swords," Elgin said, carefully running his finger along the metal. "You should see the rest of the vessel, my dear," he said to his wife. "Even Captain Morris said that nothing could equal the order with which everything is done."

"You are very kind," the pasha said. Could it be that he was speaking English with a French accent? Perhaps he had learned English from the French. Given the long alliance with France, the pasha's command of that language would be stronger than his command of English. Prince Isaac was on hand to interpret if necessary, but the pasha was getting along with the Elgins quite well by himself. His voice was deep, Mary thought. It reminded her of something that had rich, sweet overtones, like fine chocolate or certain vintages of wine.

Dinner was served on exquisite Dresden china at a table set as if for a king's banquet. The pasha helped Mary into her chair, and then the men sat down. Out of nowhere, a dozen attendants appeared with silver-domed dishes and suddenly the room was filled with the heavy scent of spices and roasted meats. Servings of dish after dish of meats and vegetables in strongly flavored sauces of butter and onions were put on Mary's plate. She worried that her stomach, in its present condition, would reject the rich foods on the basis of aroma alone, but she picked up her fork, noticing how heavy the silver instrument felt in her hand.

"Compliments to you English," Prince Isaac said, "for we use only our hands when we eat."

The Capitan Pasha muttered something to the prince, who turned to Mary. "The lady is not content with her food? It shall be changed and the cook reprimanded."

Mary felt even more alarmed. She would not have a cook's head on her conscience. "No, the food is lovely. Please forgive me. Perhaps you did not know that I am expecting a child, and sometimes it is difficult to eat."

No sooner had she uttered the information than the climate in the room changed. "The state of being with child is a holy one, say the prophets. It is one of the highest forms of worship," said Isaac Bey. "The rewards from Allah for this are so great as to be unimaginable."

She was brought a special tea that would soothe her nerves, and a spectacular shawl of woven silks in different shades of red to wrap around her. "From India," the pasha explained. "I bought it for my sister, but I know that she will want you to have it."

"Our ladies here are crazy for these items," added the prince.

When she admired the diamond-shaped coffee cups brought with the dessert, a platter of quince and pears and sweetmeats, the pasha insisted that they be sent to her as a gift. After dinner, a special mound of elegant cushions was arranged for Mary to sit upon. More coffee was served, and pipes were brought in for the men, and a plate of dates for Mary alone, which she was told were crucial in building the flesh and bones of the unborn child.

Tall candlesticks lit the circle of damask-covered sofas, and sweet smoke began to fill the air. Mary leaned against the cushions of gold, allowing her head to sink into the soft mass, and as Elgin held conversation with the men, she found herself entranced by a group of squiggling goldfish swimming in a large glass bowl.

The pasha left the men's conversation and sat beside Mary. "You like my friends? I will have them sent to the embassy. When you look at them, you will think of me."

"That is most kind," Mary said. He sat very close to her, smelling of things that she did not recognize, but liked—cloves, musk, lavender? Heavy and light at the same time.

"I want to say something," he announced. He seemed to search the air in front of him for words. Then he summoned Prince Isaac to his side and whispered furiously into his ear.

"Hussein Pasha would like to be made aware of all the wishes of Lady Elgin so that he might have the privilege of fulfilling them."

The pasha made a sign to the prince to continue. The prince smiled. "He says that if he were the Sultan and you were his subject, he would command you to tell him of your every wish. It would be an order."

Mary turned her attention from the pasha to her husband, who was staring at her, anticipating how she would respond. She could not apprehend Elgin's thoughts. Was there some request he would like her to make? Or some request that she might make that he would consider improper or outlandish? Or was he offended by the pasha's attention to Mary but restraining himself under the circumstances? Elgin waited silently for Mary to speak, but whether his face showed fear, caution, jealousy, or remonstration, she could not say.

Mary decided to be safe. She turned to the pasha and said in her most genteel voice, "Thank you, sir, you are most kind and hospitable, but I have everything I need at this moment. What could one possibly want after such a lovely meal? You have anticipated and exceeded our every need and desire."

"Do you like perfumes?" the pasha asked.

"Does not every lady like perfumes?"

The pasha said something in his language and two attendants disappeared, returning later with a black velvet box richly embroidered. The pasha took it and opened it for Mary, revealing ten small glass bottles in a rainbow of delicate colors. "The glass is from Venice," he said. "The scents inside are the favorites of my sister, and my sister is the favorite wife of the Sultan. I hope you will like them."

Mary knew that the pasha was an important military man, but she'd had no idea that he was so closely tied to the Sultan. She realized that for the length of their mission, he could provide a direct conduit to the man whose word was law everywhere in the empire. His attention to her took on new meaning and significance, and she wondered if these thoughts were running through Elgin's mind as well.

She opened one of the vials, inhaling the sweet, soft scent of rose. "Lovely. I shall use them sparingly so that in years to come, when we are no longer in your country, I will still have these delicious scents to recall the occasion of our first meeting, and your graciousness to me."

"To think that I might linger in your memory is the highest honor," the pasha said through the more fluent tongue of Prince Isaac.

Mary gave the pasha a gracious smile. She expected to see Elgin do the same, but the ambivalent look on his face had now turned more specific—to one of consternation and impatience. "We really must get back to our ship," Elgin said, standing. "We must rise early in the morning. We've arranged to tour the area that is thought to be the site of ancient Troy."

"Ah yes, that first invasion of the Greeks," said Prince Isaac. "How history has reversed itself. They plagued us for many centuries with their expansionist ideas, but we have kept them subdued for three hundred fifty years, praise Allah."

"My husband is fanatical about studying Greek antiquities," Mary said. "My lord, did you tell the pasha about your project on the Acropolis?"

"I have hired a team of artists and craftsmen to remain in Athens during my mission and to make precise drawings and plaster copies of all the ancient architectural elements to take home for our English artists to study," Elgin said.

"We will never understand the English and French fascination with the old stones of past Greek civilizations," said the pasha, shaking his head.

"You are all made to read the blind Greek poet when you are mere boys, and it inspires much sentimentality for those times," Prince Isaac said. "Here, we have our own legends of conquest and heroism, and our own sacred monuments, so I understand. But these Greek stones are nothing but rubble now, not fit to decorate the home of a slave who empties piss pots, monuments to gods no one believes in any longer."

Mary smiled, but hoped that Elgin would not see fit to explain the reasoning to the Turks, for if so, they would be on the ship all night long. Fortunately, Elgin was first and foremost a diplomat, schooled in the art of pursuing discussions that could bring about positive results, and even more skilled at avoiding discussions that might be insulting to men with foreign and otherwise strange ideas.

"If you are a fanatic for old Greek things, you will be very happy tomorrow when you visit the village at Cape Sigeum, where the local people say the battle for Troy was fought, for there is much of the old rubble there. The Greeks who live there hold it all most holy. They are still a very ignorant people," Prince Isaac said with a mixture of pity and disdain.

Elgin's mood brightened. "Then we shall take our artists with us so that they can make copies of all that we see. We found the most exquisite Italian draftsman in Sicily," he said. "It took much convincing to entice him to join us, but he agreed. His name is Lusieri. You will be hearing much about him in the future, I am sure. I believe that the work he does for me in Athens will bring him a great reputation."

Mary would not soon forget the recent, arduous journey to Messina, riding in the hot sun on an ornery donkey while four months pregnant, only to arrive to meet Signor Lusieri, who spoke no English and had to be communicated with in French, which was exhausting after the first hour or two. There were times in Messina that Mary thought she would not survive the heat, nor the journey back. But she did think that Lusieri's drawings were superior to any that she and Elgin had seen in London. Elgin was delighted that she approved of his choice because, he announced, she would have to write to her father to ask him to cover the artist's salary, as the English government would not. Dutifully, Mary did so, certain that Mr. Nisbet would understand the urgency and importance of Elgin's ambition. To her surprise, Mr. Nisbet saw things differently. Hiring a grand Italian artist was an extravagance. So Mary had to write a separate letter to her mother to plead the case, which Mrs. Nisbet did satisfactorily.

The prince interrupted her thoughts. "Lady Elgin, do you share your husband's love of the ancient Greek arts?"

"Of course. It is the duty of a wife to share in her husband's interests." Mary thought that she should make a wifely comment, at least in part to remind the pasha that she was married.

The pasha conferred with the prince in their language. "Lord Elgin, you may take whatever you like," the prince announced.

"What do you mean?"

"From the village. Take whatever old Greek rocks you wish to take. The pasha does not understand why the English and the French would have these useless things rather than bars of gold or purses full of gems, but he will not quarrel with your ways as long as you do not quarrel with ours. I am sure that, to you, we are also sometimes inscrutable."

"Do you mean to say that we have permission to remove the antiquities that we see?"

"So many English and French have come before you and done this. We doubt there is anything left worth the taking, but do as you wish, with the pasha's compliments. Consider it a sign of good faith as we enter upon the new relationship between our countries."

"And as a special favor to Lady Elgin," added the pasha.

The pasha wrapped Mary in an extravagant fur-lined cloak against the cold night air before sending his guests to be rowed over the waters back to their vessel. "I shall have it returned to you in the morning," Mary said.

"Only if you wish to insult a new friend," he answered. "It is my pleasure to give you these small gifts."

Though the air was cold, the waters were calm and the skies were clear. Mary looked up at the stars as she relaxed against Elgin's arm, but she felt him withdraw.

"What is wrong?" she asked.

"You are going to have to be careful in your dealings with these Turks," he said.

What on earth could he mean? She had just won over two of the most important men in the Ottoman Empire. How could that not serve their interests?

"They do not have the restraint of Englishmen and Scotsmen," Elgin went on. "You must resist the temptation to tantalize them. I do not want any incidents or scenes. I cannot afford any interference with the political mission."

"My husband, how can you suggest that anything untoward took place this evening?"

"Do not pretend to be naïve, Mary. You know the effect you have on men. I had to witness the way you carried on with General O'Hara at Gibraltar. I wondered if you were going to come to Turkey with me at all or if you were going to stay there and be his concubine."

"Don't be ridiculous. General O'Hara is an elderly man." Mary sniffed, hoping that she sounded outraged, but the fact was that she had flirted with the general when they stopped at Gibraltar. He was probably in his sixties—older than her father—but he still had the good looks and the manly charm that had long ago made his reputation as a breaker of ladies' hearts. Because he was forty years her senior, she did not think that Elgin would take offense. Apparently, she was mistaken.

"As for this evening," she said, "I saw the opportunity to ingratiate myself with two men to whom you might have to turn for assistance while we are in Constantinople. All that I did, I did for you, I assure you. Besides, the Turkish men seem rather courtly and most respectful of women."

"Do not be naïve, Mary. If they possessed any control whatsoever, would they have to lock their women out of sight for their protection?"

Sigeum, near the site
of ancient Troy

THEY SET OUT LONG before dawn on damnable donkeys. In Sicily Mary had prayed that she was making her last trip on one of these beasts, but now that hope seemed an innocent one. She probably had a good two years of donkey travel ahead of her, given the difficult terrain and primitive roads of the territories

to which Elgin had been assigned, coupled with his thirst for explo-
ration, adventure, and antiquities.

The Learned Men, as Mary had come to call Elgin's staff, set
out with them, Homer in hand, ready to discover the location of the
exploits that they had been reading about since boyhood. Accompanying them were Captain Morris, a few officers from the military
contingent, and several Greek-speaking Turkish guides. Mary's
own saddle could not be found in the chaotic luggage-hold of the
Phaeton, so she was stuck spending the day on a hard saddle devoid
of padding or comfort of any kind. She was past the worst of the
nausea lately, but the frequency with which the donkey needed to
defecate threatened to bring back the days when she could barely
hold her head up. Elgin had offered to leave her behind, but Mary
could not bear the idea of spending the day in the clammy air of the
ship while her husband traced the footsteps of Achilles.

The morning had begun auspiciously enough. Before he set sail,
the Capitan Pasha had sent twenty-five sheep and six oxen as a present for their ship, along with letters to Elgin. Nineteen guns were
fired in salute as the *Selim III* sailed away, and Elgin ordered nineteen guns to be fired in return from the *Phaeton.* Mary grew so
weary of the sound of the cannons that she wanted to curl up into a
little ball, but she stood on deck with her husband smiling proudly,
as if listening to the roar and blast was the most pleasant activity
she could think to enjoy first thing in the morning.

By seven o'clock they were riding across the flat plains straight
into the rising sun, which drove its rays into Mary's eyes in defiance of her broad-brimmed straw hat. In the distance they saw the
famous mounds of Troy, or that is what the Learned Men claimed,
and it looked to Mary as if it would take the day to reach them.
Still, it was exciting when Reverend Hunt waved at the sky, crying
out, "We are on the very plains of Troy, riding into Homer's 'rosy-
fingered dawn.' Imagine! By the afternoon, we shall be pouring
wine to the gods into the same soil as Achilles and Alexander!"
Despite the discomfort of the heat and the saddle, Mary felt the
chill of gooseflesh on her arms.

At noon they arrived at the tiny Greek village of Sigeum.

"Greek in populace, language, and custom, like so many of the coastal regions of Turkey," Elgin told them. After washing up at the well of a Greek Orthodox church, Mary and Masterman laid out a picnic lunch of cold meats, bread, and wine from their basket while the Learned Men poked about the church grounds. Masterman swatted the flies away from the food as Mary waited impatiently for the men to return, her stomach empty and begging for a morsel. She picked up a slice of roast beef.

"It's not for me, you understand," she said to Masterman. "It's for the babe."

"And a bit for the babe's nurse too," Masterman said, joining her mistress. "It would be a shame to die of starvation in Turkeyland before the babe is born."

Suddenly Elgin came running toward them. He was alone, and his face was flushed and excited. Mary hoped that no one had met with an accident.

"You must come! Cover the food. There is something you must see."

Mary opened her mouth to question him but he grabbed her arm, leading her toward the church.

"Stay with the food," he ordered Masterman. "We shall return."

Elgin led Mary around to the rear of the church, where a woman, perhaps forty years old, lay on an ancient-looking marble bench. A priest in a tall, flat-topped black hat and heavy black robes stood over her, reading from a book that looked like a Bible. The woman's eyes were wide like a bug's and unblinking. She writhed back and forth, clutching and twisting at her dress of dirty blue muslin. Her long black hair, unbound and streaked with gray, spread on the marble bench like Medusa's snakes. Drool ran down from the sides of her mouth. Whenever the priest raised his voice, she threw her head back and screamed. Another priest, thin as a spider, put his hand on her forehead, trying to hold her still.

"They are performing an exorcism," Elgin whispered in Mary's ear. The Learned Men stood off to the side, riveted to the scene.

"We shouldn't be watching," Mary said.

"It's just ignorant superstition," Elgin said. "There are no devils present, if that is what you concerns you."

Mary turned her eyes away. "We are intruding upon something private."

"Nonsense," Elgin said. "The Orthodox, like the Roman Catholics, perform their sacraments publicly. Besides, it is not the exorcism I wished you to see. It is the two seats. They are magnificent."

"They look rather pitiful to these eyes," Mary said. The slab upon which the woman was writhing had probably once been a pediment. As the woman tossed from side to side, Mary could see that the thing was covered in some kind of inscription, which looked almost stripped of its characters. The other seat was on the opposite side of the church door. It appeared to once have been a relief of sorts, but the sculpted heads had been chiseled away beyond recognition, or at least beyond anything that Mary could identify.

"Reverend Hunt assures me that they are of the utmost historical importance," Elgin whispered, leading Mary away from the bizarre scene, much to her relief. "The guides told us that visitors have been making bids on them for as long as visitors have come to this place, but the priests will not let them go."

"So that is that." Mary was anxious to get away from the horrible display and back to filling her stomach. She felt light-headed and dizzy, but she used her sweetest voice on her husband. "Eggy, I must eat. The baby is demanding his sustenance."

"The other visitors did not have the permission of the Capitan Pasha, now did they?"

"I don't know, Eggy. Why would we want the benches? What shall we do with such things?" Mary did not want to be in possession of these tools of exorcism and other superstitions. Surely it would not carry good luck to have such profane things in one's home, though she had to admit that the beauty of the original was still apparent. The marble was worn down to an alabaster white, and on the unoccupied bench, fragments of angular, serene faces remained like stubborn guardians refusing to abandon their post.

"They are precious relics of an illustrious history. These Greeks do not value them or preserve them as they should if they were civilized, but allow devil-struck peasant women to wriggle all over them, wearing down the inscriptions. Reverend Hunt says that the writing is in the rare, antique style where one line is written from the left to the right, and the following line is written backwards. In ancient times, that is how messages both sacred and profane were inscribed. Look at the other, with its heads chipped away, suffering the worst exposure and neglect. They require a protector," Elgin said. "They should be preserved properly."

"Whatever you think is best," Mary said. Could he not see that she was fatigued and hungry?

Elgin smiled. "Come. Let us get our baby his sustenance. Perhaps when he's had his lunch, he'll inform his mother of the significance of his father's mission to retrieve these precious specimens from antiquity."

Suddenly, all went quiet. The priest had stopped reading from his book, and the woman lay breathing heavily, eyes shut. A peasant man and two small girls, presumably the woman's husband and children, rushed to the priest, falling upon their knees and kissing his hands. The priest dispassionately accepted the gratitude, distracted, it seemed, by the sight of Mary and Elgin. Catching Mary's eye before she turned to walk away, he snatched his hand from the man's grasp and, picking up the big silver cross of strange shape that lay against his chest, raised it toward Mary, who could not discern whether the gesture was a blessing or a warning.

During their picnic lunch, Elgin, eyes aflame, speech rushed and excited, made plans with the officers for procuring the benches. He made Captain Morris swear that he would manage to load the things onto the *Phaeton,* even if it meant leaving behind some of the sheep and oxen sent by the pasha. According to the guides, numerous travelers through the years had tried to procure the benches, only to be defeated by the lack of means to cart them off and back to Europe, or by the protests of the locals.

"We will inevitably encounter some resistance, my lord," said Captain Morris.

"But they did not have my advantage of being accompanied by military commanders," Elgin responded.

Nor did they have the advantage of the Capitan Pasha being enchanted with their wives, Mary thought as she watched her husband execute his plan for capture of the benches like some mad general after coveted turf. She knew the part she had played in the pasha's permission to allow Elgin to remove what he liked. The pasha desired to establish good relations with Elgin, but it was obvious that, as a man, he also wanted to please Mary.

"And you must insist that I have permission from the Capitan Pasha to remove whatever I like," Elgin instructed Major Fletcher, handing him a coin purse to hire villagers and carts to transport the benches.

"Do you require a nap before we move on in search of Troy, my dear?" Elgin asked Mary, who was resting in the shade of a tree. "The sun will only be with us another four to five hours."

"No, no, I am quite rested," Mary lied. She was tired after her lunch, but the donkey's jerky gait would surely keep her alert.

The party packed its supplies. One of the officers would escort the captured artifacts back to the ship, while the other officers and the guides would catch up with them after the transaction was completed.

The sun was directly overhead, and the heat of the afternoon was upon them. Mary opened a fine purple parasol, finding that she could easily ride the lumbering animal with only one hand on the reins. Her arm would lose its strength soon enough, but she welcomed the relief from the sun. They were not a quarter of a mile from the village when they heard someone yelling, and then the sound of footsteps behind them. They turned to see the priest running toward them, chased by the officers, who were chased by the guides. The priest spewed a litany of angry words at Elgin, who stared impassively at him as if he were not real, but an apparition conjured at a magic show. The priest's right hand pointed to the skies as if he was invoking God. His vociferous words brought with them spittle, which Elgin leaned backwards to avoid, watching it land at his feet.

"What is he going on about?" Elgin looked up, asking no one in particular.

"He says that if you take the benches, you will bring death and destruction upon the village," translated one of the Greek guides.

"What nonsense," Elgin said.

"No, it is true," the guide said. "These were put here by the heroes of old, thousands of years ago, to honor the gods. The last time an Englishman took an old inscription from the church, the village was infested with the plague."

"Ask your priest if he still worships Apollo and Athena," Elgin scoffed.

The guide posed the question to the priest, who responded quickly. The guide translated. "No, but to think that they do not still exist and protect what was once theirs would be a mistake. God presides over the earth, but the ancient ones are angry that they have been replaced. They can still prevent the crops from growing. If you take the seats, the olives on the trees will shrivel, and the local doctors will no longer be able to treat disease."

"Inform your priest that his ideas are ludicrous and dangerous. He is supposed to be a man of God. He must act like one. These are precious artifacts and must be put under the protection of someone who will shelter them properly. If he wishes to impede us, he will have to answer directly to the Capitan Pasha."

What village priest would want to confront the second or third man in command to the Sultan? Mary thought.

While the interpreter explained Elgin's position to the priest, Elgin let it be known that the conversation had ended. He remounted his donkey, and the rest of the party followed.

They rode for a few minutes in silence, the wails of the priest lingering behind them. On the plain, there was little to see but the mounds of Troy in the distance, and a few camels grazing off the path.

"Was that the proper thing to do, Eggy?" Mary asked.

"What?"

"Remove their talismans? Perhaps the villagers will turn on the priest when they find out what has happened."

"Let them turn on their Turkish oppressors. These priests are revered. No one will harm them. Anyway, it's about time that they shed their superstitions. Such ignorant barbarians do not deserve to be in possession of things as precious as those we have just acquired."

Mary knew that Elgin was right. If left at the church another hundred years, the inscriptions would be worn beyond any recognition. Or perhaps another collector, or Napoleon, who was always threatening to invade these shores, would take them, depriving the English of the glory of possessing them, and perhaps not caring for them as only the English could.

Still, it was unsettling to hear the cries of the priest dissipating into the warm, moist air, as they left him and his village behind.

In the city of Constantinople,

November 1799

CARRIED IN A GOLDEN chair by four Turks over the muddy and uneven paths of the city, Mary wondered what she would do when, returning to Scotland, she would have to negotiate the sidewalks on her own two feet like a mere mortal. She felt like a goddess, high above the heads of those relegated to the streets, such as they were, with their ruts and dung and assorted filth that one must by-step to arrive at one's destination unscathed.

She knew that a sensible Scottish girl should not allow herself to become accustomed to being carried like a queen on a glimmering throne padded with soft cushions the colors of spices—cinnamon, paprika, clove. But her illustrious Turkish hosts would not even consider an alternative method of transportation for their new ambassadress.

At the moment, she was dressed neither as an ambassador's wife nor in the drapes of a deity, but in a man's riding habit, a beaver hat, and a bulky woolen coat, with huge epaulets, that hid both her sex and her pregnancy. Carried next to Mary on a less decorative chair was Masterman, costumed in a similar gentleman's habit that Mary had contrived for her. Masterman's pale, rigid face was pointed ahead as she tried to hold herself straight as a pin while the chair jostled back and forth on the shoulders of her carriers.

"Isn't it exciting?" Mary asked, trying to ignite at least a bit of enthusiasm in her lady's maid. "We are attending Lord Elgin's formal presentation to the Grand Vezir, who is the most powerful man in the empire next to the Sultan."

If the Capitan Pasha was the first man in the military, the Grand Vezir was the first man in the political scene. He presided over the Divan, a council of ministers that kept him informed on, and debated with him, the politics of the Turkish Empire. The Grand Vezir then took their counsel to the Sultan.

"Relations between myself and the Sultan will rely largely upon the relationship developed with the vezir," Elgin had explained to Mary.

Masterman had no response, but clutched her coat against the early-morning dampness as she continued to stare straight ahead into the slowly rising sun.

"Hundreds of important people will be present to hear Lord Elgin's speech. And we shall be the only two women among them," Mary continued.

"It's a naughty bit of scheming, if you ask me—which, to be fair, you did not," Masterman said.

Masterman had never approved of Mary's tactics, but Mary rarely took this fact into consideration. Though women were strictly forbidden to attend any court function, Mary had devised a scheme for admittance. She would dress in men's clothing and be presented as Lord Bruce, presumably a young relative of Lord Elgin, and Masterman would accompany her as a manservant. Mary knew that she would have to rise well before dawn and set out upon a long journey in heavy clothing, enduring long hours in the rituals of the Ottoman court, and she was unsure that at this stage of her pregnancy she would be able to handle the adventure alone.

She was sure that her charade was unique and that, with Masterman's support, she could pull it off, until she met a woman at a party who had attempted the same thing, with disastrous results. The woman was found out in the middle of the ceremony, and physically removed from the premises by Janissaries—"roughly," she'd said, "fearing for my life."

"I have found the Turks to be most chivalrous and respectful," Mary had said. "Upon my honor, I just wrote to my mother that I had not known politeness until I met Turks."

"That is true enough," the woman answered, "until one exceeds the boundaries set for women."

Still, Mary was not to be deterred. She had already exceeded the boundaries of her gender, and rather than reprisal, the Capitan Pasha had met her daring with admiration.

"You show no enthusiasm, Masterman, though you are literally making history today," Mary chided.

"This sort of thing makes me queasy in the middle. You might have been meant for a career upon the stage, Miss Mary Nisbet, if your father had not been a gentleman. But I am just a poor lady's maid with no stomach for pretending games."

"There is nothing to worry about. I have the permission of the Capitan Pasha to carry out my plan. I begged his indulgence for my desire to see my husband deliver his speech and to know firsthand the ways of the Turkish court. He sent his messenger with a personal response that we might attend with his assurances that all would go smoothly for me." For *her*, he had emphasized, and Mary was not unaware of the enormity of the favor.

Elgin had marveled at her pluck. He was anxious about delivering his speech and determined to make a bold impression on the Grand Vezir. He wanted his wife to be present at the event so that she might afterwards indulge in an analysis of his performance. This time, he did not object to the special favor showered upon her by the Capitan Pasha, who assured Mary that anyone who subjected her to the slightest insult or mistreatment would answer directly to him.

"The pasha is sending us his sister's lavish carriage, which he assures me is the most comfortable one in the city," Mary added. He had been concerned over a woman in Mary's condition having to ride through the city's rugged streets.

The carriage had four lovely glasses from which they could see the minarets and domes of the city thrusting up into the skies, and the houses, crowded together as if leaning upon one another for support, painted bright reds, greens, and blues. Though it was barely past dawn, in the streets, merchants in great white turbans hawked goods, while beggars hassled their clients for coin. The sheer multitude of painted surfaces made Mary think that all of England and Scotland, by contrast, contained only two colors—gray in the cities and green in the countryside.

Arriving at the palace of the Grand Vezir, the two women were escorted into a small room, where they were served coffee, and Mary was given an opportunity to speak with the official dragoman of the Porte, the court interpreter, who, though he had already met her as Lady Elgin, agreed to address her, and treat her, as Lord Bruce. From this antechamber they were escorted into the larger, grander audience room, crowded with at least two hundred men, dressed in the strange and beautiful clothing of their nations. The Turks wore robes of dazzling jewel-colored silks over loose pants tucked into high suede boots, and tall hats of many sorts—conical, flat-topped, plumed, and some wrapped in the turban style about their heads with a tiny feather jutting from the center, above the forehead. Mary could not identify the other ambassadors except for her neighbors, the Russians, who wore tailored black jackets with fur-lined lapels and dark shirts with severe high collars underneath, though she assumed that the other westerners were Venetians and Swedes, whom she would eventually meet and entertain.

At the commencement of the official ceremony, Elgin and the Grand Vezir toasted each other with delicate coffee cups. After servants took the cups, a tray of scents was brought out and Elgin and the vezir were perfumed.

"I don't imagine our Mr. Pitt sharing a spray with foreign gentlemen!" Masterman whispered, looking down her nose.

"We are in an exotic land," Mary whispered back. "We must respect their customs, as different as they are from our own."

"Different indeed! That's a mouthful," Masterman said.

"Now, hush!" Mary said as Elgin stood to give his speech. Mary's heart pounded in her chest. She did not want him to suffer any distraction. She had gone over the speech with him so many times the night before that she had to stop herself from mouthing the words as he said them. Though only she and one or perhaps two others in the room could understand what he said, her nervousness on his behalf was not quelled until he delivered the last of the words, to great applause.

Finally, the Grand Vezir delivered to Elgin his official credentials, after which two Turkish attendants brought forth great fur cloaks made of lush reddish-black sable. They draped one over Elgin's shoulders, and he motioned for his wife to stand.

Mary stepped forward, and the vezir's men placed the second cloak over her shoulders.

"Lord Bruce," one of them announced to the Grand Vezir. The attendant released the weight of the cloak onto Mary's shoulders, and she almost dropped with the heaviness of it. She had never seen such luxurious fur, much less felt it upon her small frame. Once she adjusted to its oppressive mass, she felt its soft hairs tickle her face and neck, and she had to stifle the urge to giggle.

"Lord Bruce will now be presented to the Grand Vezir," whispered the dragoman.

"Ye gads!" Mary said. By this time, she had been awake for many hours, with little sleep the night before, and almost nothing in her stomach. She feared that between the hunger and the dizziness, she would drop at the great man's feet if she tried to bow.

"Steady me, old girl," she whispered to Masterman as she stood. Blackness rose in front of her eyes, but holding on to Masterman's arm, she waited the few moments until her vision returned.

Smiling, but trying to maintain the solemnity of a man at his duties, she walked toward the vezir in his emerald green robe. His intense dark eyes seemed to command her to look directly at him. Did he suspect that the male wardrobe was a sham? Was she walking too much like a woman? With the squarest shoulders and longest neck she could affect, Mary focused on putting one foot ahead of the other until she was within the appropriate distance of the Grand Vezir to bow her head, relieved to be released from the man's stare.

"And have you any daughters?" Mary heard the dragoman ask Elgin, interpreting the question asked by the vezir. She looked up just in time to see the surprised look on Elgin's face when he realized that she had been mistaken for his son. She almost lost all composure as her eyes met Elgin's and he smiled at her.

But their moment was interrupted by what seemed a battle cry, a fierce and dreadful yell. Mary crouched, turning to see the origin of the sound, afraid that perhaps she and Masterman had been found out, and a riot was about to take place. The dragoman must have seen the look of fear on her face. He ran to her, crouching over her.

"It is a prayer for the Sultan," he whispered in her ear. It sounded to her much more like a call for war or revolution, and she was mightily relieved when the cries to heaven subsided and calm was restored.

Though the rest of the afternoon was uneventful, the journey home was long, and her nerves did not recover from the fright. She arrived at home after five o'clock in the afternoon, spent after her day of pomp, ceremony, and heavy men's clothing. Mary had never experienced the sort of fatigue that accompanied pregnancy—the kind of tiredness that could not be overcome by a positive mental outlook or a good cup of tea. It was an exhaustion that overruled one's greater intentions and demanded surrender.

"I think I'll have a nap," she said to Masterman.

"It's Thursday, remember?" Masterman replied. Thursday was the day Mary and Elgin had fixed as their weekly "public evening," when they would entertain all the appropriate dignitaries and visitors in the city. "You are hosting a supper, followed by a ball. The guest list tops out at one hundred."

"But I am exhausted," Mary protested.

"That may be so, but you have less than fifteen minutes to transform yourself back into a grand lady, Lord Bruce."

Mary greeted the guests at six o'clock as planned. As the night wore on, Elgin took those with whom he required private discourse into his study, leaving Mary to entertain the others. When she ran out of conversation, she played the pianoforte for them, and finally, in desperation, taught the guests how to dance Scottish reels. She was not certain that any of them would have left had she not instructed the servants to stop replacing the long tapers that lit much of the room. It was not until midnight that the last of the guests gave in to the message sent by the dwindling candles.

"Lordy, I have had enough of them!" Mary said to Masterman as the older woman helped her undress.

"In seven days, you'll be doing it again, mistress. And then seven days after that, and seven days after that, and on for two years," Masterman said dryly. "So you mightn't want to tire of their company so soon."

"By my calculations, I can anticipate one hundred and four Thursdays of entertaining one hundred guests," Mary later said to Elgin as they climbed into bed. "The mathematics of it defeats me."

"Ah, but you are a superb hostess, Mary. Everyone tonight has commented on it," he answered.

"Thank you, my darling. I want everything to be absolutely perfect for you while we are here," she said, not revealing to him that she felt fatigue deep within her very bones. Then she prayed quickly to God to let her have a good and refreshing night's sleep. Mid-prayer, she felt herself begin to lose consciousness. Her last memory as she drifted off to sleep was Elgin cozying up to her warm body in their bed and untying the neat bow she had made in fastening her nightgown. Whatever transpired after that was anyone's guess.

MARY WOKE THE NEXT day, put on her dressing gown, and went out onto the balcony off her bedroom to greet the giant yellow sun that so often presided over Constantinople. The Elgins and staff were ensconced in the former French Embassy Palace on the Grand Rue, the street that housed ambassadors from around the world. She looked out over the view of the shimmering waters of the Bosphorus, the strait that divided the city; the Golden Horn, its inlet; and the Sea of Marmara. She could see all of them from this, her favorite part of the lavish palace. She loved her mornings when she stole a few private moments, taking her tea tray outside as she looked over the city, all the way to the imposing towers of the Sultan's palace.

She finished her tea and went inside, pondering what she must do on this day. She was sure that she had some appointments, and she thought she would wear the little scoop bonnet she'd bought in London in the style that had recently become so popular. Where was it? Maybe she would save Masterman some time and find it herself. She went to one of the wardrobes in the dressing room adjacent to her bedroom and opened its tall doors. A scent escaped that was not familiar to her. Nor were the clothes that hung in the wardrobe.

"Oh dear," she said aloud. This was not the first time that she had discovered the abandoned possessions of the French ambassador, the palace's most recent occupant, who had been unceremoniously evicted and was imprisoned in Yedikule, the daunting seven-towered fortress. She closed the doors just as Elgin came into the room.

"We must have the servants pack up the belongings of our predecessors," she said. "I do not like to think of those French diplomats in Turkish prisons."

"Mary, do not worry. I promise to appeal to the Grand Vezir for their humane treatment. For surely they are gentlemen, victims of the politics of the time and the ambitions of their general, who does not know how to honor an alliance."

Others could say what they wished about her husband, but Mary saw his idealism and his desire to always do the right thing, and she loved him for those qualities.

"But one shift in the political tides, and the French could be back in the palace and you and I in the prison!"

"Nonsense, Mary. We have no Bonaparte to send us on the road to ruin. At any rate, you have done a splendid job of imprinting our own style upon the place," he said. "Whoever says that the French are the current arbiters of taste have not met my Poll."

"I have worked hard to rid the rooms of the ghosts of the former tenants."

Mary had already spent almost two thousand pounds of her own money refurbishing the private rooms she shared with Elgin as well as the rooms of his staff, trying to erase the memory of regimes gone by. She knew how important a comfortable environment was to her husband—to any man—and she wanted to give both Elgin and his staff every opportunity to thrive. She only hoped that when her parents saw the bills, they would share her perspective. If not, she would write to them and explain the situation. If they balked at the cost of feeding sixty mouths thrice a day, and entertaining the multitudes of Hottentots, they should take it up with His Majesty's government, which refused to pay the true costs of running a foreign embassy.

Elgin went off on his appointments, and Mary went in to breakfast, hoping for a quiet morning. Instead, she was greeted by the entire embassy staff of sixty.

"They have appointed me to speak for them," said Reverend Hunt as she ushered him into her private office. "We have threats of mutiny, Lady Elgin. Some are upset with their living conditions, some with their pay, and some with the hours at which they are to take their meals."

Hunt was so polite in the asking that even though she was annoyed at the staff's complaints, she spent the next day trying to fix everyone's difficulties with his or her rooms, and she made a schedule for dining that seemed agreeable to all. Then she reconvened the staff.

"May I remind you that those of you who make deliveries to the palaces of the Sultan and other Turkish dignitaries receive gratuities equivalent to two years of your salaries? All of you will prosper from the great generosity of the Turks, but only if you carry out your duties with a modicum of grace."

Because of the English government's parsimony, Mary was personally responsible for most of the expenses of running the embassy, and she was not about to increase anyone's salary now that she saw firsthand the riches that the entire staff might accumulate if they simply did their jobs.

"Just yesterday," she continued, "those of you who delivered the chandelier to the Sultan as a gift from Lord Elgin and the English government were rewarded for your trouble with coin five times the annual income you would be earning at home!" The men to whom she referred avoided her eyes, staring sheepishly at the floor.

How she wished that this group of whining ingrates had to perform their tasks with a baby in their bellies as she did. She wished with all her heart that she could say this to them right now, but it would be unseemly.

The week continued in the same vein—socializing, entertaining, redecorating, and attending to the complaints of the staff.

"I'm as tired as a working mule," Mary commented to Mr. Morier, one of Elgin's secretaries. "Sunday is the Lord's Day, made for nothing but services and rest."

"Oh dear," he replied. "So sorry, Your Ladyship, but may I remind you that a golden chair is to arrive within the hour to carry you to dinner at the Russian embassy?"

Exhausted, she dressed for the occasion, summoning whatever energy remained in her wrung-out body. When she stepped into the chair, she realized that the only time she ever sat down was on these excursions. Yet one was always on display. A parade of eight Janissaries, four footmen, and a dragoman served as her escort this evening. Windows all along the street opened to watch this elegant tableau as they made their way down the street to the neighboring palace.

At the dinner, the guests announced that they had heard about Mary's tutelage of Scottish country-dances and asked for a repeat performance. But she had to decline because it was Sunday, and she was not about to dance on the Lord's Day. Just because they were in the land of heathens, it would not do to throw Christian ideals out the window. She had to reply in the same way when the wife of the Russian minister invited her to sit down to a game of whist, Mary's favorite card game and one at which Madame Tamara, the Russian ambassadress, claimed to excel.

Mary was looking for an excuse to leave the party early when

Elgin rushed in carrying a letter. He took Mary aside. "You've been summoned," he said.

"Have I? And by whom?"

Elgin showed her the official letter, replete with its golden seal.

"By the Supreme Head of the House of Osmanh," Elgin said. "He who presides over the Golden Horn and all the territories from the Adriatic to the hinterlands of Persia."

"The Sultan?" Mary felt slightly queasy as she said the word and she put her hand on the small table behind her to steady herself.

"Tomorrow morning before the sun rises, you must be dressed and ready to be taken to the Palace of the Topkapi Sarayi. I suggest we make our apologies and get you home to bed." Elgin seemed giddy at this new turn of events. "It's unprecedented, Mary. You are breaking every rule and custom."

"But why would the Sultan summon me?" Mary asked.

"I suppose that he heard through the Grand Vezir and the Capitan Pasha that you were worth a look."

"Must it be tomorrow? I am exhausted," she said.

"You are the first woman from the Continent invited into the Sultan's palace," he said with pride. "Other wives of ambassadors and intrepid female travelers have merely contemplated the labyrinthine building from outside its gates. Apparently he has heard tales of both Lord Bruce and Lady Elgin, and he wishes to have a viewing."

"But why?"

"It is not up to us to ask why, Mary. When the man who lords over North Africa, Asia Minor, and the Balkans, and over great cities from Cairo to Tripoli to Baghdad to Constantinople, asks to see you, it is only proper to make an appearance at the appointed time."

Topkapi Palace,

November 26, 1799

L ONG BEFORE DAWN THE next morning in damp,
chilly air, Mary found herself once again high above men's
shoulders, surrounded by torch carriers whose wild flambeaux lit
the path to the water. Her escorts, the Janissaries, carrying mus-
kets and swords, walked alongside the golden chair, their uniforms
of bright teal blue in sharp contrast to the still-black sky. She had
learned that they composed an elite unit of soldiers, a strike force
led into battle by the Sultan himself, and trained in an atmosphere
of rigor that demanded celibacy and monasticism in all habits. In
times of peace, they served as police and bodyguards. Mary was
honored that no less than eight of these warriors were assigned to
deliver her to important occasions, when she was sure that one or
two would have done.

"I would like to talk to them," Mary said to the translator who
accompanied her. "But they do not meet my eye."

"Such familiarity with a woman is forbidden," the man answered.

"Even one they have seen as much as me?"

"When encountering an unveiled woman, they naturally, and
out of respect, lower their eyes," he answered. "Frequency of contact
does not alter the etiquette."

"Then I shall have to suppress my natural curiosity," she said,
watching the long white silks of their headdresses, folded high over
crowns, dance down their backs like the veil of a Tudor bride.

Arriving at the water, she panicked when she saw the small Turkish vessel in which she was to be transported across the river. The
translator helped her into the boat, instructing her to remain seated
and absolutely still. "Last week, a European visitor got overly enthusiastic at the sight of the palace and tipped the boat mid-river."

"Did he survive?" Mary asked.

"Yes, but he is in a rather rheumatic state from which we pray he recovers, *insh'Allah*."

Mary shuddered; she felt rheumatic enough already, having awakened at three-thirty in the morning with a tickle in the throat and a pounding headache. She was much more nervous than she'd wanted to acknowledge. Maybe the Sultan was going to admonish her for invading the all-male ceremony at the Grand Vezir's palace. It seemed implausible that a man whose realm extended over many countries would take it upon himself to punish her small, indiscreet act. But something that might be perceived as merely indiscreet to her, or an act of daring, might be seen as downright insulting, or even lawless and punishable, in this strange land, with its opaque rules and customs.

She looked out of the corner of her eye at the dark waters rushing past her, pitch-black but for little glimmers of light from the lamp that lit their path; she was afraid to turn her head lest she tip the boat. Even if she survived being dunked into the water, what would happen to her tiny unborn child? She sat, rigid, letting the cold wind hit her face, finally tucking her nose into her fur collar to preserve it from turning red, letting the warmth of her even breaths soothe her tension.

They arrived at the dock in front of the Imperial Gate just as the sky began to lighten. The sun was not yet visible on the horizon, but the slowly reddening sky forecast its arrival as dozens of people lined up to be admitted. Mary was advised to remain close to her escorts to avoid getting caught up in the throng that would rush the gate as soon as it opened.

"Is today some sort of holiday or special occasion?" she asked the dragoman. Perhaps she was just one of many who would be presented en masse to the Sultan.

"People travel many miles and from many countries to make appeals to the Grand Vezir, who hears cases for the Sultan and then presents the most urgent to him. Every morning, when the gates open, there is a scuffle to get to the head of the line. Some days, the scuffle turns into a riot."

Mary looked up at the tall gates. The inscription above in Turkish letters with their lovely curves and accents seemed to dance on the wall.

"Welcome to Topkapi Sarayi, built by Mehmet the Conqueror, after he took the city in the year 1453," said the dragoman.

"What is the inscription above the gate?" Mary asked.

"The great Mehmet declares that the palace was built with the permission of God and is secure and impregnable. He asks that God make the sultanate eternal, and declares himself the hero and conqueror of land and water, the shadow of God in two worlds and the servant of God between the two horizons. He asks God to place him above the North Star."

"A reasonable request," Mary said, immediately regretting the irony in her voice. She had found many admirable qualities in the people of this land, but humor was not among them. Perhaps they had their own sensibility on that matter.

The gates opened, and Mary joined the throng pouring inside. Though she had to steady herself against her escort as the various contingents of supplicants rushed past them, she saw flashes of brilliant mosaic fountains and well-manicured gardens. Elgin, who had arrived even earlier, found them soon enough, and hustled her into a small antechamber, where she collected herself before joining the procession into the assembly room where the Grand Vezir was sitting in state.

"I'm the only female," she whispered to Elgin.

"You should be accustomed to that by now," he replied, offering her a seat next to him so that she might observe the Grand Vezir hearing cases, pleas that citizens of the empire wished to make to the Sultan. "The Great Man is listening behind the latticework," Elgin said. Mary wondered if from behind his screen he was looking at her.

The proceedings went on for three hours. Mary had fallen asleep several times, whether from fatigue or passing out from hunger, she did not know. A merchant in a red tunic with a big white turban was imploring the Grand Vezir on some matter or other, and she took a deep breath, trying to stay conscious. She did not want to create a scene. She tried not to think of the long years stretching ahead. As the wife of a high-ranking diplomat, she would have to accustom herself to these deadening rituals.

Suddenly a bell was rung, and everyone stood. Elgin turned to her, mouthing the word *dinner,* his smile reminding her that all that she was enduring was well worth the price. What was a morning of discomfort and tedium compared to the utter bliss of being the wife of such a man?

It was ten o'clock in the morning. In the dining room, Elgin was seated at the place of highest honor next to the Grand Vezir, while Mary dined at a massive silver table with fancily dressed men, whom she assumed were important. She was starved, longing only for tea, toast, jam, and a coddled egg, but she was presented with platters of oily meats reeking of pungent spices, dishes she might have enjoyed in the evening with a glass of light wine. Starvation won the war; she could not afford to black out from hunger in front of the Sultan. But she hoped that her body would not betray her in other ways for admitting these foreign substances.

After dinner, she joined yet another procession into an open courtyard, where a skirmish broke out among a Greek contingent clamoring for the kaftans and cloaks handed out by a Turkish official. Elgin pulled her up on a small pedestal and pressed her so hard into his chest that she thought she would suffocate. From the corner of her eye, she saw fabrics fly into the air, then land in hands that pulled and tugged and threw punches. Some of the men were knocked to the ground before guards rushed in to restore order, and the culprits were escorted from the courtyard.

"There, there," Elgin said, patting her back. "Not so bad as a London riot, was it?"

"I am not very fond of those either," Mary said, hoping to keep the bits of rich meats she ate for breakfast in her belly.

"Are you ready for the audience?" he asked. Four men with stiffly erect posture in magnificent gold robes approached them with purposeful strides. Wordlessly, two flanked Elgin, and the other two, Mary. The men each with one hand over his heart, marched the Elgins into a small, dark room.

Still reeling from the ruckus, Mary was not sure of what was happening. Her eyes did not immediately adjust to the dramatic change in light. It appeared that a monster was propped up on a huge platform, one knee raised, supporting a long, droopy limb. As objects came into focus, she realized that it was the Sultan, Selim III, the Grand Seigneur, lying on an immense golden throne, which back home would be called a bed. She almost chuckled as she imagined parsimonious old King George receiving his visitors sprawled out in such luxury.

The Sultan, she now saw, was not so immense, but was wearing a yellow satin robe with a huge collar and cuffs of black sable, thus contributing to Mary's initial impression that he was a beast. Upon his head sat a monstrous turban with an aigrette of plumage sprouting from the center. Behind him on windowsills sat two additional diamond-studded turbans, perched like sparkly heads. A jumble of mosaic patterns covered the walls. Mary did not want to look as if she was gawking, so she kept her eyes focused on the Sultan, who had not yet acknowledged her.

Selim III was not a small man, and the accoutrements of power with which he adorned himself, and the pearl-studded cushions upon which he reclined, made him look even larger. His face was long, disappearing into a perfectly rounded dark beard. His eyes were slinky and almond-shaped, like those of a beautiful lynx. His nose was long and fine, and as far as Mary could tell in this dimly lit environment, his skin was smooth and flawless, as if only the rest of him had aged since the day he was born. Nets strung with rows and rows of pearls hung above his head, presumably to catch insects. A small butterfly, wings caught in the threads, struggled to escape, and Mary wished that she could free it from its beautiful trap and watch its burnt-orange wings soar out of the window.

At the Sultan's right was an inkstand encrusted with diamonds, and at his left lay his saber, covered in diamonds so large that Mary wondered where on earth they had been mined. She had never seen such huge, thumping stones, such concentrated lavishness, and could not wait to write to her mother about it. She was composing the letter in her head when she realized that Elgin was speaking through a dragoman, but the Sultan's gaze was upon her. Though he did not acknowledge her, he stared at her so attentively that she began to feel dizzy—and then terrified. Was she supposed to meet his stare, or was that considered a breach of their bizarre and contradictory etiquette?

She was not prepared for this level of scrutiny. Here was a man who supposedly had dozens of wives and concubines at his disposal, hidden away in his harem—she had been told that the word meant "forbidden place." Somewhere in this very palace was a virtual prison full of women who were on this earth merely to please this man. Perhaps he was accustomed to looking at women thus, appraising them as he would a horse for purchase.

Elgin, looking unconcerned that the monster was staring at his wife, focused upon the dragoman, who was translating his remarks to Selim. But to Mary, it was all disorienting. She put her hand to her head, and then, not wishing to appear ill or odd or insecure, she pretended to push a lock of hair away from her forehead. More words were exchanged, but Mary could not focus on the meaning. Elgin was bowing, and Mary chose to emulate the gesture. Then the two of them were whisked out of the room by their escorts and into the startling light of the courtyard.

"That went rather well," Elgin said.

"Did you not object to the Sultan's scrutiny of your wife?" Mary asked.

"I could hardly challenge the man to a duel." Elgin looked perturbed, and then he sighed. "I fear I must become accustomed to the way that men scrutinize my wife, or I must resign myself to fighting an inordinate number of duels, with men ranking from slave to sultan."

"Don't be cross, Eggy. I cannot help it if sultans find me alluring," she said. "Perhaps I should take up the veil."

"Perhaps you should, only removing it when your lord and master returns to his private harem." Elgin smiled. "I believe that I shall have the good Reverend Hunt castrated so that he may act as your eunuch and protector."

"When the Capitan Pasha comes for a visit, he shall be told that

Lady Elgin is no longer at leisure to enter into the company of men. Lord Elgin demands that he find another lady upon whom to lavish his gifts of furs and jewels and fine porcelain."

"We mustn't treat our Capitan Pasha in a punitive manner, Mary. Not when he has so very much to offer us."

Mary smiled, patting Elgin's hand. "How gracious of you to be so concerned about not punishing the good Capitan Pasha."

"For all your good humor, you look a bit tired, Mistress Poll," he said. "I am taking you home and putting you to bed, where I shall not allow you to rest at all. I want to lift your veil, as it were, and view the whole of you."

So Elgin had actually been aroused by the Sultan's attention to her. Men could be such strange beasts—animals whose sexual urges could be tweaked by the most unpredictable incidents. She was not unhappy. She had heard that some men lost interest in making love to their wives as their pregnancies progressed, but Elgin only seemed more eager, telling her always that her swollen belly made her look like some pagan fertility goddess.

Elgin called his valet, asking him to take charge of his horse. He would be taking the private carriage back to the boat with his wife.

As they drove toward home, he whispered in Mary's ear, "I want to see and touch every part of you, which even the Sultan of the Ottomans may do only in his dreams."

In the city of Constantinople,

Christmastime 1799

D R. MACLEAN'S HAND SHOOK with palsy as he removed the leeches from the pot and applied them to Elgin's sweaty face. The jar was an odd vessel to house the slimy creatures.

It was of elegant shape, and made, Mary guessed, by one of the finer china companies, perhaps Staffordshire. The word "leech" was painted in the color of teal that was so popular in the fashions of the day, and Mary thought that if one changed the word to "butter" or "sugar" or "milk," the jar would not be out of place on the most decorously laid-out luncheon table. But instead of accompaniments to one's tea, the contents of the jar were horrible, wormlike, blood-sucking creatures, the first of which now sat upon Elgin's temple, swelling as it fed upon his rheumatic blood.

"God help us," the doctor said as he withdrew his shaky hand, leaving the horrid thing to its business on Elgin's face.

Elgin had spent a whole evening out of doors in the rain, witness to one of the city's spectacular fires, as it burned through blocks of the unsafe wooden structures that housed Constantinople's cacophonous and polyglot population of more than a half-million people. The homes of immigrant Greeks, Jews, Italians, Slavs, and Russians had burned through the night along with the homes of many Turks.

"It's too dangerous, my darling," Mary had cried as he ran out the door. But he did not heed her, turning around to blow her the briefest kiss, and leaving his greatcoat behind in the fervor to see the flames that were shooting up above domes and minarets into black sky.

As he left the palace, Mary looked up into the sky, unable to distinguish the gathering smoke from storm clouds. When the heavens broke open later in the evening, she knew that Elgin would not heed his delicate constitution and come in out of the rain. He was always caught between his poor health and his natural desire for manly adventure. To remind him of the former was such a blow to the latter that she had ceased to do it, though she must resume now that he was paying the price of his recklessness. He had come home very late, soaked to the bone, and spent the following day in bed with one of his worst migraines, a condition that he blamed on Constantinople's inclement winter weather.

"How on earth can a Scot complain about Turkish winters?"

she would say to him. But complain he did about the bitter and unpredictable rains and the improperly heated rooms in which they often had to wear the furs given to them by their Turkish hosts.

Now, Dr. MacLean delivered the sixth leech to Elgin's face; all of them pulsated rhythmically as they bled him of his misery.

"I've never seen such vicious eaters," Dr. MacLean said, lifting the tail end of one of the creatures to make sure that it had fastened itself. "Their bite is much stronger than the English leech's."

Elgin winced, opening for one instant a startled blue eye and then quickly shutting it again. What must the worms look like from his perspective?

Mary hoped that the doctor was making a legitimate observation and not an inebriated one. His heavy drinking had caught up with him, and she noticed that his hands shook whether at breakfast or in ministering to the sick. She had wanted to call another doctor, but where to find a reliable one in this city of rampant disease, she did not know. She was aware, however, that she experienced a failure of nerve whenever she thought of Dr. MacLean presiding over the birth of her baby, which was now only two months away.

She was not a squeamish girl. She had played with earthworms and other insects in the gardens at Archerfield, to the horror of her nurses, who thought that she would die from the venom of some unidentified many-legged creature before she was out of the nursery. Her mettle had been tested on the open seas, under gunfire, and on the backs of donkeys through treacherous terrain, and all while carrying a growing fetus inside her. But Mary could not maintain her gaze upon Elgin's beautiful face as the leeches performed their grim duties. His eyes were shut tight—a look that she was accustomed to and loved in rapturous moments, but that now bespoke only agony. And yet she must resolve to be strong. There was no mother or father into whose arms she might collapse or seek comfort. Despite all who admired her, she was alone in this strange city. The other diplomatic wives sought her company and fought for invitations to her suppers and dances, but she knew that they also cackled with jealousy behind her back for the favor she was shown by the Sultan and his retinue of powerful men. How they would love to hear that

Lady Elgin had weakened under the strain of her pregnancy and of her husband's illness and had to be sent home.

She felt the all-too-familiar narrowing of her windpipe as the flow of air into her nostrils seemed to cease, as if the air were evaporating out of the room. She opened her mouth to breathe, afraid that she would divert the attention of Dr. MacLean—who could recognize the onset of one of her choking attacks—away from Elgin, who needed it more. Holding her breath, she forced herself to go to Elgin. Avoiding as best she could the sight of the leeches, she lifted his hand to her mouth and kissed it, smiling at him and at the doctor. She raised her index finger to signal that she required a moment out of the room—please, dear God, let them think she had to relieve herself—and then rushed out of the door. She ran into her private bedroom, struggling with the shutters that opened onto the balcony, coughing and at the same time trying with futility to push the air out of her lungs, sounding like some failing steam engine. With the last burst of her energy, she thrust herself outside, throwing her chest over the railing in case she vomited, holding on to the wrought iron, and shaking it as if the violent action would enable her to exhale. She sank to her knees, trying to calm herself, trying to release some tiny spurt of air so that she could stay alive until the choking stopped, which it inevitably did, but only after causing her to wonder, with every attack, if she would again survive.

The contractions in her throat began to diminish, until at last she could release shallow breaths through her mouth. She sat on her skirts, clutching the rail, slowly letting the air into and out of her lungs, and looking out into the night. It was cold and clear, starlight dancing upon the waters of the river. At the bottom of the hill, she saw what looked like a merchant pulling a cart loaded with bolts of white muslin, but it was a strange time of night for a peddler to be out of doors. The man was knocking at the door of a house. The door opened, and someone handed the merchant another bolt of fabric, which he tossed upon the pile. As he pulled the cart down the street, a woman ran from the house, chasing him, trying to grab the goods off the cart. She pulled at the fabric, rolling out a length of cloth as if unfurling a sail, revealing an inert body, perhaps the corpse of a boy. The cart stopped, and a man came from the house, covered the body again, and took the woman inside.

Mary had heard that the bodies of the victims of smallpox were taken away in the middle of the night to avoid outbreaks of hysteria, but she'd assumed that the disease was confined to certain city quarters far away from the elegant row of embassy palaces where they lived. Perhaps Elgin was right: though the weather was no worse than the inclemency in Scotland, there was something in the air that was making him sick. He showed no signs of smallpox, which was a relief, but that was not to say that any of them, especially her unborn baby, would remain immune forever.

THE ELGINS HAD BEEN warned against extending invitations to high-ranking Turks to visit them in their home; the Turks would simply not come, and it could present a diplomatic embarrassment. But the Capitan Pasha had heard that the ambassador was gravely ill and came immediately to see if he could be of service to Lady Elgin.

"I shall teach you my secret passion," Mary said to him, knowing she was being provocative, but also trying to protect her husband. She knew that she mustn't allow the pasha to see Elgin in his condition—the Turks' confidence in her husband had to be maintained at all costs.

"My husband has a mild croup, that is all. But you must not visit his room. He would never recover if he thought that he had exposed you to his illness," she said.

"What is this about your passion?" The pasha was smiling.

"It is called whist!" she said.

"Lady Elgin, you are in trouble. At this game, I already excel," he replied.

Mary thought that she had the evening under control. But while teaching the pasha one of her strategic moves, she found herself revealing to him her fears of giving birth in a strange land. She told him of the horrible sight of the child's body being taken from his mother, and her dread of such a thing happening to her own first-born.

"I promise, on my honor, that I will protect your child as if it were my own son or daughter." His eyes softened as he looked at her, and she wondered if he was going to produce a tear to match the ones that had welled up in her eyes.

"You need the companionship and conversation of other ladies," he said. "I have seen it before with ladies who come to us from other places. I would like to extend you an invitation to my home so that you may meet my sister."

"But is she not the wife of the Sultan?" Mary asked, reeling from both the invitation to the private home of a Turk and the offer to meet a sequestered woman.

"She is *haseki,* his favorite. But when I am at home, he allows her to live with me and keep me company and help me to manage my household. She has heard many stories of you and wishes to meet you at once."

The invitation to his home represented an unprecedented offering of friendship and honor, Mary knew. The additional gift that arrived the next day exceeded the limits of generosity. It arrived in a golden box, delivered ceremoniously by a handsomely dressed messenger, perfumed and plumed. Elgin had bathed and dressed for the first time in a week, and he peered over her shoulder as she lifted the lid, exposing a sapphire of astonishing size sitting on a little gold velvet pillow. His note read:

The poets of old believed that the heavens were a great sapphire cradling the earth. May this small gift represent my assurance of the protection I offer to you and to those you love.

The stone was a dark blue, the color of the sky just after sunset, and it was set inside a ring of diamonds that hung about it like stars round a planet. Mary thought that the sapphire itself might contain the heavens within its glittering facets. She rolled the stone in her hand, eyeing its sharp angles and icy flat surfaces. It seemed to embody some strange quality of infiniteness, and Mary felt as if she could lose consciousness somewhere inside of it. Had it been infused with some sort of spell, designed to make her love the pasha?

"I wonder, does he wish you to wear it in your navel?" Elgin asked, breaking the enchantment.

Though he had lost weight from his ordeal, and his eyes seemed to sit in a face ever more hollow, Elgin's cheeks were pink again, though he looked older now.

"My dear, the Capitan Pasha has made the most extraordinary offer," she began. "His sister is in residence at his home this week, and she has insisted on meeting me."

"Delightful," Elgin said. "You shall undoubtedly come away with yet more loot."

"The extraordinary thing is, she insists that I spend two nights at their home."

"That is extraordinary indeed," he said, his face inscrutable, as if he was trying to determine how he felt about the matter. "You don't suppose that he will take advantage of your situation and kidnap you into his own harem and raise our child as his own?"

"I didn't realize that you were so fond of the plots in ladies' novels," Mary said. "Besides, it would be a disaster for international relations. Otherwise I am sure that he would not be able to resist me. Only the threat of beheading by the Sultan could make him control himself in my presence."

"What matters, madam, is that *you* are able to resist *him*. Shall I remind you of what Julius Caesar said upon divorcing his second wife after she was merely suspected of adultery? That the wife of Caesar must be *above* suspicion?"

"If you do not think it proper for me to stay the two evenings, I will decline the invitation."

"On the contrary, I want you to go. Is the sister of the pasha not the favorite concubine of the Sultan?"

"The pasha declares that she is."

"Then do go. And enjoy yourself."

"So I am above your suspicion?" Mary slid her hand up Elgin's chest and neck and played with his earlobe. "Which I should be, since I love my Eggy above all."

"The point is, Mary, we are going to need the Capitan Pasha's influence, and perhaps his sister's as well if she has the Sultan's ear." He took her hand and kissed it, resuming his diplomat's demeanor. She did not like it when he acted in his private life in the same manner as in his public one; when he kissed her hand formally as if she were some envoy's elderly wife and not his beloved. Like all women, she instantly felt—and mourned—a severing of intimacy.

"I received letters this morning from Hamilton and the others in Athens," Elgin said. "Their access to the temples on the Acropolis is being severely restricted. The Turkish disdar in command is demanding exorbitant bribes to allow them access to the Parthenon. We will run out of funds before the simplest of tasks is complete."

"And how is the pasha to help with access to something in Athens?"

"He can use his influence with the Sultan to get us permission to set up and work at will. Months have passed, Mary, and nothing has been done. Meanwhile, the artists and craftsmen on the payroll are draining our resources. The work must be expedited or the mission will fail."

Elgin's face lost its color as he spoke. All good humor and appearance of health vanished and a deep furrow bisected his forehead.

"By inviting you to spend two evenings in his home with his sister," he continued, "the pasha is practically elevating you to membership in his family. And what would a proud and noble Turk not do for his family?"

"I shall send Duff with a reply accepting the pasha's kind invitation. And I shall miss you. Will you visit me?"

"Of course. Unless you think that my presence will intrude upon the pasha's fantasy that you are a part of his harem," Elgin said.

Mary could not tell if he was joking or not. She smiled at him, letting him think that she considered what he said quite foolish, but she wondered how far her husband—who in most circumstances quaked with jealousy when men attended to Mary—would go in letting her serve his ambitions.

In the city of Constantinople,

January 1800

THE AFTERNOON SUN WARMED the sandy-colored bricks of the pasha's home, bathing the structure in a golden glow. The house was not of palatial size—at least not compared to the Sultan's palace—but it made an imposing presence high above the banks of the river, appropriate to the fact that its occupant was in command of the Sultan's armies. The main structure of the palace complex was a domed building, with four pointy towers at the corners. High walls of the same bricks with geometrical cutouts surrounded the entire complex, including its courtyards, garden, and outer structures, small buildings that Mary supposed were used as kitchens and for sundry other purposes.

She had brought with her three maids and a lady interpreter, Madame Pisani, a very pleasant woman about forty years of age, the wife of the court dragoman, who, with her husband, was from an ancient Venetian family. A male interpreter, foreign or otherwise, who was not a husband or a blood relation would not be allowed in the same room as the Turkish women. The palace's high walls made Mary think of a medieval fairy tale, which was only fitting because that was how she had come to think of the aristocratic Turkish women—like imprisoned princesses in fairy tales of old. She was anxious, if not a little nervous, to see if the reality of the women's lives bore any resemblance to her fantasy.

Soon, however, she was in the aura of the ladies' enthusiastic welcome. Rather than feeling she was in a prison, in the women's quarters she felt as if she was being invited into a warm hive, buzzing with female activity. Surrounded by cousins, aunties, and widows of brothers and other relatives, Hanum, the Capitan Pasha's sister, greeted her. All were introduced by name, and by where they lived and with whom, and by their relation to the pasha, none of which

Mary had any hope of remembering. But each took her hand, holding it until the introduction was complete and then passing her on to the next kinswoman. Mary thought them beautiful, one and all, with their thick, dark hair—some black as night, some lighter and as luscious as honey or caramel. The eyes staring at her were in shades of brown and green, bright and shimmering like leaves in a forest before a strong rain.

Everyone was talking, and Madame Pisani was trying her best to keep up and make certain that Mary knew which lady was making which comment, but she soon gave up in confusion. Mary reached for the small gifts she had brought, English music boxes that would play pretty tunes when the tops were opened, and handed them to the ladies. As soon as the music was released, they gasped as if they were being presented with the most delightful magic, though Mary was sure that they had seen such devices before, and that sheer politeness was driving their enchantment.

The afternoon had been thoroughly planned. Mary and Hanum sat on silk-covered couches and had tea, speaking through an interpreter while the others listened. Mary did not know whether Hanum held authority over the others because they were in her brother's home, or whether it was her particular position with the Sultan, whom she referred to as the Padishah, that made the others behave deferentially. Or whether it was simply a hierarchy agreed upon in advance, under which they would present themselves to this foreigner.

Throughout their conversation, Mary's eyes kept wandering around the room, which was decorated with exquisite painted wallpaper, mosaic tea tables, and intricate silks and carpets. Birds in delicate, ornate cages chirped along with the women as they spoke. Mary showed Hanum a picture of Elgin that she kept in a locket.

"He is most handsome and worthy of the love of a great lady such as yourself," Hanum declared through the interpreter.

"Please ask Hanum to repeat that when she meets Lord Elgin," Mary replied.

A momentary hush fell over the chatty room. Mary sat uncomfortably until she realized her gaffe. Hanum would never meet and address Elgin, or any man outside of her family, unless, as she later gathered from Hanum herself, the Padishah tired of her and married her off to some respectable official in his government. She remembered what one of the Turkish interpreters had told her about conversation between men and women. *Women's voices are soft and beautiful, and the melody of their speech is arousing. Therefore, they must not be heard speaking to strange men.*

But here in the pasha's harem, the women spoke freely, exchanging stories of their families, and Mary related her impressions of Constantinople. All the while, many of the women embroidered, working with such skill that they could speak, listen, and look away while moving a needle in and out of the fabric. One of Hanum's younger cousins worked furiously on a sampler of sorts, the kind of needlework an English girl would do of a wise saying or the alphabet to learn the skill. Mary asked through Madame Pisani what the girl was working on, and everyone in the room began to laugh.

"She was hoping that you would inquire. That is why she is sewing so demonstratively," said the interpreter. "It is a quote from Mihri Hatun, a lady poet who wrote many centuries ago. 'A talented woman is better than a thousand untalented men, and a woman of understanding is better than a thousand stupid men.' "

Hanum muttered something to her cousin, something that Mary thought might not be intended for her ears. She turned to Madame Pisani, hoping for an accurate translation.

"Hanum says that her cousin is intelligent but rebellious, and as she gets older she may discover that while rebellion may be a sign of intelligence, it is not a sign of wisdom."

"It is not a sign of wisdom, perhaps, but it is a sign of youth," Mary said to the girl, wondering how she would have felt if her destiny had been cast to the will of others. What might have become of her if she had had no power to choose the direction of her life? If her father had not listened to her and consented to the marriage with Elgin? If she had never had discourse with another man and could not compare the tedious hours spent with some potential suitors with the excitement she felt in Elgin's company?

"Your baby is a boy," Madame Pisani announced, interrupting Mary's thoughts. An older woman smiled at Mary as she explained that the baby was carried low in the womb, which clearly meant that she was going to have a son. *"Insh'Allah."*

Mary explained that she would love to give her husband a son, but would be grateful for a daughter. "We are all of us daughters," Mary said, waving her hand as if to encompass all the women in the room. "My father has shown nothing but pleasure with me."

The women began to squabble among themselves until the interpreter, in her lilting Italian accent, delivered the litany of questions: Was the sickness worse in the beginning of the pregnancy, or did it worsen as time went on? Were her feet hot or cold? Was Elgin gaining weight as the pregnancy progressed? Were her looks improving, or did she look in the mirror as the months wore on and get depressed? Mary tried to answer all the questions, as if turning evidence over to a jury. A conference was held, and then the verdict was pronounced. The grandmother had been correct: the baby was definitely a boy. One of the young women stood and spoke directly to Mary as if giving her a blessing. Her words sounded like song, which she sang first in a strange language that Mary did not recognize, and then repeated in the language of the Turks, which Mary had heard enough to recognize, if not comprehend.

"Farah is the one who recites from the Holy Book. She says that God has spoken His will, and it does not matter if the child is a boy or a girl," the interpreter said. " 'To Allah belongs the dominion of the heavens and the earth. He creates what He wills. He bestows female children to whomever He wills and bestows male children to whomever He wills.' Of course, we have the same philosophy in Venice," she added.

"Please tell her that that is my belief, as well as the belief of the Scottish people. Any healthy baby is a gift."

Farah agreed, nodding her head, but added, "Though we know the word of God, some continue to celebrate only when the child is a boy and mourn the birth of another girl into this world."

Hanum, having perhaps been warned by the pasha to steer

clear of controversy or any subject that might turn unpleasant, announced that a demonstration of music and dance had been prepared for Mary.

Mary was relieved. She could not understand this strange way of life in which men and women were separated in so extreme a manner, but she did not wish to express her bafflement to these women, who exceeded all expectation in hospitality, and who were allowing her a glimpse into their secret world. As ambassadress—and as a good Christian woman—it was not her duty to pass judgment upon the ways of others, but to represent her own society in the best possible manner.

The songs were pleasant enough, played by two women on odd stringed instruments that resembled a long-necked lute or mandola. Mary could appreciate the music; she herself was a fine player of the pianoforte. But the dances reached beyond good taste, especially for women who were forced to remain chaste by being hidden away. The writhing and twirling she witnessed seemed like something Emma Hamilton would do in private for a salivating lover. How odd that these women who were to be held above reproach had no inhibitions about moving their bodies as if simulating sexual intercourse.

Mary thanked the dancers for their performance and decided that she would praise the wardrobes of the Turkish ladies, which she found to be beautiful, a swirl of colors that one would never find at home. Their skirts were made of silks in varied patterns, with complementing shawls draped over the hips or shoulders. Hanum's coat in particular was striking, a deep blue velvet with an ermine lining that folded over into a collar and lapel. Their heads were wrapped in bright scarves, with beautiful bonnetlike puffs that hung down their backs. When Mary expressed her appreciation of their clothes, Hanum's eyes lit like candles.

She had ordered two Turkish dresses to be made for Mary, one more lovely than the other, in hues of salmon, emerald, and gold. Mary held the dresses up to her body. The sunlight through the small windows at the top of the walls shone through, making the fabrics shimmer like jewels. Dark gold threads ran through the skirts, and the paisley shawls were decorated with tiny pearls. Mary was also presented with gold slippers with furry balls that matched the fur lining on the deep crimson velvet coat that Hanum was holding for her to try on.

Pleased that the coat fit, Hanum took a scarf and wrapped it around Mary's head, pulling Mary's long, dark curls through the folds. The woman's face was flushed with the pleasure of either new friendship or generosity—Mary could not guess which. But she was certain the fondness that shone in her eyes and her smile exceeded the requirements of diplomatic politeness. Though there were not two words that Mary might have uttered that Hanum would have understood, she was sure that they had achieved some means of communication.

" 'Now you are one of us,' " Madame Pisani said, repeating Hanum's words in English, but Mary had already understood the meaning and responded with an embrace of gratitude.

The entrance of the Capitan Pasha interrupted them. He looked around the room, finally saying something to his sister in their language that made her and everyone in the room laugh.

The interpreter said to Mary, "The Capitan Pasha asked his sister what she had done with you."

"Capitan, you did not know me?" Mary asked.

"I did not. You make a fine Turkish lady," he said. His face was flushed and his eyes shone with mischief. "We have a special visitor this afternoon. I believe that he is someone who will want to meet with you."

THE PASHA HAD ORDERED all the women save one to seclude themselves in a room upstairs as he escorted Lord Elgin through the corridors. The sun had already set, and a small lamp lit the room where Mary sat. She heard the voices of the two men as they approached the door.

"This is my private study," the pasha said, opening the door.

Elgin peered in. "Do excuse me, madam," he said, startled. He turned, confronting the pasha's smile.

"How polite you are to ladies, Lord Elgin," Mary said.

Elgin turned around. His wife, now out of the shadows, smiled at him.

"A fine pair you two are, playing tricks!" As she whisked by, he slipped his arm around her waist. "You're a rascal, Lady Elgin," he whispered in her ear, before letting her leave the room to follow the pasha.

Though Elgin still suffered bouts of coughing, asthmatic attacks, and migraine headaches, his spirits seemed restored since his horrible ordeal at Christmastime. His skin, however, had never recovered. No one could diagnose the illness, but whatever it was, it had started to eat away at his nose. Strangely, his nostrils, which had gotten scabby during his illness, had not healed, and in the last month, the condition had worsened. Mary had a private conversation with Dr. MacLean in which she had asked him if Elgin might have either leprosy or the pox. The doctor assured her that her husband merely had had a bout with a very bad germ, and all symptoms should clear up with time. She certainly hoped so, and prayed for it nightly. She even asked God to forgive her for asking Him to restore her husband's beauty. She did not love Elgin for the way he looked; it was just that the way he looked had made it easy to love him and to be intimate with him in the way that he desired.

"I've brought Lady Elgin's pianoforte," Elgin said as the pasha ushered them into his parlor.

"The ladies wished to hear our music, so I sent for it," she said. "I shall play it for them in the morning. I did not know that it would be delivered by such an illustrious footman."

"Will you stay for dinner?" the pasha asked Elgin.

"I have duties this evening which forbid it," he replied. "I must leave my wife to your care."

Mary was secretly pleased that Elgin could not stay for dinner, because that would have meant that the women of the house would have had to have their dinner in seclusion, and she had looked forward to spending more time with them. After Elgin left, Mary was left alone with the pasha, which made her nervous at first, as she knew the special feelings he harbored for her. She wondered if Elgin's comment before they had arrived in Constantinople had been accurate after all—that the women were sequestered because the men could not control themselves. Elgin must have changed his mind about it, because here she sat, with her husband's permission, alone with this powerful and handsome man.

Had Elgin changed his mind? Or was he willing to sacrifice Mary's honor for his purposes on the Acropolis?

"Show me how to play," the pasha said, sitting beside her on the pianoforte's bench. He put one long finger on a key and pressed, pulling back from the keyboard as he heard the sound, as if by touching it, he had done something wrong.

"What sort of music do you like? Dances?" Mary asked.

"I prefer something more serious," he said.

With her right hand, she played the melody to a sonata by Mr. Franz Joseph Haydn that she had recently learned.

"For the first lesson, one hand only, I think," she said.

He watched her, and then he imitated her fingering perfectly, four bars at a time, until he was able to string together the first sixteen bars of the melody to his satisfaction. He concentrated with great intent as he worked out the tune, as focused and serious, Mary imagined, as if he were planning a strategy for a battle.

"You are a natural talent," Mary said.

He shrugged. "You are a good teacher."

She felt uncomfortable sitting so close to the man, so she asked if they could move to the sofas and have coffee. He was only too delighted to accommodate her wishes, he assured her.

Coffee was served from a gold filigree pot studded with rubies and pearls, poured into matching demi-cups. When Mary admired the set, the pasha insisted that his servant wrap it up for her to take home. She protested, until she realized that she was insulting him by rejecting his gift.

"There is something else I wish to give to your husband. If I send it through you, he will not be able to refuse me."

The pasha commanded something of his servant, who returned with another servant, carrying a jewel-studded saddle.

"That is very beautiful," Mary said. "But I do not think my husband would refuse a lovely saddle."

"No, but he has already tried to refuse the stallion that accompanies it," said the pasha. "I wish him to have it, but he begged me to consider that my generosity was overwhelming."

"What makes you think he will accept it if it is sent through me?"

"Because I have found that it is impossible to refuse you anything at all. It must be impossible for your husband too."

For one moment, she thought she could kiss him. She got hold of herself, of course. But he was so dear, so gentle, and so flattering. He was also handsome, sometimes ruggedly so, and sometimes, as in this moment, almost winsome, like a poet or musician. It was said that the Sultan was an accomplished poet and a great lover of music, a composer who wrote delightful melodies. Apparently the Turks saw no contradiction in an otherwise barbarous man embracing pursuits that required the participation of the soul. Mary also noticed that certain military men, known for valor and toughness, such as the pasha and General O'Hara, with whom she had flirted in Gibraltar to Elgin's dismay, were particularly genteel with ladies, as if trying to balance their martial occupations.

"Lady Elgin, can you explain to me why Lord Elgin protested the gift of a superb horse, but is full of gratitude for the ancient pieces of stone from the village on the coast? I do not understand, and our relations with the English are new. Is it customary to accept only worthless things?"

"They are not worthless to Lord Elgin. I'm sure he's told you all about his ambitions in Athens."

Mary imagined that in his time with the pasha, Elgin had laid the groundwork in the event that the pasha's assistance would be required to pull off his plans. "Lord Elgin is on a mission to improve the arts in Great Britain," she continued. "His architect, Mr. Thomas Harrison, has convinced him that England's young artists would benefit and progress greatly if they had actual casts and precise drawings of the ancient Greek masterpieces. My husband has very broad ambitions and lofty goals."

"Yes, he has told me all about it," the pasha replied.

"You do not really approve of it?" Mary asked. Sometimes, she didn't approve of it either. Elgin often got more upset over problems with the Athenian project than he did when things did not go well in the international affairs in which he was embroiled.

"It is not that I do not approve. Whatever a man's passions, he must pursue them, unless they offend God. I merely told Lord Elgin that if I were in his position, I would rather spend my money decorating my wife with jewels worthy of her great beauty."

Mary was not unhappy to hear the pasha's assessment of what Elgin's priorities should be; however, she knew that it was time to excuse herself from his company to wash and dress for dinner.

In the city of Constantinople,

April 1800

GEORGE CHARLES CONSTANTINE, LORD Bruce—the real Lord Bruce, not his mother costumed as a man—gurgled in the arms of Calitza, his Greek nurse, who sat holding him on the sofa as Mary answered the correspondence that had been piling up since his birth. They had decided upon the name George in honor of the king; Charles for Elgin's late father; and Constantine for the child's birth city. The child was healthy and beautiful, and, Mary was sure, would be worth the pain that she had endured in bringing him into this world. After three weeks, she could sit again. That was a blessing. And the laudanum that she had required to see her through the pain of the birth and its aftereffects was finally wearing off. Her head had cleared, for the most part.

"He's the finest fellow ever born," Elgin had declared after the babe had been cleaned up, swaddled, and handed to him. Mary had not wanted Elgin to see her as she knew she appeared after the labor, which had lasted an excruciatingly long time. She had Mas-

Karen Essex

terman wipe her face and brush her sweat-soaked hair. The dazed expression on her face, combined with the dizzying effects of the laudanum, must have given her a beatific look.

"You look positively angelic," Elgin had said.

That is because, one hour ago, I was praying to the angels to take me to heaven with them, she thought, but she did not reply.

"Would you consider the pain I have just experienced normal?" she had asked Dr. MacLean. She wanted to know because, if it were, she would refuse to go through it again. The doctor's hands shook as he poured himself a full four fingers of brandy.

"No, Lady Elgin. I assure you that your experience was severe. I feared for you."

"But look, Mary," Elgin had said, "it is all over, and our boy is beautiful and perfect! Was it not worth the discomfort?" He beamed at her, lifting her son to show her as if she'd not bothered to look at him yet. She merely smiled.

Discomfort? She'd never known such suffering. She'd had a choking attack while she was in labor, which frightened poor, palsied Dr. MacLean. Mary, torn between the agony in her chest and the agonizing contractions, had prayed for her own expedient death. When she could breathe again, the contractions became more severe. She felt as if the baby were doing great battle with her internal organs. Was he wrapped around her insides and not safely tucked in the womb like other babies? This went on for half the day, with Mary begging for sedatives to ease the pain. Nothing helped. She clutched a blanket, terrified that the pain would bring on another choking attack. Soon thereafter, she began to push the baby out. Certain that her body was being torn in two, she said what she thought were her final prayers and hoped that Elgin would remain healthy enough to raise the child, should it survive, on his own. If not, she reasoned, her mother and father would give the tyke a good home.

Elgin himself had been miserably ill in the last months. He suffered bouts of chills and fevers along with inexplicable cold and hot fits. He sweated constantly, and his joints hurt so much that he often cried out in the middle of the night. The treatment of mercury and bleedings administered by Dr. MacLean did not adequately alleviate his pains, so he medicated himself with copious amounts of alcohol. Mary did not enjoy his changeable moods at these times, but she could not blame Elgin for trying to find relief. When she had to watch the leeches pulsing on his face, she wished that she too had the will to get drunk.

But the birth of his son improved Elgin's health and his spirits. He hadn't required leeching since the baby's arrival, and he had not complained about his joints, or taken fever either. Mary overheard him dictating a letter to his mother, the Dowager Lady Elgin, exclaiming over the health of the baby.

"Mary is lost in delight of her little brat. The pleasure she takes in caring for the young lad has obliterated any memory of the pain she'd suffered," Elgin said, composing aloud to his secretary, his voice full of mirth.

In fact, the opposite was true. Though she was enthralled with the little boy and gave prayers of thanks every day for his safe delivery and his health, she could not forget the suffering during and after the birth. Truly. Her breasts were not as swollen as they'd been, and she had regained an appetite. All bleeding had stopped. Still, she was afraid to resume sexual relations. She did not think her body could tolerate the violation and she also did not want to get pregnant again.

"Darling, give me credit for having delivered a glorious and healthy male heir. Can we not curb our appetites for a while so that I might heal?" she asked him sweetly one night. She needed to put the pain of childbirth behind before she could indulge again in an act that might lead to procreation. Thoughts of repeating the experience filled her with terror, often interrupting her sleep. But Elgin merely smiled and assured her that healthy women healed very quickly.

On Mary's twenty-second birthday, when the baby was but eighteen days old, the nurse had carried him into Mary's room. In his tiny hand he'd held a little note, which the nurse asked Mary to take. She opened it, and a lovely emerald ring fell out and onto her lap. The note read:

My Dear Mama,

*Pray accept this ring from your affectionate Bab. A green stone in a
ring is an emblem that my hopes can have no end as long as your hand
supports me.*

Love,

Your little Bab

Elgin popped his head into the room. "What do you think of
your Young Turk now? Is he not the most gallant of little creatures?"

"I think that he and his papa make me the happiest of creatures
who ever existed," she said, holding out her arms to her husband
and kissing him. Elgin's various diseases and their treatments had
robbed him of some of his boyish good looks, but not of his manly
charms.

"He's a fine young man, is he not?"

"He is. And a fitting heir to your title and all that will come
through our families. We have our heir, Elgin. The first baby is a
strapping, healthy little boy!" Mary said. She had been trying to
reintroduce the subject of using contraception, at least for a little
while, but the time had never seemed right. If she didn't work up
her courage, it would be too late, and he would be on top of her and
inside before she could stop him.

"We are fortunate, indeed, Mary. Just think! You are young.
You might give me five or ten before we're done!"

"Five or ten? I know that we have talked about having many
children, but must we think of it so soon after the birth of our first?
I would like to give Little Lord Bruce his due, after all."

"Oh, nonsense, Mary. He will always have a special place in
our hearts because he is the first. But we mustn't stop now." Elgin's
tone turned very serious. "My oldest brother passed away so young,
Mary. That is why I am the earl. We can never have enough children to ensure our line."

"But of course we can, my darling. We are not cattle! As you say,
I am young. Why must we rush? I would like to recover from this

experience before I find myself back in bed, choking, pushing, and bleeding!" She lowered her voice and raised her eyes to him. "It was frightening, Eggy. I thought I might die. So did Dr. MacLean."

"Normal jitters for a first-time mother," he replied. "Everyone says it is a frightening experience the first time, but if one comes through as you have, with a healthy baby and one's own health undamaged, the next time will be much easier."

"Yes, of course you are right," Mary said, wondering how her husband, or indeed any man not in the medical profession, might become an expert on childbirth.

"King George and Queen Charlotte have fifteen living children, and if you ask His Majesty in private, he will confess that he still does not think one of them a suitable heir. No, Mary, a man can never be sure of these things. We must look to the future. As soon as you are healed, I hope to get you with child immediately." Elgin was as confident and as formal as when he spoke to the Grand Vezir.

"Immediately?"

"Yes, of course. All practicality aside, motherhood has made you more luscious than ever."

"I do wonder whether we should have any more children in this city. Smallpox is rampant. Every time I look at our son, I worry that he will contract it."

"We shall keep him safe," Elgin replied. He kissed her tenderly on the lips, took the emerald ring, and placed it on her finger. "You are the brightest star in the city of Constantinople. Everyone knows it and remarks on it. You light up both sides of the Bosphorus, both continents of Asia and Europe, with your luminosity. I love you, Mistress Poll."

"I love you too, Eggy," she said, letting the topic she wished to explore rest, at least for the moment.

Soon thereafter, a servant rushed into Mary's study with the news that she'd tried to serve Dr. MacLean his meal in his room, as had become his habit. But when she took him his dinner, she found him lying dead in his chair.

Mary would miss the man, though she recognized his shortcomings. If she had to give birth again in this strange land, she would not even have the good doctor upon whom to depend.

In the summer of 1800

MARY HAD NOT ALLOWED herself to admit how lonely she was for her family until she saw the faces of her mother and father as they arrived at the embassy. She had hoped to rush into their arms. After all, she was their only and beloved daughter. However, she quickly learned one of the universal realities of having had a child: the grandchild trumps the child. After perfunctory kisses to their daughter's cheeks, the Nisbets whisked past Mary to witness little Lord Bruce in the arms of Calitza. Mrs. Nisbet hardly took a moment to coo over the baby before snatching him out of the poor nurse's arms as if the woman had stolen him in the night. Mr. Nisbet kept slapping Elgin on the back, shouting, "Good job, lad," as if Elgin had single-handedly produced the boy.

Mary had done everything possible to ensure that her parents' visit to Constantinople would be comfortable, interesting, and profitable. She had outfitted rooms for them, done as lavishly and tastefully as she knew their wealth and status demanded but their Scottish sensibilities would allow. She made sure all the right people entertained them—foreign diplomats, English dignitaries, and illustrious Turks. The Capitan Pasha invited them all to his home and, in the presence of both parents, took a giant amethyst out of his turban and presented it to Mary, to demonstrate to the Nisbets, he said, how much he had come to treasure the ambassadress. She spent an entire morning with her mother at the women's market, where they bought embroidered shawls and fabrics, hair clasps of gold, buttons of ivory and pearl, exotic-colored threads, and cosmetics and creams that would be unknown on the Continent. Mrs. Nisbet was impressed with the way that Mary remained unfazed with the aggressive peddlers crowding the streets, and with her fierce bargaining techniques with the lady vendors who sold the majority of the goods at the women's market.

Mary had been heavily coached by Elgin before her parents' arrival. He had a very specific agenda he wanted his wife to follow.

"There is no room for failure or delay," he had told her a few weeks before the Nisbets were to arrive. "The project in Athens grows more costly by the day. We have so many on our payroll. The Turkish officials in Athens are demanding larger and larger bribes and fees to allow access to the Acropolis. The Capitan Pasha tried to intercede on my behalf, but he was suddenly called away to Egypt."

"What has this to do with my parents?" Mary asked, already knowing the answer.

"Mary, we need more funds."

"But we have already asked them for so much!" She had been working so hard in planning their visit, trying to strike just the right note between demonstrating how nicely she had set up the embassy and how thick she was with Turkish society, and showing that she did all she did with an eye toward economy. Mary dreaded any confrontation with her father over money. Mr. Nisbet allowed his wife and daughter the luxuries necessary to maintain their positions in society but, with his wealth, could have lavished thrice the luxuries upon them. "Comfortable, but sensible," was his motto, and he had no patience for grand plans such as Elgin's.

"My father feels he has done enough. He thinks you spend too much. He won't capitulate."

"Does he understand that every cent is put forth with the heart of a true patriot?" Elgin asked. "Does he know that most of our funds have gone to aid General Abercrombie in his military efforts against the Napoleonic menace?"

It was true. Elgin had sent huge sums of money to Abercrombie in Egypt. The general had figured out that getting money out of the ambassador was easier than getting money out of the king. Elgin promised his bankers as well as Mary, who was nervous over doling out their private funds for a war effort, that the government would reimburse him. What with funding the war effort and funding the Athenian project and funding the embassy itself, the Elgins were constantly in need of cash. And only Mary had access to more.

"Does your father understand that the British government treats me like a private purse it can tap at will?"

Mary could not argue with Elgin. She thought the British treatment of her husband deplorable. Still, the man could not stop spending. Some of it was born out of his generous spirit, such as the recent gift of the enormous emerald he bought knowing that she had an affinity for the gem. She did; however, she did not require another one, especially at this delicate time in their financial lives. But what could one say to one's bright-eyed husband as he proudly presented one with an extravagant gift? She continued to thank him profusely, while writing secret letters to jewelers in London asking what the jewel would fetch. She knew that she would have to sell it one day if she was to fund the rest of Elgin's ambitions.

She hid the emerald from sight when her parents arrived, and, affecting as troubled a face as she could muster, she took advantage of the first opportunity to speak with them about money.

But Mr. Nisbet was well prepared for the discussion, and had come to Constantinople with concerns of his own.

"I do not dispute that Lord Elgin acts out of patriotic leanings, Mary. It is his other expenditures that concern me," her father said.

Mary waited for him to continue, but her mother interrupted. "He might lose Broomhall!" she said.

"What is this?" Mary asked. Elgin had mentioned no threat to his home—their home—in Scotland.

"He and Mr. Harrison, the architect, went rather mad with their plans for the house," Mrs. Nisbet said.

"Grandiose. Use the proper word, my dear," said Mr. Nisbet.

"Yes, their grandiose plans are costing fortunes more than expected," her mother continued. "His bankers are in receipt of the invoices, and they alerted us to the problem out of courtesy. If Lord Elgin does not take heed and curb his ambitions for his home, he may run out of funds before its completion and have to sell it at a loss."

"He would not be the first free-spending aristocrat to find himself in such a predicament," Mr. Nisbet said. "Indeed, clever landowners in the area are waiting for the bankers to close in so that they may acquire the property at a price."

"Of course, we hear all the talk in the county, dear," Mrs. Nisbet added. "His poor mother writes to him constantly advising him to cut back on the expenses for that house, but he doesn't listen."

"His banker sends Elgin letters of warning—which I take it he does not share with you, my dear?" Mr. Nisbet asked.

Mary said nothing, revealing her ignorance of her husband's affairs.

Mr. Nisbet shook his head. "Just like the father, God rest his bankrupt soul."

"Surely you would not allow the worst to happen?" Mary asked. "To your own daughter and grandchild?" She'd fantasized every day about returning to Scotland and taking up residence at the baronial Broomhall. Why, she'd decorated every inch of it to her satisfaction in her mind. Some nights when she couldn't sleep and felt empty inside thinking about home, she'd go over the rooms at Broomhall, matching the tremendous bolts of fabric she'd been collecting from Turkey and India to furniture, walls, and windows in her Scottish home-to-be. "Where on earth would we live?"

"A man must be responsible for his wife and child," Mr. Nisbet said. "If you recall, I did warn you."

Mary's mother made an admonishing face at her husband. Mary guessed that her mother would never allow her father to sit by and watch Broomhall be taken away from the Elgins. But Mr. Nisbet had made his point.

"I've got sixty Hottentots in this very embassy to feed every day, three meals each!" Mary let her parents see her exasperation. "You can't know how hard I've worked to economize!"

"I did hear that you let Lord Elgin's chamber orchestra go," her father said, rather snidely, Mary thought. Did he not understand that a man in Elgin's position had to have such entertainments at his disposal? Everyone expected it, but the government would never pay for it. Mary herself had so enjoyed having musicians in the house. She shed tears when she had to dismiss them to save money.

"I insulted scores of musicians in the interviews because I asked them if they would be willing to double as servants," Mary said. It had been no small task finding good musicians who agreed to her terms. Even then, after six months, she had to admit defeat and send them back to England.

"Lord Elgin has written to Mr. Harrison that he has his staff searching for immense cuts of marble from which he will have copies of the ancient columns made and sent to Scotland to be placed in Broomhall. Are such extravagances really necessary?" Mrs. Nisbet asked.

"The shipping costs alone would be phenomenal," Mr. Nisbet added. Mary did not know of these plans of her husband's. "There is talk, my dear, that his purpose in making forms of the Greek architectural elements is to make Broomhall more ornate."

"That's absurd," Mary said. "Elgin's ambitions in Athens are to raise the standards of the arts in the United Kingdom. That is all. It is a noble endeavor, and one that I stand behind. And my mother agrees with me," she said. She turned toward Mrs. Nisbet. "Or have you changed your mind about the duties of a good and proper wife?"

Mrs. Nisbet blushed. Obviously she remembered her advice to her daughter when the subject of the Athens project was first mentioned. The mother had surprised the daughter with her speech about supporting the ambitions of her husband. Her opinion had influenced Mary's every decision since arriving at Constantinople. She would not allow her mother to back out of her position now that it was expensive and inconvenient.

"I have not changed my thinking," Mrs. Nisbet said. "A wife's duty is to support her husband's every ambition. But I had no idea how expensive that support might be."

"A wife's duty is also to temper her husband's excesses," countered Mr. Nisbet.

"Has my mother had to perform such a duty?" Mary asked.

"It has not been necessary," Mrs. Nisbet answered quickly, turn-ing her eyes away.

Mary wondered if she had not sensed a little regret joined with her mother's pride at that statement.

True, Mary would have to rein in Elgin's spending. But was his extravagance not a sign of a man of passion, eager to have and consume the best of what life had to offer? Eager to make his mark by improving the larger world? Though Mrs. Nisbet could take comfort in her husband's sensible nature, had she ever experienced the excitement that a man like Elgin offered a woman, both in the bedroom and in the public arena? Mary's mother led an elegant ex-istence, free of worries, largely because Mr. Nisbet had conducted their affairs with superb judgment and constant measure. But here was Mary, the toast of the Ottoman court, feted and spoiled by men of great power, living at the very center of historic events. No, she would not exchange a life such as the one she was living for one with fewer headaches and less excitement.

THEY ARE TAKING HIM *out of her arms, pulling his limp body from her, tearing away the small, hand-crocheted white lace blanket that her grandmother had sent as a christening gift, revealing the oozing sores that cover his porcelain skin. She is not strong enough to keep him, not strong enough to hold on to her firstborn. The man with the cart is bigger and more determined, his thick brown arms reaching out from his saffron robe, pulling the inert little boy from her. Mary wants to call out for Elgin, but she is afraid of letting him see that the boy is dead. She has failed the father and failed the son. She is weak, physically weak and mentally weak. She has allowed her lust for attention from men who are not her husband to cloud her judgment. She has remained here, taking their trinkets from big, open palms, wearing exquisite silks and hefty jewels, and being carried high above heads no better than hers, when she should have been forcing Elgin to take her and the baby home. She is pulling the baby so hard that she is afraid that she will tear off his flaccid little arm, knowing that her vanity—not the plague, not the poison coursing through the veins of half the city, but the way that she has indulged her pathetic female whims—has finally done her in, and her son with her. She fights with all her strength, but the man with the cart is stronger. She can no longer challenge his superior muscles nor the chilling look of blame in his eye. She lets go, shielding her eyes from the sight of her son falling upon the other dead children, but she neglects to cover her ears. She hears the dull thump as the baby's body, the one that she had so recently protected in her womb, hits the bodies of the other dead children.*

SHE WOKE BEFORE DAWN, struggling with the heavy duvet on top of her and feeling the approach of a choking attack. She calmed herself, taking small gasps of air, which she prayed to the Lord that she would be able to expel. If she did not get too greedy on the intake, perhaps God would be more merciful this morning and make the garroted sensation inside her subside before a full-scale attack launched itself.

Elgin was already awake, lying beside her on his back with his eyes open and his hands behind his head. "You're fitful. Bad dream?"

For reasons she could not explain, she did not want to reveal her dream to Elgin. Though her healthy son was in his crib, the guilt she'd felt in the dream carried over to her waking state.

"Cat got your tongue?"

Luckily, the feared choking attack did not manifest, and she spoke. "Yes, bad dream. Something about the smallpox plague. I don't quite remember the details."

"You worry too much about it," he said. "No one in our embassy has had the slightest symptom."

"That is pure luck," she replied.

"Or Providence," he answered. "Or perhaps, to the man of reason, merely superior medicine and cleaner conditions in which to live."

"The chief wife to the Grand Vezir has lost ten of her eleven children to smallpox. I do not believe that our living conditions are superior to those of Yusuf Pasha and his family, lavishly cared for though we are."

"Perhaps not, but as far as superior medicine and habits of hygiene go, the British take the day, my dear. I believe it would be uncontested in open court."

"Not in the Sultan's court," she replied.

"Nonetheless, one mustn't worry."

"Eggy, there is a new vaccine against the disease. Dr. Scott has been informing me of it."

A most excellent and forward-thinking physician had replaced poor Dr. MacLean. Mary's confidence in the new man, Dr. Scott, was growing with every conversation she held with him. Dr. Scott was a man of ideas; moreover, his hands did not shake when he administered medication.

"The formula actually originated here with the doctors in Constantinople," Mary continued, "but our own physicians and men of learning have been improving it in these last years. Though it's still a bit controversial, Dr. Scott believes in its efficacy."

"We live in a time of magnificent scientific advancement, Mary, that is true."

"Do you ever consider that we might make a lasting imprint upon this city?"

He laughed. "You mean above ensuring the radically new alliance between our nation and the Ottoman Empire? Beyond your being the first European female to visit the private harem of one of the highest men in the empire? And to have that man's loyalty and devotion? I say, Mary, what ambitions might you hold beyond that?"

Mary did not mean to imply that she held private ambitions that could compete with or reign supreme over Elgin's. These days, he was easily upset. After a brief respite from disease after Bruce was born, Elgin now was rarely free of fevers or chills. His joints ached day and night. He suffered from the same mysterious chokings that from time to time attacked Mary. And the beautiful aquiline nose that Mary had so admired when they were courting was slowly disappearing, being eaten away by whatever disease had lodged itself in his body and was impervious to even the strongest and most advanced medicines of the day.

"I was just thinking that I might use some of our influence to inform the Turks of the vaccine."

"Darling, you are playing a dangerous game," Elgin said. "The vaccine is unproven. It might even turn out to be a danger to those who receive it. It is not based on sound medicine, if you ask me. Who ever heard of infecting the patient with the very disease that one wishes to prevent? If the vaccine is administered to those close to the Sultan and brings harm to the recipients, who knows how our relations will be affected? Who knows what blame will be slung and what punishment meted out? You let your guard down with these people, Poll, because you are a dear and tender creature, but I must caution you that, beneath the skin, they are crucially different from us. Lives are not valued. Heads are easily chopped off. Friends are thrown into the prisons at the slightest provocation and die there. Be cautious for once in your life."

"You are extremely wise, Eggy. And I am naïve, I know. But I am grieved by the way smallpox sweeps through the population here. If in a small way I could help prevent the pain of mothers' having to watch their children be carried off by the reapers of the dead, I would surely do it."

"Of course," he said.

"Shall we catch a few more winks?" she asked. The nightmare had exhausted her, and the sunlight was not yet peeking through the drapery.

"I'm afraid that there will be no more sleep for me. I received a letter yesterday that may interrupt my slumber for a time to come." He said this with closed eyes, as if opening them would force him to face some fact that he had not yet disclosed to Mary. "Napoleon is with his fleet at Toulon. Information gathered by our people is leading us to believe that he is going to carry out his threat to attack Greece. He's always intended it."

Mary felt a tightening in her middle. It seemed that war was moving closer. "What does that mean for us? Is Turkey next? Eggy, we must leave this place. It won't be safe. At least let us send the baby home with my parents."

"What's got into you, Poll?"

"I suppose that motherhood has made me skittish."

"Yes, what happened to the girl who cheered at giving chase to French gunboats?" Elgin asked as if he was nostalgic for the adventurous girl he'd married.

She knew why she was suddenly full of fears and caution. Childbirth had been a nasty introduction to suffering in an otherwise blessed life. She could not deny the ominous feelings that had suddenly descended upon her dream life and her waking life. Better to be safe than sorry in these matters. If she was receiving omens, what good would it do to ignore them?

"No need to panic," Elgin said. "I've been instructed to send someone to Greece to caution the Turkish pashas who are ruling the provinces against welcoming or negotiating with the French. You know how those people are. A few coins changing hands, and all our hard work to form an alliance with the Ottomans will be lost. Morier would be good, but he's tied up in Egypt. I believe I shall send Hunt."

"As long as his skills as an envoy exceed those as a minister. Do not let him sermonize to the pashas, Eggy, or all of Greece will soon be speaking French!"

Elgin allowed himself a tiny smile. He had finally opened his eyes, but Mary did not like the heated look coming from them.

"You realize, don't you, that we must do anything we can to hurry along the Athens project? If Napoleon lands on Attic soil, all will be lost. Our artists on the Acropolis will be thrown out or imprisoned, or even killed. The French will usurp their work, down to the last drawing. All that they've amassed, all that they've done, all that we've worked for and—my God, Mary—paid for with our own precious funds! All my efforts will have been in vain. We cannot allow that to happen."

"But what more can we do?" She had not yet informed Elgin of the outcome of her dispute with her parents over money.

"You know what we must do. While your parents are here, you must make them see the urgency. Do they not realize what is at stake?"

"I have spoken with my parents at length. They are not disposed to providing further financial aid," Mary explained.

"But that's impossible," Elgin sputtered. "Were you emphatic with them? Did you not explain our predicament?"

"I believe that I was articulate in laying out our cause. They, on the other hand, are more concerned over your mismanagement of funds *domestically.*"

She'd been waiting for the right moment to confront him over the Broomhall expenses. The idea of losing the family home had been eating away at her.

"What are you talking about?"

"My parents are afraid that you are soon to lose Broomhall through needless extravagance."

He looked at her suspiciously. "Where would they get such an idea?"

"Surely you do not think that your own wife is telling tales about you? They have heard it from your creditors and bankers in Edinburgh. Apparently, all of Scotland has been aware of this pending disaster—everyone, save your wife."

She expected Elgin to go into a sputtering fit. Instead, he composed himself. "I do wish that your parents and my wife would not listen to idle gossip."

"They are not merely listening to gossip! They are looking at invoices!" Now she was the one sputtering.

"Mary, do you not apprehend our position? Do you not see the esteem in which I will be held after our service here? General Abercrombie's war effort will succeed because of our assistance. We, you and I, will be instrumental in the English defeat of Napoleon."

"How do you know that the English will defeat Napoleon?"

Elgin sat up tall, his hand at his breast as if he were making a speech to a foreign dignitary. "Because we are a superior culture, with discipline and morality far above those of the French. It is obvious, and it is unpatriotic to suggest otherwise. When that day of victory comes, and when the casts and drawings and artifacts from Greece are safe in England, we shall be honored for all our contributions to the nation." He got out of bed and stood over his wife with his hands on his hips. "Do you not see that we will require a family seat commensurate with our position? Should we return in honor and glory to live in some shabby rented place? Is that what you want for yourself and for your children? Is that the home that those who nobly serve the king deserve?"

Mary sat quietly. Once again, she had neglected to believe in her husband. Of course Elgin had thought through all of her parents' possible objections and had made his decision based on sound judgment and faith in himself and in the United Kingdom whose interests he had been appointed to support and to represent. Yet she did not see how she could present his position again to her father. The man had already made up his mind. Another rousing speech from her would not change it.

"But you must understand my parents' view. Father has amassed his fortune through cautious management of money, not through grand acts of patriotism. He is a pragmatist."

"Mary, Hunt will need to take bags of money with him to Greece. Only money buys alliance with the pashas. In addition to that, we must redouble the effort on the Acropolis. Whatever it takes. The Turks do not value one ancient stone. They will trade the entire Parthenon to the French for mere trinkets—that is, if the French do not simply take it from them first."

Apparently, Mary did not respond quickly enough, for he added, "Honestly. You do agree with me, do you not? We have come too far to fail now."

"Then you must speak to my father directly. You must impress upon him that you are still a young man, and a reputation made for your deeds at this juncture will set you up for life in His Majesty's eyes." After all, it was not just Elgin's future anymore, but hers as well, and that of the Nisbets' beloved little grandson.

"I shall speak to your father, Mary, but I have a better idea. Let's send them to Athens while Hunt is there. Let them tour Greece and see firsthand the magnificence of the treasures. I believe that no man, not even your father, could be exposed to such grandeur and not wish to participate in this project. There is something about these artifacts. Something in their perfection that makes men want to possess them."

"You don't understand my father," she said. "He considers all of this superfluous to the necessities of life. He has no patience for romance or excess."

"I may not understand your father, but *you* don't understand the ambitions of men," he replied. "We are all the same beneath the surface when it comes to having a brush with glory. You talk with your mother. Leave your father to me."

THE CAPITAN PASHA NOTICED that Mary's spirits had sunken after the departure of her parents, and told her he was concerned over her sad countenance. He invited Lord and Lady Elgin to his home for dinner, sending in addition a cryptic message that he wished to present them with a fine bit of news. They speculated upon what it might be: Was he planning to present some elaborate gift, wishing to see the looks upon their faces? He had recently given Elgin a ship, outfitted as elegantly as any sea vessel in the world, so that Elgin might tour the territories of the Ottomans. How he could top that, Mary did not know. They'd received jewels, horses, saddles, priceless fabrics and rugs, spices from the East, and, most of all, the pasha's loyalty and friendship. Further gifts were not necessary, as far as Mary was concerned. Every time the pasha presented her with yet another extravagance, her feminine lust for finery was aroused, but at the same time, her Scottish sensibilities warned that she should limit her acceptance of such things. Or at least refrain from unbridled delight.

But this evening, after dinner had been eaten and coffee was served, the pasha did not come forth with gifts, but announced that the Sultana Valida, the mother of the Sultan and traditionally the most powerful woman in the empire, had been asking questions about the much-discussed Lady Elgin.

"Delightful!" Elgin said. "Mary, the Sultana has jurisdiction over the Acropolis." He turned to the Capitan Pasha. "You know how important my Athens project is to me, Capitan?"

"The Sultana is going to invite Lady Elgin to her quarters in the palace for a private audience," the pasha said. "She has heard tales for over one year now, and she wishes to see who is this lady who has captured the heart of her city. I wanted to give you some warning, Lady Elgin. I know how ladies like to prepare for these occasions in terms of costume and adornment."

"Is it customary for the mother of the Sultan to invite a foreign ambassadress into her home?" Elgin asked, already knowing the answer.

"Lady Elgin will be the first European woman to attend upon the Sultana in the harem," the pasha said, smiling at Mary as if she were his own protégée. "It is the highest honor she can confer upon you, or upon any lady, for that matter."

Later in the evening, when Mary and Elgin were alone again, he expressed his delight at the Valida's interest in his wife.

"The more admiration you acquire, the more we are assured of success in Athens. Time is of the essence now, Mary. My term is coming to an end. We must finish up, and quickly."

"Of course," Mary said. She tried to say it sweetly, but truly, she was annoyed at how her every resource and asset now seemed to be in the service of Elgin's ambitions on the Acropolis. "But I've been thinking. I believe I will use the opportunity of meeting the Valida to present the idea of the vaccine."

"We've gone over this," Elgin said. "Please do not lose sight of what is most important. A misstep with this vaccine business could throw everything into turmoil. The precious remains of the Athens of Pericles are at stake."

Elgin had not had very much to drink this evening, so Mary felt that she could challenge him in a light spirit. "I see that you do not follow the sentiments of Pericles, despite your great love for all that he built."

"What do you mean, Mary?"

Despite his sobriety, he had a defensive look on his face. Nonetheless she continued. "I have finished reading Plutarch's *Life of Pericles*. Do your recall what Pericles said in his famous funeral oration? That the greatest of women is she who is least talked of among men, whether for good or for bad? Apparently, all of Constantinople is talking about your wife to the extent that I have attracted the attention of the Sultan's mother, and you do not seem to mind."

"But all of Athens and beyond talked about Pericles' wife, or concubine, or courtesan, or whatever you wish to call Aspasia. Perhaps he did not mean what he said," Elgin replied.

"But Aspasia's renown eventually caused problems for Pericles. He was accused of starting a war at her behest. I wonder, has it always been unsafe for a woman to have a reputation of any kind? Was that what Pericles' warning was about?"

She thought of Emma Hamilton—*That Hamilton Woman*. Queen Charlotte was less discussed in society than Mrs. Hamilton. But as much gossip as she garnered, no one ever mentioned the good deeds that Sir William had described to the Elgins. Apparently, those were kept a secret, while the elements of her life that should have been kept secret were presented in periodicals and salons the Continent over for public consumption. It was a paradox.

"It appears to me that our sex is only discussed publicly in a derogatory manner. The respectable woman is doomed to anonymity."

"Good God, you women today—European women, in any case—have us men over the barrel, don't you? I suppose that a man such as Pericles had to appear to be the leader in his own home if he wished to be the leader of Athens. As do I, even if I am not."

"You flatter me," Mary said. "I am hardly the leader of this household, or this embassy, or this ambassador, for that matter."

"We shall try to keep it that way for as long as possible, shan't we? Despite all the attentions that intrude from the outside?"

"I think we shall," she said.

"Do not forget, my Poll, that though Pericles was allegedly in love with this Aspasia, the Athenian poets called her the dog-eyed whore. We shall have to withdraw you from all this public attention before things get quite out of hand."

"Yes," Mary agreed. "That would be a very good idea."

She wanted to ask him just where that line would be drawn, and how many of his ambitions would have to be fulfilled before he began to consider her reputation, but Elgin was yawning. Instead of pursuing that line of thinking, she kissed his cheek and turned on her side to go to sleep.

But sleep did not come, and Mary knew that it would not. She hadn't slept in three days, ever since she began to suspect that she was pregnant again. Her monthly was now ten days late, and if her body wasn't telling her that she was with child, her intuition was sending the signal. She knew, deep inside, that a tiny seed had been planted and was growing. How she knew this, she could not say. While she hadn't had a direct premonition, she did feel that certain womanly knowing that accompanies monumental events such as conception, births, and deaths.

She hoped with all her heart that the recent nightmares were merely a sign of a mother's natural concern, arising from the fact that her body already knew that she was carrying a baby and was warning her to be cautious, rather than some horrible premonition of things to come in her own life.

How to know? It was not possible to second-guess God's will. No matter how lucky she felt, and no matter how hard she prayed, why should the Lord spare her the miseries of a thousand other mothers? God had made her suffer hellish torments during her last delivery. Perhaps that was a warning to limit the number of children she and Elgin should have. But Elgin had no patience for this sort of thinking. Surrendering to such womanly fears and emotions would be counter to all logic and reason, things he prized highly as a man of his day. She tried to cheer herself with thoughts of another healthy, rosy-cheeked baby, but her normally sunny disposition inevitably withdrew when memories of suffering crept into her mind. It was as if her body still carried the frightful experience somewhere within itself.

She had nearly died. Did Elgin not love her? Was she just a vessel for his children and a vehicle for his ambitions to be fulfilled? It was horrible to let such thoughts wander into her mind. She was sure they were not true. He loved her. Surely he did, everyone said so. And yet, why did she feel this discomfort?

She wanted to roll over and interrogate him. What if he and

the little boy were left without her after another horrible delivery? This one had ended well, but it could easily have gone the other way. Would you like to be on your own? she wished to demand. Hosting your own suppers and balls? Supervising your own household and staff of sixty? Thoughts of the enormity and variety of her own duties overtook her outrage. An exhaustion born out of defeat overtook her, and instead of confronting her husband, she slid into a fitful sleep.

From the city of Athens,

June 1801

Dearest Daughter,

We are delighted to report to you that the Archbishop of Athens has presented us with a treasure of incalculable worth—and, we are told, in honor of your reputation and influence. Perhaps he was instructed to do so by the Capitan Pasha or the Sultan himself? At any rate, darling girl, we are most proud of the service you do in the name of our country and the honor you bring to our family.

The piece is a gymnasiarch's chair, sat upon by the judges in the ancient Panathenaic Games that were held every four years on the Acropolis in honor of Athena. This is the solemn ceremony believed to be depicted in the magnificent frieze on the Parthenon's exterior, sculpted by Pheidias and his team of artisans, some of which is in ruin, but much of which is still in supreme condition. But of course you know all of this. According to Reverend Hunt, you are studying the ancient Greeks like the most serious of scholars. He said that "the names of Pericles and Pheidias, to whom we owe the chefs d'oeuvre of architecture and sculpture at Athens, have so strongly interested Lady Elgin that she has studied the works of Herodotus, Plutarch, and other original historians with an eagerness I have seldom witnessed." We are very proud of you.

The chair is handsomely carved with a relief of the Sacred Olive Tree, the owl of Minerva, the victor's garland, the vase of consecrated oil and the tripod given to the winners of the games and artistic contests, and other beautiful symbols. The seat is worn, but the carvings are in wonderful condition. We are going to put it outside in the garden, where we shall enjoy and appreciate it all the days of our lives. We are most grateful to you and to Elgin for arranging for us to have the privilege of keeping this lovely piece on our estate.

We shall now proceed to Malta, where we must be quarantined against smallpox before reentering the Continent. Pray that the French do not fire upon us during our long journey.

Please give our grandson sumptuous kisses from his doting granny and granddad.

Your loving
Mother and Daddy

From the city of Athens,

July 1801

Dear Lord Elgin,

Mr. & Mrs. Nisbet were so kind as to include Mr. Carlyle and me in all their touring parties. Mr. Nisbet's connection with Your Lordship opened the gates of the Acropolis and every recess of the superb buildings it contains. With the knowledge now accumulated by Your Lordship's architects and modelers, the Athens of Pericles seemed to rise before me in all its pristine beauty.

Of the Temple of Athena, called the Parthenon, I can say nothing that would convey an idea of the effect it produces. It must be seen to know what the union of simplicity and beauty is capable of. Unfortunately, the Parthenon and the famous Great Gateway, also called the Propylaea—Pheidias' masterpieces—are all within the walls of the Acropolis, now a Turkish fortress, garrisoned by mercenary and insolent Janissaries. The insults to which those great monuments are daily subjected are almost too painful to enunciate.

The Ottoman soldiers sell off fragments of this precious monument to visitors. Every traveler coming adds to the general defacement of the statuary within his reach. The Turks have defaced all the statues' heads. In some instances, they have pounded down the statues and other magisterial architectural pieces to convert the lead holding them together into ammunition. Stones from her walls and columns have been used in the construction of the miserable, makeshift dwellings in which the Turks presently live. To witness the abuses is to die just a little.

The Parthenon of Pheidias is in an irrevocable state of disassembly. We must act immediately to preserve what is left, and to finish the important work that Your Lordship has begun. The Turkish officials put daily obstacles before your artists and modelers. The commandant has decided that they may not have access to any part of the Temple of Athena without the proper *FIRMAN*, which is a written order from the Sultan, stamped and signed. Without this firman, the great bas-reliefs, the magnificent frieze, the metopes, and the statues of the gods in the pediments—the last remaining wonders of that ancient civilization—can neither be modeled nor drawn by your staff.

Every day that they sit idle is a day that brings potential destruction to these pieces. Why, who knows what tomorrow will bring? The commandant might take it upon himself to topple a pediment statue in search of lead for his gun. Time is of the essence, I assure you.

I await your expeditious response.

> Respectfully,
> Reverend Philip Hunt

"DOES IT NOT TEAR at your heart, Mary?" Elgin asked. "Is it not unbearable to hear firsthand the sorry fate of the Athens of Pericles and Pheidias?" Elgin looked as wretched as a man had ever looked.

Mary regarded both letters, which had arrived in the same post, along with a private letter from her father to Elgin offering the funds for the Athenian project that Elgin had so boldly—in Mary's estimation—requested, on top of the money they required to continue to fund the embassy.

She marveled at how Elgin had played his cards. Her father's enthusiasm was right there on the page, in her mother's handwriting, as worthy a translator of that man's true sentiments as any, and again, in her father's own. Elgin knew exactly how to fuel the ambitions of another man, even one as measured and skeptical as Mary's cautious father. And, considering Hunt's description of the wretched condition of the monuments, Elgin must have been correct all along in his desire to preserve what was left for present and future generations.

Mary must have been wrong in judging Elgin's ambitions to be overarching. His goals must be completely worthy after all, if her father had been thus seduced into the game. Perhaps women simply did not have the wisdom or the foresight to see such lofty projects through to fruition. Women focused on small, domestic ambitions for attainable things like happiness, comfort, safety, and security. Perhaps they must leave the concerns of the larger world to men, who appeared to know no bounds in the pursuit of seemingly unachievable things. Perhaps that is what it took to make changes in the world. Perhaps Aspasia uniquely possessed this larger vision held by men, and that is what fascinated Pericles. Could she, Mary Nisbet, a practical Scottish girl, hope to hold such grandeur in her prosaic mind?

The ruins of once-majestic Athens must be saved. The glory of Athens would be preserved, its transformative beauty brought into the future by her own husband's vision. Her father's new enthusiasm validated that vision forever in her mind. He had seen something in Athens that had changed him, something so powerful that it had forced his hand where his bankbook was concerned. Whatever Mary's personal needs and desires—even her own life, if need be—she must put it all aside and remember that she was Elgin's soldier in his march on history.

The city of Athens,
in the sixth year of the
Thirty-Year Truce with Sparta

PERIKLES HAD BEEN AWAY for months, and I so occupied myself with new students and clients as best I could to avoid the perpetual longing I felt in his absence. He was with the Athenian fleet, attempting to suppress a revolt on the island of Samos. The Athenian forces had managed to overthrow the rebellious regime, installing a government cooperative to Athens. But still the Samians would not yield, and so Perikles besieged them, hoping to force capitulation. The siege dragged on and on, and had become unpopular with the people of Athens. The costs were high, in terms both of money and of human life, and as the war was happening on remote shores, most people forgot the cause and now only complained about their rising taxes.

I did not like to venture out of the house these days for fear of hearing the criticism leveled at Perikles. I busied myself tending to the romantic and domestic concerns of the men of Athens. I had developed a reputation as a counselor in matters of love and marriage. Men requested audiences with me to get advice on how to select a bride, how to tell a good matchmaker from a crooked one, and, once married, how to run a household. Fathers sent sons to me to improve their powers of oration—both in making public speeches and in making private declarations of love. I was delighted to oblige. Though legal marriage was denied me, I had formed a happy union with Perikles, and I did not like to see any young man or woman enter what would be a disastrous one.

"Do not allow Cassandra the Matchmaker to bring your son a wife," I told the wealthy father of a shy and handsome young man named Lysander. I had helped the boy memorize and recite the more familiar parts of the speeches and axioms of the Seven Sages, and I had grown fond of him. "That woman does not tell the truth about the qualities of the parties to be wed, but accepts bribes for giving false praise to an ugly bride or a foolish groom."

I always counseled prospective grooms to educate their wives if the girls came to the marriage ignorant. "The husband's activities may bring the money into the household, but the wife's prudence in matters of spending and management is what keeps it there," I would say. "I realize that most women are kept apart from knowledge of any sort, but a wife who can read and write and count so that she might keep books of the expenditures is worth her weight in gold." It was all common sense, but the men treated the information as nuggets of wisdom from a divine source.

I never accepted money for my services. If I did, I would have been doubly criticized. Sophists were sometimes despised for the very fact that they were paid. And for a woman to accept money for any activity would automatically put her in the category of prostitute. I who held a tentative place just above that on the ladder of respectability could not be too careful.

Staying indoors did not protect me entirely from Perikles' critics. The men who came to me as students and clients often brought the gossip and events of the day with them. I learned soon enough of a new rumor that was making its way across the town, and possibly across the entire federation of Greek states.

"Is it true that Perikles started the war on Samos at your behest, Aspasia?" a man who had come for matchmaking advice asked me.

"What are you saying?" I asked. I had heard the Athenian aggression criticized for many reasons, but that it had started at my behest was a new one.

"It is what they're all saying in the marketplace. I heard that it's even been suggested in the Assembly. They say that the only reason Perikles decided to crush the revolt in Samos was that the Samians declared war on Miletus. Everyone knows that's where you were born, so it is easy to make the connection."

"They can't be serious," I said. "Perikles went to war be-cause—and only because—Samos challenged Athens's author-ity. The Athenians and all their allies have charged him with protecting their interests and maintaining Athenian supremacy, but they criticize him and make up these ridiculous accusa-tions when he carries out the mandate of the people."

"I didn't level the accusation, Aspasia. I merely heard it and am repeating it to you."

"Well, it is so preposterous that it will surely die out very soon," I said, rushing him out of the house so that he would not see how upset I was.

I became even more reclusive, deliberately ignoring the passage of time. One day, as I sat in the courtyard, I noticed that the air was considerably warmer, and was astonished to realize that we were ten days into Elaphebolion, the first month of spring, and that the Greater Dionysia was about to begin, cele-brating the resurgence of life after the fallowness of winter. On the eve of the festival, weary of my solitude, I donned a mask and slipped into the streets to watch the ancient wooden image of Dionysus paraded in his chariot with the mule-headed prow, draped in ivy and decorated with grapevines and fruit.

Though women composed the core of the cult of Dionysus, they would not attend a festival in the open streets, save the streetwalkers, the beggars, and the vendors come in from the country with their goods, so I took Hilarion of Gaza, a slave boy, with me for protection. He was only seventeen years old, but of a strong build, and good with a small knife. With the entire male population stirred up on jugs of the god's wine, a woman alone would have been subjected to more than verbal insults.

We followed the procession all the way to the Theater of Dionysus, where in secret the priests would sacrifice a male goat on the altar that sat at the center of the stage. Once an animal was sacrificed, the season's theatrical productions might commence, and even without Perikles, I hoped that I would have the chance to attend at least one event. I asked Hilarion to walk me back to the house before the men got caught up in the late-night revels, racing through the streets with torches, singing hymns to the god, but also looking for trouble and a bit of anonymous wine-soaked fun.

In the following days, I did not go to any of the tragedies presented. For the past two years, I had attended the productions with Perikles, which meant that I was safe. But with the new accusation, I did not want to venture out openly without his protection. Pheidias, however, called on me and offered to escort me to the comedy on the fourth night. I thought it might cheer me up to watch the antics of the actors, slinging insults through their grotesque masks and wagging their gargantuan leather phalluses. The comedies always lampooned the high and the mighty—those hubristic creatures who were on the tip of everyone's tongue—and so were great fun to attend.

Perikles had entered the public arena by financing Aeschylus' play *The Persians,* and at that time he began to develop a passion for the theater; this I shared with him. We had spent many a day and night here enjoying the work of the finest playwrights and performers Athens had produced. Ladies were not permitted to attend theatrical performances; if they did, they were often hissed at until they hid their faces and left. Of course, men brought their mistresses, and the priestesses sat in thrones in the front row set aside for them alongside the judges and city officials. When attending with Perikles, I would take my seat next to him in one of the front rows reserved for the more illustrious citizens. Since I was a courtesan, no one cared that I sat with the men of privilege.

This evening, in deference to Perikles, his seat remained empty while he was away at war. I felt many eyes upon me as Pheidias and I walked down the steps to take our seats, but that was not an unusual experience for me. As Perikles' mistress, and a female philosopher, I was always a topic of gossip and speculation. But I had entertained so many of the men of the city at our parties that I had gradually come to feel accepted by them, at least when I was in their company. I am sure that when they were with their cronies, they indulged in coarser assessments of me, but at least they had come to treat me with dignity and respect.

As soon as we were seated, the entertainments began. We were treated to a pantomime of a boxing match, which was so much nicer to watch than an actual contest, with its body blows and blood. How lovely to experience the grace and artistry of the fighters without the damage. The pantomimists were especially good, moving with fluidity to the music of flutes and cymbals as they mocked punches and knockouts. Following them were erotic courtesan dancers, who twisted and contorted their nude bodies, with only scarves as props, writhing like snakes to the rhythm of the drummers. They so enthralled the audience that a second dance was demanded.

Finally, the comic presentation began. I adjusted myself in the seat, ready to enjoy the production. The set consisted of three housefronts, with the double roofs necessary for the spying and peeking and escape routes that were always part of a farce. The celestial balcony constructed for the appearance of the gods was gaudily decorated with fluffy clouds and boughs of flowers, an indication that even the deities who appeared would be ridiculed. I loved the twists and turns and mistaken identities of this sort of satire, where even sacred subject matter was not treated sanctimoniously. The heavy mood I had felt since Perikles left Athens was lifting, and I was ready to enjoy the entertainment.

The chorus took the stage, dozens of actors wearing masks of elderly men, their bodies padded with heavy paunches and wide, saggy bottoms. It did not take the audience long to understand that this was to be a meeting of the Assembly, what with the jokes made with the word "ass," as the actors turned to us to demonstrate the same.

"If only Perikles were here!" I said to Pheidias.

"My dear, he has wrestled with the asses of the Assembly quite enough," he quipped.

A character identified as Honest Citizen took the stage, giving the opening monologue. As he spoke, it did not take long for the smile on my face to fade. Honest Citizen revealed that he was from the isle of Samos and was a man who had suffered terribly in the war, which was perpetrated by the corrupt leaders of Athens. Since the Athenians and his government refused to make peace, he had come before the Assembly to cut his own deal.

I did not think that I could sit through a two-hour attack on Perikles.

"I came here tonight to escape all this," I whispered to Pheidias. "Would you be upset if we slipped out of here?"

"Aspasia, you are the most notorious woman in Athens. I do not think that you can 'slip' anywhere without setting off a torrent of talk," he whispered back to me. "The best thing to do is remain in your seat and laugh as if you think it the funniest thing in the world."

If Pheidias was not going to escort me outside, I was not going to leave. His assessment was correct; if I left, it would cause a stir. I settled back into my seat, resolved to remain gracious, when I heard one of the characters ask, "And what was the cause of this war to begin with?"

The other faced the audience to answer. I could have sworn that he was staring directly at me. "Oh, two playboys from Athens went to Samos and stole a drunken whore named Simaetha. But the Samatians took it to heart and got themselves all liquored up and went over to Aspasia's place and stole a pair of whores from her. That's why Greece is in this pickle. Then, what do you think happened next? Olympian Perikles got all upset on her behalf and started to thunder and lighten in his wrath, throwing Greece into an uproar."

Needless to say, the fifteen thousand spectators in the Theater of Dionysus found this utterly hilarious. The laughter rang out all around me, to the point that I found it deafening. My face flushed so hotly that I thought I would pass out. My heart was racing, and quite against my will, I let out a gasp. Pheidias squeezed my hand, and I squeezed his back even harder to save myself from either screaming or crying. The intolerable laughter was echoing in my head, driving me crazy. My eyes darted about, as if I might find some means of escape, as if some part of me was refusing to accept that I could not simply disappear into the night and go somewhere safe where this was not happening—indeed, had never happened. But everyone in our vicinity was looking at me to see my reaction.

"Laugh," he said under his breath. "Don't let them see that you're upset."

But I could not laugh. I had just begun to feel that I had made a place in Athens for myself and a place in Perikles' home and his heart. Now it seemed that I had been living in a fantasy. While I had been fooling myself that the people of Athens had begun to accept me, public sentiment had been turning on me behind my back, bringing with it a new level of scorn, one that was much worse than whispers in the marketplace. Did these people really believe that I had talked Perikles into besieging an island? What sort of power did they think I wielded?

Though the entire play was a scathing indictment of war, a good majority of the audience reacted with loud boos and heckling whenever Perikles was criticized. I felt better, knowing that he still had the support of many Athenians. My name, thankfully, was not mentioned again. When the performance was over, I clutched Pheidias' arm and exited the theater, forcing myself to keep my head erect and my eyes meeting those of anyone who dared to look at me. I stared many, many men in the face quite defiantly, but my eyes did not register anything at all. As we walked with the crowd out of the theater, I might have been as blind as Oedipus after his fall.

I HAD NO IDEA why Pheidias wished me to visit him in his studio. "I have something radical to propose," he'd whispered in my ear as he left me at my house after the performance, though he would not elaborate on what it was. I had once tried to obtain an invitation to view his work, but he'd scolded me, telling me that my womanly presence would be too much of a distraction for the artisans, and they were lagging far enough behind the schedule for completion of the colossal—and colossally expensive—statue of Athena Parthenos that was already causing so much controversy.

As if to mock my shame and my grim mood, the day was glorious. The marketplace was lively, even at this time in the afternoon, when the air warmed and the silver-green leaves of the olive trees on the hillside began to take on a wilted look. Slaves haggled with beleaguered mongers over the last few fish, which had to be sold before the heat ruined them and they became food for the wandering dogs, and therefore a loss for their sellers. Rancid bits had already been discarded, and I took a small piece of linen, perfumed with lavender oil, out of my pocket to cover my nose.

No one seemed to notice me. The few men with whom I was acquainted nodded politely before quickly walking on, but that was not unusual. Men did not want to be seen chatting with a courtesan in the agora. Gossip from Athens's network of slaves inevitably wiggled its way into the men's homes, causing trouble. Not that wives had much authority to complain about their husbands' sexual indiscretions. But no one could take away a woman's prerogative to nag about household money being spent on a whore.

Though the comedy was as vehement a statement against war as I had ever seen, the reference to me was so absurd that the audience must have taken it in the spirit of parody, and not as an actual indictment. No one was shouting accusations against me in the marketplace as I had feared. Life seemed to be going on as usual. The play would not be performed again in Athens until the next cycle of festivals, if ever. Perhaps last night's humiliation would be the end of it.

I slipped into the shade of a colonnade to escape the crush of pedestrians and shoppers and looked up at my destination. The spectacular white columns of the Parthenon glistened in the flat light of the sun. An oxcart passed by me, hauling two great slabs of marble. I knew where it was headed, so I decided to follow.

The marble was exactly as Pheidias had described it to me—quarried from Mount Pentelikon, about ten miles out-side of Athens, the finest of white stone in Greece. The temple to Athena would be built only with this particular Athenian marble, I was told. "It is smooth, with a consistent and beauti-ful grain," Pheidias had said, "not coarse and shiny like the marble imported from the islands."

"Even Athenian stone is superior to that of the rest of Greece," I had joked at the time. He laughed, but the selection of stones was, for him, no laughing matter. "Yes, Aspasia, even our marble is destined to be supreme over the other stones of the Greek world."

Pheidias' studio was a makeshift structure at the south end of the Akropolis; it had been erected there so that the marble, once carved, would not have to be carted too long a distance, lessening the labor involved in transportation and also the chances of breakage. Even if I had not known the location of the studio, I could have followed the sounds of the chisels, mallets, and hammers hard at work. I freely entered the high-ceilinged one-room building and was hit by the clouds of dust circling in the air. The artisans wore kerchiefs around their noses as they banged away at the stones. I put my handkerchief up to my nose to shield it from the flying particles, and I heard a voice ring out above the clatter.

"Welcome."

The sonorous greeting caught the attention of the workmen. The tools came to a slow silence as I felt dozens of pairs of eyes turn upon me.

"Back to work," Pheidias ordered, and the clamor started once more.

Body parts huge and small made from stone and ivory were scattered on the floor. A great white arm, as long as I was tall, lay before me, its hand turned upward as if ready to catch something that might drop from the heavens. Two sculptors shaped the formidable, sandal-footed legs, working from giant wooden models made to size. Each limb must have been at least twenty feet long.

"This might be the workroom where the gods designed the human form," I said.

"She's still in bits and pieces," Pheidias said. "But when Athena is put together properly, she will be the most superb representation of woman and goddess that has ever been made. Forty feet tall, my dear, sheathed in ivory, and decorated with more gold than a man might see in all the days of his life and his children and grandchildren in theirs. A sight for mortal eyes to behold."

"When do you think the lady will be assembled and ready for display?" I asked.

"That depends on whether we can keep the money flowing. The Assembly continues to say that we cannot both wage wars and build monuments, but we can, and we must. Have they sent you sent here to spy on me?"

I laughed. "I am not exactly on good terms with the Assembly."

"Well, it will all be finished by the Great Panathenaic Festival next year," he replied. "See how much we have already accomplished?"

He pointed to the body parts lying about. "The arms, hands, legs, torso, and feet are quite finished, as you can see. We've worked in a very industrious manner, emulating the goddess herself, who presides over skill and craftsmanship. The winged Nike that will perch in her outstretched hand is being made. Here is the goddess's shield, which will rest at her side."

The shield was fantastically large, taller than two men, and it rested on a wooden frame. On its surface, Amazon women fought their way up to the Akropolis, but Greek warriors hurled them back, protecting the citadel.

"I thought that the Parthenon was to commemorate the victory over the Persians. What do Amazonian women have to do with Persia?"

"They are from the eastern lands, for one. And they are barbaric, for another. Besides, the Persians have employed Amazon-like women in their wars. Have you not heard of Artemisia of Caria, who was a naval commander? She had the ear of King Darius more than her male counterparts. Like yourself, she quite overturned the natural order of things."

"Interesting," I replied. "I thought I might be the first woman in all history to have a man's ear."

"Now you know that you are the second."

"I hope that Artemisia was not the subject of so much public scorn," I said. I did not want to bring up what had happened last night, but if Pheidias had heard any gossip about it, I wished he would tell me.

"Oh, I wouldn't worry so much about that. You're like an Amazon, Aspasia. You are just as strong. They're quite right here to be afraid of you. Everyone knows that both in battle and outside of it, men can be quite undone by women."

"But not yourself."

"I have other vulnerabilities," he replied. He was known as a lover of men, and therefore a great companion to women such as myself, who intrigued him, but who cast no spell.

"You have left Athena's face blank as yet. How do you envision it?"

Pheidias looked at me as if I had asked a startling question. "Come with me," he said, leading me out of the studio and heading straight for the Parthenon, which was near completion. I had seen the building in various stages of construction, and each time, proximity inspired awe.

"This is your masterpiece, Pheidias," I said.

The temple sat upon the earth with quiet dignity, as if it were itself a deity. Tall, somber columns surrounded the rectangular building, rising upward as if they were living matter growing out of the earth, rather than oppressively heavy slabs of marble placed there by human hands. They tapered slightly as they rose, giving the impression of both lightness and symmetry. Though Pheidias had delegated the specifications and engineering feats to the architects Iktinus and Kallikrates, he supervised every aspect of the design. He often credited the other men, but I was under the impression that on an artistic level, he considered the temple his own work.

Some distance from the building, a small fire burned in a pit, attended by two craftsmen who kept it alive, a pot of molten lead atop it. The metallic smell was nauseating. "We mold the iron clamps that fasten the sculptural ornamentation to the building with hot lead," Pheidias explained.

"We are getting ready to place the metopes," he said, pointing to the blocks of marble on the ground, upon which were sculpted scenes of battle between centaurs and men. "Most of them are already in place above the columns, situated between the triglyphs." He gestured toward the metopes beneath the pediments that were already set on the building. In the ones remaining on the ground, it seemed that centaurs were hoisting females over their shoulders, trying to carry them away on their horse-hoofed legs, as the human men fought to prevent the rape.

"The last of these are ready to be lifted into place by those cranes," he said, pointing out the system of ropes and pulleys. "I've made ninety-two metopes in all. When the last is in place, we'll finish the roof, and then we'll fill the pediments with sculpture."

"You have made the centaurs so formidable that I am not certain who I wish to win the maidens," I joked. The bug-eyed centaurs were wild and determined in the face, bearded and hairy, with a hint of pointy ears poking from their tousled manes. As I looked at the carvings, I wondered what it would be like to be carried off by a creature with the face and torso of a man but the legs, hooves, and mane of a horse. "On the one hand, the abducted women seem to shrink in horror, but on the other hand, there is a glint of erotic desire in their faces. Do they find the monsters more alluring than their mortal men?"

Pheidias looked insulted. "I thought the young sculptors did a fine job with the mortals."

"Indeed, Pheidias, the nude figures of the men are as finely formed as any I've seen." The musculature in the chest and stomach could have made me ache with desire if I'd stared for too long. One in particular showed a beautiful naked youth, draped only about the shoulders with a cape, reaching out to capture a fleeing centaur. The heroic strain in his body as he pulled at the creature's neck seemed so lifelike and beautiful that I wanted to caress him. "Would that all men looked like that beneath their robes!"

"In my mind, they do," he answered wickedly. "Besides, it's crucial for the humans to be victorious. That figure you admire is Theseus. He was an invited guest at the wedding banquet of the King of the Lapiths of Thessaly. The centaurs, in contrast, showed up at the wedding uninvited and tried to carry the women away. Filthy creatures!"

"So once again the Greeks prevail over foreign monsters?"

"Precisely."

"Each figure in the metopes is more spectacular than the next. Your genius has once again prevailed."

"I am aware of that. I refined every one of the figures myself. I allowed the others to sketch the scene upon the stone and make the initial carvings—all after my approval, of course. But the work is truly mine. May I add that there is not a tool mark upon them."

"But they will be positioned up so high on the temple that only the gods will be able to appreciate your detail," I said.

"What other opinions matter, in the end," he responded, "if one has the good opinion of the gods?"

"Now you are sounding like a philosopher," I said, making him laugh.

He turned to walk up the steps and into the building, but something stopped me from following him. It was such a formidable structure, foreboding in its beauty. He must have read my mind.

"Come, Aspasia. The temple is not yet consecrated by the priests nor dedicated by the people. Until then, it is of no consequence to the goddess."

Inside, sunlight crept through the incomplete roof, held up by massive structural timbers of cypress. Above, I could see four men in what appeared to be precarious positions placing marble roof tiles. The temple had two rooms, the larger of which would house the statue of the goddess; the smaller one would keep the Athenian treasury. Pheidias showed me where the colossal statue of the goddess would stand. "A shallow pool of water will surround her, casting a great shimmer upon the ivory and the immense tonnage of gold that will be hammered onto the statue."

"Ah, yes," I said. "The gold that has all the tongues wagging over the expense."

"They know that they are merely exercising that organ. As Perikles has explained to the Assembly, the gold will be set so that it can be removed in the event that it is needed by the city."

He shook his head in annoyance at the pettiness of their enemies. "I prefer to concentrate on the final result, which, as you can see, will be glorious. When all those fools are dead, Athena will still stand. She will be assembled, dressed, decorated with precious gold and jewels and inlays of glass, and presented for the lucky few to see. But all will hear of the majesty of the monument."

Only the priests and priestesses and the most prominent people in the land were allowed access to the temples on the Akropolis. Because of my association with Perikles, I was considered one of them.

"I will tell you why I have asked you here," Pheidias said. "I have been pondering the details of the face of the goddess. I wish to do something different. I do not want merely to represent the goddess. I wish to give her a real face, one that has the qualities of intelligence, wisdom, compassion, and bravery. I had never seen those qualities in the face of a mortal woman, but I do see them in yours. Aspasia, I would like to use your features and expression for the face of Athena."

I was stunned by his suggestion. The idea of the face of a notorious woman representing the great goddess of the city seemed more radical than any other feature of Pheidias' designs.

"The idea came to me last night as we were leaving the theater," he said. "You walked with such dignity—beautiful, bold, defiant. But it must be done in secret, for the obvious reasons."

"Yes, your detractors must not know that your model for the face of the Mother of Athens is a woman who is often called a whore," I said. "That might not evoke a favorable reaction from Athens's more respectable citizens."

"Succinctly put," he answered without a trace of apology. "But it is true, what I am saying about your face. Perhaps the trials of your life have imbued you with more visible character than ordinary women whose fates as mothers and wives are sealed at birth. Perhaps it is your innate intelligence, or your bold but diplomatic way of speaking. Or perhaps it is that you strategize like a man—an attribute shared with Athena. Whatever the reason, I am committed to the idea. What say you?"

"Shall we tell Perikles?" Pheidias' suggestion intrigued me, but I did not know how I would keep a secret from the man I loved, though I often suspected that he kept secrets from me.

"He is away at war. Let's not bother him. He is criticized enough as it is, and, as we saw last night, even over his relations with you."

"No one minds that Perikles has a mistress," I said. "They simply do not like that I have influenced him. And I have not—not to the extent that people imagine. I listen, and sometimes I make suggestions. That is all. But one would think that I was casting spells upon him to get him to do my bidding."

"Will you be casting any spells upon me, Aspasia? Perhaps you can win friends in the Assembly by casting a spell upon me to work faster and use cheaper materials." This amused him greatly, and it amused me too. Yet a small part of me felt a sting whipping at my heart.

"Why do I have to be insulted and thought wicked simply because I have enough intelligence to converse with my lover and offer him a forum for discussing the issues that occupy his mind?" What threat did I, a woman without a dowry—a penniless orphan who lived and breathed and was fed at the pleasure of the man I loved—pose to the powerful men who whispered ugly things about me behind my back? Sometimes it seemed that they feared me more than they feared Perikles, which was nonsensical. How to figure these paradoxes of human existence?

"There is no sense in asking unanswerable questions, Aspasia."

"But as a philosopher I take it upon myself to address such

questions. There is no such thing as a concrete or satisfactory answer, but one must take comfort in the exploratory path that logical inquiry offers."

"Those are the first words of truth I have heard spoken today," said a strange voice from behind us.

We turned around to see that a husky young man carrying tools and cloths had entered the room. He bowed to us and began to polish the long plinth that would eventually serve as the base of the statue of Athena. He tried to look as if he were hard at his labor, but I could tell that he wanted to listen to our conversation. Pheidias spoke to him.

"Ah, Sokrates, I see that you have finally decided to do your work. Did your fellow workers tire of your conversation and send you back to your labors?"

He was about my age, twenty-five, and quite muscular. His hair was wild, his nose was wide, and his lips were almost crudely full. He was slightly bug-eyed, like the centaurs in the metopes, and he was hairier on the arms and around the neck than I like a man to be. It was not impossible to imagine him as a satyr, with the horns and hoofs of a goat and the giant erection with which they were often portrayed.

"This fellow could be a good sculptor," Pheidias said to me, "but he is more taken with the art of conversation and the habit of asking questions incessantly. His father, Sophroniscus, is one of the finest marble workers in Athens. The son could follow, but chooses to waste time in lesser pursuits."

"Thank you, Pheidias, but it's widely known that I am not much of a sculptor. In fact, I know very little about anything. That is why I must ask questions, for as an asker of questions, I excel. However, I did give the matter much thought last night and I decided that I could make a good deal of money as a pimp. For that is my pleasure: introducing others to those who will introduce pleasures to them."

I laughed loudly. I did not know whether this Sokrates was trying to amuse me or amuse himself.

"Here he is again, talking nonsense when he should be

working his magic upon the marble," Pheidias said in mock frustration. I could not tell whether or not Pheidias was flirting. Perhaps he found Sokrates attractive in some bestial way and was trying to groom him for a lover. It would not be the first time he had given one of his workers additional duties.

"What is the story told in the relief?" I asked, pointing to the long sculptural scene that Sokrates had been polishing when we interrupted him.

Pheidias opened his mouth to speak, but Sokrates began talking as if I had addressed the question to him. "It's the story of the creation of Pandora, the first woman, who released mischief into the world. The story is widely known. The Olympian gods were annoyed with Prometheus for stealing their precious fire and delivering it to the common man, so they decided to punish the human male by creating an irksome creature who would both enchant men and cause them great aggravation."

"A woman, naturally," I said.

"This creature was Pandora, to whom the gods gave many gifts, along with a precious box." He pointed to the figures on the pedestal that he had been polishing. "See here how each of the gods is giving her the same gifts that Athena gave to the citizens of her city? Here she is given knowledge of weaving, of learning and wisdom, of how to grow crops and forge weapons. The only caution that Athena issued was that Pandora was not, under any circumstances, to open this mysterious box. But the box was so lovely!"

"And I am sure that Athena had also given Pandora a love of beautiful things," I said.

Sokrates raised his finger straight in the air like a teacher about to make a point. "Being of a curious and disobedient nature, Pandora flung aside these gifts. She could not resist an investigation into the unknown. She opened the box, releasing all evil into the world."

"You are positing that women were irksome from the start? That women are responsible for the world's ills?"

"I merely relate the events," he said. "I did not invent them."

"I have a different proposition. Is it possible that everything that Pandora released has made the world a more interesting place? After all, how would we know what is right and good and virtuous if we did not have contrasting qualities to compare?"

"I do like the way that you have turned the question on its head," Sokrates replied.

"Pandora was perhaps the Greek world's first philosopher. For like myself, she was not content merely to accept the given, but was compelled to launch her own investigation into the order of things."

"That is certainly an interesting observation, and one that I would like to pursue with you," he said.

"For the gods' sake, please do it later and not when I am dependent upon your labors, Sokrates," Pheidias said.

"I have long wanted to make your acquaintance, madam, to witness for myself if your wisdom is fact or rumor."

"But we have yet to be introduced. How would you know me?"

He laughed. "All Athens and much of the rest of Greece knows of Aspasia—even before last night. From the moment I saw you, I knew that you could be no other."

I felt the blood rising to my face, but Sokrates was smiling, and not maliciously. Perhaps everyone was taking the comments in the play as a joke. "So there are some things of which you *are* sure, despite your earlier claim to the contrary?"

"Apparently, yes. I am sure that the gentlemen of Athens find you so wise that they ask you for advice in matters of love."

"That is true enough," I said. "It is difficult for men to apply their natural powers of reason in these matters. Intervention from an observer, one versed in the philosophy of love, is valuable, I am told."

"Madam, I am a student of the greatest teacher of the philosophy of love."

"Are you? And who is this wise man?" I asked. I had heard

of no philosopher, sophist or no, who had declared himself thus.

"It is no man but a woman like yourself, though much older and, of course, not nearly so lovely, though she declares that loveliness is in the eye of the one who looks upon it."

"Enough!" Pheidias interrupted. "Lovers of words have no place where honest work must be done. Make a time for chatter when I do not have to listen or after I have had enough wine to be amused by you. Come with me, Aspasia. If we do not leave, he'll never get to his tasks."

I left Sokrates with an invitation to my home, having expressed my desire to meet his female instructor. I thought that if he did not irk Perikles, he might amuse him. And I could not wait to meet my older and less beautiful competitor who was also spouting wisdom in matters of love.

"I must take my leave," I said to Pheidias, who, once outside, was sneezing dust out of his nose. He looked fatigued and in need of an afternoon nap. Sweat had broken out on his forehead, which was growing higher with his ever-receding hairline. He was not old, but it did occur to me that he was no longer young. I hoped that his massive efforts would bring him the acclaim he both desired and deserved while he was still lucid and living and able to enjoy the accolades.

"As you leave the Akropolis, take a moment to notice a new sculpture of the figures of the Graces. That odd fellow Sokrates is the artist. The figures are quite nice. There is true motion in them. He could be something of an artist if he had half a mind to try."

The Graces are called thus because of the qualities they represent—beauty, joy, health. Part of the retinue of women who served the great love goddess, they were supposed to enhance Aphrodite's already irresistible feminine allure. Some say they were her daughters by Dionysus, and looking at the figures that had sprung from Sokrates' imagination or inspiration, it was easy to believe that the two great deities of sensuality had indeed mated and formed these three beings. Pheidias was correct; the sculptural grouping by Sokrates showed demonstrable talent. The magical creatures were skillfully painted, decorated with glimmer that made their hair catch the late-afternoon sunshine. I wondered if Sokrates had applied the paint that gave flush and definition to their faces and forms, or the jewels that had been fastened into their necks and ears, or if another artist had come behind him and decorated the figures.

In any case, the figures were well carved. The sculptor had presented them as naked but wrapped their forms in a single length of fabric that intertwined their arms and legs, connecting the Graces in an unending nimble dance. Their arms were wrapped around one another, and their elegant figures seemed to flow together. I could almost imagine the music that moved them to sway together in their seductive dance. But even as their bodies were entangled, their faces remained disturbingly separate and disconnected. The striking face of Aglaea, goddess of beauty and charm, peeked out from the wrap of fabric, beckoning and teasing. Thalia, mistress of health and radiance, threw her head back in ecstasy and abandon. But Euphrosyne, who presided over mirth, and some said joy, stared at me as if down her nose.

I did not like the way the figure seemed to look at me, as if she had something in mind for me that she would not share. Beauty and Health appeared benevolent though remote. But Mirth appeared to have a specific message for me. Could it be that the same sneering I had endured from the comic playwright was also coming at me from this block of stone? I turned away from the creation of Sokrates, admiring his talents, though he had been quick to discount himself as an artist of any consequence. I told myself that when I again saw him, I would remember to tell him what I had imagined about his creation. Then I left behind the disquiet aroused by the mistress of mirth and I began the long walk home.

My dearest Father,

I am delighted to report that we have succeeded marvelously in procuring the proper FIRMAN from the Porte! It allows all our artists to go into the citadel at Athens, to copy and model everything in it, to erect scaffolds all round the Temple of Athena, to dig and discover all the ancient foundations, and to bring away any marbles that may be deemed curious by their having inscriptions on them. Our artists and craftsmen are not to be disturbed by the soldiers or any officials who are on the Acropolis under any pretense whatever. Don't you think this will do? I am in the greatest glee, for it would have been a great pity to fail in the principal part of our mission, after having been at such an expense.

Father, you can have no idea of the pleasure your and my mother's letters from Athens gave us. I know that you did not admire Elgin's pursuits on the Acropolis, and I, too, was against them for a time. But I feel the greatest comfort at your approval of the work. It is certainly very pleasing to hear that things are done in so superior and masterly a style. With your support, I no longer have cause to grudge them. Elgin is delighted that you *have entered so heartily into his cause. Your visit will undoubtedly restore the spirits of the artists and set them to work with renewed vigor.*

We have been at lovely Belgrade these few weeks escaping the heat and the plagues. Nothing can be lovelier than this city with its springs that give poor Elgin relief from his chronic rheumatism. The city has many shaded walks and endless gardens of flowers, all within view of the Black Sea. But I fear that we have run into a fever epidemic here and must refrain from drinking the water as Dr. Scott tells us that the water itself is quite feverish. Little Bab has been sick, and there is nothing more horrible than seeing one's Bab ill. I hear that you will soon be quarantined at Malta, and then to London and on to home. How I envy you and miss the faces of my dear own Mother and Dad.

> *Your dutiful and very affectionate daughter,*
> *M. Elgin*

August 1, 1801

Dear Lord Elgin,

The citadel is now as open and free to us as the streets of Athens. The artists are to consider themselves at full liberty to model, dig, or carry away whatever does not interfere with the works. The last few days have been particularly exciting. The ship-carpenter and five of the crew mounted the walls of the Temple of Athena, and with the aid of complex cordage and about twenty Greeks, they succeeded in detaching and lowering down, without the slightest accident, one of the statues in the metopes representing a combat between Theseus and a centaur. It has long been the admiration of the world; indeed, nothing can equal it for beauty and grace. A second, which adjoins it, on the same subject, was lowered without incident. Lusieri allows that there is nothing more perfect than these works in all the Universe.

On the western front of the Parthenon was the celebrated group of

Zeus presenting Athena as his daughter to the council of the gods. Much of it has disappeared, but being convinced that these enormous works could not have been carried off, we pulled down an old house and excavated beneath it. On digging to a considerable depth, we found the naked torso of Zeus and the greatest part of the statue of Victory. The drapery of this winged creature, which Lusieri posits might be the messenger goddess, Iris, is so light and elegant as to resemble the finest muslin and miraculously shows all the contours of the form beneath. The realism of the clinging drapery is so strong as to defy the imagination. One can hardly believe that it is made of stone! We also found there in the ground part of the body of Hermes, son of Zeus, and herald of the gods. No doubt he was on hand to announce this earth-shattering birth of Athena.

Still, my lord, there is nothing that we can do to stop the garrison from destroying what is left of the Parthenon. They are continually pummeling its parts to extract the lead that was used to fasten its clamps. I am sure that in a half century there will not remain one stone. It would be well, my lord, to ask for all that is left, or else to do all that is possible to prevent their going on in this fashion.

I do hope to see Your Lordship in Athens before too long. Until that time, I remain—

Reverend Philip Hunt

In the city of Constantinople,

Autumn 1801

LADY MARY CHRISTOPHER BRUCE— called Little Mary—was born on the last day of August. She came into the world in a much easier fashion than her brother. Still, Mary had once again found that the word "labor" had earned its literal meaning, and she had not had nearly enough rest since that long and—as she often laughed to herself—laborious event. Just two days after the birth, the French surrendered to the English and

Turkish armies in Alexandria. Elgin came flying into the house with the letter of announcement in his hand, and life for the Elgins in Constantinople accelerated at once. They were expected to attend all the celebrations hosted by the Sultan—and there were many—as well as to give a series of suppers and balls in honor of the victory.

Just three weeks after the birth of Little Mary, Mary was out on a boat every night watching the Sultan's weeklong display of fireworks. She was required to attend; Elgin was singled out in each celebration for a special honor. On one of these nights on the water, they passed the Sultan's barge. Selim acknowledged the Elgins as he drifted past them, but shortly afterward Mary turned around in time to see the Sultan staring at her through his telescope. She also saw, at that moment, the women of the harem waving to her from within their snug little prisons.

Why could they not be out on the river enjoying the spectacle with everyone else? These were the most prominent women in the empire; didn't their men want their company on such a monumental occasion? Mary could not imagine watching Elgin from a distance. No, he wanted her at his side, and she wanted to be there.

In any case, the Sultana Valida must have seen from her perch in the seraglio that the Sultan was staring at Mary, because the long-planned meeting was set for the very next day.

"The Valida is a formidable woman," Madame Pisani had told Mary while preparing her for the protocol of the harem. "Her name—though please do not utter it—is Mihrisah, which means 'Ruler of the Sun.' She is from the country of Georgia in the Caucasus, and she has been through much hardship on behalf of her son. You know it is the custom of the Turks to imprison the heirs to the throne. It is the only way that the reigning sultan might stay alive. Selim was imprisoned for fifteen years, waiting for his uncle Abdulhamid to die. For all that time, Mihrisah had been living in the Palace of Tears for widowed sultanas. Finally, twelve years ago, Abdulhamid died, Selim became sultan, and they were both freed."

"Is she the power behind the throne?" Mary had asked.

"She is probably the single greatest influence on the Sultan, more so than any one of his advisors. She is informed on everything. Nothing gets done without her knowledge or approval."

After weeks of preparation and attention to protocol, the encounter was to take place. Mary had arranged for beautiful pieces of ornamental furniture to be made for the Valida and her favorites, who included the wife of the Grand Vezir, with whom Mary intended to have an intimate chat about the vaccine. Other treats from England—chandeliers, candelabra, lace, silver trays, teas, and an elaborate samovar—were procured and packed. Mary's wardrobe had also been carefully designed. There would be as many costume changes today as in one of Mr. Shakespeare's five-act plays, and Mary would be expected to be splendidly outfitted for every aspect and ritual.

The early-morning boat ride was not pleasant. The weather was boisterous, winds whipping the water into undulating waves while rain poured down upon the passengers. Dawn was a slow, gray revelation. Mary sat huddled under the small boat's shelter, wrapped in fur, feeling as if she were engulfed by a huge bear carrying her hurriedly across some broken terrain. The weather had been damp these two months, and her chokings had returned. The attacks were not serious, but were prolonged by her being out every night in the clammy air, or dancing Scottish reels until the wee hours at the balls. Finally they arrived at the shore, and a phalanx of black eunuchs met Mary at the Great Gate to the Sultan's palace, waiting to escort her to the seraglio and the meeting with the Valida.

As soon as Mary passed by the Janissaries on duty, and the gate to the seraglio shut, the eunuchs disappeared, and Mary and her entourage of Masterman, Madame Pisani, and two servants were met by dozens of women, all magnificently dressed. Two led her by the arms while one very grand lady walked before them with perfumes smoking in an incense tray of gold filigree. The heavy scent of Indian spices, with cinnamon mingling with sweet myrrh, overwhelmed Mary's senses as she followed her escorts. They led her upstairs, where Hanum met her on the landing, screaming with joy at the sight of her. She took Mary into a small room, where she helped her arrange her clothing after the long voyage. Two women held a looking glass for Mary so that she could see herself. Mary was more interested in watching Masterman's expression on the other side of the glass than in gazing at her own flushed face. After she fixed her hair and smoothed her eyebrows, she whispered to Masterman, asking if the woman was feeling well.

"You should see the back of that looking glass," Masterman said. "You've never seen pearls and diamonds so numerous and so large!"

Once Mary had been refreshed with coffee and sweetmeats, Hanum announced that it was time to meet the Valida. She escorted Mary to a room with elaborately tiled walls, which were decorated with inscriptions that seemed to move like dancers. Mary saw a small figure seated upon a sofa—a woman with a beautiful scarlet shawl embroidered with gold spangles flung over her shoulders. The Valida was seated cross-legged—*à la Turque,* as Mary had come to think of the women's preferred posture—and the great shawl was draped in a way that made it look as if her legs had been cut off. Her hair was tucked up inside an elegant, cone-shaped yellow silk turban, with thick dark fringe across the forehead. Mary noticed that all the women in attendance had tucked up their hair as well, perhaps in imitation of the Valida's style.

"Those are real thumpers," Masterman whispered as Mary walked away from her attendants to be seated upon the sofa opposite the Valida. Masterman meant the diamonds the Valida was wearing, which were immense. Eight formed a tiara of sorts on her head, while the one on her little finger was the largest and most brilliant Mary had ever seen, even larger than the dazzling rock—worth twelve thousand pounds—that she and her mother had ogled one day in London at Rundell & Bridge. On a cushion nearby lay a watch covered with diamonds, and an inkstand and large portfolio, all studded over with rubies and giant smooth sea pearls. The Valida also kept near her a small looking glass embedded with precious stones. The lavish gifts heaped upon the Elgins by the Turks must have been mere trinkets to them.

Mary made three bows as she'd been instructed to do before she sat down. Madame Pisani immediately began to read Mary's greeting speech.

The Valida listened attentively and then reached under her sofa for a sheet of paper, which she handed to Hanum to read. Madame Pisani translated the statement for Mary. It was full of compliments, declaring that the Valida was publicly receiving Mary so that the world might know that both she and her son were under great obligations to the English. It concluded: "We cannot sufficiently express our thanks to you and to the English people, the Crown, the officers, and the army and navy of His Majesty. We hope that Lord Elgin will remain here, for his superior sense, prudence, and diplomatic abilities are needed. In excess of that, his friendship has been the greatest utility to us and to our son."

Mary nodded and gave all the appropriate thanks. Then the Valida broke with all protocol and spoke directly to Mary. She was animated and seemed quite upset, upsetting Mary, who hoped that she had not inadvertently done anything wrong or insulting. But apparently the Valida was angry over Mary's transportation that morning. She had sent—she promised, putting her hand over her heart—her loveliest and biggest barge to bring Mary across the water. But her eunuchs had somehow sabotaged this, jealous as they were that a stranger was receiving access to the magnificent vessel. The Valida was embarrassed, and assured Mary that she would seek out the offenders and punish them.

Because she had spoken directly to Mary, Mary decided to speak directly in return, hoping that she was not crossing some line of etiquette.

"No harm was done, and I arrived safely," she said. She did not want to be responsible for heads on the block. She had learned that the gentleness with which the Turks had treated her did not necessarily extend to those who caused them displeasure.

"I noticed that you were looking at our walls," the Valida said. "The tiles on the walls spell out words from the holy Koran, messages directly from God. We are in the presence of God. My son, the Padishah, is the shadow of God on this earth. We must tell the truth here because God is listening."

A shiver ran down Mary's spine. She had no intention of not telling the truth today, but she worried over what truths she would be asked to tell. But the Valida did not press her for information. Rather, she announced that it was time for Mary to tour the gardens and to be served lunch, and before Mary could contemplate anything further, she was taken by the arms and led into the room where she would change from her traveling clothes into her day dress.

The eunuchs, yelling in loud and threatening voices, preceded the women into the garden, which faced the southern side of the Bosphorus.

"They are searching the grounds, announcing that anyone caught spying on the women is risking the penalty of death," Madame Pisani said in answer to Mary's unspoken question. Satisfied that no one was present, the eunuchs allowed the women to pass through the gate and into a long avenue of shade trees that ran parallel to the high double walls of the seraglio. The women of the harem led the way for Mary. The gray skies had broken and the rain had stopped. Some of the ladies had loosed their tresses, which were also studded haphazardly with jewels. As they emerged from the shaded colonnade and into the sun, all modesty was discarded, and they happily exposed their faces, necks, and cleavage to the skies. They wandered down a long gravel path, past a grove of orange trees, and into the higher gardens, from which Mary was able to see a long stretch of the Turkish coast.

The ladies led Mary to a grand kiosk, where a meal had been prepared. She was seated on a sofa with fine Dresden china and gold flatware before her. Innumerable dishes were placed on low tables.

Hanum sat on a cushion beside Mary. "You will be waited on by all the Valida's head maids of honor, even the wife of the Grand Vezir. It is the highest honor the Valida can show you."

"Which one is she?" Mary asked.

Hanum pointed to an immense woman wearing red silk robes and matching shoes, the toes of which pointed to the sky. "Yusuf Pasha loves her above all six of his other wives. He has promised that if her son lives to the age of ten, he will banish the others and be faithful to her."

The woman was extremely polite as she presented Mary with a dish of roast chicken. Mary took a small piece and put it on her plate, asking the lady to sit beside her. Hanum made room for her. Another lady, seeing what was transpiring, came to sit near them. "This lady is the Sultan's own Key Keeper," Hanum said. "A very important position and valued by the Padishah."

Mary began slowly and carefully. If she was to speak on the matter of the vaccine in front of these two great ladies of the harem, she was not going to waste the opportunity. "I am a mother of two small children, and I understand what pain you have suffered in losing so many of your babies. I want to give you my sincerest condolences as well of those of Lord Elgin, for he, as a father, has only tender feelings toward his children, as I am sure is true of the pasha."

The woman blinked and nodded courteously as all of this was translated to her. She looked rather puzzled, though, as to why a stranger would initiate this sort of conversation.

"I would like to offer to you something that might begin to relieve the sufferings of mothers and fathers in this city," Mary continued. "English doctors have developed a vaccine against the smallpox. I had my own little daughter inoculated when she was just sixteen days old, and I am pleased to tell you that she suffered not at all, and that she is in the finest of health."

Mary recalled how jittery she was when her baby was inoculated. She watched the child for days straight, forgoing sleep, waiting for a bad reaction to the medicine. But none came. The babe ate and slept as well after the inoculation as before. She was a beautiful child, with black hair and bright blue eyes, and a perfectly turned ankle with which she would, in later years, according to Elgin, take many hearts. Mary was terrified of having her inoculated, but even more terrified of losing her to the man with the cart in the middle of the night. Mary decided that she could not advocate that other mothers take the risk of inoculating their babies if she did not do it herself.

The Turkish women talked briskly among themselves while Mary and Madame Pisani listened with care. Finally, the wife of Yusuf Pasha spoke through the interpreter, who said: "If the pasha consents, she will send to you for this Dr. Scott and she will inoculate her son. The other ladies agree. If you are so confident to experiment on your own precious child, they are confident that your heart is sincere."

The large woman put her two hands together as if in conspiracy with Mary.

"She wishes to see a picture of Elgin," Madame Pisani said. "She hears that the two of you are very fond of each other."

Mary took the locket from her neck and opened it to show Elgin's picture. If only he still looked as he did in the image! In recent months, his infection had come back, eating away horribly at what had been left of his nose.

"How lucky you are that the man you love only has one wife," the woman said wistfully.

Mary could not imagine having this woman's destiny, where all was tied to the heirs she produced. In the world of the Ottomans, however, it would not do for a man to discard wives who could produce healthy sons for a woman who had lost ten children to a disease. It was a brutal but practical way of thinking.

The women rested indoors after lunch, after which Mary was taken on a tour of the harem. She was astonished at the number of women and girls the harem employed. She visited two rooms filled with young girls embroidering fabrics or performing intricate needlework on pillows, coats, and shawls. She watched for a while unseen by the workers as gold thread flew in and out of the linens and silks stretched tight on wooden frames. In an even larger room, a dozen females were weaving highly patterned kilim rugs, the kind Mary adored.

At the end of her tour, she was treated to a performance by the harem choir. The girls were not the Sultan's lovers or wives or favorites, at least not most of them, it was explained to her, but maids and other slaves who were taught to play instruments and vocalize. Mary would have liked to hear native Turkish songs, but in her honor, and to commemorate the recent victory at Alexandria, they performed a charming rendition of "God Save the King."

By the end of the day, she had seen at least a hundred girls in the harem, each with a specific task. Where did they all come from? She couldn't bear to think of little girls stolen from their villages and made to labor the day long for the Sultan's further accumulation of wealth, and then, later, made slaves to his sexual desires. Or worse, ladies whisked from their ships by pirates—chaste, noble ladies such as herself—and forced into a life of sexual submission. And yet the workrooms of the harem buzzed with productivity. She did not see anyone forced or beaten, though she guessed that as soon as one caused displeasure, the punishment was severe. She realized that she had actually hoped to uncover some sordid tales of unwilling, captive women.

"How do these large numbers of girls come into the harem?" she asked the woman who was Keeper of the Keys, hoping to receive an honest answer. "Are they captives of war?"

"Very few. There are war orphans, yes. But most of the girls are brought into the harem because their families cannot care for them. Here, they are fed and sheltered and taught skills. They work to earn their freedom. When they are old enough, they are given to good men in marriage. That is the fate of most of them, which is orchestrated by God under the care of the Valida."

As if reading her thoughts, the Keeper of the Keys added, "Poor girls are not thrown out into the streets to make their living in disgrace as in some countries. Here, women are cared for and kept from the corruptions of men."

At the end of the day, Mary was called in once again to speak with the Valida. This time, the woman, in an ermine pelisse set on pink silk, appeared even statelier than before. Her scarlet spangled shawl was now flung over her shoulder. Mary had changed into a court gown trimmed in beads and sparkling sequins, which the Valida insisted on touching and admiring. She bade Mary sit near her on the sofa, and then asked her to remove her gloves, which Mary did. Did the woman wish to examine her fingernails? But Mary realized that the Valida was merely inviting her to stay. She complimented every aspect of Mary's appearance, and then invited her to spend the night in the harem.

"The waters are rough," she said. "I cannot have so valuable a person risking her health by crossing the river at night."

"I am not afraid of the water," Mary answered. "And I am most anxious to see my little ones at home."

"I merely wish to offer you our hospitality, and to lift the shroud of our customs for you. I know by the questions that you have asked here today that you do not understand the reasons for our seclusion from the world. Do you think that I do not know the world outside my quarters? You might think that we are restricted in our movements, but we understand that women must be kept pure. We are holy. We are the very vessels of life. God creates the baby stage by stage in the mother's womb. That is why women must remain pure."

"I thank you for your hospitality," Mary said. "But I am afraid that my babies will miss me if I do not return home this evening. I am sure that you, as a mother, understand."

"I am convinced, as is my son, that Lord and Lady Elgin must remain in Constantinople. The Padishah will build a new embassy for you, something elegant designed especially to your tastes. He is establishing the Order of the Crescent, by which he will knight Lord Elgin and a few special English friends of the House of Osmanh. The Sultan is informing Lord Elgin of these developments right now. I hope the two of you will rejoice in the friendship that we offer to you and to all English people."

Mary knew that speechlessness was not what was called for, and yet she had no idea what to say. She knew that her words would be scrutinized. Elgin's philosophy in diplomacy was when one was unsure of what to say, one must opt for either silence or brevity.

"You honor us in ways beyond expectation," Mary said.

"Now you may go, and God will watch over you," the Valida said with an air of certainty.

She called for her attendants, who laid parcels at Mary's feet for her and for Elgin. "Tokens of our friendship," the Valida said. "I beg you to accept." Then the women who had accompanied Mary were given, one by one, rolls of bills in embroidered handkerchiefs.

With the same three bows with which she had arrived, Mary took leave of the Valida and the other ladies. Once outside, Masterman and the other attendants were cackling over the contents of the handkerchiefs. Each had received English pounds, in an amount equal to twice what they earned for a year of service. Mary did not open her gifts, but put them aside, wondering all the way home if the Turks were correct in keeping their beloved females protected from the sins of man. It seemed to her a good idea in theory, but in practice it would be, for a woman such as herself, intolerable. Now that the Sultan was honoring the Elgin in new and greater ways, would the two of them be expected to remain in this strange and seductive land, where they would be spoiled beyond measure, but in which they would always be outsiders?

Exhausted from her long day, Mary let herself be helped into the boat that would take her back across the Bosphorus. The waters were choppy again, but she let the lolling waves erase all the questions from her mind, and soon she found herself dropping off to sleep.

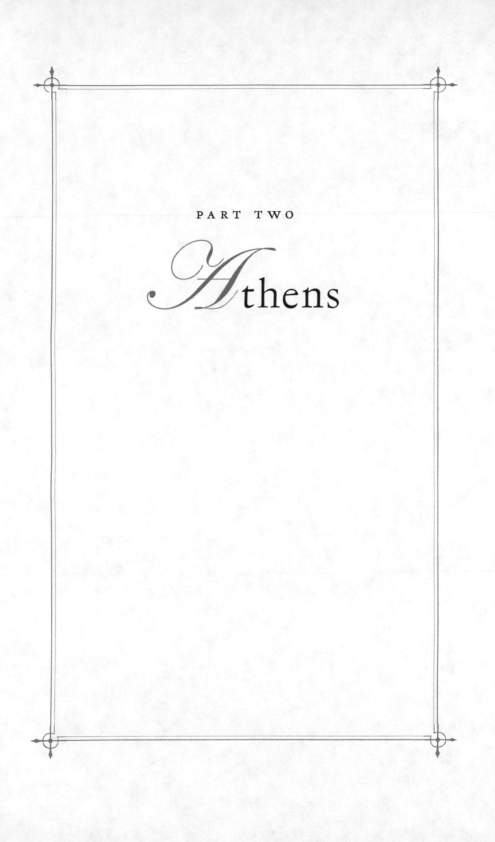

PART TWO

Athens

The city of Athens,
in the eighth year of the
Thirty-Year Truce with Sparta

WE STOOD ON RICKETY scaffolding—we privileged few of Athens—high above the floor of the Parthenon colonnade to view Pheidias' latest sculptural tour de force. Defying all logic and convention, he had designed a frieze that would be set under the ceiling of the colonnade and would run along the entire perimeter of the building.

Despite the fact that it was dark, and we were suspended in the air on slim pieces of lumber held together with ropes, we were too riveted to the display before us to feel fear. The sun was setting, leaving a glimmer of copper light on the horizon. The burgeoning night sky was glossed with a strange hue of midnight blue, and slaves held torches to light the great relief. Perikles had returned from the war, victorious, in time for the dedication of the Parthenon, and now held my arm as Pheidias addressed his small, elite audience.

"Hundreds of feet of uninterrupted sculpture, the longest frieze ever created," Pheidias said. He was not boasting, but merely stating a fact. "Unlike the metopes, which are individual works fashioned around several themes, the frieze depicts one event—one grand, continuous, dramatic event—that is to commence tomorrow at dawn. What I refer to, of course, is the Procession of the Great Panathenaic Festival."

This most sacred of rituals was performed every four years in Athens, and culminated in the presentation of a newly woven *peplos,* or robe, to Athena Polias, the small, olive-wood icon of the goddess that had not been carved by mortal hands but had fallen from the sky in ancient times to mark the location of the great city that the goddess wished to be built in her name.

"I have created a sculptural representation of the entire procession held in the year of the Battle of Marathon," Pheidias continued, gesturing toward his masterpiece, his white robe blowing in the gentle wind that had just come in from the north. "The ambitious building project conceived by Perikles and executed by myself is largely to commemorate that notable confrontation with the Persians that changed the course of Athenian history. In that year, the Great Panathenaic Festival was held a mere four weeks before the decisive battle. Fortunately, the Athenians had put on a particularly lavish show for the goddess. And that, my friends, undoubtedly is why the goddess fought with us and ensured our victory over the Persians despite their overwhelming numbers."

The audience gave the sculptor a polite round of applause. I was surprised to see some of the wives of Athens's more notable politicians present. Normally, ladies did not attend public viewings of art, even if the works were shown privately to a small group, such as the one this evening.

I was even more surprised when some of these ladies boldly addressed Pheidias, asking him about his work.

"Why did you choose to set the frieze against an indigo background?" one very finely dressed lady inquired as she fingered the gold choker at her neck.

"Because, madam, it will make the figures more visible to the viewer, who will, once the scaffolding is taken down, be gazing at it from far below. That is also why the figures of the frieze are slightly deeper at the top than the bottom. Though you are among the lucky few who will see it at eye level, for the rest of the world, this alteration in the depth will make the viewing from below a much more vivid experience.

"Only we few happy mortals and the gods will ever have the privilege of viewing it from this vantage point," Perikles added, impressing upon this small group, some of whom opposed the funding of the Parthenon, how fortunate they were to share an honor with the Divine Twelve.

"The frieze was carved in place," Pheidias continued. "Frankly, I had nightmares about watching our painstaking work slip off the pulleys and smash into pieces on the ground. The scaffolding upon which you stand has held dozens and dozens of sculptors and painters, all of the highest talent and training. The painting staff was entirely from the school of our dear, recently deceased Polygnotos, the famed painter responsible for the murals of the Sacred Oracle of Apollo at Delphi, as well as for many of the vases to be given away as prizes at the competitions this week."

We started our viewing at the beginning of the frieze, which, in content, was also the beginning of the procession.

"The horsemen prepare," Pheidias said dramatically, pointing to a long cavalcade of riders. A young man at the head of the procession motioned for his friends on rearing steeds to join him. Behind him, a long run of horsemen charged, some nude, with only capes flowing in the wind. Figures of overlapping horses carrying riders, some with helmets and armor, seemed a miracle of motion. Pheidias invited us to put our heads right up to the frieze and look down at the long, shallow relief that was only a few inches thick. "Since it will be seen at a great distance, I could not rely upon facial expressions to convey the desired excitement; hence, dramatic gestures and semblances of motion are employed to capture the anticipation of the moment."

I put my face as close to the relief as I dared and looked

ahead. I could smell the fresh paint clinging to the figures. Horses' heads rose and fell along the length of the frieze like waves, seeming to obey the same rhythm as the riders, all linked together in an unbroken dance. So lifelike were the figures that it did not take much to imagine oneself at the actual event.

Gold paint accenting the more muted colors of the frieze shimmered in the torchlight. I saw that the horses were decorated with metal rings and leather bridles, some linking the horses to the ten charioteers moving swiftly on their vehicles, whipping the beasts on. These were the chariot races, which would also take place tomorrow at the games.

We followed Pheidias as he continued the tour of his creation, the ladies shying away from the flames of the torches that lit our way. As we moved around the frieze, the rest of the sculpted procession came to life. Tray bearers carried barley cakes with honey to bait the sacrificial animals to the altar. Some of the cows seemed docile, while others—protesting, shaking their heads—were catching on to their fates. One threw its head back, mouth wide open, as if howling a final plea to the gods for clemency. The rest of the suppliants to the goddess followed—girls holding bowls to pour out the sacrifices of wine, oil, and blood, one following with a tall incense burner. Ahead of them, the elders, magistrates, and officials leaned on their walking sticks, herding the entire procession to the centerpiece of the frieze, where the Olympian gods, seated, ignored the commotion surrounding them, waiting for the Athenians to bring them their due.

Hephaestus, the lame god, crutch under his arm, sat facing Athena, who carried a spear in her right hand. She was not in warrior pose, but was reclining in leisurely fashion upon a chair, waiting to see what her people would bring. The goddess's back was turned to a mortal girl behind her who was accepting the *peplos* from the Royal Archon, the top religious official of the city. Behind him was Athena's priestess, facing young girls carrying stools upon their heads. Zeus, father of Athena, was seated with Hera, his wife, his back turned to his daughter. The other gods—Hera, Nike, Ares, Demeter, Poseidon, Artemis, Aphrodite, and Eros—rested on benches, each ignoring the suppliants.

"Pheidias?" I said. "Why did you choose to position the gods in this way, with their backs to those who are bringing them gifts?"

"Because they owe us nothing," he said, his eyes wide as he spoke. "Because we are uncertain if they are ever listening to us or heeding our desperate prayers. Because at times they seem not to pay us any attention at all," he answered, far too quickly and, to my mind, too honestly. I could hear little gasps and murmurs escape from several pairs of polite lips. Artists were always being criticized for their impiety. Pheidias, who had already received heavy criticism, did not need to add this to the list of accusations against him.

I had never seen such a decoration as this in a temple, where artistic ornamentation always consisted of scenes from the great myths or stories of the heroes. These figures represented an event in recent memory. I remember challenging Pheidias in the concept stage as to why he'd chosen something such as this to decorate Athena's temple.

"The mortals are given more emphasis than the gods, Pheidias. The idea seems more an homage to the people of the procession—some of whom are undoubtedly still alive—than to the goddess," I had said. "I hope this will not be perceived as sacrilege."

"Perhaps it is time for Athenians to be featured alongside the gods," he had answered.

"They certainly behave as if they deserve it," I had replied, and he'd laughed. I had left him that day with an anxious feeling, worried over his choice of subject and how Athens's more conservative critics would perceive it.

But as I walked around the frieze, a strange feeling came over me. It was as if I were staring into the near future, as if the very naturalistic images before me were going to take the form of flesh and blood during the night and assume their places at dawn, lining up at the Dipylon Gate to participate in the festival. I suppose that that was the effect that Pheidias had hoped to achieve.

I wondered if the odd sensations I felt had anything to do with the fact that the forty-foot statue of the goddess inside the temple, presently draped in linen, that was to be unveiled tomorrow, carried the image of my own face. I'd sat for Pheidias only a few times in the early stages of his design; all the sittings had been scheduled during the time that Perikles was away leading the expedition against Samos. I had not seen the face of the goddess since it had been painted and adorned.

Pheidias had assured me that by the time he was finished with the icon, no one would notice the resemblance. "I consider it more a spiritual likeness than a realistic one," he had said. "I imbued the face of the goddess with your qualities more than with your features."

When I said that I did not find the qualities of wisdom and boldness in my own face, Pheidias replied, "Of course you don't see them. But I see them in you. And I know it is because circumstance has forced these attributes onto your very pretty face."

I was flattered that the great sculptor of our age identified such strengths in me. But the larger question was: Would anyone notice? And if so, would people protest?

After we toured the frieze, Lysikles, a wealthy man who had made his fortune raising sheep on the immense grazing lands of his ancestors, approached me. He was a fixture at the drinking parties Perikles and I gave, and I always enjoyed conversing with him.

"My dear Aspasia, I come to you with a request that I addressed to Perikles, who in turn told me to speak directly with you."

He was a handsome man, perhaps ten years older than I. His dark skin, tanned from long hours in the sun, contrasted nicely with his deep-set blue eyes. He had lush black eyelashes that would have been nice on a woman.

"What question could you possibly have put to Perikles that he needs me to answer?" I asked.

"Some of the ladies, my wife included, are weary of hearing next-day reports of the drinking parties that you host. As tiresome as it is, many of us husbands are forced to try to recite large portions of the previous evening's conversations, which are of a very scintillating nature at the time they are had, but are not easily remembered the next day."

"Especially if one drinks to the bottom of the bowl," I said, and laughed.

"I never knew that ladies wished to hold philosophical dialogues. Perhaps they do not. Perhaps they are merely interested in observing the behavior of their husbands. But the request I bring you is from the ladies. They wish to attend one of your notorious parties."

I was surprised on many levels. Considering how much the men drank, and how often the evenings included turns taken in the bedrooms with one or more of the hired prostitutes, I couldn't believe that any honest account of these parties had ever been given.

"Lysikles, are you actually suggesting that gentlemen bring their wives tomorrow evening?"

"I do not suggest it, Aspasia, but the wives have suggested it. Because it is on a feast night, and because it is hosted by you, who are also a woman, they do not wish to be left out."

"Being a woman, I suppose that I have no logical grounds upon which to exclude other women. Tell the ladies that they may attend the party with my compliments." I nodded to Adelpha, whose eyes lit up at the suggestion. If the husbands did not need to exclude their wives, then what objection could I possibly have? It would be amusing to see the altered behavior that the presence of respectable ladies was bound to produce.

I put the idea to Perikles later in the evening. We were in our private dining room, where I usually dined on a couch— sometimes the same couch as my lover. When we entertained guests, of course, I sat in a chair. Even the professional courtesans who sometimes dined with us were of too high a class to eat reclining in the presence of men. This was a cozy room, though plain, with bare walls upon which I had hung a group of particularly expressive terra-cotta satyr masks that I liked. The room had simple stone floors, two small tables for food and drink, and a stack of blankets and furs that we used in the cold months. A lone black vase that we found amusing, painted in red figures, with a satyr plucking a young woman's pubic hair, sat on a tripod. Here in this room we often shared our most private thoughts, after which we inevitably made love.

"Do you think these ladies are secretly planning to spy on me, gathering yet more information to slander me in the marketplace?"

"No, I think that your renown has spread even to female quarters, and that they are curious about a woman who has gained the respect of the cleverest men of the city."

"We shall see. Shall we tell the prostitutes not to come?"

I worried over this. I could not imagine the reaction of the ladies when faced with brothel-dwelling whores of Athens, though we hired only the most intelligent of them to appear in our home. I always expected Perikles to slip off with one of the women during the night, but he never did. Perhaps he had women who serviced him in secret. Though we loved each other passionately in bed and out of it, I could never believe that he was pleased to have only me as his lover. But that was the way it appeared.

"If the ladies of Athens wish to attend a drinking party, I think we should allow them the entire experience," Perikles said. "If they object to the presence of the prostitutes, they will leave. But if we do not have prostitutes, I will hear no end of it from the men whose wives are not present. No, let them all come, wives, prostitutes, and whoever else wishes to attend. After all, it's the feast day of Athena. The goddess is democratic in her love for all native-born Athenians."

. . .

IT DID NOT MATTER that I was the beloved of the most powerful man in Athens; I still had to wear red at the Great Panathenaic Festival to distinguish myself as a resident alien. Anyone with the means to travel to Athens could observe the Grand Procession that opened the festival, but only Athenian citizens could participate without a special invitation.

"The goddess desires it this way," Perikles told me. "Athens literally belongs to Athenians. It is not like other Greek cities. It was not taken by conquest. We have always been here. The members of the Ten Tribes are the descendants of the original heroes—Erechtheus, Ajax, Leos, Kekrops, and the like. We are born to the soil."

Kalliope and I decided that if we were to be set apart in red on this day when all the city was present, we would adorn ourselves to be as beautiful as possible. We made dresses of the finest incarnadine linen, trimming them with gold silk ribbons. Several evenings before the festival began, Kalliope proposed that we have a rehearsal to try out our coiffures, so we dismissed the women who worked in my house and, as when we were girls, made pin curls in each other's hair. The next day, we laced red ribbons into our long locks, which we then tied up in pleasing ways, with ringlets dangling nicely around our faces.

We began the first day of the festival long before dawn. Perikles was to preside over the commencement of the procession. Games and contests would follow for five days, but today was the most holy day, the day in which Athena would receive her new robe woven by the women of the city and carried by the *arrephoroi,* adolescent virgin girls chosen from the most prominent families. At sunset, a solemn sacrifice was to be made to Pandrosos at her altar on the Akropolis. A priestess of Athena had apparently foreseen the advent of a plague, but claimed that, in a vision from the goddess, she was instructed to make a sacrifice to Pandrosos, that singularly obedient daughter of King Kekrops, that would hold the plague at bay for ten years.

Kalliope and Alkibiades met up with me at the head of the procession. My sister looked very pretty. She wore the gold necklace we had inherited from our mother, and I wore the long earrings, which I thought complemented my upswept hair. Besides, the necklace was the more valuable, and she, as the older sister, should have the privilege of wearing it on special days.

The morning was still gray, but the necklace brought color into her pale face. Hers was not a happy life. Alkibiades, many years her senior, treated her as he might a serving girl who should be grateful for her bread and cakes. When he was not around, she tried to share with me conspiratorial gossip about the horrors of men and the marriage bed—trials with which I could not, in my own circumstances, identify. I did not want to make her life more unhappy by revealing that all men are not ogres in the bedroom or outside of it, for I was sure that an old and cantankerous dog like Alkibiades would not soon change his ways. The best we could hope for was that he would not live to a ripe old age.

I did speak up once, after my sister told me that he had slapped her for spilling his wine.

"Alkibiades, I am aware that you do not respect my opinion, though the men of Athens eagerly seek it on domestic matters," I began. "But I feel compelled to advise you that a wife treated with kindness and respect will blossom and bring happiness and prosperity to a home, whereas one treated cruelly will only wither."

"I do not require your advice, Aspasia," he said coldly. "I know that a woman with noisy opinions is considered a welcome anomaly among Perikles' more perverse friends. But in my regard, you are still just a big-mouthed girl, and I do not need you to tell me how to run my household."

I did not say anything further to him because I knew that he would use whatever I said as a reason to abuse my sister again. She had very little power in her household. She was a foreigner, and therefore not an Athenian citizen; nor were her children, owing to Perikles' law. But in Alkibiades' mind, and in the minds of others, she was a cut above me in society because she had the status of a legitimate wife.

I was excited to see her this morning because I wanted to share the extraordinary news from the night before. I desperately wanted her to come to our party, so as hard as it was for me, I obeyed protocol and addressed the request to her husband.

"Alkibiades, I do not know if you are planning to attend our party this evening," I began. I was sure that he was not planning to attend because neither Perikles nor I could tolerate him and so we never invited him to these occasions. "Many of the gentlemen are bringing their wives. I invite you to bring my sister along with you, as this is a very special evening."

"Aspasia, I do not approve of my wife coming into your house when you are there by yourself, much less when the drunkards and peacocks of Athens are present, spewing their subversive ideas. Do not raise the issue again."

His face assumed its usual countenance—that of a bloated, grumpy animal. He turned away abruptly, taking Kalliope by the arm. She gave me a sad look as he dragged her off.

I rushed to rejoin Perikles, who smiled when he saw me, reaching out with his long arm to clasp me to his side. It was destined to be a very long, hot day, so I'd worn my most comfortable shoes rather than suffer the tall platform sandals that made me look more regal and compatible with Perikles, who towered above me.

Though the procession took place on the twenty-eighth day of Hecatombaion, the hottest month of the year, the air was unusually crisp at dawn. Perikles and I arrived at the Dipylon Gate just as the light was breaking. Hundreds, perhaps thousands, of suppliants had arrived to stand in the line, which wrapped around the storehouse where all the festival's accessories were kept, then staggered for what looked like miles down the road. Normally, onlookers would line the Panathenaic Way to watch as the sacred procession of horse riders, charioteers, priestesses, *arrephoroi,* gift-bearing maidens, musicians, specially chosen citizens and city officials, and the Royal Archon—all the characters depicted in Pheidias' frieze—would lead the cart carrying the *peplos* like a great sail to the goddess in her temple. Only those involved in the procession could enter the temples, of course. But Perikles had decided that this year—the year of its dedication—all Athenians who wished to do so could follow the procession up to the Parthenon, where they would be led inside by soldiers and ushered past the colossal statue of the goddess.

"Why should all Athenians not celebrate the unveiling of the great statue of the goddess since all have, in one way or another, paid for it?" Perikles had said over the objections of some members of the Assembly. Though an aristocrat by birth and by temperament, Perikles had a democratic streak that always led him to consider the common people.

At the moment the sun began to appear over the east side of the Akropolis, the ceremonies began. Perikles climbed to a podium set up for the event and addressed the people. Though his voice would not carry to the multitudes, much of his speech would be whispered through the crowd. Scribes would also copy his words and write up pamphlets of their contents to be sold in the marketplace in the coming days.

"The Temple of Athena Parthenos and the colossal statue of the goddess that will be unveiled today are public works, voted on and approved by the Assembly. True, they are magnificent in appearance and great in scale, but let me remind you citizens of the ways in which we of this city deserve such monuments to commemorate our deeds and our services to our allies in the Delian League."

With this, he commanded their silent focus. I had to stop myself from smirking as I thought about how Athenians were always ready to hear a list of their own virtues.

"These other cities do not contribute soldiers, horses, or ships to any war efforts," Perikles continued. "All they give is money, which we use to defend not only ourselves but all of our allies. We carry the burden of war for them. We have kept the Persians off our shores, evicting them from all of Greece and Asia Minor and containing them in Egypt and the east, where they still threaten to exercise their expansionist desires. We do not spare a cent in defense of those who depend upon us for their freedom and safety. Therefore, after all the funds needed to carry on the wars are dispersed, do we not deserve to apply the surplus to public works, which once complete, will bring Athens her glory for all time?

"Athenians! Think on how these projects have provided inspiration for every art, and employment for every hand. Why, we have transformed our entire population into wage earners. Everyone should benefit from the national income, yet no one should be paid for sitting about and doing nothing, and these projects have put to work men in every craft and industry. The materials are stone, bronze, ivory, and gold, along with ebony, cypress, and other woods. Those who secure and mine the materials, as well as those who ship them to us by boat or by cart, have profited. We have employed carpenters, model makers, sculptors, painters, coppersmiths, stonemasons, dyers, ivory and metal workers, embroiderers, engravers, and the like. The carriers and suppliers of all these materials—merchants, sailors, pilots for the sea traffic, wagon makers, animal trainers, drivers, rope makers, weavers, leatherworkers, road builders, and all of those who work for them on every level, and who possess every level of skill from laborers to the most gifted of artists—have prospered. We have employed those who work with the body and those who work with the soul.

"What you are about to see is imposing in size but inimitable in grace. Every artist and laborer has striven to excel in the beauty of workmanship. Yet they worked with astonishing speed and frugality so that no money or time was wasted in the construction. Those who opposed us thought it would take generations to complete what we proposed. But see, citizens, with your own eyes, that a few short years of labor and patience have given us monuments that have put wealth in every Athenian pocket and that will bespeak our glory for generations to come."

Perikles turned around, looking toward the Akropolis. The sun had risen higher, its pale morning rays beginning to gleam on the marble roof of the Parthenon, which seemed to rise as if from the center of the hill. The crowd began to applaud Perikles' words, shouting his name. As usual, he showed no emotion, but left the podium, taking his place with the magistrates in the procession.

I had been invited to lead a group of young girls, daughters of other resident aliens, sent by their parents to bear gifts to the goddess. All wore red dresses, though none as ornate as mine. They carried trays of oils, perfumes, and spices, all to be laid at the feet of the ancient sacred statue of Athena as she received her new robe.

The procession commenced, led by the representatives of the Ten Tribes, some who marched on foot carrying their standards while others showed off their finest horses. Foot soldiers in full armor marched behind, and following them were representatives from each of Athens's allied city-states carrying their armor—breastplate and helmet—on poles. So began the long walk up the Panathenaic Way. We paused to make way for a group of youths who had fetched the sacred fire from the altar of Eros and were running a foot race with it to the altar of Athena on the Akropolis. They passed us with their lit torches, and then we commenced, stopping in front of the Temple of Hephaestus to make a small sacrifice to the god of metals and swords. Across the way, the city's potters flanked the huge studio where they worked and lived. The twenty-room brothel behind it was closed for the day, and its inhabitants stood on the porch reverentially like all other suppliants of the gods. A small delegation of potters carrying vases for the goddess fell into line behind us. Later, oil from the Sacred Grove of Athena would be placed in the vases and given as prizes in some of the competitions.

At the Royal Stoa, the Royal Archon, the city's leading

religious official, joined the procession. We walked slowly and solemnly, and I was more grateful than ever to have worn my comfortable shoes. Though it was not yet as hot as it would be at midday, I could feel the air begin to warm as the sun rose higher in the sky. We crossed the way, stopping in front of the Altar to the Original Heroes, where young men who had earlier won a beauty contest laid gifts at the feet of each of the ten bronze statues. Women from the Ten Tribes had woven banners with the heroes' symbols, draped ceremoniously on the statues. Some small girls were lifted up to place garlands about the statues' necks. But the most dramatic moment came when a priest of Ares and the boys who serve him stepped forward and poured bowls of animal blood into ceramic pipes that ran deep into the ground. Believing that the spirits of the dead heroes fed on sacrificial blood, the Athenians always honored them with this ritual to appease their appetites.

Opposite the Heroes lay the Altar of the Olympian Gods, the point from which all distances in Athens were measured. A small ceremony was held and all the proper offerings were left for the great gods and goddesses; this was followed by the traditional war dance performed to drums by a group of soldiers with spears and shields.

The drummers and dancers joined the procession, and we entered that part of the agora that marked the beginning of the Dromos, where the foot and chariot races would later take place. Here the chariots left the procession, along with the cavalry riders and the cart carrying the *peplos*. The rest of the climb up the hill was too steep for the vehicles. After displaying the bright blue *peplos*—woven with scenes of the Battle of the Gods and the Giants—to the onlookers, the maidens and the priestess folded it and delivered it to the Royal Archon, who would carry it up to the goddess on the hill.

I tried to share in the excitement of the day, but I was tense to the point of nausea, afraid to see the statue of Athena. The higher we climbed along the Panathenaic Way and the more visible the Parthenon became, the more difficulty I had breathing. I wondered what would happen if I slipped out of the procession and remained with the spectators, but considering the flamboyant color of my garment and the fact that many Athenians recognized me as Perikles' woman, this would have caused much commotion. I was already criticized for so many reasons; disrupting a great religious festival would be like throwing manure on the fire.

I walked along, putting one foot in front of the other, taking shallow breaths to calm myself, until we entered the Great Gateway, manned by soldiers wearing shiny greaves and armed with gleaming swords. They did not permit even the smallest crack in their solemn expressions, which informed the passing populace of the seriousness with which they must take this rare and unique opportunity to visit the goddess inside her shrine. The grim demeanor of the guards also let the people know that insolence of any kind would not be tolerated today.

Once inside the gates, we fell under Pheidias' magic. Darkness fell upon us as we left the sunlight. The roof of the Great Gateway was painted a deep blue, like a midnight sky, against which golden stars were twinkling. It was as if a spell was cast by the gods over everyone who entered, preparing us for the sacred monuments and shrines we were about to see.

Out in the sunlight once more, I noticed that everything had been scrubbed clean for the event. Flowers and plants sat in large urns on both sides of the path. On the terrace of the Parthenon, flowering shrubs in huge pots now sat between the lovely bronze statue that Pheidias had sculpted of the god Apollo, and the rows of busts of honored men of the city, including both Perikles and his father, Xanthippus.

Beneath the Parthenon's triangular pediments, the statues that would sit inside them were on display on the ground, completed and painted, waiting to be hoisted into place. I had tried to look at them last night, but the torchlight was too weak to reveal the details that were now fully illuminated by the morning sun.

Truly I had never seen such beauty. One of the scenarios

was the birth of Athena on Mount Olympus in the presence of all the gods. The chariot of the sun god, Helios, arose from the sea, signaling that the goddess was born at dawn. Dionysus, youthful and naked, celebrated her appearance, as did Demeter and Persephone, all sensuously displayed, watching in approval as this feral deity was born. Athena appeared to be letting out a roar as she leapt from Zeus' head. She was in full armor, flashing her sword high above her head, as if her first act was to let out a battle cry. Her father held his thunderbolt, ready to let it loose, perhaps at his new creation. Indeed, she looked fierce, as if turning against her father, the god of gods, was within her power. A little girl, the drapes of her clothes showing her motion and excitement, recoiled in shock at the appearance of the ferocious goddess. At the close of the scene, the moon goddess, Selene, descended with her horse into night.

"It is theater in stone," said a spectator.

We were allowed to walk before and behind the second sculptural scene, which depicted the contest between Athena and Poseidon, each racing in a chariot to the Akropolis to perform a miracle that would establish who would be dominant. Poseidon struck a rock with his great trident, causing a salt spring to gush forth, thus gifting Athens with a supply of water. But Athena won the day, not with her battle strategies, but by making the first olive tree sprout. Again, the goddess was fierce and splendid in her snake-fringed vest, a gift from her father. On her left lay a languid, naked youth rising from water. To the right of Poseidon was Iris, goddess of the rainbow, heralding the arrival of his chariot, her garment fluttering in the air as she races through it.

I noticed that all of the figures were complete, gorgeously and painstakingly sculpted and painted behind as in front, though once they were in place in the pediments, no one would ever again see the back.

"Perfection does not take into account the viewer," Pheidias had once said to me. "It exists on its own, independent of and unconcerned with opinion or utility. Once you see the tableau finished and nestled inside the pediment, you will know the power of Divine Proportion. It is a mathematical equation I have invented that makes things appear as aesthetically pleasing as is possible to the human eye."

He had seemed very pleased with himself, and now I understood why. What I had seen thus far of his creations must have exceeded the achievements of any artist or architect who had lived before him.

AFTER VIEWING THE PEDIMENT statues, we were soon climbing the steps of the Parthenon and entering the expansive open doors of the temple. I started to feel sick again, wondering if I was going to walk in, see my face, be identified, and be chased down by the crowd. I was dizzy, falling into the man behind me, who caught me so that I did not fall down the steps. He steadied me, asking me if I was ill.

"Just the heat," I said, smiling.

I continued slowly, entering through the great wooden doors, where I was struck with the towering and divine image that presided over the room.

Pheidias stood grandly next to his statue as the Athenians slowly walked by, necks craning, to admire it. Because of its size alone, it was impossible to gaze upon the colossal work without a feeling of awe. I heard gasps of wonder as people entered the space and encountered the holy figure. A shallow pond of water surrounding the statue cast ethereal, shimmering reflections upon the great masses of gold and ivory hammered onto it.

The image of the goddess was almost blinding in its beauty. As I searched Athena's face, I did not see any of the features that I could observe when I examined myself in the looking glass. She projected wisdom and surety, but within that, her gray-eyed gaze seemed pitiless. She was a deity, deserving of worship, whereas I was merely a mortal woman, eager to please and anxious, at least at times, for love. She looked nei-

ther soft nor maternal nor compassionate. She was the antithe-
sis of the comely Aphrodite or the Mother Goddess, Hera. She
had none of a woman's vulnerability. Perhaps Zeus had created
her this way, as the son he always wanted bound in the body of
a daughter who would not challenge his supremacy but allow
him to maintain his dominance over all the gods. I realized that
I, too, had this androgynous quality. While some praised me for
being both a female and a philosopher, there were others who
believed that my logical mind wiped all feminine charm from
my visage. None of it made sense to my rational, inquiring
mind that sought the logic in all things.

But my greatest anxiety was alleviated. Adorned with jewels
and inlays of all kinds, the remote goddess looked no more like
me than she looked like any other earthborn female. None of
the observers seemed in the least motivated to declare a likeness between the statue and me. I bowed my head to Pheidias
as I walked past him, and he smiled at me as if I were just
another woman gazing upon his creation.

Relieved to have passed this moment without incident,
I followed the procession to its destination, the sanctuary of
Athena Polias, where the primeval wooden goddess-of-the-
city had resided since she fell from the sky. The ancientness of
the statue evoked an automatic reverence. With songs of prayer,
the priestess, the Royal Archon, and the *arrephoroi* unfolded the
peplos and wrapped it around the small figure of the goddess.

As I watched the ceremony and listened to the hymns, I
thought about how sharply this older, more humble-looking
icon contrasted with Pheidias' colossal one. The wood was so
worn that it was difficult to imagine her original form, but she
looked as if she had been rounder in body than the war goddess. Far from being a sinewy figure, she appeared matronly,
her pendulous breasts and protruding stomach visible beneath
a sheath of fabric. She looked as if she were truly the Mother
of Athens—as if her womb were not made of stone but had
actually given birth to someone or something. In my opinion,
the new colossal figure should be deemed Athena of the Mind,

whereas this icon represented Athena of the Body. The goddess was both female and male, but we mortals could think only in terms of one sex in one body, and required different icons to represent the various aspects of the gods.

AS THE GUARDS ESCORTED the procession out of the Great Gateway, I caught up with Perikles, and we walked to the Odeion to watch the choral competitions. This was my favorite building in all Athens. Perikles had built it to accommodate the Athenians' ever-increasing appetite for the musical competitions that took place during the festivals. Flute, pipe, and kithara players competed, as did the men's choruses that had grown so popular in recent times. Also, playwrights previewed their new works here before moving to the larger stage of the Theater of Dionysus. Athenians were mad for theatrical productions and welcomed the opportunity to see plays as they evolved; the critical comments that they gave to the playwrights and performers were crucial to the development of their works. The Odeion, like all the other buildings in Perikles' project, was also intended to serve as a war monument. It was modeled after Xerxes' great pavilion in Persia, and, for the sake of irony and insult, it was constructed of the lumber from the Persian ships wrecked by the Athenian navy.

A mild breeze swept through the audience as we watched the men's choruses deliver impassioned hymns to Athena. When the judges announced the winner, Perikles awarded the choir leader a tripod and a vase filled with olive oil, and he garlanded the members of the group. We exited the building to applause, greeted as we walked away by a group of ladies who were waiting for Perikles. When he appeared, they rushed to him and began to put garlands of flowers around his neck.

"For the victory at Samos!" one of the women cried.

"In gratitude for keeping us safe!"

"For keeping Athens supreme on land and by sea!"

There was no end to this fawning as they put their garlands

on his neck and head. He did not seem flattered, as any other man would in this situation, but rather received his glory with restraint. I had to giggle because, to my eye, he looked less like a great victor than like a prisoner receiving his punishment.

"These islanders must realize that they will never be allowed to challenge the Masters of the Sea," cried a male spectator.

"Hear, hear!" A man's voice, drunken, sarcastic, sang loudly from behind the group. "Let no one challenge the tyrant Perikles or he will find himself out of Athens on his ass, wasting away on one of those very same weak islands, drinking his wine with the weak islanders, screwing miserably weak island women, and consoling them for all the blood money they have to pay every year to the Masters of the Sea. Or is that 'Master,' in the singular? For it seems that one man's will has replaced democratic vote."

It was Stephanus, one of the sons of a conservative Athenian politician who had been the greatest of enemies to Perikles and his building project, and who had been ostracized for ten years after the other Athenians got sick of him.

"Democratic vote ostracized your father, not me," Perikles answered.

"But you persuaded them with your fancy words and your promises of grandeur. And you made good on it, didn't you?" He gestured toward the Parthenon. "As my father predicted, you used good money—our money—to decorate your city like some vain woman."

Suddenly, an old woman named Elpinike, wearing pale colors, appeared from the center of the group. It was generally acknowledged that she had had a very public affair with the painter Polygnotos some years ago; at the same time she was also reputed to have had sexual relations with several other men, including her much older brother, Kimon, a general and hero during the Persian Wars. She was aged, but still grand, bedecked in fine fabrics and jewels, undoubtedly purchased with the money of her dead lovers. Her skin hung in tiny folds from the bridge of her nose all the way to the end of her cheekbones. She had emphasized her still-bright almond eyes by drawing dark rings around the rims, which did in fact take one's gaze away from her crinkled lips.

"Just say it, Stephanus. You're drunk enough. Perikles decorated the city as he's decorated his whore. Your father knew what would happen. He warned the people, and for his truthtelling, he, like Kimon, my brother, was ostracized."

She spoke in a low voice, but I have never heard such a tone of viciousness. She hissed her words as she directed them at him like arrows.

"What brave deeds you have done in Samos, Perikles," she continued, "where so many a worthy citizen was lost, not in war with the Persians or some other enemy race, such as the monsters my brother, Kimon, fought, but against men of an allied and kindred city!"

Perikles had stood in opposition to Kimon, and this had certainly encouraged the Athenians to vote for his ostracism. But Perikles had refused to participate in Kimon's prosecution. At that time, Elpinike had lost a brother, a lover, and a means of support. She had never forgiven Perikles, even though, a few years later, he had argued for Kimon's return. Why did she not credit him with that and be done with it? But families of the ostracized never forgave. Indeed, it appeared as if they had united today in an effort to confront and embarrass Perikles.

"You should be ashamed of participating in that war," Elpinike continued. "And you fawning, mindless women who drape these chaplets about him should be even more ashamed. Let your husbands take you home and beat you, I say!"

I was still smarting from her comment about me. "Someone should take you home and beat you, old woman," I said. "How dare you call me a whore when it is a well-known fact that you have always had a crowded bed, while I have only been with one man in my life? Who is the real whore, and by what definition?"

I dared the old bat to argue with my logic. Instead she chose a different point of attack.

"Everyone knows that Perikles only went to war with Samos because Aspasia used her witch-powers in bed to convince him to defend her countrymen in Miletus. The war that shed so much Athenian blood and spent so many Athenian coins was ignoble at best."

Perikles opened his mouth to speak, but I decided to defend myself, publicly, and once and for all.

"What am I, Elpinike? Some modern-day Helen? The idea that Perikles would mobilize forty ships and risk hundreds of young Athenian lives to placate some request of mine is ludicrous."

"You speak well, Aspasia. You are known for the gift of rhetoric. Pity you do not turn your talents to speaking the truth."

"Ah, but it is true!" I smiled at everyone, looking as many people as I could directly in the eye. "Perikles might trade me for another woman anytime he pleases," I said. "He needn't go to war to keep me. Everyone knows that he is the source of my bread and wine, and most of all, the source of my beating heart."

My words drew applause. The Athenians loved debate of any kind, even if it were between a crone and a despised woman. But Perikles remained unshakable. I could not see any alteration in his demeanor or even his breathing. Finally he spoke. "When you came to me all those years ago, Elpinike, offering your body to try to coax me to interfere with the ostracism of your brother, I told you *then* that you were much too old to be able to carry out your mission. All these years later, you are still have not learned. Go home and be happy that you still have a few of your teeth."

At once her face transformed into that of a creature so mean that I thought she had become one of the avenging Furies. All she needed were snakes coiling on her arms and a lion skin hanging about her sagging breasts. Her nostrils widened and she squinted her eyes. "That never happened!" she retorted. "Everyone knows that I would never stoop to such an act, even to save my beloved brother."

A few people—the older ones, who knew her best—snickered. One man said, "Brother? You tried to save his ass to keep it in your bed!"

"How dare any of you tarnish the name of my brother? He carried the very bones of Theseus from Skyros to Athens! He was a hero the likes of which this city no longer knows!"

"And a damned good fuck, too, eh?" someone else cried out.

This brought more laughter, which only made her angrier. I noticed that Perikles, to his credit, did not join in the jokes. Still she directed her rage at him.

"I may be old, Perikles, but you underestimate me," she said. "I am not yet too old to listen when men talk. I happen to know—because, like their teacher, some of the students of Polygnotos wish to converse with me—that your harlot, Aspasia, sat for Pheidias on numerous occasions, and it was upon her face that the sculptor fashioned the visage of the statue of Athena that now stands in the Parthenon. You do know the image, correct? The one paid for with public funds?"

He looked at me, waiting to see if I would speak, but I could not defend myself. I stood there, letting the whisper spread through the crowd like a swarm of bees on its way to a target. I could not move and I could not speak. We stood there until Elpinike walked right up to Perikles and said, "Did you think I would ever forget the insults to my brother and to myself? I am not through with you. Not in the least. I will never be through with you until one of us is dead."

She turned to the crowd. "Not only did Pheidias impiously and mischievously use the face of a courtesan to represent the sacred goddess of our city, he also, as a joke—a joke on you Athenians who have made him a rich and lauded man—painted his face and the face of his friend Perikles into the shield of the goddess."

She looked at all the people staring at her, astonished at her words. No one knew what to say. Then someone shouted: "Impiety!"

"Answer these outrageous charges, Perikles!" shouted another.

Perikles took my hand and said, "What you say is ridiculous, Elpinike, the rant of an old woman. We do not have to dignify these insults with commentary."

He turned, leading me away, but she would not be deterred. She continued speaking to the shocked onlookers: "Just *try* to get an invitation to the temple to investigate my accusation. You will encounter resistance, I assure you."

The sun was now high in the sky, and the heat of the day was increasing, but I trembled as we walked away from Elpinike and her indictment.

"There is time to rest in the shade before the sacrifices begin," Perikles said.

It occurred to me that he found what Elpinike had said so preposterous that he was not even going to ask me if it was true. I wanted to feel relief, to tell myself that that was the last we would hear of it. There was little enough actual resemblance between the statue's face and mine. It would be easy to deny the charge. But I did not want to withhold information from Perikles. If the topic arose again, I would tell him that I was merely doing Pheidias a favor by providing him with a strong face, and that it was never intended that Athenians would gaze upon the face of the Goddess of the City and see Aspasia staring back at them.

I agreed to rest in the shade, but what I wanted to do was go home and hide, though on this feast day, I knew that was impossible. Perikles must have sensed my lack of ease. He spoke as if he were reading my mind. "The best thing to do is ignore it and proceed with our duties today. Her words will blow over like so much smoke. That woman has been trying to make trouble for me since the day I refused to lay my hands on her decrepit flesh."

If he turned out to be right, and Elpinike's words dissipated with the heat into the night air, never to be heard again, I would keep my secret with Pheidias. If not, I would confess.

"I suppose that no woman, no matter the age, enjoys having her advances rebuffed," I said, offering up an explanation for her vitriol and indirectly denying her charge.

"That is why the sport of conquest, like many other things, is better left to men," he said.

LIKE ANY WITNESS TO the sacrifices she performed, I was in awe of Diotima's power. Her regular duties as High Priestess of the City included the interpretation of omens, and in recent months she had divined that a plague was on its way to Athens. She had said that she could hear the disease riding up to the city as if on horses, the drumbeat of its journey growing louder and louder as it crossed the Attic plains toward the city. This prediction caused much panic. People started to close up their homes and retire to the country. A few jumped off cliffs or hanged themselves. Some women elected to terminate their pregnancies. Men wondered whether to kill their children now or go through the agony of watching the disease take their lives. To put a stop to the madness, Diotima promised that she would sacrifice a ewe at the Great Panathenaic Festival and that this would send the disease into retreat for a period of ten years, after which she would reevaluate the threat.

I had not planned to attend the sacrificial ritual with Perikles at sunset. I wanted to go home to make certain that all preparations for our party that evening were under way. However, this was the sacrifice to Pandrosos, the girl who was obedient to Athena, and therefore loved by the goddess. I begged Perikles to let me attend; I did not tell him why this was so important to me. But as the blood spilled, I would offer my own silent prayer that the potential disaster encroaching upon my happiness, like the plague making its way to Athens, would also remain at bay for at least a decade, if not forever.

During the five days of the festival, hundreds of cows would be sacrificed to Athena upon her altars on the Akropolis, but the one ewe sacrificed to Pandrosos was considered special. The story of Pandrosos was told in many versions, and the most common was this: Hephaestus, the metal-forging lame god, wished to copulate with Athena, the beautiful virgin goddess. He had done so much for her, fashioning her breastplate and her shield, that he thought she should repay him with sexual favors. But all men's sexual advances disgusted Athena. Hephaestus rubbed himself against her, but she repelled him just as his semen spurted onto her bare leg. Appalled, she quickly flicked it to the ground. In an instant, Erechtheus, half boy, half snake, the first earthborn Athenian, sprang from the earth. Athena placed him in a beautiful box and gave him to the three daughters of King Kekrops for safekeeping but told the girls not to look inside. Pandrosos obeyed, but Herse and Aglauros could not resist. They opened the box, and the sight of the snake-boy so terrified them that they threw themselves off the side of the Akropolis.

Thus the fate of disobedient women. The more compliant Pandrosos was given a sanctuary on the hill beside Athena, where men throughout the ages have honored her. The sacrifice to Pandrosos has always recalled the days when young girls were offered up as sacrifices, and so it was more solemn than most. Whereas the meat of the sacrificed cows was roasted next to Athena's altar and shared with the public, only the clergy and a select few could partake of the meat of the ewe slaughtered for Pandrosos.

The Sanctuary of Pandrosos was located in the precinct of the Akropolis dedicated to that unquestioning sister. It was very near the shrine that held the ancient olive-wood statue of Athena Polias, and it contained the original olive tree that Athena presented to the city in her contest with Poseidon. This tree was sacred to the people of Athens. It had proven its magical qualities by regenerating itself overnight after being burned down by the Persians when they sacked the Akropolis. Old men who remembered that horrific event swore that on the very next day, they saw the miracle: after being burned to the ground, the tree had already grown a shoot more than a cubit in length.

Perhaps two hundred people were packed into the temple courtyard, but I stood at the front of the crowd with Perikles and other city officials. Musicians beat goatskin drums and played haunting, hollow-toned melodies on pipes. The marble altar had been cleaned and purified of the blood and stains of previous sacrifices, but it was worn at the center. Two boys wearing snakeskin vests, representatives of Erechtheus, tended the ewe, which had been garlanded for the occasion. Women and men in attendance had draped themselves in animal skins, and some of the women had put crowns of flowers on their heads.

I was surprised to see Sokrates standing very close to the altar. I wondered how a young craftsman with no illustrious familial connections was allowed this sort of proximity. Perhaps he was the lover of someone very important. If so, he had not disclosed it to me. I was further astonished when Diotima appeared in her white robes and nodded to him as if the two of them were old friends.

I have seen priestesses rely upon young boys to straddle the sacrificial ewe to hold down its legs, but not Diotima. She was perhaps fifty-five years old, but she was tall for a female, and taut. The labor of her life was on behalf of the goddess, since Athena's attendants must, of course, not engage in sexual relations with men while in service. She was long widowed, with one adult son, yet she had none of the sag and droop that haunted the bodies of mothers her age.

I was very tired, having been awake since long before dawn, and I knew that a long evening stretched out before me. The smoke from the roasting flesh of the relentless sacrifices at the great altar to Athena filled the air, making me slightly queasy, whether from hunger or from the thick smell of it. I wanted to lean against Perikles but dared not, as it would undoubtedly be taken as a sexual overture by one of the many people who scrutinized our behavior no matter where we were. The noise too started to irritate me, and I yearned for solitude. The drumbeats quickened, and the women in the courtyard began to sway and scream in anticipation of the sacrifice. Animals awaiting their fate at the other altars were bellowing loudly. It seemed as if all parties were in competition to triumph in noise.

Finally, Diotima raised her arms, and the ritual began. The two boys pulled the ewe, rope around its neck, to the altar. There Diotima took control, placing the ewe's head on the altar and virtually mounting the animal to hold it in place. One of the boys picked up a knife and handed it to her. The priestess held the ewe's muzzle in her left hand, pulling the animal's neck back. With her right hand, she raised the sacrificial knife, long and sharp, and, bringing it down, pierced the ewe's throat. Slowly and cleanly, she slid the blade across the neck, making a straight cut. She had placed the animal on the altar in such a way that the blood ran in all directions. If the blood did not cover the entire altar, the sacrifice would not be received. Everyone watched as the thick liquid spread across the altar, slowly making its way to the four corners.

Diotima signaled for the pipes players to recommence. Accompanied by their music, she sang: "Give us a well-ordered city with women fair, where their sons revel in youthful merriment and their daughters play in dances flower-strewn, with happy hearts, and skip through fields in bloom. This is what you give us, Holy Rich Divinities."

By the time she finished singing, the blood had covered the altar, spilling over the sides into ceremonial bowls held by the two boys and two young maidens. Diotima gestured with her hands, and the children poured the collected blood back on the altar to soak it so that Pandrosos would get her due and intercede with Athena.

My eyes were riveted to the cascading blood. The acrid smell of the pots of cow fat burning on the other side of the Akropolis in offering to Athena conspired with the heavy per-

fume of the garlands around Perikles' neck. I started to feel
light in the head, and then bitter and sick in the stomach. A
dark screen seemed to rise from the bottom of my eyelids,
blotting out the world in front of me. Suddenly, all turned
to black and I felt myself fall against Perikles, who could not
catch me before my body hit the ground.

A SHIMMERING FIGURE APPEARED, *as if breaking
through the darkness. Sparkling lights fluttered behind her tall body,
gradually taking the shape of wings. She was beautiful but stern as
she stood on her griffin-drawn chariot. Those two ferocious guardians
of the divine, their immense eagle-wings spread like great hawking
shields, aimed their wicked beaks in my direction. I tried to scream,
but no sound would come. My heart pounded in my chest as the
enormous lion-paws moved toward me. I imagined how it would feel
once those black, hornlike nails were ripping at my flesh. The strange
female creature stared at me without pity as if I had done something
terribly wrong. I appealed to her with my eyes but my plea met with
no empathy. She did not move to stop the griffins, which were picking
up speed and charging at me. I tried to scramble away on my knees, but
my body was like an infant's and I could not even manage to crawl. I
was clawing at the dirt, trying to get traction and creep out of the way,
when I heard the wheels of the chariot churning behind me, closer and
closer. I looked over my shoulder one last time, but suddenly nothing
was there.*

I FELT WATER HIT my face. I opened my eyes to see
Perikles kneeling beside me, a ladle in his hand. My eyes darted
about, looking for the strange creatures of my vision, but all
had returned to the scene of the sacrifice. Sokrates was bend-
ing over me, his big eyes full of concern. Perikles took one of
my arms and Sokrates the other and they lifted me to my feet.
I felt many eyes upon me. I was light-headed, scared from the
vision I had just had, and wishing I could disappear.

I could barely feel my own body. "I must go home immediately. I must see to the preparations for the evening."

It must have sounded nonsensical, coming from the mouth of a woman who had just passed out.

"Of course," Perikles said. "But I must stay to partake of the sacrifice."

"I have a small cart just down the hill," Sokrates offered. "I can drive her there."

Perikles released me to him, and I took his arm. The last thing I noticed as he and I walked out of the temple was Diotima, her sleeves drenched in blood, staring at me with her wise, impenetrable eyes.

As Sokrates and I walked down the hill to the cart he used to carry his sculpting supplies, I described to him the details of the vision, hoping that he could help me decipher its meaning.

"I have no idea what it means, Aspasia," he said. "But I shall ask Diotima about it, and perhaps arrange for the two of you to meet."

THOUGH PERIKLES COULD HAVE built himself a more opulent home, he thought he was deflecting criticism by living in modest quarters. I do not know how many hundreds of people attended our party, but the crowd filled every interior room on both floors, and spilled out into a packed courtyard. I had arranged for the acrobats and musicians to entertain in the courtyard, but it was too crowded, so I slipped them extra money and asked them to go from room to room like the itinerant players they were.

The leader of the group was a former slave captured in some far-off Median land. A superb acrobat, he had earned his freedom by entertaining his Greek master, and had started a troupe made up of musicians, storytellers, dancers, and contortionists, as well as two flute girls, whom the men called the Anchovies, because they were slim and pale and had wide eyes, and because of the crass practice of associating women, particularly loose women, with fish. The Anchovies and the other flute girls and female acrobats often took home an extra five or six drachmas from servicing the men after their performances.

But this evening brought a new breed of guests, the conservatively dressed wives of Athens. Out of deference to these women, I had told the prostitutes and the performers to conceal their fornication and other acts of pleasure behind locked doors. I had instructed the slave girls to dilute the wine in the women's bowls, as I knew that most were not accustomed to drinking, and I did not want rumors of my corruption of fine ladies to fill the ears at the marketplace in the morning.

The ladies—draped with garlands and scented with the heady fragrances of wisteria and narcissus—were most anxious to speak with me. In doing so they covered their mouths with fans, as they were wont to do in public, unlike the prostitutes who talked with mouths wide open, laughing at times so that one could see the very last teeth in their gums. But they did not introduce any topics of conversation beyond their names and who they were married to and how many children they had. I listened politely, but beyond welcoming them to my home and offering them refreshments, I was at a loss as to what to do with them. The men did not want them in the banquet rooms, where they were lying about eating food and discussing their favorite topics.

"We do not wish to censor our dialogue, or be asked inane questions, while we are trying to achieve some advancement of the mind," one of the husbands said.

Unlike their husbands, or myself, or the courtesans, these women lived very secluded lives, speaking only to one another or their children or the household slaves. In Athens it was said that only a woman of ill repute would show a man her tongue—a convenient way of keeping a woman's mouth shut. I always thought it strange that the men who wanted their mistresses educated also insisted that their wives be kept ignorant of the arts of reading and writing, and certainly of dialogues that could challenge the mind. Of science, astronomy, medicine, mathematics, and rhetoric they knew nothing. It occurred to me that I might provide a service to both sexes if I could establish a philosophy for marriage that would bring fulfillment to both parties. I would speak to Perikles about it when I had the opportunity. Why should I dole out advice only to the men when I might speak to both members of the couple, helping each arrive at a more satisfactory state in their marriage?

In defense of the women, however, I had to admit that I was too distracted watching Perikles be accosted by some of the prostitutes to adequately focus on my conversation. Two whores had each taken one of his hands while another was running her index finger up and down his chest slowly and seductively. They seemed to be united in an effort to convince him to do one thing or another. He listened to them in his usual impassive manner, turning his head to look at whichever one was speaking. I wondered if this would be the night that I would realize one of my fears and he would disappear into a dark corner with those three witches. It was his privilege, after all. I could be angry or hurt, but I had no grounds upon which to stop him. I did not even try to catch his eye in admonition. I decided that the best thing I could do was turn away and pretend that I did not notice.

As I was about to walk away from the gaggle of wives, one blurted out the question I hoped I would never need to answer.

"Is it true, Aspasia, that you were the model for the face of Athena?"

The gossip had spread. I suppose it was inevitable. Enough people had heard Elpinike's accusations. A simple mathematical equation would demonstrate that it would take but a few hours for every pair of ears in Athens to have heard it, especially when the entire city had congregated for the biggest feast day in four years. I decided to adopt a feminine tactic and hide behind Perikles' orders.

"Perikles has decided that the charge is too ridiculous to address. I apologize. I can speak no further upon it." I said it with a serene smile, though inside, I had started to quiver.

I was relieved, and very surprised, when Sokrates entered the courtyard with Diotima. I was under the impression that a priestess spent days in meditation before and after a sacrifice. When he said he would consult Diotima and arrange a meeting between us, I had no idea that he meant this very evening.

"Forgive me," I said quickly to the wives. "I must receive the priestess."

I turned away from them and headed straight for Sokrates and his illustrious companion.

Far from the blood-soaked diviner I had seen earlier in the day, Diotima looked much like any other woman present. She had bathed, and was wearing a fresh pale blue dress with wide folds, cinched at the waist with a braided gold belt. She had crimped her hair and adorned herself with gold earrings. But still, her face shone with the radiance of one who has touched the divine. She seemed as ethereal as the statue of the goddess, though she was neither ivory nor gold but human flesh and blood. She held herself completely erect, like one who has never doubted the correctness of being in her body. I could see why even the xenophobic Athenians accepted her, a Greek from Mantinea, as their connection to Athena. She had been married to an Athenian, but when he died, she'd devoted her life to the goddess.

I approached them rehearsing my greeting in my mind, but Diotima spoke first. "I shan't stay long. May we speak privately?"

"Of course," I said.

I hurried her and Sokrates into the private dining room, one of the rooms I had closed off to guests. It was a special sanctuary for Perikles and me, and I did not want it sullied with spilt wine and the semen of strangers. A slave rushed in and lit the lamps. I sat on one of the four couches and invited Diotima and Sokrates to sit too.

"I have long wanted to unite the two great female logicians—one, master of the Philosophy of Love, and the other, master of the Philosophy of Domestic Relations," Sokrates said.

"My dear, I am told that you are very brilliant, but you are also very young," Diotima said to me. I was not prepared to be condescended to; however, her age and rank gave her permission. I smiled, and sat quietly.

"I am a diviner," she continued, not with the grandiosity one associates with clergy, but as if stating a known fact. "I see the future, and sometimes, even when I do not care to, I see deep into men's souls."

"Did Sokrates relate to you the strange vision I had?"

"Yes. The figure you saw was Nemesis, the goddess of vengeance, the one who executes the will of Athena."

"Vengeance?"

"As her chariot turns, she sets the wheel of fortune in motion. Destiny is in her hands. She's been known to crush the enemies of Athena beneath those wheels. That, or toss them to the griffins."

"Oh, help me, Diotima!" I cried. My worst fears were being realized. "I've insulted the goddess and now must pay the price."

"Aspasia, are you also a diviner? If not, then I will ask you to leave the interpretation of visions to me. How have you insulted the goddess?"

"Have you not heard the accusation against me?" I asked.

"I have heard many accusations against you, my child, but I have always assumed that they were rumors wickedly spread by the enemies of Perikles."

"But there is one that is true," I said. I explained everything to her and Sokrates—that I sat for Pheidias at his request, that no one was supposed to know, and that Perikles had been ignorant of what I had done.

"I have insulted Athena, and she has sent Vengeance to punish me," I said. "Isn't that what the vision meant? Isn't that what you came here to tell me?"

"Not at all," she said. "I came here to tell you that you are pregnant."

"Pregnant?" I had not even considered the possibility. I had given up on conception when, after nearly five years with Perikles, it hadn't happened.

"That is why you passed out," Sokrates said. "Diotima saw it immediately and insisted on coming here tonight to tell you."

In the priestess's presence, he was quieter than I'd ever thought to find him. He never suppressed himself, not even with so luminous a figure as Pheidias, but he deferred to Diotima like a lamb to a lion.

"You are very early in the pregnancy," Diotima said. "If you want this baby, you must take more rest and more food. Perikles is the father?"

"Of course he is! I thought you said that you did not believe the rumors spread about me."

"I do not. But one must always inquire if one is to know the truth. Women's morals are not what they used to be. I am sure that you've noticed."

"This should be joyous news. But how can I have any happiness when Athena has set Vengeance against me? Will she take the baby from me?"

The priestess shrugged. Why wouldn't the goddess punish me for what I had done by taking my baby? Any good tragedian would have written his play thus.

Diotima took a drink of wine. She lowered the bowl and looked into the bottom as if she were reading the entrails of a slaughtered beast for omens. I awaited her answer, but she merely smiled broadly.

"Have you had a revelation?" I asked.

Now she laughed, draining the last drops of wine from the

bowl and showing me the figure painted at the bottom. It was a caricature of a naked, muscled athlete, a discus in one hand and his gargantuan erection in the other.

How could she be amused when she was delivering a two-pronged message to me—one that filled my heart with joy and another that punctured it?

"My dear, I am the final authority on the word of the goddess, so you needn't question what I tell you. Athena is the goddess of wisdom, and therefore she loves all philosophers and all seekers of truth and knowledge. You can count upon her blessings."

"Do you not think she is angry with me for my audacity?"

"Oh, probably. But your intentions were innocent enough. And Pheidias only meant to honor her with a fitting representation."

"May I ask what Nemesis' mission might be?"

"That will require quite a bit of meditation and perhaps more than one sacrifice. It will cost you," she said.

"Of course," I replied. I would tell Perikles that I needed a new dress and he would give me the money.

"Even then, the goddess will reveal it to me in her own time, not yours. You will have to be patient."

Suddenly my thoughts shifted to Perikles. Had he already gone off with the prostitutes? I wanted to rush out of the room. Perhaps I could corner him and tell him about the baby, in which case, he might not slink off into the darkness with them.

"A dark cloud has passed over your face, Aspasia," Sokrates said.

"I must find Perikles and tell him about the baby," I said. I stood up, hoping that they would stand up with me.

"Sit down," Diotima said. I obeyed. I was in no position to argue with Athena's priestess. Sokrates raised his bowl for more wine.

"When we came inside, I was watching you watch Perikles

with those women," Diotima said. "You needn't worry over them."

"I suppose that he is like all men, willing to please himself with whoever is available for his pleasure." I felt exposed, knowing that they had seen my distress. Was it so obvious?

"That is not my point," she said, sighing. "I am going to enlighten the two of you, but you are going to have to strain every muscle and nerve in your bodies to try to understand what I am saying."

Sokrates nodded his head like an eager student, and I felt that I had no choice but to follow.

"You might think Perikles is driven by lust, but I assure you that lust is actually the soul's longing for immortality."

"How so?" I asked. I was anxious to go to Perikles and reveal the news, but her conjecture immediately engaged my philosopher's mind. "Lust seems quite firmly rooted in the body."

"The memory of immortality haunts the souls of mortals. We are never satisfied with our mortal state," she said.

"Yes, I agree. That is why we seek immortality in procreation," I said. Would this great Philosopher of Love teach me nothing new? I wondered. "That is why I am anxious for Perikles to know that I am with child."

"Oh, he will be pleased," Diotima said. "But a man like him has a greater incentive in life."

"And what is that?" I asked. I must say that I was annoyed that she talked about him as if she knew him better than I.

"The love of glory," she replied. "He seeks an eternal place in the deathless roll of fame." She said it with such finality that I wondered if she would be open to questioning.

"I do not see why you are telling me this," I said.

"Aspasia, are you a philosopher or not? Think about it. For the sake of fame, men will risk great dangers. They will put themselves in the jaws of death more than for their children. For fame, they will spend their money like water and work their fingers to the bone. Have you not observed this in your own home?"

I had to admit that she was right. Perikles had two grown sons whom he loved dearly, but it was for his building project that he risked his standing in Athens. Now she had me in the grasp of her reasoning. "Yes, you are right," I said, "especially in the case of Perikles."

"Of course I am. Do you think that Achilles would have died for the love he bore Patroklus if it had not been foretold that it would bring him immortal fame? Every man is longing for that endless fame. The nobler the man, the greater his ambition."

"Because he is in love with glory," I said.

"No!" she cried. I was afraid that she had given up all hope that I would demonstrate the intelligence for which I had a reputation. "Because he is in love with the eternal!"

Her eyes lit up, though she spoke in a lower, but firmer, register, changing the texture of her voice, as if that might help me to understand. "Erotic love and procreation are bids for immortality. But Perikles' sons and their sons, like all progeny, will die within a few generations. His building projects, however, are a more perfect bid for eternal fame than his children because they will last through the centuries if not the millennia, and they will always carry the name of Perikles."

"I see," I replied. I did see. But I was still at a loss as to why she felt the need to grace me with her philosophy. Perhaps Sokrates insisted upon it so that he and I might debate it on our own, as we were wont to do with many subjects. Perhaps she had a darker purpose. "Are you telling me that he will not care about our child, only about his buildings?"

"No, Aspasia, I am telling you that the child will not outlive the buildings. Do you understand that whereas women may touch the immortal by giving birth, men—great men—must build monuments and seek fame?"

"Yes," I said sheepishly.

"Then do you follow that Perikles has no need for prostitutes because his quest for the immortal is embodied in those
monuments atop the Akropolis? Make no mistake. This is not
hubris. This is a man trying to appease the cries of his immortal soul."

Her words rang with such truth that I could not utter a
word in response.

"Therefore, Aspasia, you may go to your lover, and you will
find out that he is not taken with the whores. At least not at
this time, for he is nourishing the desires of his soul in another
way."

"So you see how the argument is complete?" Sokrates
asked, a look of satisfaction on his face. Wine seemed not to
affect him at all. He turned to Diotima. "Good lady, there is no
worthier occupation than listening to your philosophy."

She did not respond to his fervor, but turned to me. "Go
to Perikles," she said. "Tell him you are expecting his child. He
will be pleased, of course." It was not a request but an order.
"My guards will see me home."

Sokrates opened his mouth to protest, but she said, "Stay
here and drink wine until dawn so that you will be good and
drunk for the games tomorrow."

"I have visited you in your home, Philosopher," she said to
me. "If you wish to know more, you must visit me in mine.
And you must bring gifts."

"GOOD LADY, BESEECH your husband to take pity on
a poor whore!"

I had not imagined that the prostitutes hanging on Perikles
would be delighted to welcome me, but their faces lit up as
I approached. Pheidias had joined them. He, of course, was
hopeless as a customer. He had come to the party with his
lover, Agoracritus, a talented young sculptor and one of his
pupils, whom he always suspected of not being in love with
him at all, but rather gleaning as many of his techniques as pos-

sible before starting his own studio. The younger man was flirting with some of the wives across the courtyard, and Pheidias was watching while pretending to be jocular with the whores.

"You have received an excessive amount of money for your services this evening," I said to them. I knew, for I had gone over all the expenses with Perikles' steward myself. "I do not see that you require pity."

I was eager to be rid of them so that I could tell Perikles the good news.

"But the hand of Perikles takes away even as it gives," said one of the others.

"How is that so? I see you all siphoning off wine and food for yourselves. What more do you require here?" I asked.

"They are petitioning for a reduction in the taxes they pay on their income," Perikles said.

"That's right," said the prostitute who was older than the other two. "We were present today at the unveiling of the statue of our lady. We heard a gentleman say that Perikles and Pheidias were costuming the Akropolis with these expensive monuments the way men decorate their whores. And I turned around and said to him that it was only fitting, since the taxes from whores are paying for all the fancy things that Perikles is doing up on the hill."

The other prostitutes howled with laughter at this. Even Perikles cracked a smile. I suppose the whole town had embraced the metaphor.

"Enough of this. Get back to your work," I said, pointing the whores toward the guests.

"This is the last time we will invite this sort of horde into our home," Perikles said. "Everyone wishes to mingle with us to further his own purposes, even the whores on the payroll. In the future, we shall have to limit ourselves to those whose loyalty is certain."

"Is there a reason for exercising caution at this time?" Pheidias asked. "This is our moment of triumph."

"No better time to be cautious. Triumph gives rise to

more enemies than failure, I assure you," Perikles said. "Are you aware of the ridiculous assertions we were made to suffer today? Elpinike, the former mistress of Polygnotos, has started the rumor that Aspasia sat for you for the face of Athena. And that you painted yourself and me into the goddess's shield as two warriors."

"Why, that is true, at least in the case of Aspasia," said Pheidias. "I did not think anyone would notice. The likeness is not apparent."

"Explain yourself," Perikles demanded, not of me, but of Pheidias.

"I needed a face that was young and beautiful, but that also carried the quality of wisdom. I coaxed Aspasia, and she agreed. As for the other accusation, I have no explanation. It is simply not true."

Perikles turned to me. "You did not confide this in me?"

"We did not intend for anyone to notice the likeness," I stammered. "The sittings were done in secret. We wanted to protect you from the information. There is enough talk about me."

"Yes, that is true," he said. I could tell that he felt I had betrayed him. "Neither of you will speak about this to anyone. If asked, you will continue to say that the charges are absurd. Elpinike's long, vicious tongue is carrying the rumor to the four winds. Say nothing about it. Nothing. Now if you'll excuse me, Aspasia, I will leave you to bid goodbye to our guests. I am going to bed."

He turned around, leaving Pheidias and me to stare at his back as he made his way across the courtyard, speaking to no one. The party had grown wilder. Two discus throwers who had placed high in the day's competition were tossing one of the Anchovies between them, the girl laughing crazily as she flew through the air. Perikles mounted the stairs, oblivious to this, or to the acrobats performing tricks or the people trying to get his attention, leaving me to wonder if I had just sealed an unhappy fate for both my bastard child and myself.

I do not recall the passage of time from that moment until the one when I realized that Alkibiades had entered the court-yard. By the time I saw him it was too late. Before I could make a move to hide from him—for in my present condition, I did not want to speak to so disagreeable a man—I saw a look of shock register on his face. Then I saw it transform into anger. I followed his gaze. The discus throwers had stopped playing ball with the Anchovies, and both girls were now straddling the standing athletes, who were cupping their buttocks. It took me a moment to realize that the athletes were bouncing the girls up and down on their erect penises, much to the delight of the other guests. Some of the ladies were watching with utter glee, as if they hoped that they might have the next turn with the men.

Alkibiades did not speak to anyone. I doubt that any of the others even saw him or registered his unspoken outrage. Everyone was so enthralled with the performance that they were oblivious to him. Without comment, he turned away, leaving in as much of a hurry as he had arrived. He stormed off into the night, but I knew that his thoughts were not san-guine, and that they would lead to trouble.

The Ottoman-occupied city of Athens,

April 1802

MARY LEANED CLOSE TO the frieze as Elgin had instructed, looking down the length of it. Though she was in her third and most sick-making month of pregnancy, she had climbed the laddered scaffolding so that she could see the acclaimed piece of sculpture in situ before it was taken down. They had brought big saws with them on the voyage to Athens; Mr. Lusieri had required them to remove the gigantic slabs of marble from where they had rested since the hands of Pheidias' workers had hauled them up and put them in place. The Greek sculptor had fortified each piece of his relief with a thick backing, which made it far too heavy to be transported; Elgin's workers were hacking the sections away from their backing so that they could be more easily taken down and shipped to England.

"Is it not the most astonishing piece of sculpture you have ever seen?" Elgin asked. "Can you not envision the procession?"

"Oh yes, it's so lifelike! It's like watching a parade." Or a ballet, she decided upon further reflection, what with the wavelike crests of the heads of the animals and the cavalrymen who rode them. She had to look away quickly, though. The lumber beneath her feet shook as the workers on the other side of the building did battle with a metope that apparently did not wish to be dislodged. Mary felt the motion all the way inside her belly, and she did not intend to be sick here at the location of her husband's grand project.

"Come round," Elgin said. "Let us check on their progress."

The workers numbered in the dozens and included a group of masons. Amid a web of ropes and pulleys, the team was working tools into the masonry to loosen the marble slab, which was fixed between the triglyphs that decorated the perimeter of the temple's exterior. While the masons chiseled away, other workers worked thick ropes around the metope as the temple loosened its grip on the ornamental sculpture.

The metope was a particularly gorgeous one, Mary thought, of a centaur abducting a woman. The woman, however, to Mary's eye, looked willing.

"Have you ever seen such beautiful delineations of the body?" Mary asked.

"The woman?" Elgin asked.

"No, the beast! I declare, Pheidias made the creatures irresistible. In some of these metopes, it appears to me that the centaurs are seducing the girls, rather than abducting them."

"Seduction makes abduction so much easier," Elgin said, smiling. Mary wondered if he was musing on some past conquest or talking about his courtship of her. He had seduced her and then abducted her to foreign lands.

"And now, thanks to us, the world will have an opportunity to view these magnificent things," he said, kissing her on the forehead. "The French made off with a few of the metopes, but they shan't get any more. Now that they are once again on the loose, we must hurry our mission before they try to intercede."

Elgin had not been so happy in months. The drier climate seemed to agree with his health, and seeing the progress of his artistic team boosted his spirits. He had easily taken over supervision of the removal of the marbles, rising before dawn each day to preside over the work. Nothing escaped his notice.

Mary felt the planks beneath her tremble again. She looked down to see Dr. Scott climbing the scaffold and arriving at her side. "Lady Elgin, should you be at this altitude on such a precarious construction in your condition?"

"I wanted to see the frieze before it was taken down," she said. "Besides, who knows how long these ladders will remain in place."

The artists had had to remove the scaffolding on the Parthenon walls once before when the Disdar had accused them of building it to spy on women who lived in the adjacent temples, now converted into harems. He informed them that the offense was punishable by death, which made them desist at once. But with the new firman, the artists were able to rebuild the scaffolding required to remove the metopes, the frieze sections, and the pediment statues that Elgin wanted. The Disdar seemed to be in Elgin's pocket—literally. Even with the firman, he required daily bribes to refrain from interfering with the work.

"Dr. Scott, please keep Lady Elgin company," Elgin said. "I must see to the work being done on the ground. You cannot trust a soul with these treasures. Would you believe that when I ordered the houses around the Parthenon to be razed so that the grounds might be excavated, the old fool who built them gleefully told me that he had ground up the fallen pediment statues and used the materials to build his hut!"

"Do see to your duties, then, Lord Elgin, before more treasures are lost forever," Dr. Scott said. "Lady Elgin and I shall tour the frieze together."

Elgin disappeared into the hubbub below, but Mary was grateful to be above the chaos and dust. The view from her vantage point was spectacular, on one side looking out over the plains that surrounded Athens, and on the other, upon majestic Mount Lycabettus, where she had attended Easter Sunday services at a Byzantine chapel just a few days ago. But she could not ignore the rude huts and run-down cottages and mounds of modern rubbish that interrupted the loveliness of the ruins and the landscape.

The Turkish occupiers were living atop the Acropolis and had pitched tents everywhere. The higher officials and soldiers of rank had admittedly built houses using rubble that had fallen from the temples, those glorious monuments conceived by Pericles and designed by Pheidias that she had been studying. Sometimes, imagining their original condition, Mary could barely look at the ancient buildings, which now were mere carcasses, ravaged by time, by war, and by negligence. In between the huts and tents and the ruined temples, the Turkish occupiers had planted gardens of fruits and vegetables, which seemed to thrive despite the lack of rows or any semblance of order, adding to the general disarray of the place. Every Turkish soldier had a servant, who was cooking his master's dinner in a pot over an open fire. Billowing smoke choked the air. Merchants—did they follow every army on earth?—hawked food and supplies and other goods, adding a hectic noise to the general feeling of pandemonium. Amid the tumult, men squatted in whatever shade they could find, mumbling prayers. Here and there, a few scraggly cypress trees clung to the ground, like stalky symbols of more serene times.

The Parthenon, however, was somehow still venerable for having survived all of its wounds. The portico had been walled up to store military supplies inside, and the walls of the cella had long ago been pummeled for their lead. Yet it retained a chaste grandeur, and the Turks had come to appreciate the temple, or at least recognize its inherent holiness. They might have torn the whole thing down; instead, they had built a small mosque inside, which was still intact and in use despite the work that Elgin's artisans were doing on the exterior. Mary had been informed that her viewing of the frieze had to take place between prayer times, for no woman could be in the vicinity of the building when men were praying at the makeshift mosque.

"These are the pavements once trodden upon by gods and heroes," Dr. Scott said dramatically, looking downward. "Doesn't seem right, does it?"

Mary shook her head. "How does a civilization once so mighty have such a fall?"

"It did not happen all at once," Dr. Scott said. "The degradation of the monuments began when the Romans conquered Greece.

Tiberius Nero raided the Acropolis and took most of the standing statuary for his personal gardens."

"Oh, I know the decay has taken centuries. I suppose that I've been reading so much about the days of Pericles that I started to imagine that it all happened quite recently. I would not have been surprised to find the Assembly in session, with him at the podium," she said.

"But this old girl still stands," Dr. Scott said, waving his arms around as if to encompass Athena's temple. "And in her many incarnations, she's served many gods. The Visigoths may have sacked the Acropolis in the third century, but all of her lovely bones survived. Then the Christians converted her into a church. Perhaps all who have gazed upon her columns and pediments have been spellbound enough by her beauty to preserve it."

"Imagine seeing it in its original splendor," Mary said. She tried to picture it without the small dome the Turks had built in the center of the roofless ruin. "Quite honestly, Doctor, I would prefer it to have remained a good Christian church. I'll wager that those early Christians didn't sell off its rubble to passing visitors," she said, feeling proud that she could defend the actions of her religious forebears.

"Far from it. They saw it for the holy shrine it was. Though the Greeks, like the rest of the civilized world, converted to the ways of Christianity, they never lost pride in their grand past. When Emperor Theodosius the Great declared Christianity the religion of the Roman Empire, he ordered the destruction of all pagan temples. But the Athenians ignored his edict, merely changing the identity of the presiding lady from Athena to Mary. Quite a refined way to make a transition, when you think about it."

"Whatever happened to the colossal statue of the goddess carved by the hand of Pheidias?" Mary asked.

"That, with the wondrous Athena Promachos raved over by Pausanias, was removed. Some say both were destroyed in earthquakes. But others say they were taken to Constantinople to serve as symbols of the new empire, where they were lost in one of that city's great fires."

"Now, *that* I can believe," Mary said, laughing. "Whatever goes to that city eventually burns."

One of the primary reasons the Elgins had decided to come to Athens was that their embassy had been badly damaged when fire broke out in the city. "I watched as one hundred buckets of water were unceremoniously dumped over our beautiful furniture and carpets," Mary said. "When the Turks go to put out a fire, nothing is spared!"

Elgin had taken it as an omen that they were to leave the city while repairs to the embassy were being done. Of course, Mary knew that he had been searching for a reason to leave his duties in Turkey and visit his master project in Athens.

"We cannot blame the Turks entirely for the Parthenon's disintegration. When they took it over, they didn't destroy a thing, but merely whitewashed its walls and mosaics. They added the minaret, but did not harm the building any more than it had already been harmed. Its grandeur must have spoken to even the most barbaric among them," he said wistfully.

"I thought you respected the Turks," Mary said. She caught a whiff of meat roasting and put a handkerchief over her nose.

"Within limits," he replied.

"After all, it wasn't the Turks who truly destroyed the temple, but the Venetians," Mary said. "In 1687, a foolish Venetian general fired upon the building, shattering the structure. The grand building exploded, killing all its inhabitants."

"Lady Elgin, you've studied your history. I am impressed," Dr. Scott said.

"A duty to my husband," she answered. "And to the monuments themselves, Dr. Scott. Can you bear seeing them in this state of disgrace? Especially when we consider what they once represented?"

"That is why your good husband is going to such lengths to rescue them," he said. "What is left will be safe in England."

During their conversation, the scaffolding had been shaking, and Mary had been trying to ignore it. The metope that the men had been trying to remove all morning had been giving them difficulty, as if it did not want to be dislodged from its home. Though it made her nervous, she was determined to see what was left of the frieze here in its strange location high above the ground where only birds and the gods could have seen it. She had read the geographer Pausanias' descriptions of the Parthenon, written in the second century of the Christian era, but he did not mention the frieze. Now she understood why: from his vantage point on the ground, he may not have seen it.

Key pieces of the relief had been removed already and were wrapped and waiting at the docks. Those, she would have to see out of context and in England. But the rest, she wished to see as the tableau Pheidias had conceived and executed. Already, the gaps were making it difficult to reconstruct the grand procession. The artists had described some of the missing slabs to her, and some she had admired in their drawings. She had particularly wanted to see the portion representing the gods with their backs to the processionals, but it had already come down.

Mary realized that there was not one representation of Athena left on her temple. The image of the great goddess that had once been everywhere on the Acropolis, looking out over her population with her protective and wise gaze, was now nowhere to be found. The statues of the goddess that had been in the two pediments on the Parthenon, one representing her at the moment of her birth, the other in her contest with Poseidon, had long ago been destroyed. No one knew exactly how it had happened, but none of the excavations performed by Elgin's staff around the Parthenon had yielded images of the goddess.

Perhaps the Turks had used the very statues of Athena, fallen from the pediments, to build their houses. Mary was sickened to think of Pheidias' beautiful statues pummeled to nothing and lodged with ordinary concrete and mortar, holding up the walls of these unsightly buildings.

Even on the metopes where Athena appeared, the face of the goddess was damaged. Mary realized that nowhere in the city called Athens had she been able to look upon the face of Athena. Someday, in a faraway and unimaginable future, would the face of Jesus be wiped from the earth? She shuddered at her own morbid—and perhaps sacrilegious—thought.

Suddenly the lumber beneath her feet shook violently, throwing her into Dr. Scott's arms. She heard the screams of men and
the sound of ropes flying around pulleys. In an instant, something
crashed to the ground with a thundering noise.

"Are you all right?" Dr. Scott asked, looking her in the face.

"Yes, quite," she said, escaping his grasp and racing around
the scaffolding as fast as she dared to see what had happened. She
prayed that the beautiful metope had not met a disgraceful fate.

Pheidias' lovely sculpture rested safely on the ground in a single
piece. But the workmen's endeavors had loosened a part of the ad-
joining masonry, a finely made cornice, shattering it into white
marble fragments now littering the ground. The Disdar had taken
the pipe out of his mouth, which was wide open in either astonishment or disgust. "*Telos!*" he yelled. It was one of the ten Greek
words that Mary knew, and it meant "the end."

Mary looked at Elgin, who did not see her, but was shading his
eyes from the sun with his hand as he stared at the corner of the
building. Mary looked up, following his gaze. Blocks of concrete
stuck out like jagged teeth in the empty space where the cornice had
been ripped from its anchor.

THE JOURNEY TO ATHENS had not been a pleasant
one. Why was it that she had twice agreed to travel on tumultuous
seas in miserable ships when she was in the early stages of pregnancy? Had she not learned her lesson the first time around on the
trip to Constantinople? This time was none the more pleasant for
having had the experience before. But it could not be helped. As
bad as her condition was, she was nowhere near as sickly as Elgin.
A month ago, on the day of their third anniversary, Dr. Scott had
had to amputate a good portion of Elgin's nose. It sickened Mary to
see her beautiful husband so disfigured, but after months of blister-
ing and wounds about the throat and nose that drained incessantly,
she agreed with the doctor that there was no alternative.

Elgin had gotten sicker as the months in Constantinople wore
on. He blamed the dampness and the coal fires that were every-

where in the city, and allowed that he required a warmer climate in which to heal. Mary could not deny that her husband was terribly ill, but she also knew that when he lobbied to be in a warmer climate, he meant that he wanted to go to Greece to supervise the crucial and final stages of his Athenian project.

She sensed that it was all that he thought he had left. She'd had no idea of how diplomatic service used up the diplomat for the purposes at hand and then discarded him. It had been a delicate and serious mission from the start, and a less experienced and skilled man could easily have destroyed the nascent relations between England and the Ottomans. Elgin's great diplomatic dexterity, combined with Mary's ability to charm the most powerful Turks in the empire, had saved the alliance more than once. But after the French were expelled from Egypt, the Sultan saw no more reason to remain alienated from his former allies, and the English saw no reason to placate their ambassador.

The British didn't seem to want to reward Elgin. He requested that the enormous sums of money that he and Mary had contributed to the war effort in Egypt be reimbursed and, astonishingly, was turned down. When that plea failed, he requested a peerage, thinking that this was the very least that the British government could do for him. If granted, he would automatically become a member of the House of Lords and could circumvent the elections. In this too he was turned down. It seemed that neither Parliament nor king bore under any responsibility to their ambassador.

In December of the previous year, after the truce with France, a young French officer, Horace François Bastien Sébastiani, arrived in the city, announcing himself as Bonaparte's cousin and his representative in the Levant. Mary and Elgin received him graciously. Though it was difficult to stop thinking of the French as enemies, Mary was easily taken with his rakish handsomeness and urbane manners. He always wore tight breeches, a colorful waistcoat, heelless shoes, and a cravat tied several times around his neck. His hair was long. "Unkempt!" Elgin declared, but Mary informed him that the style had come into vogue with the Revolution. Sébastiani and Mary were the same age, and the young Frenchman seemed intent upon impressing her.

Besides blatant fascination with Mary, Sébastiani began to put ideas into the heads of both Lord and Lady Elgin. The young marshal, soon to be on his way back to France, tantalized Mary with the idea of how glamorous it would be for *her* if Elgin—now that there was peace—were to be appointed the next ambassador to France. She had never been to Paris, and he was whetting her appetite for culture and luxury with exotic tales of that city. With Elgin, Sébastiani painted grand scenarios of the rewards that would be due the ambassador that the British government would now require in order to do business with Napoleon.

Elgin was intrigued with the idea of going to Paris. One evening at a ball, however, he was so distraught at Sébastiani's attentions to Mary that he marched right up to him and said, "My dear sir, may I remind you that the lady's husband is in the room!"

Sébastiani had laughed, answering that it was Elgin's presence that allowed him to pay such tribute to Mary. "It is the truly wicked man who attends to the ladies behind the husbands' backs."

Then, much to Elgin's dismay, Sébastiani began to visit Mary at times when he knew that Elgin would not be present. Mary was annoyed at her own fascination with the officer's charms at a time when her husband, ill and disfigured, needed her more than ever, but she could not resist Sébastiani's sophisticated company. His racy stories and jokes, and the way that he bothered to kiss her hand whenever possible, charmed her. One night, after avoiding Elgin in the bedroom for weeks and weeks, she felt so guilty for her attraction to Sébastiani, and for her repulsion for the bleeding, oozing wound that sat in the middle of Elgin's once-handsome face, that she made wild love to her husband. That little mistake had landed her here, in the middle of the sea, pregnant once again and wishing for death as the ship rocked in the waves.

But before they'd set sail, her flirtation with Sébastiani had culminated in an exchange that left her feeling at once sordid, frightened, and titillated. The bold young Frenchman had gone so far as to suggest that once Elgin's appointment was accomplished, he and Mary could begin an affair.

"It is destiny," he said, his brown eyes dancing as he ran them up and down her body. He had a way of flipping his long, dark hair that one would have thought would have made him seem effeminate, but only made him more desirable.

She was about to pour him another glass of wine, but she demurred. "I think you've had enough," she said, trying to sound reprimanding. She withdrew the bottle. He grabbed her arm and rose to his feet, kicking the chair behind him, toppling it backwards. Mary felt a thrill rush up her spine.

"Why should you deny yourself a lover?" She could feel the heat of his breath as he whispered into her ear. "Your husband has had women."

"How can you say that?" she said, pulling away.

He sighed. "The evidence is on his face. The nose, the sores. It is syphilis, *n'est-ce pas?*"

"No, it is rheumatism, aggravated by a strange virus he contracted in Turkey," she said, conscious that the shrill tone in her voice made her sound more defensive than convincing.

"*Mais oui,*" he said, sneering. "In France, we call that virus '*la syphilis.*'"

He was laughing at her. He must have thought that she was naïve.

"I have heard these ugly rumors, monsieur. My husband's enemies put them about all the time. I did not think that you were among their number. I assure you that I have addressed this with both my husband and his doctor. Lord Elgin is being treated for his ailments with mercury, which agrees with him, but which can also eat away at the flesh."

"Ah, mercury. The same medication given for syphilis." He would not let it rest. "Come, Lady Elgin—Mary, *Marie*—I never argue on the opposite side of beauty. Let us be frank with one another. English men do as they please. Why not the women? When you come to Paris, you will not be able to resist me. I am even more *charmant* on my home terrain." He kissed her hand, and she was too flustered to stop him.

"Sir, you must go now," she said, not looking at him.

He smiled, giving her the famous French shrug, so dismissive, yet so attractive at the same time. She turned away from him and marched upstairs, where she took a strong dose of laudanum, to make sure that his insinuations did not bring on a choking attack, and went directly to bed.

The next day she demanded a private conference with Dr. Scott. She told him what Sébastiani had said, and she insisted that he be frank with her. "After all, my own health is at risk."

"Mercury is used for many ailments, Lady Elgin," he said, taking her hand and patting it in his reassuring manner. "It may exacerbate some of Lord Elgin's symptoms, but it is giving him relief as well. You must ignore these prurient suggestions. Why must the French insinuate their loose morals upon the rest of us?"

Sébastiani left Mary grateful that she had thwarted his advances—she would never take a lover!—but admittedly, with a growing desire to see Elgin made ambassador to France.

"If we've been able to make a strong impression in Constantinople, imagine what we could accomplish in Paris," she said to Elgin. "The British government owes you, my darling. If you press just a little for the appointment, I am sure it will be ours."

Elgin liked the idea. He thought that he was just the man to help sustain the delicate peace between Napoleon and the English. That is, if Bonaparte did not resent him for interfering with France's acquisition of certain antiquities.

"If the little Corsican is any sort of gentleman—which I doubt— he won't hold it against me that I sent my man to confiscate that fantastic inscription," Elgin said.

As soon as the French were defeated in Egypt, Elgin had sent his secretary William Hamilton to enter negotiations with General Jacques-François de Menou for the antiquities that Napoleon's team of archeologists had accumulated. Elgin knew that many pieces had yet to be transported back to France, and there was one that he desperately wanted to claim for the United Kingdom.

Hamilton was instructed to keep an eye out for an invaluable inscription, which Napoleon's scholars in Egypt had called the Rosetta Stone. The expert linguists and archeologists declared that this dedication, written in three languages, could be used to decipher the ancient Egyptian hieroglyphs. Elgin had been miffed since Napoleon announced his acquisition some three years prior.

"It serves him right. He could not resist making his grandiose claims when the stone was discovered. Good boy, that Hamilton. He discovered that General Menou was hiding the precious item, covered with blankets, in a warehouse, trying to pass it off as his private property," Elgin said, every bit the proud mentor.

Mary remembered when she had to promise Hamilton that he would not starve in their service. The young secretary had come a long way in the past two years.

"Hamilton promptly informed Colonel Turner, who seized the stone and is bringing it to England as we speak," Elgin continued. "When it's presented to King George, I shall be certain to let him know that it was my secretary, acting in my service, who rescued it for England."

Given His Majesty's latest dismissals of Elgin's requests, Mary doubted that King George would care, but she let Elgin have his moment of fantasy. It occurred to her for the first time that her husband considered himself in a private race with Napoleon in these matters. She was happy to let him participate, but the price for his ambitions was escalating.

To transport his collections from Athens, Mary had bought Elgin a ship, the *Mentor*. The vessel had already sailed from the port of Athens with ten boxes of molds taken from the Parthenon, several extremely heavy marble torsos found from the excavations under the western pediment of the building, and a portion of the frieze. The loaded ship was on its way to pick up William Hamilton from Alexandria, and could not be used to transport the Elgin family to Athens. Despite the expense of travel, once the house had caught fire, Elgin would not be deterred from visiting Athens, no matter how Mary protested on account of her condition. She easily acquiesced, knowing that in the face of the insults from the Crown, which he had served so well, Elgin needed more than ever for his legacy—as the man who enriched the English empire with ancient treasures and monuments and elevated all aspects of its arts—to be preserved.

ON MARCH 28, AFTER leaving directions with the staff who would oversee the repairs on the embassy, the Elgins set sail in the direction of Athens. Traveling with Lord Bruce, who was barely two, and little Mary, almost six months old, they were accompanied by Masterman; the servant Andrew, whom Mary had just disciplined for giving her toddler son wine for breakfast; and Calitza, the fat nurse who now tended to little Mary. Elgin was in a favorable mood, looking forward to seeing the progress in Athens and desperate for dry warmth, but Mary's old battle with seasickness, coupled with the familiar morning sickness, began immediately. The horrid voyage brought the old fears into Mary's mind again. Being stuck in the rank cabin of another vessel, vomiting into a bowl while Masterman held back her hair, bathing her face in vinegar, and taking thrice-daily doses of laudanum reminded Mary not only of that horrible initial voyage to Constantinople, but of her near-death experience in labor. Did that time on the ship contribute to the difficulty she had in delivery? She asked Dr. Scott, who said that it was possible, but not probable. Yet he could not explain why her second child, conceived and carried on dry land, had come into the world with much more ease.

"Second babies are often easier to deliver," Dr. Scott said.

"What about third babies?" she asked. She felt as if these questions were an admission of timidity, a thing she prided herself on not possessing. But once she was pregnant and on the open seas, memories of the delivery of beautiful little Lord Bruce began to haunt her once more.

This was not a topic she could share with Elgin.

"At least pregnancy is a normal condition, and a temporary one," he said once, touching the small mask that he had to wear all the time now to cover what remained of his nose.

Henceforth, she realized, there would be no complaining about her own health. Still, she had to be adamant about certain things. Dr. Scott traveled with them to Athens, as Mary would not trust the safety of her unborn child, nor of her living ones, to foreign doctors. Further, though Napoleon's navy, for the time being, had been drastically diminished by Lord Nelson, the seas were rife with pirates, so the journey to Athens was made with a small convoy of vessels. Near Patmos, they were caught up in storms, which swept two crew members overboard and flooded the ship's quarters. For two weeks Mary and the others tolerated the damp, smelly conditions. When the dank cabins and the ship's motion became unendurable, she insisted they camp for a night, though she would have to travel by donkey—so unpleasant when one was expecting—to arrive at a campsite. They spent one blissful evening away from the vessel, but hearing stories of pirates in the vicinity carrying off women, they rushed back to the ship fearing for the safety of the children.

Another night, they traveled six hours over land to arrive at a village, where Mary was elated that they would finally sleep comfortably, only to be awakened in the middle of the night by fleas, which had infested her bed as well as the children's. The next morning, she was informed that they were still a nine-hour ride from Athens. Back on the asses they went, with the children carried in baskets, firmly attached. Luckily, the little ones slept almost the entire way, probably from exhaustion. The night before, they had been unable to sleep, what with fleas dancing in their hair.

Mary was delighted to finally reach Athens on April 3, having no idea of the sorry conditions, the turmoil, and the potential danger that would greet them on the mainland. Riding into the city, they passed two lone columns, remnants of the aqueduct built by Hadrian.

"Shall we have a look around?" Mary asked.

"Thieves are hiding everywhere, waiting to rob unsuspecting travelers," said one of their guides. "Everyone must stay close."

She could not have imagined the state of degradation in Athens. She had realized, of course, that the Athens of the Golden Age that she had studied in the ancient sources was long diminished, both by age and by its many invaders and occupiers. But nothing prepared her for that once-mighty city's condition of utter ruin.

The city's population had dwindled to barely one thousand inhabitants, half being Greeks, half Turks, with a few Albanians. The streets were narrow, crooked, and unpaved. There were no hotels or inns, so that the Greek who served as the English consul in Athens had to vacate his home to accommodate the Elgins. Mary had inquired about accommodations and taverns for her staff, but was told that none existed.

Sparse dwellings dotted the landscape until the streets narrowed and the buildings became more densely set. A Doric portico stood over the unpaved street. Houses looked uninhabited. Except for the storks flying lazily overhead, the streets were desolate. A lone seagull, the neighborhood's sole citizen, nested on a severely tarnished bust of some Caesar or other—one of Greece's many conquerors—in the nook of an old building.

Upon arrival at the home of the Greek who was acting as the English consul, along with refreshments they were served the information that the country was ripe for a revolt against its longtime occupiers.

"We are sick to death of their oppression," the man said. "Our language is no longer the official language of our country. They make our children learn the foreign tongue. Our daughters are sent at early ages to the harems. We are not free, in most cases, to practice our religion openly."

"If the French can throw over their long-standing monarchy, surely we can eject these foreigners from Greek soil," said another man.

Reverend Hunt, who had been on a tour of the Peloponnese with the twofold mission of seeking antiquities that might be removed and taking the political temperature of the country for Elgin, chimed in. "Secret societies are being formed everywhere. The leaders are in league with the Russians, who, as you know, would love to topple the Ottomans once and for all."

The next morning they set out for the Acropolis. "First-rate weather," Elgin said. It was warmer and drier out than the climes they'd encountered on their travels, and Elgin was in a cheery disposition, turning his face up to the warm sun, and gazing up at the monuments on the hill he had dreamed about for so long. That mighty and ever-present rock that had presided over the city since time out of mind still lorded over the terrain. The bones of the Parthenon and the other ruins stood against the morning light, columns rising majestically from the center of the hill.

"One must look upon it with awe," Mary said as they approached, and Elgin smiled and patted her hand. At last they had arrived at the place he had dreamt of for so long.

But as soon as he saw the condition of the citadel, his mood began to shift.

Turks in robes and turbans, holding prayer beads, were sitting with their backs against the ancient columns of the Great Gateway.

"Why would they choose this location to say their prayers?" Elgin asked. Mary did not think that he expected an answer from her, but she nonetheless gave one.

"With every bead they invoke another attribute of God," Mary said brightly. "God most Holy, God of Mercy, God of Truth, God of Infinite Wisdom. I think it a lovely way to pray, no matter the location."

Elgin ignored her comments, staring at two turbaned fellows slouching against the grand columns, bleached to a bony yellow.

"Disturbing, isn't it?"

"What?"

"To see that Turks have commandeered the monuments of the Greeks."

"Would you prefer they were French?" Mary asked provocatively. What had he expected? They were in Ottoman territory.

"Of course not. But *we* are more the spiritual descendants of the Age of Pericles, Mary. Not the Turks."

"Yes, but *we* are not in English territory."

She had hoped—prayed—that Elgin would be pleased with what he saw on the Acropolis. She did not think that his spirits would hold up against another disappointment such as those he had suffered with his own government.

Lusieri met them outside the Parthenon, where he had set up a camp for the artists to work. Happily, Elgin's mood improved once he saw the artists and workers rushing in and out of the white tents with their tools and supplies, and the scaffolds climbing the walls and columns of the Parthenon. Dozens of workers twined with a complex system of ropes were busily removing its pieces to send to the warehouse he had rented at the docks.

Inside one of the tents, Lusieri had made a lovely display of the work he had done over the past two years. He and the other sketch artists and painters had made dozens and dozens, perhaps hundreds, of drawings and paintings of the ancient temples, from magisterial representations of the whole of the Acropolis to individual pictures of the monuments, and fantastic drawings of every architectural detail.

"When we met you, I said that your drawings were superior to anything I had seen in England, sir, but you have exceeded yourself," Mary said. "Generations of artists and designers will cherish the work you have done here."

"I must tell you something important," Lusieri said. "Louis Fauvel is out of prison and he is coming back to Athens, this time as a representative of Napoleon."

Louis-François-Sebastien Fauvel, a cutthroat antiquarian art collector and dealer, had been in Athens for years, trying to garner as much as he could for himself and Bonaparte. He was arrested by the Turks, along with the rest of the French, when Napoleon invaded Egypt, and was sent to Constantinople. The officials on the Acropolis happily gave Lusieri the use of all of Fauvel's sophisticated excavation equipment, including a large cart and tackle without which the removal work could not have been done.

"Dear God," Elgin said. "Will we have to give back his equipment?"

"If I lose the equipment, I can do nothing, Lord Elgin!"

Lusieri looked on the verge of hysteria at the thought. "That

French dog managed to sabotage our operation even from his prison cell," Lusieri explained to Mary. "He had his agents in Athens cut off our water supply time and again, slowing the work down. Now he has the use of Bonaparte's money! He has already tried to bribe our artists into giving him the drawings that we have done for you, Lord Elgin. The French are going to do anything they can to reap the benefits of your labor."

He leaned in close to Mary and Elgin. "I have used the gifts you sent me to gather information. Greeks and Turks alike enjoy a little cash or trinket now and then. The Greeks say that Napoleon is already sending spy ships, disguised as merchant vessels, to look for everything you have collected at the docks. Even now, they are trying to find where you stored the treasures."

Later that night, after she put the children to sleep in the make-shift nursery upstairs, fashioning a gate across the stairwell so that the adventurous Lord Bruce would not set out on an expedition in the middle of the night, Mary voiced her concerns to Elgin.

"Is it safe here for the children?" she asked. "What with brewing revolts and Napoleon's spies everywhere?"

"Oh yes, rebellions are discussed for years and years before anyone lifts a finger. The Russians have been trying to get the Greeks to oust the Turks for forty years. I have my informants, Mary, and they are paid well. If there were imminent danger, I would send you and the children away at once."

"Would you not come with us?"

"Not until my work here is complete," he said. "As you have heard with your own ears now, we must move very quickly."

MARY STOOD IN THE hot sun under a parasol, gazing in wonder at the latest object of her husband's grand ambitions. The temple called the Erechtheion, dedicated to Athena Polias, the ancient olive-wood icon; the snake-boy, Erechtheus; and his faithful governess, the obedient Pandrosos, had been damaged in the same explosion that had blown open the roof of the Parthenon. Mary had been keen to see the temple complex described in the books of antiquities she had been reading. Since she had been acquainted with the myth of Pandrosos, the king's daughter who was honored forevermore for obeying Athena's command, she often reflected on it. She too thought of herself as an obedient daughter. But she was also a curiosity seeker and a natural-born adventurer. Would she have obeyed the goddess and not looked inside the basket, or would she have disobeyed and found herself jumping over the side of the Acropolis with the more curious sisters?

The Erechtheion was one of the four main buildings designed by Pheidias as part of Pericles' master building plan. It too had lost its roof, and the interior, packed with rubble and huge blocks of marble, was impossible to negotiate. The structure was smaller than the Parthenon, and its primary feature was a south-facing porch that was supported by Caryatids—statues of solemn ladies in flowing robes—which served as columns. The Caryatids' faces were elegant and noble, as if the women were bearing the burden of the heavy building from a sense of duty.

The Caryatids—along with the ornamentation of the cornices and capitals, thought to be unsurpassed works of design by the world's experts in architecture—were the most extraordinary things Mary had seen thus far in Greece. Originally, six Caryatids had held up the porch, but Elgin's crew had removed one of the sisters, leaving a rather sad gape in the configuration, or so Mary thought. The symmetry of the structure had been destroyed, but it was more than that.

"It appears as if a family member has been ripped from the clan," Mary said, looking at the gap where the sixth sister had stood for two thousand years.

"That is sentimental nonsense and not worthy of you," Elgin replied.

The lone statue in question was now at the dock at Piraeus awaiting means of transportation back to England. Elgin revered the Caryatids. He had just shooed away three servants lounging in their shade. He could not bear to see the elegant Greek ladies sullied by the attentions of such fellows.

"The Erechtheion, holiest of holy temples on the Acropolis, was most recently used by the Turks as a harem," Reverend Hunt said. "But that was long ago."

It looked to Mary as if ages had passed since it had been inhabited. "It looks more sacked than abandoned," she offered. "According to Pausanias, the temple was just about the most lavish thing. It was jam-packed with statues and frescoes and gilded ornaments— all still there when he wrote about it, five hundred years after the days of Pericles, and now, all gone!"

Elgin folded his arms.

"I think we should take the entire temple," Elgin said matter-of-factly.

"Splendid idea," said Reverend Hunt. "Why not remove it and rebuild it back in England?"

"If we were supplied with a man-of-war, it would be possible, wouldn't it?" Elgin said.

"But the costs in labor and transportation would be prohibitive," Mary said, trying to imagine the letter she would have to compose to her father for his financial contribution to the project. He had been happy to help since his own trip to Athens, but the transporting of an entire Greek temple was sure to test the limits of any Scottish landowner.

"We are having difficulty finding transport for the one Caryatid we've got!" Mary added. "I have already spoken to Mr. Lacy about it."

"If I may, Lord Elgin?" Thomas Lacy had been quiet the entire day. He was a captain in the Royal Engineers, whom Elgin had managed to steal from service in Egypt to come to Athens to supervise the transportation of the treasures. "Captain Dick of the *Cynthia* cannot be persuaded to transport the Caryatid. I thought I had him convinced, but he sent someone to the docks to estimate the weight of it and decided it was too heavy."

"What was he persuaded to take?" Elgin asked.

"In fact, sir, he looked at all the marbles and declined to transport any aboard his ship. He said that he was under no direct order by either Admiral Lord Nelson or Admiral Lord Keith to perform these services. With pirate ships plaguing the seas, he thought it too dangerous to be weighted down by the statues."

"Is Nelson interfering with the transportation of these items?" Elgin asked.

"Not to my knowledge, sir. But neither is he encouraging the captains to comply."

"What are we to do?" Mary asked.

Nearby, headless, fallen statues that had appeared to have been of goddesses leaned against one another as if for support. Elgin pointed to them as an example. "Do you wish these great ladies to suffer the fates of those crumbling pediments? Bonaparte has got no such thing from all his thefts in Italy and Egypt. I shall write to Admiral Lord Keith immediately and ask him to send a ship of a size to accommodate the most valuable piece of architectural art at my disposal. Surely he will understand that I am doing a very essential service to the arts in England!"

"If he is a man of vision like yourself, Lord Elgin," said Reverend Hunt. "And if we succeed in procuring the proper ship, there is also a fetching little temple to Pandrosos on the Peloponnese that we might take."

As with Athena, Mary thought, soon there would be no sign of Pandrosos in Greece.

"What is the mood outside of Athens?" Elgin asked. "I hear that the collector Edward Clarke ran into some difficulty in Eleusis."

"Yes, he was determined to procure the statue of Demeter that had stood in the field there for, oh, several millennia. It predated the Age of Pericles. He hired one hundred fifty men and chartered an enormous ship to carry it off. But the villagers protested that if the lady with her basket were removed, their crops would fail. Demeter was goddess of the corn, or some such nonsense that they still believe though they are supposedly of the Orthodox faith," Mr. Hunt said. "The villagers said that the statue of Demeter was older than the world, and anyone who took it away would be punished by the goddess."

"All Greeks are peasants and do not deserve to possess these masterpieces," Elgin said.

Mary was afraid that some of the hired Greek workers might understand enough of the English language to overhear. "What did happen to Mr. Clarke?" she asked Reverend Hunt.

"Ah, the superstitions of the Greeks were confirmed! As they were clearing away the soil to take the colossal statue, an ox broke loose from its yoke and went careening in the field, which sent the villagers into a panic. The priest declared that it was an omen, and that Clarke would pay the price of insulting a goddess. The ox went mad; nothing would stop it. It finally rammed itself into the statue."

"Imagine a rational man going on about a pagan goddess," Elgin said in disgust.

"Later, the ship Clarke had chartered was battered in storms and got stuck in the seabed, and it took weeks—and an awful lot of manpower and money—to get her to sail again. At that point, I believe, even Mr. Clarke was convinced that Demeter did not want to abandon her people."

"Pausanias claims that when Demeter is neglected, barrenness comes to the land," Mary said, chiming in.

"Why is it so easy for women, even the most intelligent among you, to lapse into superstitious nonsense?" Elgin said.

"I did not invent the myth, my dear, I am simple relating it to you," Mary replied, though her husband had read her thoughts correctly. Something deep inside her was beginning to question this wholesale acquisition of Greece's treasures. Perhaps she had read too much mythology. She knew, for example, that Poseidon, the sea god, was lovesick over Demeter, who sometimes took the form of a mare. Poseidon had transformed himself into a stallion in order to seduce her. "But don't you think it's easy to see why the villagers would conclude that Poseidon had teamed up with Demeter to take his revenge on Mr. Clarke? After all, they had been lovers."

"We mustn't allow the backward mentality of the Greeks to interfere with our mission, Mary," Elgin admonished. "We must behave as the enlightened creatures we are and stay the course."

Mary knew that Elgin was correct. It would be a shame, perhaps a crime, to allow the treasures to remain here where they might be pummeled for ammunition or building materials, or shipped away to put coins in the Disdar's pockets. What if there was another war in Greece? Another siege? Another explosion? They had ample evidence that much of Greece was ripe to join in a revolt against the Ottomans.

"I shall write to Lord Keith immediately, making a case for him to put a man-of-war at my disposal," Elgin said. "If he complies, I shall set about preparing to transport the Erechtheion—every last glorious Caryatid and cornice and column—to England."

MARY WALKED AWAY FROM the men and the rubble to collect her thoughts. She was sure that Lord Keith would have nothing to do with the transportation of Elgin's treasures. In fact, it was becoming increasingly clear that no one wanted to participate in the endeavor. From all reports, every sea captain feared the cost to his ship and to his crew if burdened with the tons of marble that Elgin had been collecting and amassing at the port of Piraeus. In addition to all that had already been shipped on their private vessel, the *Mentor,* the collection was growing: six more slabs of the Frieze were removed, and another was found in excavation. Slabs of frieze from the Temple of Athena Nike, also on the Acropolis, were discovered built into the walls around the citadel. Massive examples of architectural detail that Elgin insisted were crucial to the elevation of art and design were collected—pillars, bases, cornices, capitals, and other details from all of the Acropolis's temples and shrines— and waiting for shipment at the dock. The stacks of metopes piled up, sitting in the storeroom alongside the lone Caryatid, and all the casts that the artists had made of architectural details that could not be removed from the buildings. Coins, inscriptions, busts, heads, and a staggering number of vases—anything found that was considered of worth—were put into Elgin's storehouse.

When the grand prize from the Parthenon—the horse's head from the chariot of Selene, the moon goddess—was lowered to the ground, Mary had been sure that Elgin's ambition would be sated and they could return to Constantinople.

But she soon learned that this was only the beginning.

"We must make a tour of all of Greece," he had announced. She wondered if he'd noticed that she was pregnant. "Mary, we shall cut quite the dash all over the country. We must do this now, while I am here in an official capacity. The opportunity will not come to us again. The French have been released from Turkish prisons and will soon be crawling all over Greece. They'll sabotage me at every turn, don't you know? We must see what antiquities are available to us in the other Grecian territories. Reverend Hunt says that Athens is just the tip of Greece's treasures!"

The excitement Elgin used to display during sex he now reserved for his Greek acquisitions. Not that his enthusiasm for sex was gone. Now that Mary was pregnant, she acquiesced whenever he desired her. Though he was no longer handsome, she still enjoyed being in bed with her husband, especially since she did not have the fine-looking Sébastiani to compare him to. If there was no risk of pregnancy—already done!—she enjoyed it even more. Whereas her eyes used to remain open, they now enjoyed the rapture in the dark.

She sat on a pedestal in the sun, disquieted by his words. The sun was high in the midday sky. Dr. Scott had warned her that though it was spring, the relentless Greek sun could pose a danger to a woman in her condition. She did not believe him. She had traveled half a month aboard a damp, stinking ship, and half a day on a donkey "in her condition," and had survived. Still, the heat and the glare made her feel a sudden fatigue, and she looked for a patch of shade that was not taken by a crouching Turk.

Through an opening in the wall, she saw a scraggly olive tree. She climbed over the mounds of concrete and peered inside the temple. Most of the roof had been blown off and light streamed inside, illuminating a flat chunk of marble. She climbed through the opening. The room was fairly empty but for weeds growing out of the old stones and a pile of rubbish in the corner. She heard a noise come from the trash, and fearing it was a nest of rats, moved away from it.

The chunk of marble sat on a pedestal and was worn at the center. She had to resist the urge to give in to her fatigue and lie down upon it. She envisioned herself doing so and realized that she would look like a human sacrifice, whereupon the idea struck her that the thing had once been an altar. It was not ornate, not by the standards of the art that her husband was collecting. The pedestal was plain, and the altar itself was without adornment. There was something primitive about it, as if it did not belong in the ornate building that housed it. It was devoid of the kind of design that had gone into Pheidias' creations. No, this was the sort of place she had read about where the mysteries must have been performed.

She put her hand on the cold marble, where, she thought with a chill, blood had undoubtedly been spilt. She felt very dizzy, and so hot that she knew she had to find some shade and sit down. If she could return to Elgin and the others, the men would somehow see to her comfort. Maybe she would call for Dr. Scott after all. She turned around, but fell back against the slab. She steadied herself on it with her palms. She could fight the urge to rest no longer. She thought for a moment that she heard the distant sounds of drum-beats. Was that possible? It seemed to get louder as her head started to spin and spin. Was it part of the Mohammedan call to prayer? She turned and fell forward on the altar, and managed to lie on its cold surface before the world went black.

THE CAVE WAS DARK, *but torches lit its craggy walls and low, jagged ceiling. Mary tried to crawl along the passage but the stones hurt her knees. Her dress kept catching on rocks, and the faster she tried to move, the more difficult it became to make her body obey her own commands. She felt as if she were trying to crawl through thick molasses. She was running away from the terrible screeching noise that seemed to be chasing her. What sort of creature, what unearthly beast, could make such a sound? It ripped through her ears, making her head feel as if it would burst. She looked up. Elgin stood at the opening of the cave, the light from outside forming a halo around his body. He held out his hand to help her, but the noise overtook her as she heard a horrible fluttering and flapping behind her, gaining on her, as if some winged creature were after her. She flattened herself against the ground to try to protect herself and the baby inside from whatever monster was chasing her. She could not imagine what it was, or what she had done to incur its wrath. She tried to cry out to warn Elgin, but her mouth would not make a sound. She had lost all ability to move forward or to talk. The screeching became louder, intolerable now, and she covered her ears with her hands, afraid to look up, but knowing that she had to find a way to help Elgin, who was still holding out his hand. Suddenly a huge wingspan—was it a demon from hell, one of Satan's creatures?—appeared in front of her, blocking her view of her husband and of the entrance to the cave. In the dark, she heard Elgin cry out as the creature enveloped him. "Mary," he cried. "Mary!" A woman, also with great black wings, appeared, watching impassively as the beast attacked Elgin. "Help him," Mary called out. But the woman ignored her, and Elgin's voice grew weaker and weaker. "Mary! Mary!"*

"MARY!"

She opened her eyes. Elgin stood over her. The sun was streaming down on him, and he was still in silhouette. All was quiet. Dr. Scott was behind him, peering over his shoulder.

"Where am I?" She clutched Elgin's sleeve.

"Captain Lacy was concerned that you were wandering off alone," Elgin said. He helped her sit upright. "You mustn't, Mary. This is not London! There is danger everywhere, especially for a female."

"I was tired. I suppose I fell asleep."

"Lady Elgin, we are all aware of your extraordinary stamina, but how many times must I tell you that a lady in your condition needs to rest during the heat of the day?" Dr. Scott reflected Elgin's stern look.

"That is precisely what I was trying to do, Dr. Scott," she answered.

"But we found you laid out on an altar like some maiden sacrifice," Elgin said.

"Stay with me for a moment, Elgin," she said. "Send the others away."

"We will see you back at the encampment," Dr. Scott said. "I would like to examine you further, Lady Elgin. We mustn't take chances where your health is concerned."

"As you wish," she said, anxious for him to leave. She did not want him to hear what she had to say. It was one thing to risk acting the foolish female in front of one's husband, who expected such behavior of a wife. It was another to display vulnerability to his staff.

"Something terrible happened, Eggy. I'm afraid. Terribly afraid."

"What on earth, Mary? It's not the baby, is it?" He put a protective hand over her stomach.

"No, the baby is fine, I am sure. I needed to rest. I was overtaken with dizziness. I thought I would pass out, and I did. On this horrible slab!" She looked down at the worn marble with its eddy of colors—yellow, orange, white—and wondered if some of what she saw were ancient bloodstains. "I had a vision of sorts. It felt like one of my presentiments. It was horrible. You were being attacked by some monster, some mythic beast with wings and a beak!"

She described the entire scenario to him. He listened patiently, holding her hand, but the look of skepticism did not leave his face.

"You fell asleep, Mary. It was a bad dream, nothing more. Though God knows I have my enemies. Was it Napoleon? I wouldn't be surprised if the little monster had wings." Elgin laughed. Mary could see that he was not going to take the warning seriously.

"I'm afraid that something bad is going to happen to you. I can't explain it, and I do not want you to blame it on foolish superstition."

"Do you honestly think the Olympian gods are taking revenge? Why wouldn't they be grateful that we are saving what remains of them?" He threw up his hands. "Dear God, now I sound as foolish as you and Lacy!"

Of course he was right. It was ludicrous to think that pagan idols had ever been real, or were still stalking the earth. But she could not deny that Elgin's health had suffered terribly since he undertook the Athenian project. Not to mention that the rewards he was virtually assured of for his service were not forthcoming. Why was his luck not better? Yet she had no rational way to discuss these things with him.

"I'm sorry, my darling. I had a fright. That is all. Of course you are doing the good and proper thing here."

"Now that you have seen the place, is it not all perfectly clear, Mary? Athens was once the seat of genius and liberty. What nation wears the mantle today, Mary, if not England? How many times must I explain myself?"

"I am in full agreement with you. You will never have to defend your actions again, at least not to me."

DIFFICULT TO DECIPHER ITS original plan," Elgin said as they walked the path above the Theater of Dionysus, looking down upon its ruins. The theater had been stripped of almost every bit of its famed marble. If any remained, it was obscured by centuries of piled debris. Dirt and rubbish sat in lumpy mounds covering what was once the proscenium. Feral cats snooped the heaps, but quickly grew discouraged in the heat and ran for shade. A brazen dragonfly persistently tried to strafe Mary, and she batted it away with her fan while she tried to maintain her balance on the uneven path.

The wrecked theater was yet one more discouraging sight.

"Where is the Odeion?" Mary asked the Greek guide.

He pointed to an insurmountable mass of rubble.

"Are you sure this is it?" Mary asked.

Yes, he replied, he was quite certain that the unsightly heap had once been the Odeion, the music hall Pericles built to house competitions, modeled after Xerxes' mammoth pavilion.

"But this was the location of the music contests and at times the law courts," Mary protested. "It was so important! Oh, and the theater, where Sophocles and Euripides debuted their magnificent plays!" Perhaps her pregnancy was contributing to her sentimental state, or perhaps she was weary of seeing irreparable ruins.

"They say that the buildings that used to sit on the hill above the theater toppled in an earthquake and rolled into the audience, covering the great hemisphere of theater seats," said Reverend Hunt. Indeed, but for a partial row of carved marble chairs that must have been for judges or dignitaries, the seats that once held the audience were entirely covered over. "It appears that the Odeion met with the same fate. Completely collapsed."

Using walking sticks for balance and to scare away the critters that ran wild in the ruins, they made their way down the hill to the few remaining chairs in the theater. The ornaments were in miraculously good condition, and the marble, a swirl of gray and cream.

"They're lovely," Mary said. "So like thrones."

"Can you identify the carvings, Mr. Hunt?" Elgin asked.

"Oh yes, quite. On this side, I believe we have Theseus or some other hero slaying an Amazon." They walked around to view the back. "These are olive wreaths, the symbols of victory. And here we have the shield of Athena. All symbols of Athenian democracy and freedom."

"Let us sit down for a moment," Elgin said. Mary sat in the most perfectly preserved chair. The marble was warmed by the sun and felt good on her tired back. Elgin sat next to her, and they both looked up to see the sole vestiges of the theater's grandeur, two imposing Corinthian columns flanking a headless colossal statue.

"That fortification is called the Wall of Cimon, after one of the heroes of the Persian Wars," Reverend Hunt explained.

"Oh yes, Cimon! The enemy of Pericles, and the brother of Elpinice," Mary said. "A good man, if I read my history correctly."

"Lady Elgin, I believe you know your Plutarch," Reverend Hunt said. "After having him ostracized, Pericles remembered Cimon's worth and lobbied for his return."

"Those splendid columns in front of Cimon's wall and the statue of Dionysus were added by the citizen Thrysallos, oh, some hundred years after the Age of Pericles."

"Poor Dionysus," Mary said. "No longer able to look out over his theater. Is there a god's face left in all of Athens?"

"Nonetheless, the body of the statue is a marvel," Elgin said, ignoring her sentimental comment. "Arrange for me to have it, Reverend Hunt."

"Of course," the reverend replied before qualifying his answer. "I will have to see if the Turkish officials will interpret that the firman extends to the artifacts on the slopes of the Acropolis, or whether they will try to cause us trouble. The Disdar is still quite upset over the cornice that fell from the temple."

"Perhaps a little gift will help," Elgin said. "Give whoever the Disdar reports to a good horse, and perhaps a cape and saddle to match. That should do it. Throw a few coins to the Disdar as well. He might like a bit of tobacco for his pipe."

"We are being drained of our funds!" Perhaps it was the heat again, or the overwhelming enormity of Elgin's project, or the money it was costing her, or simply the peak emotions that accompanied this stage of pregnancy, but Mary felt herself growing impatient. Since the disturbing vision on the altar, she was determined to support Elgin's efforts, and by God, she would see this project finished as soon as possible so that they could be done with it. She was anxious to go home—not to Constantinople, where she hoped they would soon go to pack up the embassy, but to London, and then on to Scotland, where they could embark on the life that Elgin had promised, the one in which they lived in beautifully renovated Broomhall, with her parents near and their children growing up in fresh country air.

"Listen here, Reverend Hunt," Mary said, "and give this message to Mr. Lusieri as well. If there is the slightest hint of opposition, tell the officials that I have procured an even more far-reaching firman from the Sultan. It is well known that the Grand Seigneur; his mother, the Valida; and the Capitan Pasha are all personal friends of mine. I doubt you will be opposed. Lord Elgin and I will have no further impediments to our plans."

"Yes, Lady Elgin," said Reverend Hunt.

"That's my Poll." Elgin had not used his pet name for her in months. "Let us be done with everything before it is too late. The French are trying to sabotage me. And if the Greeks do manage a revolt, the Turks will destroy every remnant of their civilization before they depart."

"Quite right, Lord Elgin," said Reverend Hunt, ever eager to agree with his employer. "Let us not leave one thing for them to deface."

"Not what remains of that glorious statue of Dionysus. Not the Caryatids," said Elgin. "And certainly not that beautiful chair my wife is sitting in. Have it removed and sent to the warehouse too. It will look splendid in our gardens at Broomhall."

"LORD BRUCE! You are a little torment. You must eat your vegetables if you want to be big and strong."

Mary sent her son to bed without the rest of his supper. He would eat nothing but meat, eschewing the array of greens that Dr. Scott prescribed to maintain good health. Elgin had convinced Mary to accompany him on a tour of the Peloponnese, leaving the children in Athens with their caretakers. In their absence, Little Mary had grown fatter and happier. But Bruce, left to the devices of Andrew, the manservant who treated the two-year-old as if he were a grown man and had already inherited a fiefdom, had grown unruly.

Still, he was her beautiful firstborn, and Mary had to turn away from his huge, questioning blue eyes whenever she had to correct him. She was on her own now in Athens. Elgin had devised a second tour for them, this time through central Greece, but she begged him to go alone. She could not leave the children again, nor could she face more time on an ass's back. She'd ridden those beasts through treacherous mountain paths, climbed on all fours through archeological sites, and slept long nights in miserable huts and tents. Now she was in her seventh month of pregnancy. Her body had become big and unwieldy, and her choking attacks had returned. Perhaps it was the encroaching summer heat, which seemed to agree so well with Elgin—though he was not with child—but Mary was suffering once more. Thankfully, Dr. Scott had an ample supply of opium, which calmed the nerves and seemed to dissipate the attacks. At least she could sleep.

"One line from you will bring me back, dearest," Elgin said to her upon his departure. He was once again at his manly best after so many weeks riding and climbing through mountains and rocks and being out of doors in the sunlight.

"I shan't call you back, no matter how much I want to," she said.

Besides, she had a secret mission that she thought would be easier if her husband was out of the way. The antiquities—tons and tons of them—were stacking up at the docks at Piraeus. They'd gotten everything down from the Acropolis. From the Parthenon alone had come five hundred twenty-four feet of the frieze, fifteen metopes, and seventeen statues from the east and west pediments, counting the gigantic horse's head. Four relief pieces had been taken from the Temple of Athena Nike. Many of the molds, casts, drawings, inventories, and measurements remained in Athens. The Caryatid still awaited shipment, as did the big marble chair from the Theater of Dionysus. The fate of the rest of the Erechtheion was in question until ships could be found to transport what had already been gathered. Now, the dozens of pieces that Elgin had collected, large and small, were coming in from the tour he had made of the Peloponnese, and he was on his way to Thebes to accumulate more.

But Lord Nelson continued to refuse their requests for even a single British warship to transport the acquisitions. And Lusieri was worried that the Turkish officials in charge of the Acropolis had started to panic at the steady stream of marbles leaving the citadel.

Mary feared that if Elgin failed in the Athens mission, he would turn back into the sickly, rheumatic man he had become toward the end of their days in Constantinople. She saw an opportunity to help him, and she set about putting her plan in motion.

Young Captain Hoste, the twenty-two-year-old skipper of the *Mutine,* whom Mary had entertained in Constantinople, arrived at

Athens with his ship and a life-threatening case of consumption. Mary took him into the house where she was living and gave him a comfortable upstairs room. The poor boy was sure that he was going to die, but Mary fed him a steady diet of milk and whey, and assured him that as he was a favorite of Lord Nelson and of such value to the British fleet, she would not let him perish so far from home. He'd been at sea for nine years without seeing his family, and Mary thought that loneliness might be aggravating his illness. She cared for him as if he were her child, though he was but two years younger than she. He improved under her care, and when he was well enough to go back to his vessel, she accompanied him to the docks and showed him the crates that needed a lift back to England.

Well, what could he say?

"You are headed straight to Malta, Captain," Mary said. "I checked with your lieutenant. There will be no enemies to encounter. You would be doing me a very great favor."

He looked upon his caretaker and vowed to take as many crates as would fit in the hold. "Nothing would please me more than to oblige you, madam. But it is a Greek holiday this week and no one will work. How might we get this massive cargo on board?"

But she had already thought of that problem and had solved it. "Not to worry, Captain. I have offered a little baksheesh to the dockworkers and they promise to do our bidding."

She went to Lusieri and demanded that he stop his work and have the men immediately fashion crates for everything that remained atop the Acropolis awaiting transportation to the docks.

"I have never seen anything like this, Lady Elgin," Lusieri said as she explained to him what he must do. "I am all astonishment at you."

As cautionary backups to her plan, she was also entertaining Captain Donnelly, whom she needed to take the family back to Turkey, and Captain Cracraft, his commanding officer, who sailed the *Anson*. Mary paid particular attention to Cracraft, though he was older than Hoste and Donnelly and wore a constantly crooked wig over his bald, shaved head. It came as no surprise to her when

Captain Cracraft offered to take whatever remained of their collection if there wasn't room on the *Narcissus* as a personal favor to Lady Elgin. And just in case there was yet more—for who could predict what Elgin would find?—she was entertaining other naval officers, like Mr. Dickey Johnstone and his mates, with bottles of wine and the last of her nice wheels of cheese. When the *Mentor* returned with William Hamilton, she would see if there was any space left in the hold for whatever Elgin was undoubtedly bringing in from his latest travels.

She felt utterly victorious. When all was done, she wrote to her husband:

Everything is down from the Acropolis, and we may now boldly bid defiance to our enemies! I have arranged shipment, and so neatly that it will not cost us a penny, much less the prohibitive amount that we feared!

As usual, female eloquence succeeded. This is all my doing, Elgin, and I feel proud. Do you love me the more for it?

And this last bit, she could not resist:

I am now satisfied of what I always thought—which is how much more women can do if they set about it than men. I will lay any bet that had you been here, you would not have got half as much on board as I have.

Her parents were in Paris, and she had arranged for them to meet with Sébastiani. How she would have loved to see her mother's face when having tea with such a French gallant. Mary wanted her parents' approval, or at least their good opinion, on a stint in Paris at the embassy for Elgin. England had sent word that Elgin would not be recalled from Constantinople, so that he was free to remain or to leave, an extraordinary position of freedom for a young ambassador to have.

When Mary took stock of her life, she was pleased. She was not yet twenty-five years old. She had a happy marriage and two beautiful, healthy babies, with another, God willing, on the way. She was young, energetic, and eager for more—more life, more experience, more adventure, more happiness. The smallpox vaccine, a cause so dear to her heart, had taken hold in Constantinople, and, according to all reports, Turkish children were now being inoculated. Elgin had performed brilliantly as ambassador, and at only thirty-four years old was undoubtedly at the very start of a long and important career. She was anxious to get this leg of the journey of their lives wrapped up along with the statues and things from the Acropolis and get on with the next epoch of what she was sure would be their wonderful life.

Greece,

June 15–29, 1802

THE HEAT WAS INTERMINABLE, even at night, and even by day at sea as the Elgins sailed aboard the *Narcissus* toward Marathon. Though she was sick to death of ruins, after all that she had studied about the historic battle that took place on the Marathon plain and the victory that had inspired the monuments on the Acropolis, Mary was excited to view the locale. She hoped that after so many centuries, something interesting remained.

She was not disappointed. As they sailed toward the site, the great tumulus under which the dead lay was plainly visible. Something about the mound of earth, covered now in grass, weeds, and scrub, sent a shudder up Mary's spine. She had been conversing with Captain Donnelly about the battle that had taken place on the fields there; once the party went ashore, he had his crew pitch a tent for her, surrounded with pillars that they had found scattered around the grounds. She felt like an ancient Athenian lady as she disembarked and walked toward the site.

William Hamilton, arriving on the *Mentor* from Alexandria, had arranged to meet up with the Elgins at the site. The *Mentor* had docked at Athens, where the vessel was loaded with as much of Elgin's collection as would fit in the hold, but the captain would not enlarge the hatchways to accommodate the bigger crates. This infuriated Elgin.

"We have accomplished so much," Mary said, patting his hand. He'd been so happy lately. She did not like that he was sent back into misery with this news. "We shall find a way. The captain has packed all but four large cases. Surely we can find transport for that!"

It was morning. The day was not yet miserably hot, and Mary wanted to enjoy being in the open fields. Mountains surrounded the empty plain. Trees—olive, cypress, and other evergreens—grew in sparse groups, huddled together as if against the sun.

Hamilton and Reverend Hunt were walking the battlefield, trying to mark the positions of the armies.

"The Athenians were outnumbered two to one," Hamilton said. "The Spartans had promised to send reinforcements, but they sent a messenger asking the Athenians to wait several days because, according to their gods, they could only wage war on a new moon, or some such nonsense."

"The Persians numbered twenty thousand," Hunt said. "The Greeks could have retreated, but instead chose to advance on the enemy. Imagine what guts it took."

"The Persians thought the advance by the Greeks was suicidal madness," Mary said. The men looked up. "That is what Herodotus wrote."

"Excellent recall, Lady Elgin," Hunt said, as if congratulating a child on its lessons.

"I imagine that these warriors were mere boys," she said as they looked at the mound of the dead. "Snatched from their homes, their tribes, their mothers' breasts."

"By my calculations, the Persians would have been buried over there, under those grassy mounds," Hunt said, pointing. "Their own commanders would have left them to be exposed to the vultures. That is what Darius did with the corpses of the warriors who disappointed him!"

"The Greeks were nobler than that," Hamilton said.

"Rather like English gentlemen," Elgin said.

"Wouldn't the burial mounds of the Persians be much larger, if so many had died?" Mary asked.

"An excellent question. The Persian bodies would have been burned to ashes and buried without a marker."

"They buried the Persians as a courtesy, Mary," Elgin said. "Obviously they intended the tumulus of the Athenian heroes to stand out and to last the ages, which it has."

They walked to the middle of the plain and began to circle the tumulus.

"About six hundred feet in diameter, I'll wager," Hunt said. "And forty feet in height, though we must allow that the centuries have eroded it. It must have been much higher two thousand years ago."

The men examined some big holes, which exposed dry, claylike soil and some scattered shards of pottery.

"The local people say that every night you can hear the sound of horses neighing and men fighting. They say it is not good luck to be here."

"Well, gentlemen," Elgin said, ignoring the comment and looking around, "shall we have a dig?"

"Why not?" Hunt said. "Someone's already had a go at the burial mound."

"I'll bet it was that French devil Fauvel," Elgin said. "He's preceded me everywhere. But I shall have the last word."

Out came the shovels.

"Is it wise to dig near a burial mound?" Mary asked. Mary had begun to feel sick at the idea of walking over the dead, much less excavating the area where they had rested since 490 BCE. But she did not want the men to make sport of her womanly superstitions, so she remained, watching them sink their shovels into the earth and turn it over.

After not too long, the men turned up some pottery shards, too small to allow them to speculate on the originals, and a mass of silver that had been rudely welded together. "Difficult to say what this might have been," Hunt said.

The small pieces of things were encouraging enough to make them dig deeper. Soon they began to uncover bones. Whether they were the bones of the warriors, they could not say.

"What else could they be?" Mary said.

She had to turn away. These were the bones of the noble heroes, without whom there might be no democracy in the world. If the Persians had won, conquering Greece, there would have been no Parthenon, no frieze, no pediment depicting the birth of Athena, no Erechtheion—none of the monuments that civilization had admired these thousands of years; none of the things that Elgin had been so passionately trying to preserve. There might have been no Greece at all, no Golden Age of Pericles, no grand western civilization. The entire world might have been different. Greece might have been ruled by Persia, as today it was ruled by the Ottomans.

All that these men, including her husband, had considered good and noble in the world was a result of the sacrifice of the men who lay buried under the mound. And here they were, digging away at the grave, tossing aside the very bones of the heroes.

The men soon tired of the excavation efforts, gave the shovels back to the servants to be packed away, and asked that lunch be served.

In the afternoon they rode to nearby Rhamnous, where Elgin wished to explore the ruins of the Temple of Nemesis.

"According to Pausanias, the Persians, confident of victory over the Athenians, arrived in Greece with a great column of marble from Paros, which they intended to use to make a trophy of their conquest," said Hunt. "After the battle, the Athenians seized it and brought it to Athens, where Pheidias sculpted a colossal statue of Nemesis. The Greeks built the temple to the goddess of vengeance near the battle site and placed the statue inside."

"A bit of well-earned gloating," Elgin said.

"According to Herodotus, the arrogant man commits follies because of his nature," Mary said. "And the gods punish him for his hubris by unleashing Nemesis. She is Divine Retribution."

The temple was situated to overlook the gulf of Évvoia, sparkling in the late afternoon sunlight. It was a glorious setting, Mary thought, conducive for the Athenians to revel in their revenge. Not much was left of the original compound but the remnants of its many-sided walls, the marble floors, a few bases of what had been the interior columns, and fragments that outlined the rooms. Weeds grew everywhere and the scrub covering the area was rampant, making it difficult to walk. But on a sunny day, it was not hard to imagine the sanctuary's former majesty.

"The colossal statue would have sat here, in the middle of the cella," Hunt explained. "Another great work by Pheidias lost!"

The men were digging in the dirt in the areas where the marble blocks had been removed, hoping to find fragments or small statues that might have escaped the temple robbers. It was the time in the late afternoon when Mary often experienced fatigue; it had been so with the first two pregnancies, and this one was no exception. She sat on the remnants of a column near the center of the room. A little pile of dirt partially covered the marble floor tiles, which looked as if they might have an image on them. She brushed the dirt aside with her feet, exposing the image of an animal with a large beak and huge paws like those of a lion. The beast was fastened to something, its body held taut by reins. There was something familiar about the creature. Mary slid off the column and got down on her knees, but felt a little dizzy. She put her back against the column for balance, and then tore at the dirt with her hands. Wiping it away, she thought she might be tearing her hands on the jagged relief of the tile, but she didn't care. She brushed all of the soil aside, using her nails to claw away the dirt lodged in the grooves of the relief.

A female figure, nude, with a slackened belly and a great expanse of wings, stood on a chariot drawn by two of the strange creatures. Held high above her head was a globe, presumably the earth. Beneath the wheels of her chariot was a man's head, his eyes wide with agony, his long tongue protruding from his mouth.

"Ah, there she is, Nemesis, the goddess of vengeance," said Reverend Hunt, looking over Mary's shoulder. "She is in her griffin-drawn chariot, taking revenge on some pathetic creature who insulted Athena. That is the wheel of fortune in her hand, Lady Elgin. She controls Destiny and punishes acts of hubris as well as insults to Athena."

Mary brushed more dirt aside, hoping to expose something that would change Hunt's analysis of the scene.

"Should you be on your knees, milady?" he asked.

But Mary did not answer him. She did not want to move, and she could not look up. The winged female and her two pitiless familiars were the same creatures that had attacked Elgin in her dream.

WHY DID A LOVING God condemn a full half of his flock to suffer so?

Mary knew that it was blasphemous to ask these questions, but as she lay on her bed trying to coax another child out of her exhausted body, she could not help but challenge God's wisdom. Why did she have to endure the torments of hell to bring these beautiful children into the world?

"Many ladies suffer," said the attending midwife. Mary had not seen this woman before, but she was English and had come highly recommended by the Russian ambassadress. "Only lucky ones give birth to living children, such as you have."

It was not what she wanted to hear at this moment when the searing pain overtook her again and she bit hard on the rag between her teeth so that she would not bite off her tongue. The midwife had probably put it into her mouth to shut her up. Mary wouldn't doubt it. She'd been screaming the entire day since hours before dawn when she awoke to use the chamber pot and the waters came rushing out of her. Now it was getting dark, and the attendants were lighting the lamps and shutting the curtains, blocking out the last of September's lazy rays of sunlight. Little Mary had come into the world much more easily than this, and Mary had hoped that each new baby would be easier still. But this agony recalled the birth of Bruce, during which she had prayed to die, just to put an end to the intolerable pain. Dr. Scott was on hand as usual, dosing her with laudanum and kind and encouraging words, but neither palliated the suffering.

She tried to think of all the lovely things that had happened on the journey back from Greece—the unsurpassed whiteness of the marble of a temple on the very tip of Cape Sunium as the light passed through the ruins; the nine daughters of the consul of Zea dancing the minuet to make Mary smile; the sweet water of the stream that ran next to the Cave of Pan and the fragrance of the oleanders and myrtles in bloom that grew wild; and the fountains and cascades in the orange groves at Paros. But the terrifying aspects of the voyage kept rushing in too, washing away the lovely memories—the storms at sea that sent her below, sickened; the violent attack upon their ship by pirates and the three hundred thundering rounds of cannon fire that Captain Donnelly sent flying over the sea, making the villains leap from their ship into the raging waves as the vessel sank. Mary had hugged her little ones in the cabin below as the captain took the pirates on board, tying them to one another and interrogating them as they protested their innocence.

What more could happen? she had wondered at that moment. She soon found out.

They docked at Smyrna, where the sailors claimed that the heat was worse than in India, and where a gloom hung over the city because mothers and fathers were losing all their little ones to the whooping cough. Mary watched the tiny corpses, covered in flowers, carried off to their premature graves while desperate parents called upon whatever God—Christian or Mohammedan—to help their young. The body count of the little ones continued to climb, which sickened her at heart if not in body, and she could take it no more. It seemed that the dank, narrow streets of Smyrna were specifically designed to contain the pestilence that was killing the children within it.

Elgin, on the other hand, was begging her to stay. "I must meet with General Stewart and Lord Blantyre and I am very unnerved by it," he said.

"But what if I go into labor here in this diseased place?"

"It is early yet, Mary," he answered calmly, and she knew that he was about to lay out one of his incontrovertible arguments.

"The doctor says the baby will come within weeks, Elgin. Babies are not necessarily on our schedules! It could be any day."

"Then better not to risk travel," he countered.

"Better to risk travel than to risk delivering a baby in the center of a whooping cough plague," she said.

That was the end of it. She made up her mind to leave Smyrna, but all the warships in the area including the *Narcissus* were being recalled to Alexandria immediately.

"Oh please, please can you not take us to the Dardanelles?" she begged Captain Donnelly. "We can make our way by land from there."

"Lady Elgin, you are the single person in the world for whom I would entertain disobeying a direct order of the British navy. But I find that though my affection and admiration for you run deep, I cannot risk the court-martial."

Desperate, she set off to travel back to Constantinople by land— without Elgin, who still had diplomatic business in the area—but with Reverend Hunt, Masterman, the children, and their entourage of secretaries, maids, and other embassy staff, to make the five-day journey in the dead heat of the summer. She had to rise at four in the morning every day to make arrangements for the party of fifty, causing Reverend Hunt to declare her "the best general was ever seen." They rode over rugged terrain until midday, when they had to pitch tents and wait out the heat. If she didn't lose the baby on that journey in the eighth month of her pregnancy through the miasma of roasting temperatures, humidity, and disease-ridden air, she would not lose it now.

"YOU HAVE TO PUSH now, Lady Elgin," said the midwife, holding Mary's knees apart.

"No!" Mary cried. "Pushing brings on the blood!" How vividly she remembered the sight of ladies carrying off blood-soaked rags while she, choking, pushed with all her might to deliver Bruce. She did not want that to happen again.

"No, Lady Elgin, pushing brings on the *baby*. Now be a good girl and listen to me."

She wished she'd hidden Elgin's knife, the one that the Capitan Pasha had just given him that he'd taken from Napoleon. It was set with diamonds and rubies and pearls and who knows what other treasures, but its blade was sharp. She would not hurt herself with it, nor her soon-to-be-born baby, but right now she'd like to stab the midwife who was coaxing her knees apart against her will and barking orders.

The pains were coming every two minutes. She was shaking and shivering, though it was very warm in the room. She could feel the pressure—unbearable, really—pushing at her from deep inside her bowels. She knew that it was time to push the baby out. But she could only think of the pain with Bruce, and all of her fears that she would die, leaving him a motherless child.

"Really, Lady Elgin, you are fighting your own body. When the contracting pain subsides, you must push the baby out. Just a few times should do."

"Come now, Lady Elgin. Mustn't disappoint the earl." If Dr. Scott thought that those were the correct words to say, he was mistaken. She wanted to hiss something horrible at him. It was the earl who was responsible for getting her into this dreadful condition. But even lost in this well of pain, she knew that that would be unseemly.

Oh, if only her mother were here. She missed her mother so much. She'd written her a forty-page letter, spotted with sweat, while she was on her miserable journey back to Constantinople. It was indecent that a girl should have to suffer these indignities of womanhood without a mother's wisdom and experience to guide her through. Mary would always be on hand to help her daughters through these trials, she was certain. Girls needed their mothers!

Perhaps she didn't have the strength and fortitude—the sheer *gumption*—to withstand the long years in the Foreign Service as the wife of a diplomat after all. Perhaps she should have turned down Elgin's offer of marriage and wed a good Scottish lad who would have enabled her to give birth to their children in her own bed with Mrs. Nisbet holding her hand, and the doctor of her childhood at her side, and her beloved aunts in the next room. No, she must withstand these terrors in this strange land where, outside the walls of the embassy, no one understood her language, much less knew or cared about the customs and rituals and the very people she held dear.

"Oh, dear God, help me!" she cried, fully aware that God might not be listening. How many futile prayers did women offer during childbirth?

She saw that a maidservant was taking away the dreaded blood-soaked rags. Mary's fears were warranted after all; she had started to bleed—perhaps, this time, to death.

"Now, now, all ladies lose a little blood at this stage," said the midwife. Dr. Scott poked his face over the woman's shoulder and nodded at her with owl-wide eyes, though at this point, so deep into a long day of labor, he had drunk so much brandy that Mary could only assume that he did not want to be sober when he had to tell Lord Elgin that his wife was dead.

The pressure down below was getting more urgent, and she could resist no longer. The contraction took her over, erasing all will to live. She bore it—what choice did a woman have?—and as it began to subside, she summoned her courage and pushed with all her might.

"There! A little head is crowning. I see some nice brown hair!" The midwife spoke as if she were singing a song to a child.

Mary breathed deeply as she felt the next swell of pain swallow her up. At this point, what did she have to lose? She hoped that the innocent inside her would survive and be taken care of nicely by her parents and by Elgin.

"That's it, Lady Elgin. Little Lord Bruce wants to see his little brother."

She would remember to have the Capitan Pasha execute this midwife, or at the very least have her tongue cut out so that she could not expose other women to her taunting.

She pushed again, hoping that the harridan was right and that the baby was a boy. If Mary died, Little Mary would be sandwiched between two protective brothers, whereas if it were a motherless girl, she would be a burden to her older sister all of her life.

That would not be fair. Oh please, dear God, she begged, let me live through this final labor and deliver us of a healthy baby, and then I will convince Elgin that it is Your will that we stop conceiving children. Surely the God who loves His children was too merciful to inflict this upon her again. It could not be normal that with a third baby, the labor would take the entire length of a day. Surely this was His sign to her that she must stop conceiving or she would lose her life and perhaps the lives of the children. She wondered if this pain was His punishment for the pleasures of the marriage bed, and if so, she wondered why it was only the women who had to suffer and die in the service of pleasure.

But a contraction took her over again, obliterating any thoughts from her head. She let it wrap her inside its authority, taking her into the depths of a pain that she should not be able to endure. But it finally began to release her from its clutches, and with all her might and will, she pushed as hard as she could, not caring if her internal organs fell out along with the infant. She pushed so hard that she felt as if that had indeed happened. When she stopped pushing, it seemed that ice was breaking out over her face and chest, chilling her to the bone. She was too weak to call for a blanket, too exhausted to care whether the breath she was gasping for was her very last.

"Well, if it isn't a big fat healthy girl!"

She caught a glimpse of the bloody creature as the doctor held it up. She worried that they were lying to her and it was dead. It looked like some pathetic war-ravaged beast. But as the midwife cut the cord, the baby issued its first cry—a howl, really, so strong that Mary was sure that the little creature would survive whether her mother did or not.

"Someone send a messenger to Lord Elgin." Mary heard Dr. Scott's order, and she closed her eyes, ready to let herself be carried away into peaceful darkness—to die or to sleep, she didn't care.

But the horrible midwife patted Mary's clammy face. "We're not done, Lady Elgin. Have you forgotten? It's only been a year since Little Mary was born! Remember what we must do next?" Damn this woman and her babyfied singsong voice. "One more push! One more and you're done."

Mary mustered whatever strength she had to get the afterbirth out of her body so that she could rest. With one more push, she was done with it. Now, at last, she would be able to sleep. But instead her body began to shake. It's so unfair, she thought. Her body was betraying her. She didn't remember shaking after the other two births. Was this something new and dangerous?

Dr. Scott looked concerned. Mary was shaking so hard that she could not make out what he was saying to the midwife, but she knew it was to do with the bleeding that followed the after-birth. She was hemorrhaging. Perhaps she would die after all. The inside of her froze with the thought, but the outside still shivered uncontrollably. What would happen? She tried to dismiss her fears. What would the Lord want her to believe? She had lived a good life, and her children would be well cared for. It was all one could ask of a mortal lifetime. Many were not as fortunate as she. For the multitudes, life was short and brutal. She, Mary Nisbet, Countess of Elgin, had lived a brief but privileged and exciting life. These were good thoughts to think as she felt the doctor push against the place inside her that seemed to be gushing obscene amounts of blood.

What did it matter? The soul was eternal. Was that not what Reverend Hunt was always saying in his sermons? She had made fun of his dry, uninteresting preaching, but now she hoped that everything that he had said was true. She was thinking these thoughts when she faded out of consciousness.

"MARY! MARY!"

Elgin was holding the swaddled baby—beautiful and serene but for the squashed nose that Mary knew would soon straighten out.

"She's a champion!" he said, handing the child off to the nurse. "Well done!"

Mary mustered a smile, though she felt nothing but exhaustion. Every inch of her body was weak. She tried to take in a deep breath, but found that she could manage only a shallow one. She attempted to lift her head, but found that she could not and rested it back against the pillow. She felt defeated. But even in this condition, she could not help but notice that something in her husband's words was forced, as if he didn't mean what he was saying about the baby.

"Elgin, tell me, is there something wrong with the baby? I want to know the truth."

"No, no. Harriet—if you still wish to call her that—is as healthy as the finest horse, the good doctor assures me. And you need your rest, but you will be quite fine too."

"I lost blood."

"Yes, but not a dangerous amount," he said, smiling weakly.

She must not have been asleep for very long. It was dark in the room, but Elgin was still wearing his street clothes. She could tell from his odor that he had just come in and had not yet washed and changed for dinner.

"Elgin, you cannot hide from me. I insist that you tell me what is wrong. I see it on your face and hear it in your voice. Is it the French? Has Bonaparte gone on the attack again?"

"No, dearest Poll." He stared at her as if making a decision about whether to spill his information. "Can you take a bit of news?"

"Of course, my dear. What could trouble me now, after what I have been through only to find myself alive and my daughter healthy?"

He took a letter out of his pocket and waved it at her. "I received word this afternoon. The *Mentor*, on its way to Malta, met with an accident off the coast of the island Kythera, situated at the south side of the Peloponnese. The captain and crew were saved, but all of our treasures from the Acropolis, and all of Lusieri's beautiful drawings and molds that were on board, are at the bottom of the sea."

The gods are ironical in nature. Where had she just read that? Was it in one of the ancient sources? Her body was too weak to register an outward response, and her mind could barely comprehend the magnitude of what he had just said, much less the consequences. Were all of their labors and investment lost? Had they just rid the world of some of its greatest treasures? More immediately, what would this do to her husband? And, as a result, to herself? What would her parents say? These thoughts raced through her fatigued mind as she tried to formulate the best thing to say to him, but the exhaustion soon won over her desire to be either useful and comforting or angry and admonishing.

"Elgin, dear, what are we going to do?" Mary said softly, trying to reach for his hand. But he saved her effort and took her cold hand into his warmer one.

"Why, we must recover them at any cost."

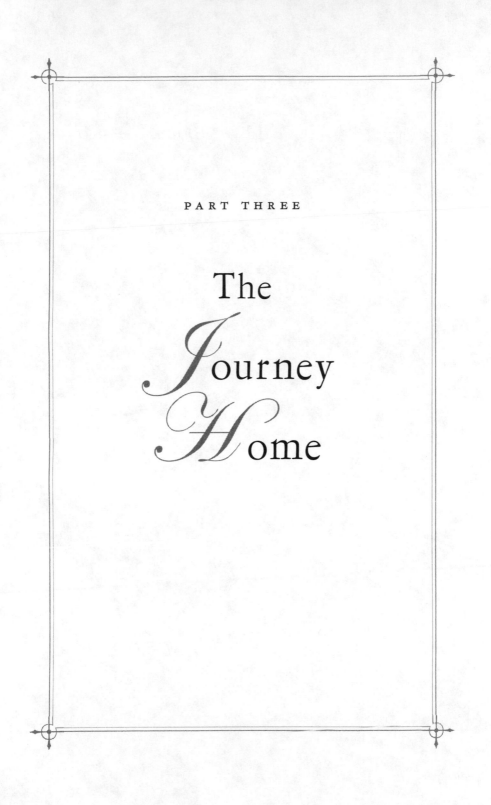

PART THREE

The

Journey

Home

Aboard the Diana,

Winter 1803

A S M A R Y V O M I T E D I N T O a bowl, Masterman held back her hair and sleeves.

"The only thing that changes is that more of my brats are added to the ships' rosters," Mary said wryly, once she collected her breath. "At least *they* do not get sick at sea."

"At least it's the rocky sea and not the stench of the vessel that brings on the illness this time," Masterman said.

The *Diana* was the most luxurious vessel they'd traveled in, and Mary counted her blessings. She had often said that she would have given anything to get home to Scotland; now that the journey was under way, she'd made up her mind not to complain.

"At least the captain is handsome and not a toothless dog of a pirate," Mary said, continuing their game.

"At least the crew is not dying of scurvy."

"At least I am not pregnant again."

"At the very least, *that!*"

"At least we are going *home.*"

"Aye, *home*." Masterman sighed. "Milady, I did not think we would get out of there alive."

Mary laughed, but toward the end of their tenure in Constantinople, she had shared the sentiment. In October, a woman who lived at an inn near the embassy died of plague, and then the fresh drumroll of death began. The Elgin children and the new baby had been inoculated against smallpox, but this new disease swept in from Egypt when sea communication between Alexandria and Constantinople recommenced, terrifying the helpless population and invading every class and quarter of the city.

Precautions were available, but they created tremendous work for Mary, who was trying to recover from childbirth in order to regather her strength and pack the contents of the embassy so that they could leave by the first of the year. Mary had the embassy fumigated every day. The thick smoke left a revolting acrid smell, but she was not going to take chances with her health and the health of her children. Bedsheets and linens were laundered daily, and anyone who ventured outdoors had to have himself and his clothing cleansed with vinegar. Once again, from her balcony, Mary watched the bodies carted away at midnight to be taken to Pera for burial. The plague spread rampantly to the Russian ships docked in the harbor, and just as the Elgins were to leave the country on the *Diana*, rumor spread that eighteen of that vessel's crew members had perished in the epidemic. Travel had to be postponed until Elgin could investigate the story, which turned out to be false. Nonetheless, the city was losing almost one hundred of its inhabitants every day to the grim reaper, and one could not be too careful.

On January 17 they were able to leave the city. Mary had bidden a tearful but happy goodbye to Hanum, for whom the Sultan had just built a magnificent palace, and to the Capitan Pasha, her own most loyal ally and admirer. She was thankful to be away from the disease that threatened her family. She would soon see her dear parents and plant her feet firmly on familiar soil.

But once they sailed through the Dardanelles, the waters became excessively stormy, and her fantasies of a swift voyage home were quickly replaced by the reality of sea travel.

"Mary, I've spoken with the captain," Elgin said. "We will make good use of the bad weather and stop at Athens."

"Must we?" she asked. She knew what he was up to.

"We must see to the safety of the marbles that remain at the docks at Piraeus," he replied.

"Are you not grateful that the captain of the *Mentor* refused to take them? Thank God we did not press the issue further. All the statues from the pediments, the tableaux of Athena's birth and the contest between Athena and Poseidon—the last remaining works of Pheidias—would all be at the bottom of the sea with the rest."

"I am not about to give a man credit for inadvertent good acts," he said.

"I do not think that the captain deserves the credit, but only God, who works in mysterious ways."

"In any case, these very stones of Pheidias, whose attributes you extol, are of immense value. We've yet to find shipment for them, or for the colossal statue of Dionysus from the theater, or the Caryatid, among others."

Yes, Mary thought, and thank the Lord that she was not paying for the recovery of those massive stones too. The rescue operation of the *Mentor* and its cargo, which had been going on at her expense since October, was costing a sad sum of money, and with limited results. The drawings were lost forever. The statuary and the frieze pieces had sunk straight down to the seabed, which the Greeks were measuring at ten fathoms. Elgin had wasted no time—or money—in trying to salvage the marbles. He authorized William Hamilton to make a staggering offer to the Greek divers for the recovery. With winter coming, he made a contract with Basilio Manachini from the isle of Spezzia, in which a vice-consul's nomination was dependent upon Manachini's success in overseeing the rescues. Dozens of divers were hired and paid extraordinary sums to work through the autumn months when the waters grew more frigid with each passing week.

Mary agreed to stop at Athens. It would be good to spend a few days off the boat. Bruce could play with the little Greek friends he had made over the summer, and Elgin would be pacified. But the storms made it impossible to dock. For two days they anchored in the Bay of Milo where the ship was battered by the winds—and Mary's stomach with it—until landing was safe.

Finally, they disembarked, settling at the same house where they had lived during the summer. At the first opportunity, Mary and Elgin went to Piraeus to inspect the stones that remained. Mary had long associated Athens with intolerable heat, so she was surprised to find herself wrapped in her warmest cape, with woolen hat and gloves against the wind, as they made their way to the docks. The winter weather was not temperate. The day was blustery and gray, and Mary pulled her wrap up high to cover her nose against the bitter sea breezes.

William Hamilton, who had been overseeing the operation since his return from Alexandria, joined them.

"Lord Elgin, I am able to greet you with good news in the extreme. I have negotiated with a sea captain whose vessel is being repaired at Piraeus. He has agreed to take the stones aboard his ship, the *Braakel*."

"Capital work, Hamilton," Elgin said. "You rival my wife in negotiating with sea captains, and you are operating without her more alluring charms." Elgin had become increasingly dismayed at navy officers' attentions to Mary, even though he and his project had benefited enormously by her ability to pry favors from them. At recent suppers and balls where the sea captains were present, Elgin had buzzed about, blocking the men's efforts to pay respects to Mary or to dance with her.

They arrived to find Greek dockworkers digging the immense statues out of the sand.

"I hoped that Your Lordship would not object to my methods," Hamilton said. Elsewhere on the beach, the workers raked aside piles of wet seaweed.

"This is a bizarre sort of excavation," Mary said.

"It is no excavation, madam. I had the workers bury the most valuable statues in the sand and cover them with seaweed. Lord El-gin's nemeses are many. As you know, the French are everywhere in Greece and Turkey again. The native Greeks despise the English now that Britain is an ally of the Ottomans, and we are afraid that they are in conspiracy with the French to steal the marbles. With Napoleon's spies lurking about, we thought it best to bury the trea-sures until we found transport."

Massive ropes on pulleys were wresting a gigantic torso of a god out of the beach; headless, it rose up through seaweed and wet sand, like some monstrous titan being born.

Hamilton paused to witness the bizarre sight before continuing: "Greek scholars in exile from around the world are writing letters of protest against the removal of the marbles. I have a letter from an Athenian artist in Venice who is putting about word that the Parthenon now looks like a noble lady who has been robbed of all her jewels."

"One simply cannot satisfy these Greeks," Elgin said. "In Peri-cles' day, they criticized him for decking out the city like some vain woman. Isn't that the line from Plutarch?"

"Yes, precisely." Mary nodded, pleased that he recognized her greater proficiency with the ancient texts.

"Now they are upset that the vain woman has lost her décor. If these Greeks wanted to protect their monuments, they should have revolted against the Turks centuries ago. I daresay the modern Greeks have nothing to do with their noble ancestors."

The winds picked up, kicking wet sand across the beach and into their faces. Mary turned her face away from the wind, her eyes stinging with the gritty invaders. She took out a handkerchief and wiped the grains away. Elgin, whose eyes had been inflaming again, cursed the winds. But the winds were indifferent; they howled and wailed and whimpered, carrying small drops of rain as they as-saulted the shore. Mary huddled against her husband.

Suddenly, one of the ropes around the torso of the god snapped and the statue fell against the beach with a hollow sound. It did not break. The Greek workmen, scarves wrapped around their faces to protect themselves from the wind, uttered muffled cries. They closed ranks, forming a hive of sorts, and talked nervously among themselves. Then they stood back, away from the fallen god, as if forming a wall of resistance.

Hamilton asked the foreman to interpret.

"They say that they heard the goddess Athena moaning as they tried to lift the god. It is a statue of Zeus, her father, and she does not want it removed from Athenian soil."

Elgin shook his head wildly. "That is absurd! I will not allow this work to be stopped over ignorant superstition, Hamilton. The captain of the *Braakel* is giving us our very last opportunity to ship the marbles back to England where they belong. I have been at tremendous expense these many years. I will not fail now, especially over this nonsense. Are these not good Orthodox men? Ask them if they dare to defy the Christian God by worshipping the pagan goddess."

The foreman conferred with his workers, who did not seem to be backing off from their positions. They stared defiantly at Elgin.

"The men say that they worship the One True God, but they also know the song of Athena, who still lives and who walks the streets of Athens, bemoaning the fate of her temples and her people. They heard her cries as they carried off the Caryatid lady from the temple on the Acropolis. They say that Athena would help the Greek people if she could, but her time is over. They do not wish to insult her. Those who do pay the price."

Mary had not disclosed to Elgin the identity of the monstrous woman and her creatures that had attacked him in the vision. Of course it was all plainly ridiculous to entertain, but the pieces of the puzzle kept forming in her mind, and she could not help but conclude that, with the sinking of the *Mentor*, and now this, Elgin was somehow being punished.

"Tell them they shall pay the price of not putting food on their tables," he said to the foreman, "and they and their families shall starve if these statues are not packed for shipping by nightfall. I can make absolutely certain that they will be denied employment for as long as they live."

The foreman reluctantly carried the message back to the men, who spat and grumbled, but eventually went back to work. Feeding the family trumps conviction every time, Mary thought, a basic law of the human condition. She was sure that Elgin, if faced with a similar ultimatum, would have made the same choice.

One lone man, older than the rest, with deep crevasses around his eyes and a skeletal physique, threw down his ropes and tools. Before he walked away, he looked at Elgin and spoke in furious Greek, punctuating the end of his words by spitting in the sand.

"What did that impertinent old man say?" Elgin asked as the others shuffled back to work, trying to salve their bruised pride by patting one another on the back.

Mary was surprised that he bothered to ask. But something in the man's demeanor, some certainty in his righteousness, must have impressed Elgin.

"He says to remind you that after they fought each other in a contest for the city, Athena and the god of the sea began to work together for the common good of all Greeks. That is why your ship hit the rocks in the storm and your marbles are at the bottom of the ocean."

I DON'T SEE A THING, do you?" Elgin scanned the gray waves through the spyglass. Giving up, he handed it to Mary.

"No, I don't either. Show us again, please," she said to Captain Maling, who took the glass from her and used it to point.

Mary followed his direction. In the distance, she saw the very tips of the masts of the sunken *Mentor* bobbing out of the choppy water. Mary had hoped that they would not have to pass the remains of the *Mentor* on their way to Malta, but it was unavoidable. She anticipated the gloom that would descend over Elgin if he saw the sunken vessel.

"There she is, all that remains of her," said the captain.

Mary saw that Elgin winced. Gathering himself, he said, "When the weather warms, we shall raise and repair her." He peered again through the glass.

"The cost of repairs would greatly exceed the value of the vessel,

Lord Elgin," said Captain Maling. "I'm afraid she'll never be sea-worthy again. Pity."

The recovery work had stopped; the winter waters, even in this southern part of the Aegean, were too frigid for the divers to withstand. The day was dark, and the shoreline was desolate. The craggy cliffs of Kythera hovered protectively over the bay.

Elgin looked miserable. He had had few happy moments since he'd heard the news of his sunken treasure. Now, as if in elegy to the ship, he took a letter out of his pocket and read the list of the ship's contents given him by Hamilton and now buried in the waters over which they sailed.

"The relief pieces from the Temple of Athena Nike. The ma-jority of the Parthenon frieze. Many statues and columns from the Parthenon and surrounding areas. An undetermined number of torsos gathered in excavations near the Parthenon." His spirits sank as he pronounced each lost item. Nonetheless, he continued.

"The two great slabs of the Parthenon frieze recovered in the walls of the Acropolis. Multiple porphyry columns, miscellaneous fragments and inscriptions from the Parthenon, and, worst of all, the marble gymnasiarch's chair given to your parents by the Arch-bishop of Athens."

This last truly upset Elgin, whether because it was one of the crowning jewels of the ancient world, or because ownership of it had kept Mr. Nisbet's money flowing into the Athens project. Elgin crumpled the letter and shoved it back into his pocket. Mary had been writing letters of misery and woe to her parents about the cost of the recovery, not certain that she would do Elgin's bidding and press them to contribute. She had tried to soften the blow of the ex-pense of recovery by writing to her father with the news that they had finally taken all the artists off the payroll save Lusieri, who re-mained in Athens to carry out Elgin's wishes. That would please Mr. Nisbet. But more stones were on the way to England, and yet more were making their way to the docks at Piraeus. To her dismay, Elgin instructed Lusieri to continue to excavate new sites. Where would all of this tonnage of stone be stored? She and Elgin had barely discussed what would happen to them once they had arrived, mainly because he deflected her efforts to be specific.

"I've arranged for my mother and your father to meet the shipments." That was all that Elgin wanted to offer on the topic. Did it mean that he had also arranged for those parties to accept financial responsibility for their storage and care?

She had received no letters of protest from her father, but it could be that the letters were not reaching her. She decided that she would not press the issue with Elgin. By spring—and it was just a few months away!—they would be happily ensconced in their true home, Broomhall, where, relaxed and reunited with their families, they could sit down with the Nisbets and make some significant and reasonable decisions.

Mary took a deep breath, comforted that her parents would be on hand during these discussions. She did not want to argue with Elgin's absolute conviction that no amount was too excessive to spend in the retrieval of the marbles. He had taken the sinking of the *Mentor* as a crushing defeat and a boon to his enemies, but had vowed that ultimately he would not be defeated, not by the French or Napoleon, not by jealous Englishmen or Greeks, and not by acts of nature. Mary admired his perseverance, but she did not want to commit an amount of money to the salvage operations that would prove detrimental to their financial health.

"Is all of this even possible?" she asked as they sailed beyond the sight of the broken masts of the *Mentor*.

"Is what possible?" Elgin asked.

"Oh, men diving into these freezing, tempestuous waters to haul up thousands of pounds of marble and stone? Admittedly, I do not know how these things are done, but the chances of success seem rather remote."

"These sorts of things are done all the time, Mary. We shall hire experts, nothing like that group of inveterate drunks who worked for us before." Elgin had come to despise the crew of workers originally hired for the task. "I assure you, my dear, that if the proper resources are committed, success is guaranteed."

For five long days, they were tossed about in contrary winds, until they reached the island of Crete, where the captain announced they would dock for five days to restock and to wait for more favorable winds. Mary went ashore every day just to feel solid ground beneath her feet. They drove into the town of Khania, where they encountered lepers living by the side of the road. Mary was shocked by the sheer numbers of them, humans looking as if they had been partly eaten by other creatures, and forbidden to enter the city, banished to live among those like themselves. She tried not to turn away from them; the poor things were undoubtedly shunned by every passing rider. Besides, she was accustomed to looking at her husband's half-eaten face, and felt she could afford the lepers a kind smile.

Favorable winds did not come. At last Captain Maling set sail in the best winter conditions one could hope for, though it took eight days of hard sailing to make the relatively short trip to Malta.

At once, though, Elgin's spirits rose. "Finally, we are returned to Christendom," he said, ebullient despite the news they'd just received.

The French had protected Malta until Lord Nelson defeated Napoleon in Egypt. At that time, the English took it over and made it a way station for travelers coming into and out of the East, owing to its excellent hospital run by the doctors of the Knights of St. John. The Elgins were ordered to submit to a twenty-day quarantine in Malta before they could proceed to the Continent. It was the same for everyone who had been in plague-infested territories in the East.

Still, Malta felt more familiar to them than any of the places they had been to in three years. The island was crammed with English people whom they knew from London who had also been traveling or stationed in foreign lands. It was not going to be an unpleasant quarantine. The Elgins would have to continue to live aboard the *Diana,* but were granted permission to walk about the grounds of the old Borghi Palace, a medieval fortress with beautiful gardens, though the French had blown the castle to bits. The Elgins pitched tents in the gardens, where they could take lunch in the fresh air, and on one special day, were able to sit on the grass and raise their faces to the sun and dream of the future. Bruce was playing swords with Andrew, using long, reedy sticks they'd found. Masterman was teaching Little Mary a nursery rhyme, and Harriet slept in her bassinet nearby. Mary sent up a quick but sincere prayer to thank God that after all the horrible days at sea, her children were a sturdy bunch, with rosy cheeks and excess energy when they might have been pale and feverish.

"I've written to my mother, Elgin," she said. "I want her to employ the best upholsterer she can find to turn the Turkish and Indian fabrics I've been collecting into curtains for the parlors and dining hall at Broomhall. I sent her sketches and samples. I'm having Mr. Poston paint the wallpaper to match the fabrics. Remember the Turkish orange and gold that you so liked?" During the stormy days at sea, Mary had distracted herself from the misery by mentally redecorating Broomhall with everything beautiful that they had collected while in the East.

"You did like the colors?" she continued. "Oh, Elgin, if you didn't, you should have spoken up before I ordered the wallpaper!" She slapped his hand playfully. But his mind seemed focused on some distant thought.

"I've decided that we must stop in Italy and France before we return to Broomhall," he said, not looking at her.

She did not think that she had heard him properly. Surely he was not proposing that they extend an already difficult trip?

"What do you mean, exactly?" she asked.

"The Continent is at peace, at least for the moment. I would like to go to Rome and see about the renovation of the marbles. Then I thought we'd have a stay in Paris. Lord Hawkesbury keeps making noise about appointing me to France."

She did not respond.

"I thought you wanted to go to Paris. Or was that simply an infatuation with that snake Sébastiani?"

"No, my dearest, of course I wanted to see Paris. But we have been so long at sea, and so very long away from home. Do you realize that I was able to live as mistress of Broomhall for one week before we left for the East? I am yearning for home. Think of the children. They have survived these long travels and the seas and the inclement weather and the pestilences! They must be settled in our home before our luck runs out."

Now it was his turn to be silent. He did not respond to her, but watched his little boy as he tumbled across the lawn with Andrew.

"Elgin? Everyone says that the peace with Napoleon is tentative at best. Do you really think we should expose the children to more danger? If war broke out again and we were in France or Italy, what would we do?"

"You are correct; the journey over land is too dangerous for them. We must send the children on by sea with Captain Maling. Your parents can meet them at Portsmouth."

"No!" The word sprang to her lips to counter the unthinkable. "I will not be separated from my children! Elgin, it is too cruel. Harriet is barely six months old! Aside from one visit, they do not know their grandparents. They will be frightened to be left at sea, and then with strangers!"

"They have their nurses, with whom they are most familiar," he said calmly.

"But I don't want to go. I want to go home." She realized that she sounded like a child, but she was so astonished at his suggestion, and so offended by the idea that she should leave the children, that she could formulate no coherent response.

"The fate of the marbles is at stake," he said. "Now, Mary, before you protest, do listen. We must go to Rome to meet with Antonio Canova. I've arranged it all by letter. I want his opinion on whether the marbles should be restored, or whether we should leave them in their present condition."

"Do you mean at the bottom of the sea?"

He did not smile. "We are the keepers of the world's greatest treasures. Does that mean nothing to you?"

"My children are my greatest treasures," she said. "Stone, no matter how old, means nothing to me when compared to their welfare."

"Mary, you must look beyond the immediate. It is only a matter of weeks. Please, do not be selfish. The marbles are of perpetual importance. We must be their servants."

SHE COULD NOT IDENTIFY the precise moment when she knew beyond a doubt that she was pregnant again. She might have known, but didn't, when she said goodbye to her children at Naples. The weather was bad in March, and Dr. Scott thought it best that the children not leave the boat to bid their parents farewell. Mary found a painter in Naples who specialized in costumes and portraits. She dragged him onto the ship so that he could make a likeness of her three that she could have with her in their absence. Little Mary could not understand why her mother was so upset. Mary tried to hide her tears, knowing that her sorrow frightened her two older children. Elgin had explained the entire situation to three-year-old Bruce, "man to man," and the little boy dared not shed one tear. He bravely kissed both his parents on the cheeks, and then retreated to Andrew, who got on his knees so that he could embrace the boy at his own level. The servant might be a drunk, Mary thought, but he took good care of her son's tender feelings. Mary covered Harriet's cheeks and toes with kisses, stopping only when she knew that one more would bring heaving tears.

She turned away from her three little ones and felt a blow to her stomach. She thought the breath was knocked out of her. She tried to recover so that the children would not be worried—so that the last sight of their mother was not of the broken-down creature she felt inside. No, one must be brave for one's children. She stood upright, though she could not manage a full breath, and forced a smile as she waved goodbye. Calitza raised Harriet's tiny hand, waving it back, and Mary thought that she would die.

Nor did she suspect that she was pregnant when she and Elgin were at the studio of Antonio Canova, discussing the fate of the marbles. The handsome sculptor from the Veneto had been in Rome for twenty-four years studying the works of antiquity, though he did not look very old to Mary, not even forty. Elgin and Mary had studied his two great marble works, *Theseus Vanquishing the*

Minotaur and *Three Graces*, which they found elegiac and balletic. Canova's opinion regarding the marbles was the most considered that Elgin could find.

"True, it is lamentable that the sculptures have suffered so much from time and barbarism," the artist said. "But they are the work of the ablest artists the world has ever seen. I am flattered that you would choose me to perform the restoration, but it would be a sacrilege for me or any man to presume to touch them with a chisel."

Mary had walked away, overtaken with nausea, but she attributed the feeling to relief that she would not be paying Canova the fortune he would have charged to work on the marbles. Later, in the bumpy carriage ride to Florence, as she was jostled and tossed, she began to get a clue as to her condition. But she did not speak up. She was still hoping that all her upset and fatigue was due to the bad roads, the miserable food served at country inns, and the exhaustion of travel.

On the way to France, they heard reports that Napoleon was ambushing English ships passing through French waters and confiscating the cargo. Mary was terrified for the children. There was no way to know if they had already passed through and reached Portsmouth.

"I do hope that my mother was *tempted* to travel to claim them," she said sarcastically. She had been in a foul temper, but as they were traveling with Reverend Hunt, she had tried to keep it to herself.

Elgin could plainly see how upset she was.

"Of course the children have arrived by now, Mary," Elgin said. "It's been three weeks since we left them at Naples. They are much better off where they are. We sent them by sea under the care of a first-rate captain and a superb doctor because it was safer than traveling by land. At any rate, the French are not looking for small Scottish children. But they undoubtedly know that the marbles are onboard an English warship. I just hope that they have not caught up with the *Braakel*."

Though she was annoyed that Elgin was, once again, more interested in the safety of his statues than of his children, she assured herself that his reasoning was correct. She had to try to console herself; it would probably be another month before she got word about the children's arrival.

Had it really been three weeks since she took leave of the children? That would mean that it had been eight weeks since she'd had her monthly. And that could mean only one thing. She pushed it to the back of her mind.

"Perhaps we should not cross the border into France," she said. She did not care if she had to use war with Napoleon as an excuse to terminate this tour. She wanted to be in their garden at Broomhall with the children running about and her mother sitting beside her, knitting, in a wicker chair beneath one of the big oak trees. This was especially so if she was indeed pregnant again.

"I have diplomatic immunity, Mary," Elgin said. "I have connections with *Talleyrand*." He pronounced the name of the man known as the Prince of Diplomats with assurance. Talleyrand was France's iconoclast—aristocrat, revolutionary, cripple, priest, and philosopher. He had miraculously survived the French Revolution to become Napoleon's prime minister. "His office has assured me of our safety. What more security do we require? The French abide by the international rules of war. They are not barbarians."

"But if all you and everyone else say about Napoleon's fury that you 'stole' the treasures of the Parthenon out from under him is true, should we risk traveling through France in these delicate times?"

"Lord Whitworth, the current ambassador to France, is still in Paris, dining with Napoleon and Talleyrand, attending the opera and who knows what else. Cavorting with dancing girls, for all I know. As long as all of that is true, I do not see how we will meet harm on French soil."

They arrived in Lyon on May 17 to find that the atmosphere had become thick with tension. The British refused to abandon their claim on Malta on the grounds that the French had not quit Germany and the Lowlands. Everyone believed that war was inevitable.

"We will shorten our stay in Paris," Elgin said. At this point, all citizens of Great Britain traveling in France were under scrutiny.

"We will not be allowed to turn around and go back to Italy. All we can do is persevere until we are home."

They made their way to Paris as quickly as possible. Elgin had written ahead to Talleyrand to reconfirm his security, and Talleyrand had responded, assuring Elgin that they might remain in France as long as they pleased, and that their passports out of the country would be available to them at any time.

They rode into Paris, arriving utterly exhausted at the Hotel Richelieu, an elegant facility done up in red granite, and intending to rest for forty-eight hours before collecting their passports and leaving for Calais. When they arrived at the hotel, they were met by Mrs. Dundas, a Scottish woman whom Mary knew from Edinburgh.

"Oh dear, oh dear, oh dear," the woman said, seeing Mary and Elgin and kissing both of them on the cheeks. "I should be happy to see you, but how can that be so in light of what is happening?"

"What is happening?" Elgin said.

The woman's eyes grew wide and her voice low. "Lord Elgin, how is it that you have not heard? Bonaparte, the blackguard, has declared war."

"Has he?" Elgin tried to sound calm.

"Yes. He *yelled* at Lord Whitworth! Called the English ambassador to France into his office, presumably on official matters, and yelled and screamed like a person who should be confined to an institution. Lord Whitworth stormed off. He's left France! I heard it all from the American ambassador."

"When did this occur?" Elgin asked.

"Just days ago," she answered. She leaned close to the Elgins, whispering. "Bonaparte sold half a continent called Louisiana to the Americans and pocketed fifteen million. He's going to use it to take us on again. The French have been gathering up all the English males between eighteen years of age and sixty. You are all to be *détenus* until Napoleon says otherwise. Oh, praise God that I am leaving town with the American ambassador!"

"*Détenus?*" Mary repeated. "Detainees?"

"One and the very same thing," said Mrs. Dundas.

Elgin tried to collect himself. It would not do for an ambassador of the highest order to receive news secondhand through a civilian friend of the American ambassador. But they had been traveling in a cramped carriage for days and had heard nothing of war's being declared. Mary clutched her husband's sleeve, but he quickly patted her hand.

"I am sorry to hear of your English friends, Mrs. Dundas, but as an ambassador, I have diplomatic immunity. Now, if you will excuse me, I must find Lady Elgin's rooms. She is exhausted from the long journey."

As they followed the French porter to their rooms, Mary could not breathe. "Elgin, is it possible that we are to be kept here?"

"Nonsense, my dear. We have the word of Talleyrand himself. Next to Napoleon, he is the first man in France."

Elgin's unflinching calm—and her own exhaustion—helped Mary to spend a peaceful night in the big feathery bed in their suite. She knew that they would soon have to pick up again and travel, and no matter what happened at sunrise, she would be better able to face the situation if she had a good night's sleep. She lay on her back next to Elgin. He dosed the both of them with laudanum, left with him by Dr. Scott, and he chased it with a large glass of French cognac. "May as well enjoy the local delights while we can," he said.

They lay together in the darkness, their feet touching. They had slept this way since their wedding night, and to Mary it was more comforting than all the Janissaries or militiamen or armed guards in the world.

THEY HAD NOT DRAWN the curtains, and in the morning, the sun came creeping into the room much sooner than Mary would have liked. As she was adjusting to the wakened state, she heard a rap at the door. Reluctantly, she opened her eyes. Elgin was already up and in his dressing gown. Before she could say a thing, he was out of the door to their bedroom. She got up quickly and stood at the door.

"What is it?" she heard Elgin say.

She heard a male voice, official in tone, emotionless and clipped. She hoped that her French was rusty and that she was misinterpreting what the man said. She peeked out of the room. The messenger was not of the hotel; he was in military uniform. Elgin did not respond to anything that was said, but shut the door. He turned toward his wife. His face was haggard. He did not sleep with his nose mask, and his poor stump sat pitifully on his face. His lovely blue eyes were encircled with black rings.

"Orders from Bonaparte, Mary," he said. "I must turn myself in today as a prisoner of war."

MARY IMMEDIATELY WROTE TO her mother to explain that though Elgin was officially a *prisonnier de guerre,* and they were detained in Paris, he was not jailed. On the contrary, detention in Paris had taken on a social air, what with fourteen hundred Englishmen prohibited from leaving the country, and a substantial portion of those detained in Paris staying at the hotel. Their passports were confiscated, and Elgin was closely watched. The Hotel Richelieu had a lovely garden, which Elgin walked in every day. He was free to move about Paris, but could not leave the city.

But Elgin would not leave the garden. His spirits sank lower and lower as the weeks passed and no news was given them about when they might leave France.

"I am not a man to live in an indeterminate situation, Mary," he said.

Their lives were full of uncertainty at present. The divers in Greece had been working since the spring, and it was difficult to get word on their progress. The French were patrolling Greece looking for Elgin's treasures, while many of the large pieces still awaited shipment in Piraeus.

"If you are worried over transportation, shouldn't you order Lusieri to stop excavating and collecting?" Mary asked. It was a matter of common sense to her. Why continue to collect if shipment was a problem? Now that England was engaged in full-scale war with

France again, Lord Nelson would surely not allow even one warship to shirk its military duties in the service of Elgin's obsession. How they would find transport for the rest of it, Mary did not know.

"You've never understood it, Mary! Never!"

He was short-tempered these days, especially with her, but she made it a point not to respond to angry pronouncements of this sort. She had done so much to help him, and even to this day was financing the salvage effort. She had persuaded her father to pay the customs on the cargo when it entered England—a fortune by the standards of any man—in addition to her parents' paying for the care of the three children. On June 14 she had received word from her mother that the children were safe in her care. Mary had parted with them in Naples in March, and it had been a torturous three months of worry over them.

"Mother says that your mother is so taken with the children that she has presented them to King George!" Mary said, waving the letter, trying to cheer her husband. "Even though she calls them 'little Greek savages who do not know proper English,' she is still the doting grandmother."

"I would expect nothing less," Elgin said. "Does her letter report anything on the arrival of the marbles? The entire collection could be in the hands of the French by now! It's intolerable not to know."

It was true that correspondence, never swift from country to country, was now blocked at every turn because of the war. The French officials opened correspondence that the Elgins tried to send, and also opened any letters they received. Mary had tried to send letters home with Lady Tweeddale, who had received rare permission to return home. But that good woman was stopped at the border and all her correspondence and papers confiscated before she was given permission to cross the Channel. Mrs. Dundas offered to carry letters back to England with her, but also cautioned that women travelers especially were searched for papers. Mary was despondent, yearning for news of the children. She kept the painting of them by the bedside and kissed it whenever she felt blue.

"They must think we abandoned them," she said.

"Nonsense. They are sensible children," Elgin said. "They are in good care. Neither your father nor Dr. Scott will allow them to harbor any such thoughts."

Mary started to host teas, hoping that the flow of English and Scottish guests would bring Elgin out of his mood. But they only seemed to deepen his gloom. The weather in Paris was miserable, raining every afternoon and thundering so loudly that Mary had a daily headache. One day, along with rare shockingly sunny weather, they received a surprise visit from Count Sébastiani, Mary's old admirer. Sébastiani had heard of their predicament and had come to offer his services.

"I will speak with Napoleon on your behalf, Lord Elgin," Sébastiani promised. "He is against you, as you know, but I have influence with him."

Elgin seemed happy to put aside his old rivalry with Sébastiani in order to gain his freedom. He even left Mary alone with the Frenchman while he took his garden stroll.

"I have dreamt of having you in Paris, Lady Elgin, but not under these circumstances. I am very sorry," Sébastiani said when they were alone.

"We appreciate your assistance, Count Sébastiani," Mary said as formally as possible, remembering their tawdry exchange in Constantinople, when he declared that she should become his mistress. He had not lost any of his good looks nor his charm. The man was dangerous.

"I have been filling the ears of Josephine with stories of your beauty and your intelligence. She is intrigued with you, Lady Elgin. I have been whispering these things to her so that she might speak with Napoleon about your husband."

"We are most grateful," Mary said, remembering how good he was at whispering in a woman's ear.

"Some evening, you must go to the opera. Josephine will see you, and I will attempt an introduction. I am sure she will help you. She is tenderhearted, and she likes me."

I'll bet she does, Mary thought, looking at his winsome eyes. Oh, he knew just how to look at a woman to make her feel desired. Time was only serving to help him perfect his art. But he was a true gentleman. He did not attempt to use Mary's situation to his advantage, but put himself entirely at her service, which made him all the more attractive.

Mary told Elgin of Sébastiani's plan, but he refused to go out in the evenings. Unwilling to sit at home alone every night and mourn their situation, Mary invited the exiles and detainees to their rooms to play whist. Word of the card parties spread quickly through Paris. All the English who were stuck in the city—and soon the entire international diplomatic community—were angling for invitations to Lady Elgin's card games. One night, a Scotsman who claimed to know Elgin from childhood showed up without invitation, carrying his own deck of cards.

"Lady Elgin's reputation for the game precedes her," he said as Elgin welcomed him. "I have brought my own deck for luck, hoping she doesn't clean me out of cash and take the family lands with it."

He turned to Mary, presenting her with the deck without introduction. She did not extend her hand—he was a Scot, after all, she knew by the unmistakable accent—but he reached for it and brought it to his lips. It did not seem an improper act, not coming from this man. She knew immediately that he was not being forward; rather, he appeared to be driven by an inner urgency. Elgin did not seem to like the gesture. "Too much time on the Continent, old boy," he said.

"*Au contraire*, Elgin, not nearly enough." He released Mary's hand. "Robert Ferguson of Raith, Lady Elgin. It's a miracle that this is the first time we have gazed upon each other. As a boy, I could have looked across the Firth from out of my windows at Raith and waved to you at Archerfield."

"A pleasure, Mr. Ferguson," she said. She knew the name, of course. "But I believe that you left Scotland when I was a girl."

"True. I had no taste for lethargic country life. I am a geologist by profession and a man of cities and travel by passion."

And a radical by reputation, she remembered from local gossip— always an embarrassment to his conservative father.

Robert Ferguson was tall, even taller than Elgin, and handsome, but not quite as handsome as Elgin had been before his disease ruined his looks. Ferguson's features were strong. Though he looked youthful, his hair had receded. His clothes, however, were impeccable—not quite dandified, Mary thought, but selected with great care.

"Are you still fond of speaking out against the Crown, Mr. Ferguson?" Elgin asked. He was smiling, but Mary detected an edge to his voice. Elgin did not take kindly to antimonarchist sentiments.

"At every opportunity. I did so last evening in Madame de Staël's parlor. Have you read her essays on the matter?" Robert too was smiling, but Mary thought he was matching Elgin's edge.

Mary shook her head politely in the negative, but Elgin was more responsive, almost laughing. "Really, Ferguson, you do push the limits!"

"Have you never been invited to Germaine de Staël's evenings?" Ferguson asked.

"Of course I was, as was every other bachelor in Paris, including, at one time, your Mr. Pitt," Elgin said. Elgin, a Tory, was strictly against Prime Minister Pitt, a Whig, an adversary of King George and, Elgin always said, an appeaser.

"What the devil, Elgin. We are all allies here against the common enemy, are we not?" The two men shook hands, slapping each other on the back. Politics receded as they began to talk of home. Ferguson remained after the other guests had departed, and he had a glass of port with Elgin.

Soon Ferguson had Elgin out of his rooms and into the streets of Paris, haunting the city's many dealers of fine arts and antiques. Within weeks, Elgin had accumulated a collection of fifty-four Old Masters paintings, along with furniture, chandeliers, candelabra, and urns and vases. He had also become acquainted with the wine merchants of the city, buying dozens of cases of their finest to bring home to the cellar at Broomhall. Pottery, porcelain, silver, and plate had all been accumulated in recent weeks.

"Mr. Ferguson has excellent taste," Mary said to Elgin one day. "But he certainly is free with his money." She was actually trying to caution Elgin about his own spending. Though they were not allowed to leave France, they were responsible for their own expenses while there. The hotel was very expensive, and Mary had proposed taking a house in Paris to try to cut costs. But now she worried that with all the sumptuous goods for sale in the city, no matter how much they saved, the costs of Elgin's shopping would outweigh their savings.

"Mr. Ferguson is terribly rich, Mary. I cannot believe that a man of his wealth, who is going to inherit the vast estate of Raith, goes on about reforming the government and the economic system. He's a gentleman, to be sure, but he is a bit unstable for a Scotsman, if you ask my opinion."

Ferguson had become an object of fascination for the two of them. Without an embassy to run, and without children to look after, they had little to do but talk about their new acquaintances. "How has the man remained a confirmed bachelor?" Mary asked.

"Oh, there are rumors. He had a scandalous affair with a married German countess, on whom he sired a son. The lad is supposed to be in boarding school somewhere."

"Is there no hope of them ever being together openly? Does the lady love her husband?" Mary asked.

"Not at all! But her father left his considerable fortune to her husband, so that she cannot leave him. She would be destitute, and she is not willing to be in that condition, though I daresay that Ferguson could provide for her."

"How tragic!" Mary said. It was the stuff of a romance novel.

"Oh, Ferguson is always falling for one woman or another. And the women always seem to reciprocate."

"He has a generous spirit," Mary said. Ferguson had deciphered Mary's tastes, and he had begun to bring her gifts—porcelain cups and other expensive trinkets, delightful French chocolates, and rocks of fascinating colors from his enormous collection of rare minerals. "And, for a political extremist, he has the ways of a gentleman."

"But his odd democratic leanings and his detestation of societal conventions prevent him from settling down. He doesn't want to live in Scotland and be 'lord of a great estate,' " Elgin said, imitating Ferguson's way of speaking. "Though what is wrong with that, I do not know. The mature man should wish for nothing else."

ELGIN'S HEALTH BEGAN to deteriorate in the damp Parisian climate. He thought it might be a good idea to go to Barèges in the southwest corner of France and take the mineral waters, famous for their curative powers. Mary appealed to her friend Sébastiani, who appealed to Napoleon. In a few weeks, permission was granted. Elgin was delighted, and proposed that Robert Ferguson join them.

At Barèges, Comte de Choiseul-Gouffier, a former French ambassador to the Ottomans, visited them. Elgin was amazed to receive a visit from this man who had been his enemy for years. Choiseul-Gouffier was one of the biggest collectors of antiquities in the world, and he had spent all of his years in the East attempting to lay his hands on the Parthenon's treasures. Here was the man who had sent his spies and agents to sabotage Elgin's efforts; who had made no secret of his envy; and who had vowed to capture the antiquities for Napoleon—who would purchase them for an enormous sum—and for France.

From the moment he entered the room, the man was practically in tears. "Lord Elgin, I have come to beg your assistance. Though we are enemies, we are both men of the same driving passion."

Choiseul-Gouffier explained that since the Revolution, when all noblemen's properties in France were confiscated, he had kept his own collection of marbles hidden in Greece. "I have spent my fortune—all the money of my family and my estates—to collect and maintain the antiquities. I am entirely bankrupt. Napoleon had agreed to purchase everything from me for the Louvre and to transport the objects here. But Lord Nelson attacked the warship that was carrying them and he has confiscated everything for England!"

Elgin explained that while he sympathized, he was a prisoner in France and could do little. But he did agree to send a letter to Lord

Nelson asking for the return of at least some of the pieces, which were still the personal property of the count.

"*Merci,* my lord," said Choiseul-Gouffier. The poor old gentleman was so moved by Elgin's offer that Mary thought he was going to kiss her husband's hand. "I am ruined! Utterly ruined. I spent my entire life collecting these magnificent treasures and now they are gone and I have nothing!"

"I will do what I can to help," Elgin assured him.

"I must warn you," the count said in parting. "Napoleon is furious at the loss. He will try to retaliate."

After the count left, Mary was silent. All she could think was that she and Elgin were destined to share the count's fate. Elgin had at last received word that some of the marbles had been recovered from the sea. Despite the superstitions of the divers, the men had overcome their fears, thanks to the huge sums they were being paid, and had developed a system for retrieval. Sixteen cases had been brought up, and the foreman at the site was optimistic about recovering all of the pieces of stone. But that did not solve the problem of the time and expense it would take to ship them to England, and to hide them from the French in the meanwhile. The drain on the Elgins' bank account was enormous. Their time in France too was costing them a fortune—in addition to the fortunes they had already spent keeping up the embassy in Turkey, gathering the marbles in Athens, and now salvaging those very same things.

Trouble had started to set in. Lusieri wrote from Athens to say that Elgin's banker in Constantinople was refusing to forward any more funds. In France they were able to operate entirely on credit, as men of rank normally were. But Mary knew that eventually the piper would have to be paid. Elgin continued to purchase enormous amounts of things all over the French countryside. His mood had improved from taking the waters for two hours every day, but Mary's had not. She missed her children more than ever.

Elgin too was agitated after the count left their company. "Did you hear him, Mary? If I am not vigilant, I will end up just like that. We must do what we can to hurry the rescue efforts."

"How might we do that?" she asked. She knew what he was

going to say: Hire yet more workers. Buy another vessel to transport the stones. Spend more money that we do not have. But she had another plan. She would take control of their finances from her seat of power back home.

"I've been in touch with Sébastiani," she said. "He thinks I might get my passport if I were to go back to Paris. He has convinced Napoleon that I must be allowed to return home to have the baby."

"But without me?"

"They will not release you, my darling. Our little ones have no mother," she said. "I want to have the baby at home, with Dr. Scott and my mother attending me. Oh please, Elgin! After the babe is born, we shall all return to Paris and be a family of detainees!"

"That is true, Mary. If you are in London, you can receive the shipments as they arrive. It will be easier for you to correspond with our agents from there too." Elgin was eagerly adapting to the idea, and Mary was delighted that it was not going to be a struggle to convince him.

"I will be happy to escort Lady Elgin back to Paris," Ferguson said that evening at dinner when they told him of the pending plans.

"That would be quite gallant, Mr. Ferguson," Mary said. He had seen all the art and furniture dealers in the area, taken the waters, and was bored, she knew.

"Will you not come back to Paris?" he asked Elgin.

"My health is as much improved here as it was in decline in the city," Elgin said. "Besides, if Napoleon does not see me, perhaps he will forget about me, and my papers for release will slip through."

WHEN MARY AND FERGUSON arrived in Paris, there was no passport awaiting her. Ferguson saw that she had started to tremble and offered to investigate. He left the hotel for hours, and when he returned, his face was ashen and his countenance severe.

"What is it, Mr. Ferguson? Must we write yet more letters begging for my papers?"

"You cannot leave, Lady Elgin. I have been to Napoleon's office, so what I am about to tell you is not rumor, but truth. Please do not panic. I am here to help you, and we shall find a way through this, I promise on my name and my honor.

"The English have arrested General Boyer, the commander of Napoleon's infantry," Ferguson said. "Napoleon has decided to seek the worst possible vengeance."

The world stopped at the sound of the word "vengeance." Vengeance. Mary closed her eyes, remembering the horrible sounds of her nightmare—the great wings of the mythic creatures flapping as they flew over her, and Elgin's cries for help as they engulfed him in their monstrous bodies.

"Lady Elgin!" Ferguson patted her hand sharply. "Stay with me, please. Lady Elgin? Mary!"

It was his use of her Christian name that jolted her out of her vision. She opened her eyes and looked at him. "Tell me," she said.

"He has arrested Lord Elgin and locked him in the fortress prison at Lourdes."

In the city of Paris,

Winter 1803–1804

ARE YOU SURE THEY won't hurt him?" Mary asked Ferguson. They had both moved to the Hotel Prince de Galles on the rue Saint-Honoré after the Hotel Richelieu had gone bankrupt, owing to the huge numbers of detainees forced to live on credit.

This evening, Robert had escorted Mary to an opera, and now she sank heavily into the big stuffed chair in the parlor while Robert helped himself to the last of Elgin's cognac. In the evenings, though the difficulties of the latter months of pregnancy were now taking root in her exhausted body, the two of them often attended opera and theater performances where they knew that either Napoleon or Talleyrand would appear. Through the connections of Ferguson and Sébastiani, Mary had now had conversations with the wife of the most powerful man in France and the wife of his feared second in command. The two women sympathized with Mary and promised to take up Elgin's cause with their husbands.

"I have discussed Lord Elgin's treatment with the highest officials and the most respected men in France," Ferguson said, dropping into the chair beside hers. She could see that he too was fatigued. Ferguson had been working round the clock to get information on Elgin's status as a prisoner. "I have used my connections in the scientific community to gain entrée to Napoleon's morning meetings. The most forward-thinking scientists and intellectuals in France gather there, and I made a personal appeal for fair and humane treatment for Lord Elgin."

"I cannot thank you enough," Mary said. "I know that my husband will be greatly moved when he finds out how much effort you have invested in his cause."

With Mary, Ferguson had written dozens of letters to every influential person within their spheres, which meant that they spent the larger part of each day writing letters pleading to anyone who may be able to help. Mary met regularly with Sébastiani, whom she begged to remind Napoleon that Elgin had petitioned for merciful treatment for the French prisoners in Constantinople, which they undoubtedly would not have received at the hands of the Turks without his influence.

"You needn't thank me," Ferguson said. "What would I not do for a fellow Scot and his beautiful wife?"

"Still, you have given me two months of unrelenting effort. We remain in your debt," Mary replied, embarrassed at the compliment. "I cannot bear it, Mr. Ferguson, when I think of the rumors of violence and torture occurring at the prison at Lourdes. It is said to be a foreboding, dank medieval fortress."

"I have spoken to men in French intelligence to find out what methods would be used to interrogate Elgin in prison. I have been assured that even at Lourdes, they would not use torture on a high-ranking man like Elgin. But they will interrogate. He will be kept awake all night long in an effort to get him to confess to one thing or another."

"But his health is weak as it is," Mary said. "You don't know Elgin. He is sicker than anyone realizes. He requires medication."

"These are the tactics of men at war," Ferguson said, pouring her a cognac. "Drink up, Lady Elgin. It won't hurt Lord Elgin if you minimize your own suffering at times. You must remember that your husband is Napoleon's most prominent prisoner. Mercy, in these times, is rare."

Weeks later, Ferguson found out that the French had tried to set up Elgin by passing him letters allegedly written by a fellow English inmate with whom he was supposed to be conspiring.

"But they say that Lord Elgin destroyed the papers unread, and told the messenger that he would do the same with any further 'secretive' correspondence," he reported to Mary. "Thus far, he's outsmarted them."

She put her hands over her big belly, hugging Elgin's unborn baby, and cried. Ferguson offered his handkerchief—did the man have any left? Mary wondered. She had cried so often in recent months in his presence.

"What with all his ailments, Elgin must be feeling near death, and yet he still had the presence of mind to outwit those conspiring against him," she said. She had entered the sleepless portion of the pregnancy, which she did not even mind, since she was sharing the sleep deprivation that her husband was being subjected to. What must he be going through? She was so tired these days that if accused of conspiracy, she would probably confess to anything. "I shall write to Lord Elgin's mother immediately and tell her how proud we must all be of her son."

AFTER MONTHS OF tireless efforts, Mary received two signals that their luck was about to change. She had managed to engage Napoleon in a round of personal correspondence, and today

his answer to her latest plea had arrived at the hotel with a minia-
ture painting of himself. Days later—no accident, she was sure—
she also obtained a personal audience with Talleyrand. She and
Ferguson had worked out a plan to ask the prime minister to exchange Elgin for General Boyer. To her immense surprise, Talleyrand agreed to the terms.

"Bonaparte sends his regrets to you, Madame Elgin," Talleyrand said. He was severe and polite, and something about him
encouraged Mary not to be as afraid of him as his reputation warranted. He was said to be the single greatest cold-blooded conniver
in French history, but here he was trying to help. "He cannot meet
with you personally, though he would like to do so. He would like
to help you, but his first allegiance is to the people of France. We
are at war, and Lord Elgin knows that he is simply being made to
play his part."

Mary left the meeting elated. She wrote to her mother, to Elgin's mother, and to Lord Hawkesbury, all of whom she begged
to petition the king. She was certain that in a matter of weeks,
Elgin would be free—just in time for him to witness the birth of
his fourth child.

Downing Street,

December 23, 1803

Dear Lady Elgin,

*I have received the honor of Your Ladyship's letter, which I lost no
time in laying before His Majesty. It would have given His Majesty the
most sincere satisfaction to have contributed to the release of Lord Elgin
by allowing his exchange for General Boyer, but a sense of duty renders
it impossible for him in any way to admit or sanction the principle of
exchanging persons made prisoners according to the laws of war, against*

any of his own subjects, who have been detained in France in violation of the Laws of Nations.

I assure Your Ladyship that it is with very deep regret that I find myself unable to render you the assistance you desire. I should have felt the greatest pleasure in contributing by any practicable means to Lord Elgin's release and to the deliverance of Your Ladyship from the very unpleasant situation in which you have been placed by arbitrary proceedings of the French government.

I have the honor to be, & etc. Lord Hawkesbury

WAS THE PLAIN TRUTH that Lord Hawkesbury did not consider Elgin as important a prisoner as General Boyer? Once again, Mary had to watch the British government demonstrate that it did not value Elgin, and she now regretted that she had written to him about the agreement.

Mary also received letters from both her mother and Elgin's mother, but the contents were not what Mary had expected—some modicum of praise and support for her relentless efforts on her husband's behalf, even while she was suffering the last stages of pregnancy. Mary's mother accused her of abandoning her children by remaining in Paris. Did the woman not understand that she was not free to leave? And the Dowager Lady Elgin had written a particularly accusatory letter asking Mary to stop attempting to be "the belle of the ball in Paris, unseemly for a pregnant mother of three." Did she not understand that Mary socialized in the evenings to try to make contact with important French people who could get Elgin released? Apparently, nasty-minded English detainees had written to Lady Elgin that they had seen Mary out "a bit too much in the company of a certain Scottish bachelor to maintain the propriety of a married woman." Worse, Elgin's mother passed the vicious rumors on to her sleep-deprived son, asking him to restrain his wife in the "city of excess." If the woman only knew that Mary had to force herself to bundle up and face the bitter Paris dampness every night when she would prefer to be resting at the hotel with a cup of hot tea. Yes, she enjoyed being in the company of people. But if she was seen out too much in the company of a certain bachelor, who had in recent months devoted himself to aiding the wife of his childhood acquaintance, it was only because she was diligent in trying to procure her husband's freedom.

Elgin did not see it that way. His letters took the tone of harsh recrimination:

I know Paris, Mary. I know its charms. I know that the city and its inhabitants, especially the roués who prey upon innocent women, can seduce one into unthinkable behavior. I have been informed that you are seen constantly at the opera. I don't begrudge your being amused, but God knows it is not natural. Your behavior hurts me more than my imprisonment. I am frankly appalled that you receive men alone and that you are seen in public with them. I am appalled that you make shopping expeditions with a man who is not your husband. I am shocked that you have allowed this man inside our intimate marital sphere. According to all reports, you are constantly in the company of men, and never in the company of other ladies. I cannot specify all that has come to my knowledge, but you would not believe the facts about your behavior that I have learned since we parted.

Mary was stung by his accusations and wrote back in kind. The only men whose company she kept were men who could see to Elgin's release. If he knew of the company of any ladies who could help his cause as much as Napoleon and Talleyrand, she encouraged him to send their names to her forthwith and she would cultivate their companionship.

As far as Mr. Ferguson, whom you suggest is engaging in improper behavior, never have you or I had such a devoted friend. He has become rather like a brother to this brotherless girl.

After months of her indefatigable effort, Napoleon agreed to release Elgin from the prison at Lourdes, with the caveat that he remain nearby in the town of Pau, where he would be under constant surveillance. Napoleon sent a note to Mary apologizing for keeping Elgin so far away, but he could not afford for him to be seen free and running about Paris.

Immediately, Elgin ordered Mary to come to him:

As Bonaparte has seen fit to keep me detained in the provinces, you must come to me immediately. It is the only seemly thing to do. I am now out of prison and able to live with my wife, albeit not in the capital. You must cease and desist your gallivanting about town, using the excuse that you are working on my behalf. I am no longer incarcerated. You have no more excuses to be seen with men not your husband enjoying the nocturnal pleasures of Paris.

"But I am about to give birth," she protested to Ferguson when he delivered Elgin's letter.

"He's not himself, Mary," Robert said. He had taken to addressing her informally when they were alone. "Once he recovers from the harsh conditions at the prison, he will come to his senses."

Still, she was hurt over her husband's mistrust. With Robert still in her rooms, she wrote back:

What a wonderful style of writing, Elgin, ordering me to leave Paris today or tomorrow. Do you not understand that I will be giving birth any day now? Do you really wish me to risk travel? Do you not care about me at all, Elgin? That is all I have to say. Your letter has hurt me too much in every respect to be able to answer it.

"Here, have this answer delivered to him," she said, folding up the letter and sealing it with her personal stamp. "I will not be commanded about, not even by my own husband. I will not risk the health of an unborn baby to satisfy the wishes of a grown man who is acting like one!"

Robert took the letter from her and smiled. He clicked his heels together and saluted her in the formal, Austrian style, a style with which he would be familiar after his time with his German mistress. "Yes, Lady Elgin. Command of me anything that you wish and I shall carry out the duty."

FROM THE MOMENT SHE saw him, bloodied and flailing about like one of the war-wounded, though the only battle in which he had engaged was with the birth canal, Mary knew that Baby William was different from the others.

The midwife held the baby close to Mary's face so that she might see him through the haze of her own misery, and through blurry eyes, she met the sight of the love of her life. "Why are you crying, little boy?" she asked aloud, smiling at him. "It is I who went through the pain."

When the midwife swept the infant away to clean and swaddle him, Mary felt a pang of loss and realized that she could not wait for him to be back in her arms, where she might stare at him for as long as she wanted.

"What is the date?" Mary asked the girl from the hotel who came in to bring fresh linens.

"It is the fifth of March, madame," the girl replied. "And the hour is eight and one half in the morning."

"Then throw the curtains back and let in the sun," Mary said. "Henceforth, this shall be my favorite day of the year."

She had been in labor the entire evening. Miss Gosling, her maid, had brought her a light supper at seven o'clock in the evening, and before Mary could take a bite of her potato, the water broke and the contractions began. It had been a horrible twelve hours, causing the same sort of agony and fear as the other births—at times even more so because she was alone, without husband or family, in this foreign country. But the little baby's knowing blue eyes made the ordeal worth it.

"I'm grateful that I survived your birth," she whispered to him when the midwife brought him back to her arms. "Because now I can get to know you. I am Mary, Countess of Elgin, from the village of Dirleton, by the Firth of Forth. It's a beautiful place that you shall grow to love. But you, my darling boy, are a Parisian by birth, and shall always have the same rakish handsomeness that you are displaying at this moment."

He was beautiful. All her babies were beautiful, but William had the bluest eyes, more like the waters of the Aegean in the summertime, and sheltered by astonishingly long black eyelashes. He was rosier, fattened in the womb by the rich sauces of Parisian cuisine. And unlike the others, he looked at her with the gravest curiosity and an acute intelligence, as if she were an object of fascination.

Though she was still too weak to get out of bed, when the wet nurse arrived to feed him, Mary refused to hand over the child. She had heard about an outbreak of smallpox in certain quarters of Paris. Who knew where this nurse had come from? Mary made the instantaneous decision that she would defy all convention and decorum and breast-feed this little miracle herself.

As soon as she could sit up in bed without pain in the lower regions, she sent off letters to her parents, to the Dowager Lady Elgin, and to Elgin himself, to whom she wrote that in addition to their three Turks, they now had a little frog. She did not mention too many of the tribulations of the birth, though she was as weakened and as ill as when Harriet was born, and she did not address any of the accusations he had made about her behavior prior to the baby's birth. Perhaps they might put that unpleasantness behind them. But she did announce the news that she would be her own baby's wet nurse.

This scandalous information brought anger and criticism from everyone, even the doctor who was attending her. Her parents and Elgin's mother were outraged that Mary would put herself in a servant's position. Have you lost all dignity? the parties wished to know. She wrote back to her mother:

Please do not scold me! You have scolded me enough. I have been alone and ill. I have worked toward no purpose but my husband's freedom. I have not seen my precious three Turks in twelve months. If I wish to preserve my baby's life by taking this precaution, I will do so!

But no reaction was more puzzling than Elgin's. He sent contradictory responses. Sometimes he chastised her severely for breastfeeding like a peasant woman, and sometimes he sent lurid missives about wanting to share her undoubtedly ample breasts with the baby. Thoughts of sex and its consequences at this juncture of her life made her completely ill. But she did not have to worry over that. Surely, with four healthy children, Elgin would not need to add to the count of his heirs. At the moment, though she was lonely and in exile and pining for her other three children, she was also free to pour her love for all of them into this small body of a boy. With his merry disposition, William was her sole consolation and the life of the household, the single factor existing between Mary and encroaching blue moods.

YOU MUST TAKE THE fresh air, Mary," Robert said, arriving at her door on a rare, sunny Monday morning. She'd been pale and weak since the birth, and all she could manage was lying in bed, nursing her baby and cooing over him. The rainy Parisian spring weather and her physical condition had precluded spending time any other way. "Alas, your time as a shut-in must come to an end. The air is fresh, the month is June, and the parks are beautiful. Let us take a stroll."

With little protest, Mary dressed herself and the baby. It was a pleasure to walk the parks of Paris with Robert, who identified the opulent blooms, trees, birds—even the insects—as they strolled. The walks became a daily ritual, weather permitting. Mary thought that Robert must be standing by his window at all times, for whenever the sun popped out from behind the rain clouds, he appeared within minutes. They continued this way quite pleasantly until, one morning, a French lady stopped them to take a look at the child and congratulated Robert on siring such a beautiful son. Both Mary and Robert were too embarrassed to correct her.

Days later, he announced his departure from Paris.

"Sir Joseph Banks has interceded with Bonaparte," he said. Sir

Joseph, in addition to being Ferguson's mentor, held the admiration of all men regardless of national allegiance. The famous botanist had explored the Pacific Islands with Captain Cook, was director of the Royal Botanic Gardens, had islands named after him, and was high on His Majesty's list of important minds. "I have my papers. I must take the opportunity to return home."

"Home?" Mary knew she was being selfish, but she could only think of how her own condition would be diminished if he left. "But Mr. Ferguson, you have not lived at home in many a year."

She hoped that he noticed that she had reverted to addressing him formally.

"I must go, Mary. You know that I must go, and I will not compromise you by explaining the reasons."

She continued to walk, but she was so shaken by his remark that she did not know how she was managing to keep moving. She was afraid to look at him, afraid to see his intense eyes staring at her, waiting for a response to what he had said. She wanted to speak, but did not want to address all that was implied in his comment.

"I have no right to ask you to remain here," she said. "You have made the impossible tolerable, and I hope that you will remember Lord Elgin's cause when you return to Scotland. He and I will be most appreciative of your efforts."

"I shall never neglect *your* cause, Lady Elgin," he said. He waved for a carriage. "Hotel Prince de Galles," he said to the driver, opening the door for Mary and then putting the baby and his stroller inside.

Mary could not bear the look of loss, of things that must remain unsaid, upon Robert's face. He had done so much for her. Where would she be, alone in this city with a baby and without him? What could she say to thank him without addressing the host of emotions—silent, yet visceral and real—that had passed between them?

"Forgive me for not seeing you all the way home." He raised her hand, which was now ice cold and trembling, and kissed it gently. "Adieu."

*The city of Athens,
in the ninth year of the
Thirty-Year Truce with Sparta*

PHEIDIAS' TRIAL WAS A sham, but the only way
to expose that fact and to prove his innocence was for him
to go through it. I did not attend. A woman's presence at a trial
is scandal enough, but my particular presence would not have
helped his cause. I was the harridan who had tempted him
into the evil of which he was accused—not the allegation in
the court, but the accusations in the marketplace, where public opinion flew across the square along with soot and smoke
from fires and other dark and bitter things. As people talked
more and more about that scandal, the crime became not his
but mine. It was I who wanted my face desecrating the temple
of Athena Parthenos, and I who used my witchery and my
influence with Perikles to bully the great artist in appeasing
my thirst for impious acts.

Under Perikles' orders, Pheidias and I continued to claim
that I had not posed for the statue of Athena. Our enemies tried
to press the charge, as well as the idea that Pheidias had painted

his own image and that of Perikles into the shield of Athena. An assembly of selected magistrates visited the Parthenon to see if any resemblances either to the two men or to me could be found, but they had to admit that whatever characteristics we shared with the images were vague at best. Deflated, Elpinike, the ringleader in this escapade, and her new accomplice, Alkibiades, began to look for other means of attack.

Rumors persisted that Pheidias had skimmed a goodly amount of gold off the statue while gilding it, until he was brought to trial on charges of embezzlement of public funds. The trial was being held today, and we had no idea what the outcome would be. The magistrates from the Office of Weights and Measures had ordered the statue stripped of its gold so that it could be weighed. Pheidias was worried that they might have been bribed to misrepresent the weight, and if that happened, then undoubtedly Perikles would also be blamed.

Elpinike had made that clear when we saw her at the games that took place on the day after our party. She had made a point of walking across the stadium so that she could pass in front of our seats. I had seen her coming, and had nudged Perikles with my foot, warning him that she was approaching us. I heard him take a deep, exasperated breath.

"You sent my brother into exile, Perikles, and I will not rest until you suffer the same fate," Elpinike said to him. He ignored her, but I thought that the force of anger coming from her was so strong that she would have to get some sort of vengeance before it dissipated.

But Perikles ignored my fears. "She is old. Perhaps she will simply die before she has the opportunity to get this revenge upon which she is so determined."

That was one month ago. I was so nervous over the outcome of Pheidias' trial that I decided to go to Diotima to get a reading on what the gods were thinking. While I had continued to deny any wrongdoing, I was still under constant attack for posing for the sculptor. After the horrible vision of Nemesis and her monsters taking revenge, I could not lose the idea

that Athena was on a mission to punish me for my crime. I was
also worried about Pheidias. Had he insulted the great goddess
by suggesting my mortal face as hers? Who knew what moved
the gods to anger? The best we could do was guess.

The sacrifice of a lamb for the purpose of reading its
entrails to determine outcomes and omens is costly. I sent a
slave into the marketplace to pawn some jewelry that I did not
like so much, hoping that she would not betray me to Perikles.
I bought cheaper varieties of fish for dinner and skimped on
other household expenses until I had enough coin to present
to the priestess. All of this took quite a bit of planning, with
Sokrates taking the role of intermediary between Diotima
and me.

I was grateful that Diotima preferred to perform the killing in private. I did not want to see a lamb slaughtered. Since
I'd discovered I was pregnant, my stomach was much weaker
than usual. I was eating nothing, but growing bigger by the
day. I did not think that I could withstand watching the flow
of blood.

When Sokrates and I arrived at the temple on the Akropolis, two young girls greeted us, ushering us to the small altar
where private sacrifices were performed. The room was dark.
A heady incense burned, spilling smoke into the air. I could
not identify the smell, but it threatened to upset my stomach.
There was no animal in sight, but a bowl of what looked like
organs was sitting on the altar. Diotima sat on big cushions,
eyes closed, as if in a trance. The girls pointed to chairs where
we were to sit, and then wordlessly backed out of the room.
We sat in front of the priestess for an uncomfortably long time,
waiting for her to open her eyes and acknowledge us. At last
she took in a deep breath and awakened from her state.

"Aspasia, I do not know why you are having dark visions of
Nemesis. Athena is not seeking vengeance upon you for any
misdeed."

Diotima has a way of phrasing things with utter certainty.
I wondered if she was so very sure of her interpretations or if

she wanted to do as little work as possible for her pay. I hated suspecting a priestess, but she spoke with the kind of emphatic finality rarely expressed by a woman.

"But why, then, would she send the goddess of vengeance to me in a dream?"

"I have no idea. The animal's intestines are as clear as a new-born baby's. The liver is pink. There are no tumors or growths. Perhaps your pregnancy is causing these strange visions. You would not be the first woman to experience this sort of thing. I was haunted by dark images when I was carrying my son."

"Were you married?"

"Oh yes, I was married to an Athenian citizen. I was fortunate enough to have come to Athens before Perikles passed his law that keeps you in the unmarried state. Otherwise I would not be a widow and high priestess of the goddess, but perhaps a courtesan like yourself. Strange, how human fate hangs by such precarious threads."

"She is never wrong, Aspasia," Sokrates said.

"How would you know, my friend, when you admit that you are certain of nothing but your uncertainty on all matters?" I had a bit of sarcasm in my voice. I did not want to attack my friend, and I certainly did not want to push Diotima into giving me an unfavorable reading, but I felt shortchanged.

"I am not certain of anything that I know," he answered. "I am certain of what Diotima knows, and of what her powers are." He did not like my questioning his teacher.

"So that is it?" I said to Diotima. "I will not be punished?"

"Not for any insult against the goddess. It is not foretold, and therefore it will not happen."

There was that officious tone again. Why did I dislike it so? Could it be that I was like the men who criticized me? Could it be that I did not like the voice of authority coming from a woman?

Diotima poured the entrails of the animal out on the altar. "Here, Aspasia, lest you doubt me. Look at the organs. Pink, clean, and clear."

I pretended to scrutinize them, but I was not allowing my eyes to focus. I knew that if I did, my stomach would be upset.

"There was one irregularity, but it has nothing to do with you."

I looked up at her. This was my reading. I had paid for it, and I wanted all information derived from it.

"I want to know all," I said.

"The animal had only one testicle. Strange."

"What can it mean?"

"It means that the goddess is going to punish someone in connection with defacing her temple and her images, but it is not you. It is a man."

"Pheidias?" I had been afraid of this—afraid he would take the brunt for both of us.

"No, no," she said dismissively. "He has already had commissioned a sacrifice and had his own reading. Did he not tell you? Perhaps he did not wish to frighten you. The sculptor only intended to honor the goddess with his temple and his statues. Athena is most pleased with him, and I believe that at this moment she is present at his trial, winning the jurors over to his side. A favorable outcome is foretold."

"Is it Perikles? Please do not tell me that something bad will happen to him."

"Perikles is in good stead with the goddess. She is pleased with his monumental marble homage to her on the Akropolis." I could tell that Diotima was getting bored with us, or perhaps just with me. That was the way with the wise ones, I noticed. Those of us who were younger and seeking their wisdom wore them out with our impatience and our ignorance.

"Can you not supply me with any more information that might put my mind at ease?"

"I do not know what to tell you, Aspasia. I am not in the business of giving comfort. Anyone who insults or defiles Athena will be punished. That is a guarantee. Look at what happened to the Persians after they destroyed her temple. She

is one to seek revenge, that is certain. She will dole out punishment, and she will send Nemesis to do the deed. I do not
know why she revealed this to you in a vision, but that was
her message, and you were correct to investigate whether it
was you or someone with whom you are connected. I do not
know why the goddess is being so secretive, but who are we
to question the ways of the gods? Someone—a man—will pay
for something egregious done to the goddess, but Athena has
chosen to keep hidden his identity. If I were you, I would let
the matter rest. Be happy that neither you nor your loved ones
have been singled out."

She stood up to signal that our time together was over. As
we were leaving the temple, I asked what had happened to the
sacrificial animal.

"The slaves are preparing it for my dinner," she said, before
showing us to the door and turning away.

I HAD NOT SEEN my sister or brother-in-law since the
day of the Grand Procession. After my reading with Diotima,
I was feeling optimistic, so I decided to stop by their house on
my way home. I dreaded coming face-to-face with Alkibiades
after he had burst in on our party, but I wanted to share with
my sister the news of my pregnancy. I had not told anyone yet,
not even Perikles, but it seemed appropriate for a motherless
girl to reveal her first pregnancy to the woman who raised her
before revealing it to the man who got her into the condition.
Besides, Alkibiades was undoubtedly at Pheidias' trial, snoop-
ing around with the rest of the old men.

After returning from exile, Alkibiades had moved into his
family's house in the city. The house was already occupied by
his mother, one of her widowed sisters, and several female relatives. Some of the younger women were also widowed, and
their children, along with Kalliope's children, ran through the
house at all times. I remembered how delighted I was when
Perikles moved me into his house. Though I had been insecure

as to my place in his life and whether he would keep me for a long time or throw me out after he tired of me, at least, at his quiet home, I could think, read, and write.

Two female slaves who remembered me from my tenure at the house were sprinkling buckets of ash from the kitchen fires around the garden plants to fertilize them when they saw me coming. "Please tell my sister that I have come to visit her," I said.

Both women hurried inside the courtyard as if it would take two to make known one guest. But that was the way with slaves, always trying to get out of work by any means possible, no matter how obvious. They did not return, nor did my sister. I waited, and then I heard the voice of Alkibiades announcing his hostile mood.

"Where is that woman? How does she have the audacity to come to this house where respectable women reside?" His bark was like that of an old dog who could no longer attack on behalf of his master, but was left only with the ability to growl. He had been in the middle of his meal and had not bothered to put down the bread he was eating. He came at me, shaking the loaf in his hand as if it were a weapon.

"You will not enter this house! You will not corrupt my wife as you have corrupted other ladies of Athens!"

Truly, he did look like one of the mangy old dogs that haunted the marketplace.

"What inane things are you going on about, Alkibiades?" I asked. "I have come to see my sister, whom I love. I know that she wishes to see me."

Kalliope came running out of the house, catching up with him and grabbing his arm, making him drop his bread.

"See what you've made me do?" he said to his wife. "Now pick it up and go inside. I will deal with Aspasia."

"But she is my sister!" Kalliope protested. More slaves and other women of the house came into the courtyard to see what the excitement was about.

"And you will never see her again!" he yelled, casting her

off of his sleeve. She stumbled backwards, and I was afraid he was going to hit her.

"Go inside, Kalliope," I said. "I will talk to Alkibiades. Everything will be fine."

She backed out of the courtyard, taking the other women with her. When they were inside, Alkibiades turned to me, snarling. "I saw what happened at your house with my own eyes. I always knew that you were a troublemaker, but I never dreamt that you would ply your trade to corrupt innocent women!"

"You must explain yourself. I have no idea what you are talking about. I shall have to assume that you have finally gone insane, a fate that I predicted for you long ago," I said. "Or is it merely old age?"

He wanted to strike out at me, but he dared not for fear of Perikles' wrath. That was all that stood between a black eye and me.

"You invited married women of Athens into your home to turn them into prostitutes for Perikles' pleasure. Pheidias siphoned off gold for him, and you procured women for him. All of Athens is being made to serve the needs of your lover. It is out of hand, and it is going to stop."

"How have you invented this story out of what you saw? No women were serving the needs of Perikles. He was in his own bed, fatigued with company," I said. Would I actually have to refute these fantasies of his in order to visit with my sister? "Come now, I have come to share some personal news with my sister. It is family business, women's business. You needn't concern yourself with our mundane conversation." I tried to placate him so that I could have a few words with Kalliope and go home, but he was not backing off.

"You gave the women bowls of wine to subvert their judgment, such as it is, and you staged acts of fornication to excite them so that you could send them into the bedroom to please your lover. Some of your guests witnessed everything. It's an outrage, but it does not surprise me that you cannot satisfy the man and that his need for other women grows. What man wants a woman like you? You will leave my premises and never return. We are done with you, Aspasia."

His accusation was so outlandish that I could not respond. I had to go home to try to sort it all out. Would he really keep my sister from me? For the rest of our lives? I did not want to irritate him further, because whenever I did, Kalliope paid the price, often with a bruise to her arm or her face. I would have to let his ire fade. Perhaps in a few weeks I would be able to see her again.

I did have one question for him, however. It baffled me that he was at home on this day.

"Why are you at home and not gloating at the trial of Pheidias?" I asked.

"The trial is over," he said, snickering. "It did not take long."

"And the outcome?"

"I won't give you the satisfaction, Aspasia. You will have to find out for yourself. But let me make myself clear. You won't get off so easy. You defiled the goddess. You defiled the women of Athens. You are a dirty, evil girl. If left to run loose, you will turn the world upside down. Never show your face at my house again."

SAYING GOODBYE TO PHEIDIAS, just one week after the outcome of his trial, was one of the saddest things I have ever had to do. Once the gold was removed from the statue of Athena and weighed, and the evidence presented at his trial, he was easily acquitted. His accusers tried to argue that he had mixed a worthless material in with the gold to make the weight appear to be correct.

"I fear that Pheidias will be brought to trial again, Aspasia," Perikles said, the evening after the verdict came in. "This is Athens, and Athenians love nothing more than exercising their right to prosecute fellow citizens. Pheidias' acquittal has done nothing to quiet the vicious tongues. I am sending him off to Olympia on a commission to make another ivory and gold colossal figure, this time of Zeus, at the temple. Of course we shall miss him, but it is for his own good."

Once Perikles made up his mind, there was little anyone could do to sway his thinking.

"And my good too?" I suspected that in sending Pheidias away, Perikles was trying to protect me. If someone succeeded in bringing him to a second trial, on charges of impiety, the name on everyone's lips would be mine.

"Yes, and yours too," he answered. "I have already discussed it with Pheidias. He is not overjoyed at leaving Athens, but he sees the wisdom in my decision, and he hopes that you will come to see him before he leaves."

The next day, I found Pheidias in his studio packing his personal belongings. He looked miserable.

"Are you not happy to have another lucrative commission, Pheidias?" I asked.

"I am being sent away from the very city I rebuilt," he said. "Ironic, no?

"But the gods are ironical in nature, Pheidias. We do not have to attend the theatrical presentations of the great tragedians to know that."

"The gods are mocking me, Aspasia," he said bitterly. "Look at Agoracritus!"

The young lover was surrounded by a dozen of Pheidias' students, showing them, with great animation, some drawings.

"He is so happy that I am leaving him with the commission of the statue of Nemesis at Rhamnous that he's not even paying attention to the fact that I am leaving him."

I looked at the drawings that Agoracritus was holding up for the students, who would become his assistants on the project. Everyone in Athens had awaited the statue of Nemesis that Pheidias was to create out of the huge piece of marble from Paros that the Persians had arrogantly brought with them to Marathon, intending to create from it their victory statue. The colossal figure of the goddess of vengeance was to go into the temple to Nemesis up the coast from the site of the battle.

"You cannot do everything," I said, knowing that his sorrow was less in leaving the commission than in learning that his lover wanted the commission more than he wanted Pheidias. But what did these older men expect when they took ambitious underlings into their beds?

"I must tell you," I added, "that the image he is holding does not resemble Nemesis." The drawing showed a serene female without any aberrations such as wings. She held an apple branch in her hand, and on her head sat a crown with a small deer and an image of Victory. "I have seen the goddess. She is fearsome, with great wings and a frightening countenance, and is always accompanied by her griffins, the monsters that do her bidding, as she does the bidding of Athena."

"Agoracritus, come here!" Pheidias called, glad to have a reason to talk to his lover. "Aspasia says that the image of Nemesis does not fit the goddess. Tell him, Aspasia, what your Nemesis looks like."

I explained to Agoracritus that I had had a vision of Nemesis, which no less an authority than Diotima assured me was accurate. I described it to him in detail, and he smiled. "Oh, I am certain that your description is correct, Aspasia. But no one wants to spend enormous amounts of public funds to make an ugly or frightening image."

"But why should anyone fear Nemesis when she looks as if she would not harm the smallest creature? How is that fitting?"

"So as not to insult the goddess herself, I will make a promise to you. Somewhere in the temple, I will make an image of her that is consistent with what you have described to me. I will even take the sketches for it to Diotima for her approval. But the grand statue of the goddess that will preside over her magnificent temple by the sea must reflect both the beauty of the building and the beauty of the landscape that surrounds it. Don't you agree, Pheidias?"

"Oh yes," he answered indifferently. "I see that you were actually listening to me when I talked."

Agoracritus kissed Pheidias on the cheek, must as one would do to an elderly grandmother, and went back to his new, adoring pupils.

"And thus the torch is passed," I said. "Come now, Pheidias, you enjoyed his assistance on your projects and his beautiful body in your bed. What more do you want? I never took you for a romantic."

He sighed. "I suppose you are correct. It's just that I do not want to leave Athens before my work is complete. My masterpiece is the Parthenon, but I have designed something much more radical, which I will not be able to see to completion."

He unrolled master drawings for a building, spreading them out on his table and weighting the edges with stones. "This temple will house the holiest of holy icons. It will replace the old temple to Athena Polias and shelter the olive-wood icon of the goddess. This level will house and protect the rock that Poseidon struck with his trident in the contest with Athena, as well as the sacred olive tree that she planted."

The temple was most unusual. It had many different levels and rooms, and was highly decorated with friezes and rosettes. I found it to be very beautiful, but in contrast to the solemn Parthenon, it appeared almost gaudy.

"Do you recognize this altar?" he asked.

"Should I?"

"Yes, dear, it is where you passed out at the sacrifice to Pandrosos. I am building this part of the temple around that sacred site. The temple is going to be dedicated as the Erechtheion, in honor of Erechtheus, the first earthborn Athenian. On the very site where the goddess fell from the sky, where she fought Poseidon, and where she flung the semen of Hephaestus to the ground to create the first citizen, the most beautiful and sacred of all temples shall be made. I only wish I would be here to see it."

"Surely you will visit it, Pheidias. You are going to Olympia, not Hades!"

"Yes, but it won't be the same as being present while it is being built," he said. "The design is my most intricate yet. I hope the architects will complete it to my specifications and not take the easy way out."

I pointed to a row of solemn-looking maidens that seemed to be holding up one of the porches. "Who are these ladies?"

"Ah, the Caryatids. My masterpieces. Are they not lovely? For me, they represent the burden of women, who must carry blame for so many things of which they are innocent." He put his hand on my face and kissed my forehead, and I started to cry. He was old enough to be my father, and I had been deprived of paternal love for so long.

"Please do not cry," he said. "I was doing so well stifling my emotions, only allowing myself to show a sour face, when I am feeling grave sorrow."

"May I give you some news that might put a smile on your face?"

"You may try," he said, his eyes still focused on his triumphant protégé, whose color seemed to rise as he gathered more of the staff around him. He would be a good leader of men, I thought, but I didn't have the heart to say it to his heartbroken mentor.

"I am going to have a baby," I said.

What is it about the prospect of new life that brings such gladness? For the first time today, Pheidias let a smile creep across his face. "How I would like to make a statue of you when you are hugely pregnant!"

"Scandalous, Pheidias. You are naturally impious, just like me. A statue of a harlot pregnant with a bastard! That would set the tongues wagging, wouldn't it?"

"What does the father say?" he asked.

"He doesn't know yet. I have been waiting for the right time to tell him."

"Aspasia, do not lose a minute," he said, hurrying me out of his studio. "Perikles should not be deprived of this happy news for one moment more."

. . .

IN TRUTH I WAS afraid to tell Perikles about the baby. He had gradually forgiven me for posing for the statue of the goddess, and we had even come to refer to it humorously as my "little indiscretion." He understood that neither Pheidias nor I had meant any harm, and he regarded the furor over the incident as ridiculous. Nonetheless, he had many enemies, and he did not like giving them cause to fan the flames of political opinion against him.

Still, the baby I was carrying was illegitimate; therefore, its fate was subject to the goodwill of its father. Like me, it would be completely dependent on Perikles' affection, which though it seemed consistent at least in this man, was subject to whimsy in most men. The baby and I had no legal status in Athens. That was the whole truth of the matter. I had to pray to the gods that Perikles' love for me would extend to the little creature blossoming inside me.

What if it were female? A thousand prayers begged that it was not. A father was more likely to accept a male bastard. The insults and terrible destinies that awaited a female child without a proper family or name were too numerous to entertain, though entertain them I did in my darkest hours.

Perikles was already at home when I arrived. "It is unusual to see you at home so early in the day," I said. Normally he was kept busy with his duties well into the evenings.

"Did you see Pheidias? How did you find him?" Perikles asked.

His voice had taken on a formal tone. I could see that he was upset with something.

"Why do you ask?"

"I am concerned that he does not agree with my judgment in sending him away," Perikles said. "That is all."

"He is more concerned over leaving that blond Adonis he calls his lover," I said. "He is quite sorrowful, of course, but he will survive. I am sure that the young apprentices of Olympia are as beautiful as Agoracritus."

"Oh, I am certain that they are even more handsome and manly," he said. "Our Pheidias will be well taken care of."

"Is something troubling you?" I asked. Lately, the Spartans had been making noise over some of the alliances that Perikles had forged in what they considered Spartan territory. This had been weighing heavily upon him.

His brow furrowed and the corners of his mouth turned downward. "I was hoping to spare you this news until I could get to the bottom of it."

"What are you talking about? You are not going away again, are you?"

I had had long months of loneliness and worry while he was away at war with the Samians. I did not want to experience that same despondency while pregnant. Besides, with Perikles away, who knows what insults I would be subject to as the pregnancy became more apparent?

"I heard a rumor today, and I hope that it is not true, though I fear that it is."

"And what rumor is that?" I had heard so many foul things about myself lately that I imagined myself immune to whatever Perikles had heard.

"They say that you are going to be prosecuted by that acerbic bastard, the comic poet Hermippus."

"Prosecuted! Me? On what charge?"

"As you know, he is a friend of both Elpinike and Alkibiades, as well as many other people who do not like my policies. The man has made a career out of lampooning me in his plays. He is charging you with impiety for defiling the goddess of the city, and for procuring innocent Athenian women for prostitution."

I did not know how to respond. I stood still, my arms limp at my side, like the cheap dolls for sale in the agora.

"We will survive this, Aspasia. I will not let them do this to you."

I put my head against his chest. I was too shocked and too weak to cry again. "But they already are doing it to me, my darling. They have been working toward it for a very long time, and it has already begun." Then I added: "Perikles, I am pregnant."

He did not reply but looked at me in astonishment.

"Do you have a response to this news?" I asked.

Still he did not reply. I cannot say it was hesitation. He had the same look I have seen many times when he was weighing the pros and cons of an argument presented to him, or when he was surprised with a request.

"You are not pleased?" I said, and heard my voice tremble.

"Of course I am pleased, Aspasia. It is a gift from the gods."

"Then why are you not rushing to hold me?" I cried out.

I couldn't move. I was hurt by his lack of emotion and his immobility at this holiest of times.

"You have shocked me, that is all. It is my second shock today."

I did not care if he was shocked. I wanted to hurt him back. "If it is a girl, should we keep it or should we expose it?"

"Are you out of your mind, Aspasia? Why did you say such a thing?"

"Because the fate of illegitimate girls is too grim! Because I do not want to put love and tenderness and care into a creature who could be turned out of her father's house and sent into a brothel!" I started to cry, at first softly, and then in great heaving sobs.

Perikles put his arms around me. "Would I allow that to happen to my own daughter?"

"No, not while you are alive, but if something happens to you, there is little recourse for either the child or me."

He led me to our private dining room, where he put me on the couch and covered me with a blanket, and sat with me for a long time, soothing me by patting my head as if I were a child. "I will not allow anything such as what worries you to happen either to you or to our child. Now, that is just silly, Aspasia, and not worthy of a rational thinker such as yourself."

"I am more human than rational," I said. But I was embarrassed over my outburst. Just as I was collecting myself, however, I remembered that I, a mother-to-be, was also going to be tried before a jury—an Athenian jury that already would have made its mind up about me, a concubine and a foreigner.

"We will find our way out of this, Aspasia. If my enemies think that they can hurt me by hurting you, they are mistaken."

"But you are sending Pheidias away!" I said. "What if they convict me, and you have to send me away?"

"If any attempt is made to separate us, I will play Achilles. I will let it be known that if the Spartans attack, I will sit in my tent until my woman is restored to me."

In the countries of France and England,

1805–1806

"YOU ARE MY DEAREST angel, and I beg your forgiveness," Elgin said when Mary met him at Pau with the baby. He took his son into his arms and gave him a kiss on each cheek and one on the forehead. "Robert Ferguson is the most loyal friend a man could hope to have. I must write to him and thank him for his kindnesses to you. I will do anything in my power to make up for my harsh judgments against you."

"You wounded me most severely," she said. "I had naught on my mind but obtaining your freedom."

"You cannot imagine the immense cruelty I was made to suffer, Mary. The French interrogators tried every trick to make me confess that I had come to France as a spy for the English." The lack of sleep for weeks at a time, the frigid conditions in the prison, the absence of medical care for his various ailments, and the horrible letters from his mother and the English gossips prying into their lives and reporting on Mary's social appearances in Paris in the company of other men—free men, handsome men, men who could care for her—had all conspired to make him lash out at his precious wife.

"I was not in my right mind, Mary. I hope you will acknowledge that and forgive me."

Mary was touched by his suffering and by the withdrawal of his recriminations against her. She tried to remember all of the things that she loved and admired in Elgin, but it was not easy for her to rekindle her affection. She could forgive his accusations, now that she knew the extent of the physical and emotional pain he had endured, but still, his angry words written in the long letters delivered for her to digest still rang in her head. In addition, he was simply not the same man. His health had deteriorated in prison, and his condition was worse than at any time before. Mary remembered reading the historian Thucydides' harrowing description of the symptoms of plague and she wondered if Elgin had contracted it at Lourdes. The signs were frighteningly similar: fever, thirst, bile, blisters, ulcerations, vile breath, and the stench of the sufferer unbearable. Along with these, heat in the head, inflammation of the eyes, coughing, spasms, pustules, and intense prickling sensations on the skin such that the sufferer cannot tolerate the feel of his own clothes or his bedsheets. Elgin had all the symptoms. Ashamed of her own suspicions, she asked the doctor if it was possible that Elgin had contracted plague. The doctor assured her that, though her husband was a very sick man, his illness had other causes.

His horrible physical condition repulsed her, but it also drew her sympathy. Away from his captors, Elgin resumed his gentlemanly behavior. They returned to Pau, where the healing waters had helped him so much in the past, and again he grew healthy. Despite his appearance, which was only one part of a man, she reminded herself, she let him into her bed again. It was not his fault that he suffered a disease that had left him disfigured. The man had been tortured, at least mentally tortured, by his captors, yet he had remained a true patriot. When Mary felt appalled by his appearance, she reminded herself of his noble character, and it made her feel more affectionate toward him.

It was a quiet time in their lives. Mary found herself feeling utterly domesticated. She learned how to embroider to keep herself occupied when William was napping. Otherwise, she was wrapped up in the baby's care. Though he was not yet one year old, she was convinced that he understood how to play poker. Thanks to her constant efforts to teach him the use of utensils, he could hold his own spoon. He had tipped over more than one bowl of soup in the learning, but Mary did not care. His every advance in development delighted her. But nothing was more pleasing to her than the private times between them, when she held him to her breast and watched him nourish himself. Why did women deny themselves this pleasure? Why must this intimacy between mother and child be given up to nurses, who may or may not give a fig about the welfare of the babies? If she had known how delightful it was to care for one's own baby in this way, she would have nursed every one of her children.

William seemed smarter than the others for all the attention she gave him. Well before he was a year old, he could toddle around the room and clap his hands to a song. His first word was not "Momma" or "Dada," but "Hark!" which he said with one finger up in the air like a statue.

"Watch this!" Mary said to Elgin one day when he came home from taking the waters.

William was sitting in his high chair with pieces of apple in front of him. Mary leaned over and looked her son in the eyes. "*Embrassez-moi, monsieur,*" she said. And in answer to her request, he pursed his little red lips for her to kiss.

"Is he not perfection?" she asked Elgin.

"If he were not my own son, I would be jealous of his ability to captivate the attentions of his mother!"

Elgin began to open the letters that had come that morning in the post. "Look at this, Mary," he said. "Oh my, he's already had his stationary redone!"

Elgin showed Mary the letter from the office of Napoleon, which now carried the stamp of a good-sized crown and read, "From the Emperor." Months earlier, Bonaparte—formerly a man of the Revolution—had conferred the title upon himself.

"I suppose that declaring himself Imperial Highness has made him feel more magnanimous," Elgin said. "He's finally given me permission to reenter Paris."

"Do you think this might be a step toward allowing us to go home?" She did not want to become excited, for Napoleon had disappointed them before. But the thought of being home was intoxicating. "Think on it, Elgin. Our Turks will be united with our frog!"

"It is too soon to tell whether he will give us back our passports. But it would be a brilliant time for us to return. The first shipment of marbles has arrived at the East India docks in London. I've written to my mother repeatedly about trying to stage an exhibition, which she seems to think would be a 'vulgar undertaking.' I must go take care of these things myself."

"Perhaps she is merely overwhelmed at the enormity of the undertaking," Mary said. She had no desire to defend her mother-in-law after the trouble that woman had caused between Elgin and herself by her letters full of vile gossip, but she also knew firsthand how overwhelming responsibility for Elgin's collection could be. "She is, after all, getting on in years."

"Yes, precisely. Another reason to take advantage of this unexpected opportunity Bonaparte has thrown our way and pack at once, before His Imperial Highness changes his whimsical mind."

IT DID NOT TAKE Mary long to close up the house at Pau. On William's first birthday, they were well on their way to Paris, traveling through Toulouse, Montpelier, and Nîmes. They arrived in the city on April 1. As soon as they got there, the baby developed a fever. Mary did not panic; William had had terrible fevers when he was cutting his teeth, worse than any of her other children, and he'd recovered. She nursed him carefully for a week, with an attending physician who never left their side. She thought he was improving, but one night he started to convulse, and suddenly he stopped breathing. Nothing that she or the doctor did could make him breathe again. It was midnight. She would always remember hearing the chimes from the cathedral as she held the still baby in her arms.

William—tiny, delicate, beautiful William—was gone, taken from her forever.

It had all happened so quickly. The sudden reversal of fortune had descended with such alacrity and fury, taking the only thing in the world that mattered. Everyone suffered heartache in this life, but why must one have so much of it at once, as if God were in a hurry to cram all the worst pains one is meant to suffer into as brief a period as possible? She was separated from her home, her beloved parents, and her other children, and now, this dear one was dead.

With William's life went Mary's will to live. "My soul doted on him from the moment he was born," she said to Elgin. "Why did he go away and leave me here?"

Elgin could do little to console her. He was wrapped in his own grief.

"I believe that bastard Napoleon had not yet done with heaping suffering upon me, Mary," Elgin said. "He has denied my request to go to Scotland to bury our boy. And yet he has granted permission for you to go." Elgin looked at her suspiciously. "Why would he give permission to you and not to me? Is he trying to put a rift between us?"

"Oh, dear God, are you accusing me of being in love with Napoleon?" she asked incredulously.

He did not answer, but squinted his eyes.

"Or him with me?"

"No, Mary, of course not," he said softly. "It's just that at this time, I do not think we should be separated."

"But who will see to William's funeral? Who will bring him home? Surely you do not want to bury our son in France?"

"Of course not. But I cannot leave, and I do not believe that I shall survive if we are separated," he said.

"What are we to do?" She could feel herself growing hysterical. She would not be able to go on if she could not take her baby home and bury him properly.

"We have just received a letter of condolence from Robert Ferguson," Elgin said. "He is here in Paris on personal business, Mary, and he is offering to help us in any way that he can."

Robert arrived at their temporary quarters not an hour after she and Elgin had sent him a note. Solemn and full of compassion, he offered to escort their child's body back to Scotland, where he would see to his burial in the Elgin family crypt.

Mary bought a little navy blue suit with woolen breeches for William to wear, embroidering his initials on the jacket herself. Why she was driven to do this, she did not know, but it seemed a task of the utmost importance. She let the Parisian officials prepare the small body, but she insisted on wrapping William in a blanket that her favorite aunt had given her as a gift when she was a child. Then she placed him carefully with her loving mother's arms in the tiny oak coffin in which he would be transported home. When Mary saw the private carriage that Robert had leased to take them to Morlaix, she panicked.

"He cannot be carried atop like cargo!" she said to Robert. Elgin tried to calm her, but it was no use. She sobbed until Robert spoke with the driver, arranging for the body to ride inside the carriage all the way to the ferry that would take them to Southampton. From there, Robert would travel with William's body by land to Edinburgh.

"I shall care for him as if he were my own son," Robert said to Mary. "I shall guard him with my life, and lay him safely to rest. You needn't worry over a thing."

NOT LONG AFTER MARY had to say goodbye to her baby, she discovered that she was pregnant again. She was numb to the news, barely reacting, whereas Elgin was joyful, trying to console her for the loss of William with the fact that they could produce more children. Mary did not say anything, but secretly she hoped that with the delivery of the next child, she would die.

Eight months into this unwanted pregnancy, relations between France and England deteriorated, and Napoleon once again ordered Elgin arrested and sent to prison.

Mary, frantic and vulnerable, assured Elgin that she would meet with Talleyrand again and beg for his release, but the night before he was taken away, he gave her the most surprising reply to her desire to be near him and to try, once again, to see him free.

"No, Mary, I have told you before, though last time you managed to elude me and remain on your own. You shall not wander about Paris again and say it is on my behalf. It is unseemly. Once again, you are obviously with child and belong in seclusion, not meeting with strange men, or allowing the same to escort you to theatrical presentations like some debutante!"

Mary was stunned to hear him bring up the old accusations. She had worked hard to wipe his unnecessary cruelty out of her mind so that she might love him again. If he started the same treatment now, she might not ever recover her feelings.

"We have been through all of this, Elgin. Why do you not believe that all I have done, I did for you, and do for you?"

"Be that as it may, Mary, I won't let things get out of hand again. Your behavior sets every tongue from Paris to London wagging. I cannot have it. This time, I am petitioning Napoleon and Talleyrand to issue a passport to you. You are going home at once."

"Elgin, look at me. You know what happens to me in these last weeks of my term. I cannot travel over the Channel in the winter weather. There will be storms. I will be so ill!"

"I have said the last I am going to say upon this issue," he replied. "You shall do as I say. I know what is best for you. Did you not beg me to let you return home when you were pregnant with William? You would be at home right now if Bonaparte had not denied you a passport."

She winced at the mention of her dead baby's name. How dare he invoke that angel to manipulate her emotions?

"I believe that you wanted to have the baby with your mother and Dr. Scott attending? Do you recall that?"

She glared at him. How would she control herself? How would she prevent her hands from reaching out and clawing his eyes? Whatever strange disease he contracted had taken his nose; she was in the mood to destroy the rest of his face.

"Now you shall have that wish," he went on. "After you have the baby, you can help my mother receive the cargo that is arriving at the docks. Someone must do an inventory. I think that you are the most appropriate person to complete this, don't you?"

Prior to this moment, she had been feeling a fury rising deep from within, a fury that she knew could kill or maim if she released it. But suddenly, it dissipated, and she felt utterly calm. This must be what it is like to be dead, she thought. Dead, and beyond care for the living.

"Whatever you say, Elgin. Though one can hardly expect this unborn child to survive the journey. But if it dies, so be it, as long as it prevents me from having more of your children."

STORMS BATTERED THE inn at Morlaix where Mary stayed for three days waiting for the skies to relent so that the *Elizabeth* could embark for England. She had never been so miserable. With nothing else to do, she spent the interminable hours writing letters to Elgin. She did not care what happened to him when he read them. The last time he was incarcerated, she suppressed any fears or unpleasantries in all of her missives to spare his feelings. She'd been so careful to sound cheery so that any good humor he had might be preserved in his difficult circumstances. Now she did not care about his state of mind. She wanted to make him as unhappy as he had made her. She was alone, and yet not at all in control of her circumstances. Others were charting the course of her existence, determining her destiny, regardless of her wishes, her feelings, her health, even her very life.

She was in hell.

But by the time the boat docked in England, the sun was breaking through the gray skies. It had been six years since she had touched British soil. Being tossed about on the boat without relief for a full twenty-four hours had left her exhausted. Yet when she walked off the boat she realized that she was neither angry nor numb, but anxious to move in whatever direction she would now take. She had exorcized her madness and left it somewhere in the stormy waters of the English Channel. She still had three living children and was expecting another child. There was ample reason to live, whatever Elgin decided to do; ample reason to live even if he died in prison.

She heard horses' hooves upon the brick road that ran alongside the quay. The sound, coupled with the idea of immediate further travel, made her nauseous.

"I cannot possibly bear the motion of a carriage," she said to Miss Gosling, the lone servant traveling with her. "Find us nice rooms in Portsmouth. I shall rest a day or two before moving on to London."

It would take weeks for her mother and father to arrive in London with the children. She should recuperate slowly from the trip. She wanted to be vibrant when she saw them, not the sallow and sickly feeble thing she felt right now. She sat on a bench waiting for Miss Gosling to return with news of lodging. Though it was late in October, England was breaking its own tradition of perpetual gloom and letting in the sunshine. She heard the carriage drivers shouting at the porters who were weighing down their vehicles with luggage. Girls hawked flowers, pigeon eggs, warm buns, chestnuts, and other items to passengers who were waiting to take the next boat. After so many years in foreign lands, Mary was startled to hear, ubiquitous, the sound of her native tongue. A man next to her inquired about a schedule, and apparently not receiving the answer he wanted, he sighed heavily and sat down next to her.

"Pity that the sun shines on a day of sadness," he said.

"Of what sadness do you speak, sir?" she asked, hoping that she had not met one of those travelers who seek a stranger to trap with their saga of woe.

"Have you not heard, madam? Days ago, off the coast of Spain, Admiral Nelson was mortally wounded fighting the French. It was a great victory for the navy, but a great loss for England."

"Oh dear, Lord Nelson. I had the privilege of knowing him," Mary said. She thought of her poor impression of the small, battle-scarred man, and of Emma Hamilton, who at this moment must be suffering terribly. Mary almost wished that she and Emma could have a good cry together. They'd both been through so much, and though Elgin was still alive, he could be as lost to her as Nelson now was to Emma. "But you say that England took the day?"

"They say that the battle will go a long way to defeating Bonaparte once and for all. If that is true, then all the world will be much improved, will it not?"

"Indeed, sir, it will," she said. She took a deep breath of the crisp autumnal air. It had been a long time since she had breathed so deeply. She was home. And both she and England were undoubtedly changed forever.

SHE HAD NOT SEEN them in two and a half years. The only child whose face she could firmly place in her memory was William, and each time she allowed that to happen, she remembered that he was gone. She was anxious to reunite with her three Turks, and not as some visitor in their lives, but as their mother and prime custodian. She would be eternally grateful to her parents for taking care of the children when she could not, but she did not want them to continue as the caretakers. Rather than live with her parents at their London residence at Portman Square, she took a house in London on Baker Street. She knew that they would disapprove of the arrangement, but she also hoped that, with a little time, they would be happy to have peace and quiet in their home.

As she waited nervously for the three children to arrive, she tried to anticipate every possible reaction on their part, even rejection. But when they saw her, they ran from their grandparents and rushed into her arms, clinging violently to her. Five, four, and three years of age, they were beautiful.

"You are elegant little angels," she said, hugging her daughters. It was impossible to decide which one had prettier eyes or fairer skin or thicker ringlets.

She wrote to Elgin daily, giving him as many details as possible on the children's growth and progress, especially that of Bruce, since he was the little hellion of the family, dropping his trousers and inviting no less illustrious a being than his grandfather to kiss his "backside" when the latter had smacked it for disobedience.

What say you to that specimen of elegance? Really, I never saw a finer boy than he is—healthy, manly, excessively active, and uncommonly tall and well made, just like his father.

She knew the things that would bring a smile to Elgin's face no matter what his present circumstances, and she concentrated on filling her daily missives with these morsels.

Mary is certainly remarkably clever and elegant. Her little head is beautifully shaped. Harriet is the mildest little beauty I ever beheld. "I am a bonny creature," she says, repeating what others tell her about herself. Our children are dear things and have excellent hearts and violent attachments for one another. They pray every day for their dear father's health and that they may soon be reunited with the one whom they know loves them dearly!

Elgin did not respond to these letters as Mary had hoped, but reprised his condemnation of her behavior:

Why have you taken a home separate from your parents in London? Why do you not live under your father's roof like a proper girl? Once again, I have been made privy to your comings and goings. It seems that you entertain gentlemen at your house on Baker Street, and that you are often seen in their company in the evenings.

She responded:

Honestly, Elgin, I am the mother of children and not a child. I will not be treated as one. My parents have taken responsibility for our children for two and a half years. Is that not enough? Do you know how noisy and active three children can be? Do my parents not deserve peace and quiet? Moreover, you never seem to acknowledge the suffering I endure in giving you these children. After all the worries to which I have subjected my parents, I do not wish to add this to the list. I do not want them to have to act as my chief nursemaids when I am recovering from the labor. As for my gallivanting at night and entertaining men in my home, I am once again doing so in yet another effort to obtain your release. I have worked like a slave for you, Elgin, and my efforts are only rewarded with your recriminations.

"Mary, dear, might I have a word?"

Mary put down her pen, happy to hear her father's voice. She welcomed the relief from these eternal missives to Elgin, answering his ridiculous fantasies of what her life was in London. Did he really imagine that, with three small children whom she had not seen in long years to get to know again, a husband whom she must try to get out of prison, and an enormous belly holding another baby due in weeks, she was flitting around the social scene like a debutante?

"I've been round to see the bankers," Mr. Nisbet said. This was rarely an introduction to good news. "As you know, Elgin seriously misrepresented his income to me when he asked for your hand. It is about ten percent of what he told me."

"I know, Father, but we have been over this. There is nothing I can do about a falsehood told by an eager beau so many years ago! He was desperate to marry me before he left for Turkey."

With all of her problems, she did not want to return to the same territory they had trampled time and again.

"That is not my point. We should be grateful that he represented himself as amply able to take care of you, Mary. Otherwise, I would have given him much more control over your money. As it is, the rumors of his spending that predated your marriage, combined with the seven-thousand-pound annual income that he claimed, caused me to guard your own fortune. And that, my dear, is why you have a fortune left. Elgin has spent everything of his own. The bankers have been selling his stocks to pay the creditors, but there is nothing left. Elgin's complete worth is down to a few hundred pounds, and he owes tens of thousands."

· · ·

THE PORTER OPENED THE door for Mary, and she walked into the bank.

Mr. Coutts, Elgin's banker, wasted little time on the formalities. "Lady Elgin, we are acting as magicians here, using one debt to pay another. It has to end."

Mary scoured the ledger books listing the debts that Elgin had accumulated. His purchases in France were far more extensive and expensive than she'd realized. He had commissioned furniture makers and other artisans to create whole suites to fill Broomhall. He had collected paintings and tapestries to cover its many walls. And he had yet to pay for any of it.

But these sorts of debts were trifling compared to the expenses of running the embassy in Constantinople. The British government still refused to reimburse them for one cent spent over their meager annual allowance, which had covered very little of the cost. Mary and Elgin had generously purchased and shipped food and munitions to the troops in Egypt, certain that they would be repaid for being patriots at a crucial time in their country's history. But despite Mary's appeals to the most powerful people she knew to intercede, the government's position remained unchanged. Mary explained all of this to Mr. Coutts.

"There is nothing to be done about that," said the banker. "Lord Elgin's decisions have left him many thousands of pounds in debt, and I see no hope of assistance from His Majesty's government. That is unfortunate.

"But there is a larger issue at the moment. I understand that it was always the strict position of Parliament that Lord Elgin himself would fund the artistic endeavors in Greece. It was always going to be an expensive venture, but once the project turned from making drawings and molds to excavation and acquisition, costs mounted exponentially. Are you aware of the ultimate costs of the salvage efforts? Those alone surpass all the other debts combined.

"Now the marbles are arriving, and the import duties must be paid. The sums are enormous," he said, showing her the invoices from the docks. "There is simply not a dime with which to pay. As you are undoubtedly aware, Lord Elgin has asked William Hamilton to find a suitable space so that he might make an exhibition of the marbles. Mr. Hamilton has suggested Buckingham House, or perhaps Gloucester House."

She was not aware of this fact at all. She had thought that Elgin's mother was arranging for storage. The two houses mentioned were among the most palatial in London. What was Elgin thinking? Where did he think the money would come from to pay for these things?

"Lord Elgin informed Mr. Hamilton that you would be paying for the leasing of the exhibit space out of your private funds," Mr. Coutts went on. "Is that correct, Lady Elgin?" The man peered at Mary over his monocle.

"No, that is not correct. My husband is mistaken," she said, embarrassed, for she had disclosed a disagreement between husband and wife, something that should always remain private. That was the way that she had been raised. But her parents did not make these sorts of extravagant decisions independently. As the government thought that Elgin was a purse it could tap, so Elgin thought the same of his wife.

"I see. I did speak to your father about it, as Lord Elgin also suggested that he might pay for the exhibition, but he too declined, citing the fortune he had already spent on the acquisition," Coutts replied.

"There is another matter," he said. "Reverend Hunt called upon us yesterday. He has not been reimbursed for any expenses he incurred on Lord Elgin's behalf. He is quite destitute. He presented a great ledger of things, all of his travels throughout Greece and Turkey. But he had no promissory notes. Even if he did, I'm afraid there is not a dime with which to pay him. He has quit Lord Elgin's service and is going to work for the Duke of Buckingham. I advised the fellow to make a formal, written contract."

Elgin had not had a more loyal, enthusiastic, and knowledgeable member of his staff than Hunt. After Mary settled all of the debts, she would see what she might do for poor Mr. Hunt. In the meanwhile, she had just a few weeks before she would be confined. After the birth—she knew from experience—she would have no energy for these matters. She must see to their finances before it was too late.

"Do not worry, Mr. Coutts, I will see to it all. My husband and I received quite a treasure trove of gifts in Constantinople. I do hate to part with such lovely things, but I am quite certain that they can be sold for ample money to cover what my husband owes."

"There is only one piece of news that gives us hope that the debts will stop mounting," Mr. Coutts said. "We have received letters from Mr. Lusieri asking for his salary. We cannot pay him, of course."

"That is not good news, Mr. Coutts," Mary said. The situation was embarrassing enough. Was he going to heap more humiliation than necessary upon her?

"No, Lady Elgin. The good news is that the new British ambassador to the Porte has reneged all permissions for Mr. Lusieri to operate in Athens. He's been kicked off the Acropolis. There will be no more marbles other than what has already been collected and shipped appearing at customs."

IT ALL WENT UP for sale—the irreplaceable diamonds and jewels given her by the Capitan Pasha and the Sultan; the furs and ivory; the china, silver, and crystal; the precious ebony boxes; the exquisite glass. All gone, all lost. Mary had barely a shawl left to remember her days in the East. She felt disloyal to the friends who had given her such extravagant gifts, and disloyal to her children, especially her daughters, who would not inherit the beautiful things, and who, unless given in marriage to a sultan themselves, would probably have no means to acquire such unique items. She remembered the night that she had cried in front of the Capitan Pasha, afraid to deliver her first baby in a foreign land. To demonstrate his friendship, he had sent the magnificent sapphire the very next day. Mary thought of her friend as she looked one last time at the brilliant blue gem, surrounded by diamonds, still sitting on its pillow of gold Turkish velvet. What would the pasha think if he knew what had become of the Elgins? How sad he would feel if he saw his exalted Lady Elgin pawning her jewels to pay her husband's debts. Though she knew that the extravagant gold-threaded costumes that Hanum had given her would fetch a good price, Mary hid them away, determined to salvage at least one memento of the warm and unlikely friendship that had helped to sustain her in a foreign land.

There were other worries. The Dowager Lady Elgin, who had been inexplicably cold to her daughter-in-law since she'd arrived back in England, had managed to store the main shipment of the marbles, the first fifty crates that had arrived on the *Braakel,* at the home of the Duke of Richmond, but that man was getting impatient at having his estate used as a depository for tons of marble. Elgin wrote long letters to Mary demanding that she find them a new home.

You must take an inventory, Mary, and then agree to take responsibility on the lease of a house, which Hamilton is hunting for at this time.

Why did he think he could order her to do this and that as if she were just another member of his staff? Did he not remember that she was with child? The cramping had already begun. There was no way to tell when the baby would come, or how it would come—whether it would be a horrible labor or merely a terrible one. She was determined to settle their finances before she was incapacitated. She did not want to face further embarrassment. Word of debts and of unpaid staff spread like a plague through London society, and these days, people did not need one more excuse to gossip about young Lady Elgin.

Her letters began again:

Your cash is going to the dogs! You know that I like pretty things too, Elgin, but think of the disgrace of it. All your stocks are gone, thousands of pounds are owed, and people are constantly demanding their money! You know what I am capable of when I take matters into my own hands, but you must give me unlimited powers until I have got everything in order, and above all, you must not buy one more item! Please, Elgin, take my advice and listen to me. If only you knew what I have been through since I have been home, how bad is our condition, and how much it has put me into despair!

Word must have spread of Elgin's dire financial condition. Mary received a letter from His Majesty's government inquiring about the purchase of the marbles Lord Elgin had collected while serving in Constantinople. But no monetary sum was mentioned.

How was she supposed to fix a sum? What on earth might they be worth?

Luckily, a friend appeared in London, just when she most needed his counsel.

"I need your help, Mr. Ferguson," she said. The words were out of her mouth before she could stop them. She had not taken the time to inquire of his health or his family, or how he found his homeland after an absence of so many years. She was so exquisitely happy to see his face at this time and to know that, with only weeks at most to get her affairs in order, she could depend upon him.

"At your service as always and forevermore so long we both shall live and breathe, milady," he said without taking a breath. He had not lost an iota of his intensity, Mary could tell, nor had his feelings for her diminished. He did not have to say a word; his delight in seeing her shone in his eyes.

She told him that the government had finally expressed an interest in buying the marbles.

"Mr. Ferguson, I have no idea how to proceed. If I propose a figure, it might be far beneath what the stones are worth. After all the pain and expense we have been through with these marbles, it would be a great tragedy to undersell them."

Ferguson sat rapt, listening to everything she had to say, as if nothing in the world were as important as grasping her needs and attending to them. What sort of man was this, who made himself completely available to a lady? He was like some knight out of a medieval romance, with his chivalrous behavior, for which he had never demanded a thing in return.

"I shall be entirely honest with you," she said, feeling a bit appalled that she was about to reveal to him the truth of her position. "I need the money to cover Lord Elgin's debts, which have been made exponentially worse by what we have spent on the marbles. I must say that it would be a great relief to sell them and to let the government see to their care."

"I have observed for some time that you have been exhausted with the burden of Lord Elgin's obsession," he said.

"Then I am aghast at my own indiscreet behavior," she replied, though she was gratified that someone had seen and acknowledged all that she had done for Elgin.

"There is no need, milady. We spent much time together. I would be aghast if in those long hours of working side by side, I did not recognize the toll your labors were taking on you."

Was ever a gentleman so kind? But she was uncomfortable pursuing this line of dialogue. She needed his help right now, not his sympathy.

"I do not wish to make a hasty decision on the sale of the marbles, Mr. Ferguson. I believe that Lord Elgin and I would regret it for years to come. And that is why I need your help."

She wondered if she was playing a dangerous game, depending on this man who so doted on her every wish while her husband was imprisoned and she was feeling so vulnerable and tired. But Elgin himself had written to Robert asking for his assistance in several matters. Elgin had agreed that horses and other livestock he owned should be sold to cover some of his debts. Even Elgin, in his circumstances in which he seemed not to regard his wife at all, knew that a pregnant woman should not be left to see to these transactions. Ferguson, a man of the world, easily arranged for the sales, as well as arranging to have some paintings and other items sold discreetly at auction.

"I am so sorry to have to trouble you with my affairs," she said, eyes downcast.

"Nonsense!"

It embarrassed her to look directly at him. He seemed so eager, like a tiger about to lunge at its dinner.

"Would you please sit down and have tea?" she asked.

He looked so fidgety that she wished she could get him to drink a good dose of brandy to settle him down. Could his feelings for her have intensified in absentia? She had been so wrapped up in her own difficulties in recent months that she had hardly thought about her poor Robert. Elgin had said that Robert was always falling for one woman or another. When last they'd spent time together, she had assumed that she was merely one of many, that Robert fell for whatever attractive—and unattainable—woman was in his vicinity. What exuded from him now hardly seemed like a passing flirtation.

"Once again, I am dependent upon you," she said.

"I would serve you all the days of my life if allowed," he answered.

She had no idea how he could find her alluring in her present state. She was swollen beyond normal. Even her face had begun to lose its attractive angles as her body grew in size. She was exhausted these days and could hardly stand the sight of herself in the mirror.

There was something emphatically different about him now. But whatever had transpired in his heart, whatever feelings were present, no matter how strong, she could not encourage them. She needed him. And she must let him know that the pressing needs of the moment must take precedence over anything else he might be feeling or thinking.

"Mr. Ferguson, you are the only person I know in England who has enough influence with the French to work for Elgin's release. You are the only person both Lord Elgin and I trust to dispose of our property. You are the only person I can depend upon to help me negotiate my way through the maze of a business transaction with the government on the marbles. It is unseemly to be so overly dependent upon one person, but there it is."

"Sir Joseph Banks will be happy to help us again. If any person in England knows who can give us an accurate appraisal of the marbles, it is he. He is universally admired. I shall speak to him forth-with."

"Thank you. I do not know how we shall repay you, but mark my words, it shall be done!"

Robert leaped out of his seat as if he could not wait another moment to start the process of helping the Elgins. Mary almost laughed at the fervor he displayed. Hurriedly, he kissed her hand and rushed out the door.

Feelings were a minor detail in the ever-unfolding drama of her life. This was not an opera or a romance novel. Mary would contain this man and his ardor, which had radiated from his eyes. She had managed the feelings of the fantastically handsome Count Sébas-tiani, the Capitan Pasha, and other powerful men. Surely she could manage Robert Ferguson.

I simply cannot have any more children, Elgin. I have never suffered so much in my life. I would do anything in the world for you but this. The horror began long before the labor and continues now long after it. Life is nothing but a burden to me under these circumstances. This is the fifth time I have undergone this pain. I am worn out and would rather lock myself up in a nunnery for life. I leave my fate in your hands. If that is your decision for me, I will live wherever you like and never see a soul, but this agony I will no longer endure.

Your wife who continues to love you, Mary.

When William died, Mary thought she had lost the will to live, but as she was defying her husband and taking her stand, she real-ized that she had entirely regained her desire to be in the world.

William had come to her while she was in labor. She had passed out, and in that moment, her fondest wish was met. She was sit-ting in a beautiful garden in France in the sunshine. Her dress was open, and she was nursing William, staring into his beautiful blue eyes again, watching him watch her. Was any child ever so alert, so curious, so in communication with his mother? As he quietly sucked at the breast, he delivered a silent message to her: *Mother, you must live.*

She had suffered worse than ever before in the labor to produce Lucy—another pretty little girl—and the aftermath was the worst she had ever experienced. But rather than praying for death, after the visitation from William she had prayed for life. As the weeks wore on and the blood and the pain kept coming, she continued to pray that she might live. It was her little boy's last request. Even when she did not have the strength to get out of bed, she begged God to let her remain on this earth and see it all through.

That is when it occurred to her—no child would ever replace William. Though Mary ferociously loved all of her children, William was special. Perhaps it was because she had been in exile, away from her other children, when he was born, or because she had nursed and cared for him herself. She realized that even if she produced another dozen children, none would ever replace William. She wrote as much to Elgin, giving him daily accounts of the children's progress, but making her stance clear.

He never answered her letters. She pleaded with him to affirm that he had received these missives, read them, and understood her immutable decision. She tried another tactic, the sort that he responded to in the past:

I am not refusing you pleasure, my darling. But there are ways to have pleasure that do not result in pregnancy. We have practiced them many times, and I do recall that you enjoyed it every time. You will have your Mary, your tasty morsel, as you love to call me, but we will eliminate the aspect that leads to the unwanted thing.

But he did not reply to her seductive missives either. She agonized over the lack of response. She wrote to him that the moment she could travel—and at this point, weeks after Lucy's birth, she still could not walk—she would return to France to be near him.

He sent no response. What would she do if he refused her terms?

In May, when the weather had cleared and Mary was recovered,

Ferguson came to visit. Slowly he entered the drawing room, a smile plastered on his face, waving a letter. "Fantastic news, Mary."

"But you look as if you have just learned of the death of a be-loved pet," she teased.

"Do I? No matter, Mary, we have succeeded. Napoleon has bent to our pleas, thanks to the numerous letters written by our more influential friends. Our efforts are rewarded. Lord Elgin has permission to leave France."

The news was unexpected. Mary did not know how to respond, especially in front of Robert. It had been so long since she had heard from her husband.

"You have nothing to say on the matter?" Robert had delivered the news with a grim countenance, and now Mary was aware that she had received it with the same. He must think her insane, after all they had been through together to obtain Elgin's freedom.

"I am surprised, that is all. I suppose that I had given up."

"I have some news of my own. I have made a decision. I am re-turning to Scotland to run for Parliament."

"You are leaving me again?" she asked. The words tumbled out. What right did she have to ask him to do anything further for her? Why did she say that?

"The Whig party has returned to power, Mary. I see a unique opportunity to push for the reforms in which I so firmly believe."

Before she could prevent it, she started to cry.

Robert sat on the sofa next to her and took her hand. "Mary, ev-erything will be fine. You have four lovely children. Your husband is coming home. I have done my best by you. Sir Joseph promises that the marbles will receive fair appraisal as soon as the customs are paid and they can actually be seen. Do you see, dear girl? All is well!"

Some intangible quality in warmth of his skin and in the sooth-ing tone in his voice caused something inside of her to break, some wall that she had kept solid and strong so that nothing from the outside could breach it, some barrier to a place in her heart or her mind that no man should breach but Elgin. A sacrosanct place that married people kept private but for each other. But Elgin was not present, and Robert was, and the wall came tumbling down.

She told Robert everything—the way she had suffered, which he and not Elgin had witnessed on his many visits before the baby was born; her decision not to have more children; and Elgin's silence on the matter.

"I want him to come home, Robert. Oh, God knows I do not want my own husband imprisoned indefinitely. But I am afraid. What if he refuses my terms? Whatever shall I do? What can any woman do? Must I choose between my husband and my very life?"

"The thought that you would endanger your life again arouses every indignation inside of me, Mary. I couldn't bear it, though I have no right to insert myself into the matter." Robert stood, pacing around the room as if this were another of her problems for which he might find a solution. He turned to her several times, and then turned away and recommenced his pacing.

"There is nothing to be done about it until my husband is at home and allows his thoughts on the matter to be revealed," she said.

"No man in his right mind would refuse you," Robert said.

"Then let us hope that when Lord Elgin arrives, he is indeed in his right mind."

In the city of London,

June 1806

MARY PREPARED THE CHILDREN for Elgin's return by telling them stories every day about their brave and important father, who, though held captive by the enemy, did not betray his country. She had worried that between his long absence and his odd appearance, what with the mask covering his missing nose, they would shun him as a stranger. Bruce claimed to remember his father, but Mary did not see how the girls could have any memory of him. Little Mary had been without him for much longer than she'd been with him. Harriet had been an infant when he parted with her, and Lucy he had yet to lay eyes on.

"He pictures his children in his mind, and that is what gives him strength and courage," she told them every day, demanding that they sit still and listen. The paterfamilias was returning to his rightful position as head of the family, and she wanted the children to acknowledge it. She would acknowledge it as well. She intended to uphold every form that was expected of her as his wife, at least publicly, but it would be more akin to staging a lovely play for others rather than actions proceeding from the directives of the heart.

She wanted everything to go smoothly once Elgin was home. It would not do to have explosive confrontations. Yet no matter his response to her demand, she was firm in her resolve. Elgin could apologize as he did when he was released from the fortress at Lourdes. He could improve his health and his appearance and return to his well-mannered ways as he had done in the past. But this time, his repentance, should it manifest, would not win him entrance to her bed.

She thought that she was doing him enough of a favor by training the children to admire and respect him and by refraining from pouncing on him with the realities of their mounting debts. When he finally appeared at her Baker Street home in London, she presented him with one beautifully groomed and turned-out child after the next.

"Why, look, it is my brood of little Greek-speaking brats!" he exclaimed, opening his arms to gather the children in.

"Lord Bruce, have you managed to learn a word or two of English in your father's absence?" he asked his son, smiling at him.

"Yes, sir," the boy said proudly. "I read the language too, sir. And Mother and I are working on my French."

"Then you shall have the gift I bought for you, young man." He presented the six-year-old with a shining French saber. *Not sharp-*

ened, he mouthed to Mary. "Thank you for being the man of the family while I was away."

To the two older girls, he presented porcelain dolls dressed in elegant French finery. He held and approved of Lucy, ever the proud father when another of his heirs was delivered into his arms. "Why, she is as small and delicate as one of the bisque dolls I brought from Paris," he said.

The children gathered around him for the rest of the afternoon, competing for his attention, and the older two demonstrating everything they had mastered since he'd last seen them. Bruce parried swords with the manservant Andrew, and later read from his primer. Little Mary had just learned to make the first tiny stitches in a sampler, which she proudly showed her papa. "I shall make the entire alphabet, Father," she said. "And I have taught Harriet how to say her letters."

"I am proud of all of you," Elgin said, kissing each of them before they were to go upstairs and be readied for bed. "You are exemplary children."

"I too shall go to bed now," Mary said to him. She was tired, and in no mood for serious discussion. She also wanted to set an example for what their relationship was to be henceforth—one of good form and friendship.

"I shall be upstairs shortly," he replied, giving no indication of whether he had read her letters or not, or of whether he intended to join her.

"As you wish," she said, and went straightaway up to her bedroom.

He might have been trying to keep her in the dark about whether or not he had accepted the proposed arrangement, but she was prepared for any eventuality. She dressed for bed, but asked the new lady's maid to lock the door from the inside and remain in her chamber. Mary did not explain her reasoning, but told the girl to sit in the chair by the window until Mary decided that she could take her leave.

Within the hour, Elgin knocked on the bedroom door. He

twisted the doorknob, but found it locked. "Mary? Please open the door," she heard him say.

Mary had to get out of bed to awaken the maid, now slumped in the chair.

"Open the door, tell Lord Elgin that I am sound asleep, and stand in front of the door until he leaves," she whispered to the girl. "Then, go to your room."

"Yes ma'am," the girl said, jumping up and curtsying, and rushing to the door.

"Asleep, is she?" she heard Elgin say.

"Yes, Lord Elgin," the girl replied. For a few moments, there was no movement. Then Mary heard Elgin shuffling away, and the girl's quicker footsteps moving in the opposite direction.

THEIR SOCIAL LIVES resumed immediately. Everyone wanted to see Elgin and to hear about his experiences. A man who was once held prisoner was always, at least for a time, an object of fascination in society. Mary declared that she had no time to digest her food between the luncheon and dinner invitations from so many curious Londoners. Even Lord Grenville, the new prime minister, invited the Elgins to dine with him.

"They have reconsidered reimbursing my expenses, because of all that I have endured on behalf of my country," Elgin speculated as they rode in a carriage into Whitehall, past Buckingham Palace toward Downing Street.

Mary had not yet brought up the subject of Elgin's ruined finances. She thought that a man deserved a little time to readjust to life at home. Elgin had not been on English soil in seven years. If Lord Grenville authorized a generous reimbursement of embassy expenses, the subject of Elgin's debts would be much easier to discuss.

"Perhaps he is going to make a firm offer for the marbles too," Mary said.

"Undoubtedly. And to offer me another position. There is talk about us going to Vienna, Mary. And also Russia."

At one time, the idea of venturing into foreign lands had been exhilarating to Mary. But now, so many years and miles later, the thought of moving their belongings and their brood from country to country exhausted her.

"It would be lovely to return to Broomhall," Mary countered. "I have dreamt of it for so long."

"We shall see what the evening brings," Elgin said. "We are young, Mary. We might spend some years in the Foreign Service before retiring to our home."

The evening began well. In addition to the Elgins, Lord Grenville had invited Richard Payne Knight, a world-famous collector of antiquities.

"I am certain that Lord Grenville has consulted with Knight on the marbles," Elgin whispered to Mary. "I'll wager that some serious discussion shall be had after dinner in the brandy room!"

But as soon as the subject of the marbles arose, Knight uttered an unwanted, unfounded opinion. "Your labors are for naught, Lord Elgin. Your marbles are overrated. They are not Greek. They are Roman, of the time of Hadrian."

The man spoke with shocking authority, Mary thought, though he could not possibly have known what he was talking about. The marbles were still in crates, sitting on the docks.

"But you have not even seen them. No one has," Elgin replied, trying to control his temper. "Oh, let me retract that statement. Antonio Canova, perhaps the greatest sculptor in the world, has seen pieces and has proclaimed them masterpieces by the hand of Pheidias."

"I do not have to see them, Lord Elgin," said the antiquarian. "Many a collector has been deceived by excellent Roman imitators."

"Sir, I beg you to cease this line of argument," Elgin said. "I was present when the pieces came off the Parthenon. They had sat in place for two thousand years!"

Elgin turned to Lord Grenville. "I assure you, Lord Grenville, that there is not a piece of marble taken from the Parthenon that was not carved by the hand of Pheidias!"

"That is for the experts to decide, Lord Elgin," Grenville said calmly. "Of course, lack of authenticity would alter the price."

"But they are authentic!" Elgin protested again.

Lord Grenville smiled politely, and then turned to the person next to him and began to discuss weather patterns. For the rest of the evening, he coolly deflected any talk of the marbles, making it clear that the government had greater concerns at present, such as containing Napoleon. Lord Grenville also offered no hint that the government had changed its position on paying any of Elgin's expenses.

"I might have sold the entire collection at any time I was imprisoned in France," Elgin said stiffly. "God knows that many offers were made, some of them quite extravagant. I believe that is why Napoleon kept me confined for so long. It is no secret that he has an obsession with obtaining the treasures yielded by the Parthenon."

Elgin looked at Knight with venom. "I do not think that Bonaparte would be obsessed with obtaining fakes! His team of one hundred sixty-nine scholars would know better—better than one man who has never seen the pieces."

He turned away from Knight, forcing Lord Grenville to pay attention to him. "Bonaparte thought that if he kept me locked up long enough, I would betray my country and capitulate. But I did not, sir! No, I did not. I have only and ever wished to serve my country and improve upon the condition of its Fine Arts."

Lord Grenville indulged Elgin by briefly—far too briefly for Mary's taste—expounding on his excellent service to the Crown. Then he quickly turned the conversation in a different direction.

Later, when the men went to the parlor for brandy and the ladies rested upstairs, Mary hoped that Elgin would get somewhere in a discussion of monies owed him, at least for the food and supplies he had sent to His Majesty's army in Egypt. Mary knew that diplomacy was a rich man's game, and that she had been expected to supplement Elgin's ambassadorial expenses. But she had not known that the patriot was expected to feed the military as well.

"Not a sou." Elgin was glum on the ride home. "That is my reward for all that I have done."

"Did he mention a specific amount in connection with the marbles?" Mary asked.

"He did not, only that the intention was to purchase them from me at a time opportune for both parties. And he made it clear that the time was not the present. He must have no idea of the magnitude of the collection, and that imbecile Knight did not help us by saying they were fake!"

"Is there the slightest possibility?"

"Of course not! You were there, Mary. How can you even ask? Knight is one of nature's freaks. The man made his reputation writing a treatise on phallus worship, and another condemning Christianity. I'm sure he has some hidden plan of his own, some personal gain he hopes for, by discrediting my collection. These rival collectors always seek to undermine their competitors."

Mary was afraid that if Elgin continued in this angry vein, his already fragile health would suffer. He looked as if he was on the verge of a seizure. He turned to his wife with wild eyes. "That is why we must put all our efforts into a grand exhibition. If they could see the marbles all together, displayed properly and in a proper setting, they would realize what I am offering!"

"But how are we to pay for such a thing?" she began before he cut her off.

"Do not be a shortsighted female, Mary. Do not worry over petty expenditures at this crucial juncture. We must prepare for an exhibition."

She knew that it was not smart to address her concerns about money directly, for men despised women who confronted them in this way. She knew that the smart wife, especially one no longer willing to parlay sexual favors, would find a way to bring up unpleasant matters sweetly, pouring honey all over the problem before showing it to the husband. But she was out of patience.

"Elgin, I have not said one unpleasant thing to you since you have returned. It is time we discussed the very real problems before us."

"You have avoided me in the bedroom, madam," he said coolly. "That is unpleasant enough."

"That should be the least of your concerns! Do you have any idea of what I have done for you in your absence?" She sat back in the carriage, trying to rein in the shrillness in her voice. She would try to be calm. "Do you have any idea how bad your financial condition is?"

"You have done what a wife should do!" he said. "I should have hoped that you would have outgrown your adolescent need to feel special by now."

She had misjudged him. He was not going to play along nicely with her arrangement. He was going to do what he had always done—demand that she serve him until every drop of her blood and every dime of her money were spent. But this time, Elgin had come home to a very different woman. She would have to make him see that.

"Lord Elgin, you are outrageously ungrateful," she said. "Another woman might have fallen apart under my circumstances! Instead, I have gotten a firm hold on our finances. How did I do this? By what means have I made up for your reckless spending? By selling off all the beautiful things given me that I should have had surrounding me all the years of my life and then passing on to our children. I had to turn my face away from the selling agent who came to collect the things for auction so that he would not see my tears and my shame!"

"You always claimed to have been indifferent to extravagance," he said, sneering at her.

"Along with all of the treasures I sold went all of my lovely memories of our time in the East and of the many friends we made. Do you think I am indifferent to those things too? Unlike you, I am a practical person. Do you think that *any* woman could have survived all the pregnancies and deliveries and health crises and plagues and travels that I have endured since I have been married to you? Do you think that *any* woman could have recovered her will to live after burying her favorite child?"

"What were your choices, Mary? To take poison?" He was treating her as if she were ridiculous. She would not let him get away with it.

"I have put your affairs in order, Elgin, even though the bankers thought it impossible. If not for me, you would still be in prison in France, where you would have remained for many more years. And if you were ever released, you would have gone straight from French prison into debtors' prison. I used every stitch of my charm and every last resource on your behalf. I have worked to exhaustion to bring us to a place where we might live without fear and chaos. And all you can think to do is spend yet more money on your marbles, which no one even wants! You always knew that diplomacy was a rich man's game, and yet you pursued it, because you knew that I would pay and pay and pay where you could not. You knew that I would pay for the collecting and shipping and salvaging of your tons of marble. But how you think we will afford an extravagant exhibition is beyond me!"

He looked at her with exasperation, as if he too were weary of suppressing something that simply must be said, something so tedious and obvious that he did not deign to utter the words. And finally he said it. "You know how we will afford it, Mary. You will pay for it. You will pay for it out of your father's immense fortune, all of which he is leaving to you since you have no brothers or sisters. You will pay for it because it is your duty to me as my wife."

"Is it? Is it my duty to race through my own money as you have raced through yours? Then where shall we be, Elgin? Debtors' prison? I have let you lead me all over the globe, but that is one place where I refuse to follow you."

"Your fortune is unlimited, Mary. Why do you insist on withholding it from me, whom you declare you are devoted to? Why do you allow your father to keep the control out of my hands? Every decent woman allows the control of her money to pass from father to husband. It is only right and proper. You and your father keep me in this humiliating position of appealing to you for money all the time, money that is rightfully mine."

After all the years of suspecting it and suppressing the horrible thought, she allowed it to come fully to the surface and express itself. "You married me for my father's money."

He looked at her as if she had just said something so nonsensical that he should not condescend to reply to it. But reply he did. "You were the prettiest and the cleverest of the wealthy girls."

Did he mean for it to be a compliment?

"I will not negotiate with my wife for the money to do the things I must do. I will not stoop so low again. You will speak to your father and explain that we are going to exhibit the marbles in order to display them to those who will be offering on them. This is a practical matter, Mary. I forbid you to question me on it. You must cease challenging my judgment. It is undignified."

What was she to do? This was her husband. This was the path she'd chosen over the objection of her father. This was the sire of her four children. It was too late to change the past. Elgin was her present and her future, and she would make the most of it. But she would get what she needed too.

"As long as we are listing our demands, what do you say to my terms, Elgin? I can speak to my father and get you the money to display your marbles, if that is what it will take to keep the peace between us. But I too am decided upon a course for our future. You did not answer my letters. Perhaps you thought that I was merely reacting to the present circumstances, but I am emphatically decided. I will not suffer again. I will not bear more children."

He did not even take a moment to ponder, but looked her dead in the eye. "I trust that you are aware that as my wife, you cannot deny me the privileges of the marriage bed, which include its logical conclusion and ultimate purpose, procreation. It is not simply *my* purpose, but that of God."

He had obviously read her letters and considered what she proposed. This was his response, and it sounded as immovable as her resolve to the contrary. She knew enough about Elgin to know that he would not renege. His voice was firm as he spoke, as solid and cold as ice.

"If you cannot agree to my terms for marriage, then I cannot agree to yours." She hoped that she sounded as firm and as frigid as he had.

In the country of Scotland,
July to December, 1806

T HE CHILDREN HAD SPENT much of their time
apart from their parents at Archerfield, so they were immediately at home on their grandparents' estate. They had been away from their father most of their lives, and the separation from him caused them no grief. They were told that Lord Elgin had duties he needed to fulfill in London, and would see them when he returned. Mary had little to do now but spend her days playing with them in the same gardens she had played in as a child, and walking with them along the same beaches, where the firth opened into the North Sea, collecting shells, and going into the water when the weather permitted. Owing to long walks with his mother and his grandfather, Bruce was becoming adept at identifying the coastal birds, and went into blue mood for an entire day when he saw a stout, black great skua devour a small, defenseless puffin. But being a little gentleman, he hid the reason from his sisters. "They might have bad dreams if they knew, Mother," he told Mary when she went into his room to bring him tea and to comfort him. "Little girls love little birds."

The girls were sensitive creatures, but they loved their fun. Mary loved to watch them laugh hysterically as the lady's maids put them into the laundry baskets atop the fresh unfolded linen sheets and swung them in the air. They could be alternately playful and terribly serious, as when they were at work on their stitching or creating elaborate scenarios with their dollies. As long as the children were around her, Mary had enough happiness to face the long days and the uncertainty ahead. She had no idea what would happen between her and Elgin; at the moment, she was content simply to be at home with her children, trying to make up for the long years of separation, and away from their father and his ever-pressing demands upon her money and her body.

She knew that Robert Ferguson was once again in her vicinity. He had won his bid for Parliament, and he had settled at Raith in order to execute his duties. Upon hearing that she was at Archerfield and alone, he began to petition to visit her.

The Nisbets were not pleased.

"We did not like his visits in London, Mary. He knew that you were another man's wife, and under the pretext of helping your husband, he took advantage of your situation to remain in your company unsupervised and late into the evenings." Her mother's voice took on the same quality that she used with her grandchildren when they displeased her. Mary had not heard quite so admonishing a tone directed at her since she was a child.

"But, Mother, he did help Elgin. If Mr. Ferguson had not persuaded Sir Joseph Banks and other influential men to act on our behalf, Elgin would still be in France. Why must I endure criticism, even from my own mother, when all I tried to do was get my husband home?"

"I was not criticizing you, dear, but Mr. Ferguson. His feelings for you are most obvious. Even your father, who notices nothing if it isn't livestock or banknotes, has commented on it. Ferguson is a good but dangerous man. He knows no social boundaries, and he has always been one to seduce married women!"

"I assure you that nothing untoward passed between myself and Mr. Ferguson in London. We were heavily engaged in aiding Elgin's release, and in disposing of my property to pay my husband's debts."

"Besides," her mother added, "I do not think that Mr. Nisbet would like to see him here, what with your present circumstances undecided." Clearly her parents had discussed the matter between themselves. Mary had seen Mr. Nisbet's frown when the letter addressed to Mary arrived from Raith, with Robert's insignia. Mary needed her parents more than ever. Initially they had been upset that she'd left Elgin, but when the full range of his crimes against her and disregard for her was revealed, they had promised their complete support.

"You are quite correct, Mother," Mary said. "We do not need Mr. Ferguson's passionate and controversial presence complicating our lives."

She wrote him a polite letter thanking him for his generous help in the past, but firmly saying that she did not think it advisable for them to meet at the present time.

IN SEPTEMBER, WITH THE weather turning cool and crisp and the cultural season commencing, Mary decided to spend a fortnight in Edinburgh. Mrs. Nisbet wanted to accompany her daughter into the city, but Mary longed for time alone. She would see some city acquaintances, attend the theater, and buy fabrics to have winter clothing made for herself and her growing brood. Bruce, especially, appeared as if he would take after his father and grow tall. His woolen breeches, put away since the spring, no longer covered his knobby knees.

Mary declined invitations to stay with friends at their city homes and checked into Fortune and Blackwell's Hotel. When she came downstairs to the dining room for her supper, she was seated at a table next to Robert Ferguson, who was eating alone. He did not look surprised to see her.

"Lady Elgin, may I join you?" he said.

"Of course, Mr. Ferguson. Please sit down," she said.

He left his food on the table and sat down with her, bringing with him only his glass of wine, which sloshed over the rim in his rush to arrive at her side. He looked so anxious that she allowed herself to laugh, despite her promises to herself to retain the utmost semblance of propriety should she ever run into him in the cosseted nest of Edinburgh society.

"How well you look, Mr. Ferguson," she said slyly. At the moment, he did not look well at all. He was wiping droplets of red wine from the bottom of his glass with the tablecloth and flinging the rest of the spilt liquid from his jacket sleeve. "What a great coincidence to see you here."

A waiter interrupted them. "Sir, shall I bring your supper?"

"No, no, I am finished," Robert said. The waiter looked at the barely touched roast beef on the plate and shook his head at the waste. He took the plate away, probably intending, Mary thought, to have it straightaway for himself.

"Mary, it is not a coincidence at all," Robert said. "Surely you know that. I have been watching as best I can your movements for the last four months. I have been mad to see you. Why will you not receive me?"

"What, no small talk, Mr. Ferguson? Should you not ask how things are at Archerfield and listen patiently while I tell you of the children's growth and my father's gout?"

"Dear God, I am a member of Parliament now. Do you not think that I have had my fill of small talk these many months? The joy of our friendship has always been the depth of our communication. I have missed it greatly," he said, taking the liberty of leaning closer to her.

She laughed. "Perhaps you should have eaten your dinner. You look as if you are about to devour me." She knew that she shouldn't be flirting and teasing with him, but she had done nothing in months but play with children—she, who had attended suppers and balls with the most powerful people in the world, and who had been the toast of every society she had entered. She was lonely for the attention of fascinating men like Robert.

"I must speak with you, Mary. I won't be put off. May I see you in your room?"

"Are you mad?" she said, whispering. "This is Edinburgh, where we are both well known. I will not be the subject of gossip so close to home."

"Then I shall take a room on your floor. And I shall come to you this evening at nine o'clock. Hear me out, Mary. You shan't be sorry."

"No, you mustn't. I am going to the theater tonight," she replied, flustered. She had thought that she'd prepared herself, should she encounter him in public, but he had found this ingenious way to talk to her alone so that she could not hide behind politeness.

"Then I shall arrive at eleven."

She started to object, but he stood. "It has been a pleasure to see you, Lady Elgin."

He picked up his hat from the table where he had left it, and before she could reply, he was gone.

Mary was filled with anxiety when she took her seat at the theater. How on earth would she be able to concentrate these two and a half hours? She'd been wanting to see the play, a comedy by the Irishman Oliver Goldsmith, about a woman of wealth who poses as a serving girl to seduce the man she wants to marry. But as the play progressed, she found herself not laughing at all. Her friend Catherine sat on one side of her, fanning herself repeatedly after overheating her face and bosom with laughter. Catherine's husband sat on Mary's left, and Mary watched his big belly convulse throughout the play. But Mary found herself increasingly annoyed. Why did women have to dissemble to gain a man's love? If she agreed to disguise her true self, as this character was doing, and agreed to behave exactly as Elgin wanted—as a servant— she would once again have his love.

"You do not find it hilarious, Mary?" asked her friend.

"Oh yes, but I feel a touch of croup coming on," she said. She was desperate to be out of there, though she was terrified of what the rest of the evening would bring. "Perhaps I should leave."

Over Mary's objections, Catherine's husband accompanied her out of the theater, hailing her a hackney carriage, and delivering instructions to the driver. When she arrived at the hotel, she saw Robert in the gentlemen's lounge, sitting in front of the fire, sipping a brandy.

"Good evening, Lady Elgin," said the high-hatted doorman as she walked through the reception area.

Robert looked up immediately. It was as if his senses were heightened, like those of a falcon at the hunt. Mary met his eyes, but quickly turned away without acknowledging him.

"Good evening," she said to the man, and then hurried up the stairs to her room.

She hoped that Robert would wait a respectable amount of time, but within ten minutes he was at her door, knocking softly. She opened the door and let him in.

"I am here to reveal my deepest thoughts and feelings to you. There is no sense in equivocating," he said. "I have made up my mind to speak to you. Please sit down."

"These are my rooms, I'll thank you to remember. It is I who should invite you to sit down, and I am not certain that I am going to do it," she said. "I am rather tired of men imposing their wills upon me. I am my own person. I shall decide whether or not I wish to listen to what you have to say."

He took a deep breath and sighed. "Yes, you are quite right. I do apologize. May I sit down? May I speak frankly with you, Mary?"

"I don't see how I might stop you," she said. "I suppose it is best to get the deed done. You seem determined, even if you are on the path of destruction for us both."

"Good. I have neither the time nor the inclination to destroy us. Here is what I have to say. I love you, and I want to spend my life proving it to you. I will give you everything that your husband will not. I ask nothing of you. I do not require your money. I do not require you to have more children. I want nothing of you but the opportunity to see you every day, to walk down the road with you in this life."

He went on, listing her fine qualities and reviewing the escalation of his feelings since the time he first met her in Paris. She let him talk.

"That is a fine speech, sir. I see that your time in Parliament has improved your already sharp oratorical skills. But your vision of our life together can exist only on some elevated plane, where the unadorned facts will not intrude upon your fantasies." Her cool demeanor belied the thrill she felt on hearing his passionate words. "My mother believes that I am just another married woman you wish to woo."

"That is unfair, Mary. I believe that I have proven my devotion to you." He looked genuinely hurt. His eyes probed hers, daring her to challenge his love again.

"When I married Elgin, I was certain that he was mad for me. I have had to face the sorry fact that he was mad only for the ways in which I could benefit him. Might you have purposes yet unrevealed? I will not be a foolish woman yet again. Frankly, I will not allow myself to be another of your conquests."

"If it is time that you require, Mary, then I shall give you time. I only ask that I be allowed to visit you. I do not think I can live if I do not see you."

"You are very dramatic, sir. I believe that you would endure on this earth whether I return your affections or not," she said, trying to bring the conversation around to a reasonable tone again. "I must control myself and contain whatever feelings I might have. Elgin is my husband. I am the mother of children. You are a member of Parliament. All that we have hoped for in our lives might be destroyed if we yield to our emotions."

Robert did not hesitate. "What I hope for in my life is you. Nothing else means rats' blood to me. You know me, Mary. I despise the conventions of our society. I despise any capitulation at all to the opinion of others if it keeps you tied to this man. I will free you from him if it's the last thing I do."

He knelt beside her, taking her hand and softly kissing and stroking it. It had been so long since she'd felt a man's affection that she did not pull away. She felt entranced by this simple action that was igniting the sensuous part of her that she'd feared would lie dormant forever, now that she had rejected her husband. Robert put her hand to his cheek and held it there as if it were the most rare and precious of objects. "Oh, Mary, let me love you. You will not be sorry. We are meant to be together in the eyes of heaven, and heaven shall work out the details of our union. We must have faith."

She wanted to taunt him again, reminding him of his lapsed faith, but the heat of his face on her hand, and the intense look in his eyes, made her keep quiet. He sat next to her on the sofa. He kissed her hand over and over until she sighed. Then he slipped his hot hand behind her neck, bringing their lips together.

It was like nothing she had ever felt before, though she had kissed her husband a thousand times. This was a merging of lips that felt as if they had been made to fit together. He kissed her bottom lip, and then the top one, and then took her bottom lip between his teeth ever so gently. She'd loved her husband for a long time, and had loved his touch upon her, but she'd never felt this sort of perfect absorption in another being before.

He did not leave her room. He stayed all night, kissing and caressing her and talking to her. "Do you see, Mary? I will do nothing to hurt you. It is enough to be next to you, to touch you and smell your sweet smell and taste your sweet lips."

They talked late into the night, and then slept side by side for a little while. He awoke before dawn, waking her with soft kisses on her temple.

"I must go, before the staff is awake and haunting the halls," he said.

Suddenly she felt as if she were in a play about an adulterous wife; as if she were some comedic character without morals, deceiving her husband. "What have we done, Robert? We must forget this evening. It can come to no good. I will close my eyes, and after you are gone, I will erase all memory of this night from my mind. I insist that you do so too."

She felt ill, knowing that she had broken down the wall that had protected not only her reputation, but also the moral and societal codes that she had been raised to obey and had lived by. She felt adrift, as if she could no longer define herself. She was no longer the person she always thought she was and would be—a respectable woman, protected by her honor and her actions. What was she now? How was she different from Emma Hamilton and all the other scandalous women in the tabloids? Even if no one ever found out, she would have to live with her transgression.

"What have we done? We have begun our lives, Mary. Nothing in my life mattered until now. You shall see. There is nothing we cannot endure if we are together."

. . .

SHE ALLOWED HIM TO visit. Briefly, at first, and always in the presence of her mother and the children so that servants and neighbors, eager to impress others with their knowledge of the much-talked-about Lady Elgin, could not spread evil rumors of their conduct. Soon, though, the visits became prolonged. A sense of ease existed between them that she had not experienced with Elgin. Robert was content just to be in her company. She did not have to work tirelessly on his behalf. Unlike the lady in Mr. Goldsmith's play, she did not have to dissemble in order to gain his love. He didn't seem to want her to do anything at all but be his.

It had been two months since their encounter at the hotel. They had restrained themselves, but Mary had longed to feel the perfection of his kisses once again. She had heard nothing from Elgin. He was away in London, doing God knows what. She found that she did not much care what he was up to so long as he left her alone.

Robert had no problem describing his hopes and expectations. While a gust of November wind blew against their faces, muffling their voices so that the children could not hear, he painted possible scenarios that might arise, leading to their ultimate happiness. Elgin was her husband, true, but he was in poor health and could die. "I am prepared to wait for that eventuality, if necessary," Robert said. "I have known Elgin longer than you have, Mary. His arrogance will get the best of him, if his health doesn't do him in first. If you continue to refuse to produce heirs, he will find someone who will. He will divorce you."

"What? He cannot do that! That is unheard of. Sir, you are fantasizing."

"He will not simply live in celibacy. He is a man, after all. He might just find a mistress and leave you alone for the rest of your lives. Many married people enter into that sort of arrangement. I was a third party in that sort of thing, remember?"

"It is one thing for Elgin to take a mistress. It is another entirely for me to be someone's mistress. I could not live under such veiled circumstances, Robert. I simply could not."

"Then we shall have to wait and see what Elgin proposes. Mark my words, Mary. He will propose something. It is up to you to be prepared for it, and for us to take advantage of whatever it is."

Late in November, without warning a letter arrived at Archerfield. Mary felt herself grow faint as she read it. Elgin was arriving at Broomhall within the week and he hoped that she and the children would be there in their rightful home when he got there. He would give in to her request and try to live with her on her terms.

MARY SCRAMBLED TO GET the house ready for Elgin and for the children. After so long a time away from him, free of his demands, she was resentful at being expected to once again work round the clock to make things nice for him. When they were in Constantinople, she would spend long hours dreaming of the day that she would make Broomhall their home. Now she dreaded living in its chilly emptiness. There was no money to fulfill the decorating plans she'd made long ago, and she was not about to borrow from her parents to create a warm and beautiful home for a man she'd come to despise. What was she to do? The thought of Elgin repulsed her, but she comforted herself with his words in the letter. *I shall try to live life with you on your terms.* That meant only one thing: separate bedrooms and no physical contact.

Robert was crestfallen when she told him what Elgin had proposed. He tried to talk her out of agreeing to the arrangement, but as she pointed out, she had little choice. She would not give Elgin any cause to take drastic measures. If she refused to live with him, he might be able to find grounds upon which to sue her for divorce. He might also find grounds for taking the children. She had to attempt to cooperate.

"He won't last," Robert said. "Mark my words, Mary. Stand firm and refuse him your bed, and he will be gone in a fortnight. You must exasperate him. You must let him know that you consider his approach a violation of your person. That will force him into a separation, I assure you."

She had no idea what to expect. Elgin returned to Broomhall, making a great show of his willingness to adhere to Mary's terms. For the first few days, he did not seem to mind the situation. He behaved magnanimously, as if he were trying to impress upon her his acceptance of her terms. He smiled pleasantly at anything she said, but he did not seem to be truly listening to her. He was very affectionate toward the children. He spent long hours in his office or library, reading a book or buried in papers of one sort or another. They dined together politely, but his conversation was minimal and impersonal.

She was sure that he had a mistress with whom he must be quite preoccupied, and she found that she did not care. If that was to be their arrangement, so be it, as long as it kept Mary from the marriage bed—which, frankly, she did not think she could endure with Elgin, so far had her feelings for him fled—and its consequences. They would live together as friends. It was a fate that other couples happily endured.

After the first week had passed, he became perturbed. He started to send barbs her way about "a woman's duty." His health got worse—always a sign of unhappiness. His coughing fits returned. He would get up and leave her company without excusing himself, locking himself in his room for hours upon end.

"Tell Lord Elgin that I am going to visit William's grave," she said to his valet. In the last few days, they had started to communicate exclusively through the servants.

"Shall I ask him if he wishes to join you?" the man asked as a formality. He undoubtedly knew the answer. One could cut the tension between Lord and Lady Elgin with an axe these days, and no one was quicker to pick up on tension between the masters than a house servant.

"No, I wish to go alone," she answered.

The Dunfermline Abbey was a somber place on any given day, but on this gray, blustery morning in December, it cast a particular gloom. Mary did not often visit William's crypt. Memories of him put her in a state of melancholy that she did not like her other children to witness. Sometimes, the very touch of those warm, living children, animated and glowing, kindled a memory of William, which would send Mary's heart sinking and her body back to a darkened bedroom for the day. She hoped that this would eventually pass. *Life is fer tha living,* her old nanny used to say whenever someone mourned excessively. Mary knew that was correct, but she had no control yet over the way that thoughts of her lost little angel overtook her.

William had been laid to rest above Elgin's oldest brother, after whom the baby had been named. That boy had been Earl of Elgin for only six months before he died. They might have thought about passing on the unlucky name, rather than trying to obey tradition and honor the dead earl. Had that mattered? Mary did not like to be superstitious, but she always looked for any reason that God might have punished her by taking away the child she loved most.

Mary passed her hand over the face of the crypt, running her finger over the boy's name, which seemed the only way that she could touch him. He was surrounded by members of Elgin's family, but it had been Robert who had placed his little body in the crypt. Elgin had upset her after William's death by ordering an extravagant crypt for his little son, which would have entailed rearranging the bodies of his ancestors. Mr. Nisbet had intervened to prevent that unwise move. The last thing that Mary had wanted was to be reminded of her baby's death by going into even deeper debt over his burial. Everywhere she looked on the monument she saw the name Elgin. Elgin, Elgin, Elgin. Here was her little tyke lying among all the dead Elgins, people he did not even know.

There was something unsettling about William's place of rest, though Mary could not identify it. It seemed as if he did not belong there, lying for eternity amid ancestors he had never met. She thought that she might propose to Elgin that they move the body, but to where? Suddenly, it occurred to her: She did not even consider William to be Elgin's baby. Though the child had, in fact, been sired by the Earl of Elgin, in her heart she had always imagined him, albeit unconsciously, to be Robert's child. It was Robert who had aided her during the last horrid days of the pregnancy and the long weeks of recuperation. It was Robert who had held the infant in his arms, and it was Robert who had promenaded proudly with the two of them through the parks of Paris, his strong arm supporting Mary as she slowly recovered her strength. She had leaned on that arm so many times over the years when Elgin's demands, on top of the normal demands of being his wife, overwhelmed her. For the last few years, ever since the moment that Elgin was incarcerated by the French, she had gradually begun to think of Robert as her heart's companion.

Mary pondered her grim situation. She was twenty-seven years old. What if she lived to be seventy, like her great-aunts and other dowager ladies seen about the world, long widowed, alone, and hobbling about to events on the arms of patient and indulgent nephews? Was she to spend the next five or six decades without love? The only reminder that her fate need not take this turn were Robert's letters, which he sent via messenger almost daily. She did not need the reminder. All she thought about was Robert. She knew that she had to find a way for them to be together. Someone of her temperament could find peace in a passionless marriage for only so long. Whenever she tried to bury her emotions, a letter would come from Robert, reawakening memories of what it was like to be loved. Yet what were her choices? Divorce was unthinkable; it was impossible for a woman to initiate unless her husband was monstrously cruel. Even then, divorces were rarely granted. People of her class—of her character—did not divorce. Divorced women were marked, tainted, shunned. Mary would not do that to her children, to her parents, or to herself, not even if she had the legal grounds to do so, which she did not.

She went home and locked herself in her room and began to write.

Today I went to see my beloved William's grave. Friend, it was you who placed that adored angel there. Perhaps if he can see and know what is passing in the world, he can intercede for us. Elgin is agitated with me and doesn't speak. He is keeping his promise, but I hardly think he can adhere to it for long. For our sake, I hope he will not. Friend, I do know how happy we can be together. As soon as Elgin tires of our arrangement and abandons me, which I assure you he will, for I know the man, I will be yours. We shall yet be happy. I am never away from you. Every instant of the day, my thoughts shall be on you. I shudder to think sometimes that nothing but death can free me. I do not wish to compromise you now that you are an M.P. Yet I cannot bear the idea that people think of me as Lady Elgin, living with him, and not you. God in heaven blesses you and honors you, my dear Robert. Let us be patient and pray.

Your own Mary

An answer came immediately, but Mary did not receive it, nor did she see it until Elgin burst into her room waving it in her face and reading aloud its contents: " 'Now I know that my Mary loves me and ever will love me until she sinks into the grave! Oh, most adored of beings, we shall forever enjoy the delight and happiness which only hearts united like ours can feel. I shall wait for you and upon you forever.' "

Elgin looked at her with fury in his eyes. "I knew it!" he hissed. "You have been deceiving me for years. I knew it in Paris, but I allowed you to convince me to the contrary. You are a betrayer and an adulteress. Neither William nor Lucy is my child, and you know it. Dear God, women are not to be trusted."

He paced about her room, giving her relief from his eyes, which were full of hate. "I allowed you too much freedom. That was my mistake," he said, as if trying to work out a problem. "Women are fanciful creatures, unleashing their emotions and their lust wherever they are allowed. None of you should be let loose to prey upon the feelings of men!"

"Elgin, I have not committed adultery, though with the way that you have treated me in our marriage, it is a miracle that I did not do so. You will find nothing in my behavior to contradict that. I am nothing to you, it is apparent. Why did you come back here? You know that you want nothing to do with me."

"You exhaust me," he said. "I should have been a sterner husband. I shan't make the same mistake again."

He left her room, and refused to speak with her. She wrote him a long letter explaining that she had committed a sin in her heart, but her body had been his alone. She begged him to believe that for so very long, her love for him had been pure and unadulterated, and that though her heart had wavered, she had remained chaste.

She could not have him tag her with the sin of adultery. She would be an outcast for life. She was no entertainer like Emma Hamilton. She was the daughter of a respectable and wealthy man, the great-granddaughter of the 2nd Duke of Rutland and granddaughter of the beloved Lady Robert Manners, who could trace her lineage to the Plantagenet kings. She was thought to be the essence of all that was good and decent in a young woman. But if Elgin was bound and determined to paint her as an adulterous woman, everyone would be on his side. He would have cause to bring legal action against her, even to remove the children from her custody.

She had no choice but to humble herself and play the repentant wife. No judge would care that her husband had driven her to infidelity. For a woman, there was no excuse for falling from grace. But all of her words, no matter how impassioned, fell upon deaf ears.

"I shall cast you out of my life forever. You shall have the separation that you and your lover yearn for."

Those were his last words to her. He left immediately for London, leaving her to wonder what his next move might be. She kept the children close to her, encouraging them to sleep with her at night, so afraid was she that he would try to claim them. Weeks later, she received a letter from his lawyers. If her trustees transferred enough money into his accounts to relieve all of his debts, he would divorce Mary quietly. If not, he would pursue a public trial that would bring shame upon her and leave her ruined in society.

"What man would do that to his children?" Mr. Nisbet asked.

Her father had been wavering in his support for her. He could not imagine the circumstances that would cause a married woman to stray. Mary knew that both he and her mother wanted to believe her assurances that she had not committed adultery with Robert, but they remained somewhat skeptical. Both had witnessed his attention to her in London and at home, and it had made them uncomfortable. Both had warned her that even if she was innocent, her behavior was bound to be misinterpreted by anyone who knew how much time Robert spent in her company, and the manner in which they ran about town like a married couple.

"Elgin is in London seeing to the inventory of his statues. He is desperate to exhibit them, but he does not have the money to do so," Mary said. "The marbles are his grand obsession. We must give him the money immediately. If he can finally display them so that all the world may see what a great service the 'visionary' Lord Elgin has done for mankind, he will be placated."

Mr. Nisbet looked perturbed. "He seduced me into underwriting his folly. I should have known better at the time. It is unseemly for a grown man with responsibilities to indulge in this sort of venture. But I shall send him what he asks for. Neither my daughter nor my grandchildren must be subjected to public disgrace that would haunt them all the days of their lives."

Mr. Nisbet wrote to Mr. Coutts in London, arranging for Elgin to receive the money he requested—a huge sum, thought Mary, one that might keep a sensible man in comfortable means for the rest of his life. Of course, it would not last in Elgin's hands, but Mary was relieved that she had saved her children, herself, and Robert the humiliation that Elgin might have heaped upon them all. By the time he arranged for the exhibition and paid the rest of his debts, she would be done with all negotiations between them. Elgin would probably take a diplomatic position in a faraway capital, and they would never see each other again. When he came to Scotland, she could arrange for the children to visit with him while she remained discreetly absent. When the children were older, they could travel to wherever their father was serving his government, thereby expanding their knowledge of the world.

These thoughts helped her make peace with what had seemed an impossible situation. She had no idea what Elgin would do next, but she guessed that the proceedings would move quickly and quietly. With enough money to care for the marbles and display them, he could turn his attention to his obsession and be done with her, except when he needed more money, which her father would have to send him if he wanted to continue to avoid scandal. It could have been worse. At least Elgin was willing to be paid off.

Perhaps he would divorce her quietly. She would be stigmatized, true, but her lineage and her father's power and money could protect her from a certain amount of public abuse. And, as Robert pointed out, after a year had passed, she would be free to marry her beloved.

Archerfield Estate,

in the county of East Lothian,

June 22, 1807

BECAUSE OF HER FATHER'S wealth and connections, Mary discovered the horror that awaited her before it came knocking on the door. The sheriff of East Lothian had known Mary since she was a baby and had enough respect for Mr. Nisbet to give warning of what was to happen—had to happen according to the law, but he was mightily sorry to be subjecting such noble persons as Mr. and Mrs. William Nisbet and their daughter to the ordeal.

Nonetheless, on the appointed morning, the man announced himself at Archerfield and read the document that Mary could not believe truly existed.

The sheriff looked miserable as he read the words: " 'The right honorable Thomas Bruce, seventh Earl of Elgin and eleventh Earl of Kincardine, is petitioning for divorce from Mary, Countess of Elgin and Kincardine, on grounds of adultery with a man or men known not to be the said Thomas, Earl of Elgin, and on further grounds of being an unfit mother. The charges shall be proven in court and followed by an Act of Parliament. From the marriage, five children were procreated, of whom four are alive today. Those children are hereby given in sole custody to Thomas, Earl of Elgin, and shall reside with him and under his care, not to receive contact or visitation from Mary, Countess of Elgin.'

"I am sorry, Lady Elgin," the sheriff said. "But this is the law."

They had barely finished breakfast. The servants were skulking about, eavesdropping, under the guise of cleaning or making tea or seeing to the needs of the children. They knew all too well what was happening. Stories of children being torn from their adulterous or otherwise unfit mothers abounded. Most of the maids—and not a few of the aristocrats—entertained themselves with gossipy pamphlets laying out the sordid details of the lurid affair between Lady This One and Sir That One that led to the lady's never seeing her little ones again. "And to think, a lady who had exhibited none but a pious nature before she met the dastardly seducer who would be her downfall, would choose satiating her lusts over her own beloved little ones!" That was the sort of thing they all read, and now, that scorned lady would be Mary.

"But we paid him off!" Mary cried. "He swore that he would avoid this if we gave him the money. That lying, deceiving Scot!"

"It isn't the first time he's been duplicitous," Mr. Nisbet said. "No matter how many ways he reveals his dark nature, it is always a shock."

"Pardon me. The children?" the sheriff said. He might as well have been asking for his tea. He looked at Bruce, who was tearing through the parlor, being chased by Andrew.

"I don't wish to go to Father!" Lord Bruce protested. "I want to stay here and play soldiers with Andrew!"

"Well, you must go," Mary said, her voice quavering. She fell against her father, putting her face into his shoulder so that the children could not see her fear. She was not crying—not yet—but trying to quell her terror so that she could calmly, and temporarily, she was sure, tell her children goodbye. "Your father wishes to spend time with you this summer; it is a great surprise."

"My father can kiss my beautiful little behind," the boy said, and then ran off through the hallway. Mr. Nisbet signaled for Andrew to run after him. Andrew caught him, and the boy's cries could be heard echoing all the way from the garden. "Pack a few things, Andrew," Mr. Nisbet whispered as Andrew carried Bruce over his shoulder and up the stairs.

Little Mary, who imitated her big brother's every word and

motion, hid herself in her grandmother's skirts. "I don't want to go either. I want to stay with my sisters."

The little girls were upstairs in the nursery. "Are you taking all of them?" Mary asked the sheriff. "Is this really necessary? I shall ride to Broomhall at once and talk to Lord Elgin."

"You do not want to do that, Lady Elgin," the sheriff said. "It could be taken as a hostile act or a threat and would be used against you in the courtroom. I have seen it many times. No use in giving in to hysteria. It's one of the very signs of an unfit mother."

"Is that how the law operates?" Mary cried, her voice uncontrollably shrill as her daughter ran from her grandmother's skirts to her mother's. "Take a woman's children away, and then call her hysterical and unfit when she protests?"

The sheriff shrugged. "I do not make the laws, Lady Elgin, I only enforce them as I am ordered."

"Don't call me that!" she said. "I never wish to be called Lady Elgin again."

Elgin, Elgin, Elgin. How she had loved the sound of the words "Lady Elgin" when she first was married. She had paraded around with Masterman, clowning on the morning after her wedding, forcing the woman to call her Lady Elgin at the beginning and end of every sentence, and then falling into a fit of giggles on the bed. Now the very sound of the name revolted her, arousing memories of her noseless husband lording it over her, even in bed, where his disfigurement was sickening, but not so sickening as the way that he tried to control and manipulate her outside the bedroom.

Mrs. Nisbet called Little Mary's governess, who took the protesting child upstairs. Mary had never let her children be torn away from her. Never. Only under Elgin's orders, as when she, brokenhearted, had to part with them at Naples so that Elgin could have his tour of Europe—the very tour that landed him in prison and their marriage in ruins.

"Elgin is trying to frighten you, Mary," Mr. Nisbet said. "Get hold of yourself. We will sort it out. I'll wager that if a big wad of money is transferred to his bank, he will release the children immediately. The extortionist!"

"How dare he bring scandal upon this house?" Mrs. Nisbet said. "What sort of man would do that to his own children? Drag his wife through a divorce court? It's unspeakable."

"Our outrage will not change this outcome," Mary said, calming herself. "Now, sheriff, what can we do?"

The sheriff put his head down, shrugging his shoulders. He played nervously with his hat. "There is nothing, milady."

"Nothing? Nothing a mother can do to reverse the loss of her children?"

"If the father wishes to claim custody of his children, there is nothing anyone can do to contest him. That is the law. I have seen this many times. I wish I could help you. Now, if you'll cooperate, I must escort the children to Broomhall and deliver them to the custody of Lord Elgin, or I will lose my badge."

*The city of Athens,
in the tenth year of the
Thirty-Year Truce with Sparta*

ONE CAN EITHER PROVOKE or charm a jury, Aspasia," Sokrates said. "I advise the latter, of course. The mere fact that your body wears the evidence of Perikles' love will win them to your side. All the world loves a pregnant woman, even if she is considered a harlot. Do nothing to provoke and you will walk away acquitted."

"This is wise advice, my friend," I said. "But they have done so much to provoke me that I wish to return just a little bit of the sentiment."

"One can either be right or be happy," he said. "I leave it to you to choose which is more important to you."

Sokrates had taken a keen interest in my trial, coming to console and advise me as soon as he heard the news. "Your brother-in-law and his accomplice Elpinike are running around town saying that you turned the home of a citizen into a fuck-factory, and that you attempted to seduce free women into prostitution, a charge that, if proven, is punishable by death!

This is the most interesting—and strangely prurient—prosecution in recent history. I'm fascinated!"

I was happy to have a friend to help me lay out my strategy. The charges were impiety and procurement, and we were convinced that neither could be proven according to Athenian law. Perikles agreed, and acted with such complete confidence that I would be acquitted that he was difficult to engage in the discussions. We were aware that I was being persecuted for being a foreign woman with influence over Athens's most powerful man, and—as Alkibiades had warned me years ago—for opening my big mouth and letting my wisdom fly out of it.

"That is not a crime in itself," I said to Sokrates. "For nowhere in the laws is it written that a woman must keep her mouth shut."

"True. But it is considered natural law that she should. And you are a woman who is threatening to overturn the natural order of things."

"By speaking?"

"Yes! You are the first woman who will be allowed to be present at a trial. It is unheard of, you realize. Speaking is your biggest fault, as far as the men of Athens are concerned—speaking as a philosopher, or speaking on political matters with Perikles."

"But what about Diotima? She speaks as a philosopher."

"Diotima is protected by the office of High Priestess. When she speaks, she is speaking with the authority of the goddess, so no one minds. When you speak, you are usurping the man's right to supremacy. When you advise Perikles, you are usurping the rights of his male peers. When you boldly move about town going where you please and conversing with whomever you choose, you are threatening all men by raising the possibility that their wives will find reason to do the same."

"Let us put this to rational inquiry," I said.

"Only if you call for more wine," he answered. We were sitting on a new couch in the courtyard of my home. I'd had it made for me to lounge on during the heat of the day, when my pregnancy made it uncomfortable to nap indoors. Here, under an awning made of sturdy white linen, and propped on comfortable cushions, I could rest.

I called for more wine for my friend, and proceeded to lay out my thoughts. "If the goddess of the city whom all good men worship and honor possesses all of the qualities that men cherish and wish to emulate, such as wisdom, boldness, courage, strategic thinking, and the like, and if Athena is a female, then is it not logical that females possess these qualities?"

"It would seem to be so," Sokrates said.

"And if females possess these qualities, then should female opinion not be heard and listened to? Should women not operate freely in society as men do?"

I could feel my face flush as I spoke, embracing my own argument, and wanting him to follow my thinking.

"I cannot argue with your logic, Aspasia. But your logic will get you nowhere with an Athenian jury. All I can tell you is this: Just be a good girl. That is what the jurors will need to see. If you show them the brazen whore of their imagining, they will convict you. If you show them the good girl, the obedient one, they will acquit."

"Perhaps I should make a special sacrifice to Pandrosos to help me learn obedience," I said sarcastically.

"Perhaps that would be a good investment," he replied without a trace of the usual irony.

"Do you not see the contradiction? You are asking me to play the role of the good and obedient girl. But if I do so, I cannot challenge these ridiculous charges."

"You must challenge them by proving them untrue, unreasonable, and immoderate, and by presenting yourself as reasonable and moderate, two virtues that we Greeks allegedly value above almost all others. 'Nothing in excess,' commands the god Apollo. You must show no undue emotion. This is crucial. You must drop this line of inquiry on the inherent virtues of women that we must all recognize and honor."

"But my argument is logical, and Athenians value logic," I said.

"But those ideas make your face go red and your voice go shrill. If you allow yourself to become emotionally charged, you will be seen as a Medea, a foreign woman out of control. I am telling you this: Athenians believe that foreigners and women are full of unrestrained emotions and unbridled lust. If left uncontrolled, such people will destroy this reasonable and civilized society that we have built for ourselves. You are both a foreigner and a woman, and neither of those attributes is working in your favor. Therefore, Aspasia, try not to show off when you defend yourself, or I promise you it will get you in trouble."

The baby inside of me began kicking, as if to punctuate the correctness of Sokrates' argument. I knew my friend was right; promoting the virtues of women based on the virtues of the goddess would not refute the charges against me, but would merely challenge the notions that kept us quiet and invisible in the public sphere.

"You realize that no one would ever prosecute a man on these charges?" I said.

"Of course no one would. All sorts of men have posed for sculptors, provoking no outrage," Sokrates replied.

"And that men invite whomever they please to their homes and are not held responsible for the behavior of their guests?"

"That is so, Aspasia, but entirely irrelevant to the matter at hand."

"Your strategy makes sense, Sokrates, but I am baffled as to how I might carry off this charade of being a good and obedient woman."

"Personally, I am always guided by an inner *daimon,* which tells me how to behave at all times. I am convinced that all human beings have a spirit of this sort who resides in them, and who will direct words and actions to the highest possible outcome. I encourage you to find yours, and allow it to carry you through the trial."

THE TRIAL COULD NOT be held in any of the usual courts. Nosy men had awakened long before dawn to stand in line to serve on the jury or to attend the proceedings. Athens was widely known for its "court-o-philes," those old men who were addicted to observing litigation and serving on juries. But the case against me seemed to turn the entire city into that caricature. Two thousand potential jurors showed up and insisted upon being selected for the trial. No one wished to be denied the privilege of seeing me tried for my alleged crimes, and no official wished to be the person who denied the citizens. Even the Odeion was too small to accommodate the hordes of spectators. The Pnyx, where the Assembly tried its cases, was rejected in favor of the Theater of Dionysus, perhaps to give the good citizens of Athens the theatrical production they anticipated and hoped for.

Here the prosecutor, Hermippus, the nasty, one-eyed, foul-tongued comic poet, would feel most at home, since one of his plays had been produced in the theater earlier in the year. In it, he had created a character named Perikles, who was an inveterate carouser, taking his pleasure while enemies invaded Athens. Nothing could be further from the truth, of course, but the parody of Athens's leading citizen did garner quite a few laughs, even from Perikles, who always considered himself to be above redressing such attacks on his character.

Magistrates sat in the row of marble seats decorated with all the symbols of Athens—olive wreaths; the goddess Athena with her owl, the embodiment of wisdom, perched on her shoulder; and the goddess's impregnable shield. I heard little gasps from the nearby spectators as I was led to my seat. Sokrates had been correct; the presence of a female at her own trial was unprecedented. Yet I saw Elpinike seated with those who had gathered to testify against me. Undoubtedly the prosecution had been informed that I, a woman, would speak in my own defense, so, in the interest of balance, another female could be called to speak against me. The court official pointed to the chair in which I was to sit. Carved upon it was an image of the hero Theseus running his sword through an Amazon.

"How fitting," I said to my escort. "Another woman being slaughtered."

I sat down, self-satisfied, allowing the marble warmed by the rising sun to soothe my back, which had been hurting these last weeks—a typical ailment in pregnancy, I was told. In the center of the stage sat a huge altar, common to many theaters in Greece. I imagined myself lying upon it by the day's end, the sacrificial victim offered up to assuage the anger of Perikles' enemies. I had sat in this very seat several times, next to Perikles, as we enjoyed theatrical presentations. Would this be my last time here? Though no one thought that I would be executed for my crimes if convicted, some thought that I might be banished from the city. If Perikles were ever ostracized, I would accompany him into exile, and we would remain together, whereas if I were sent away from Athens, he could not possibly follow. The threat of this outcome grieved me the most.

The proceedings were not ceremonious. Hermippus, his one eye squinting in the morning sunlight, repeated the charges for the jury—impiety and procurement. The two witnesses for the prosecution, Alkibiades and Elpinike, sat on the opposite side of the row from me, along with several young men whom I recognized as Pheidias' apprentices. Alkibiades would not meet my eye, but Elpinike had no problem staring at me like a wolf would stare at wounded prey. But I was not wounded, and she would know it by the time the trial had ended.

I was filled with confidence. Perhaps pregnancy brought with it special powers. Women had to protect their unborn children, and with that responsibility came a feeling of ferocity, at least for me. In the beginning, I had felt vulnerable and ill; now, six months later, I felt full of life—bursting with it, and with love for my unborn baby. I had taken Sokrates' advice and called upon my inner *daimon*. I felt that the creature would make itself known to me today and, just as my friend had said, would guide me through the ordeal.

Perikles did not sit next to me, as we did not want it to appear that he was on trial with me. I had only one witness to call in my defense, Diotima, who sat in the usual chair reserved for the High Priestess. None of the men whose wives had attended the party would testify. Anger against them for allowing their wives to commit that grave transgression was running too high, and some of the men said they had been threatened with ostracism. Diotima looked mightily annoyed that she was to spend her morning occupied this way. I only hoped that the sun would not rise too high before the trial was over. She could easily decide that she was getting too warm and get up and leave before giving her testimony.

I was also disquieted by the presence of the Board of Ten, the council responsible for keeping highways open and clear. The board also set the price for streetwalkers and mediated disputes between men who fought over them, or between a girl and her customer. The councilmen had no regard for the girls; in every case, the customer was right—and not least because the councilmen were often customers. Why were they present at my trial? I supposed I would soon find out.

Just as Hermippus was about to call his first witness, Sokrates entered, waving at me as if we were running into one another at the agora. Was he going to make a surprise plea on my behalf? It would be just like him to enter unannounced and make a verbose case for my innocence. He should have asked my permission if he wished to speak on my behalf. Instead, he took a seat next to Elpinike. I felt rattled to the core. I would never have dreamt that Sokrates would betray me and agree to be a witness for my accusers. I hoped I could get past the hurt and the anger I felt over his outlandish treachery in time to defend myself. Wasn't it he who advised me to eschew emotion when presenting my case? Surely he would have anticipated the anxiety he would cause in appearing thus. My confidence, surging just moments before, began to fizzle into a case of nerves.

Elpinike was the first witness to speak. "Since Aspasia arrived in Athens, she has brought nothing into this city but evil. The blood of Athenian war heroes is on her hands! Everyone knows that Perikles besieged the island of Samos to appease her when she complained of Samian aggression against her native Miletus. As if that were not bad enough, she used her friendship with Pheidias to imprint her own visage upon the face of the Mother Goddess."

Hermippus nodded his head in agreement. "A council of magistrates has declared the likeness of the statue to Aspasia to be negligible," he said. "But it is the defendant's intention that is on trial here. She intended to offend the goddess, and any insult to a deity is an act of impiety, which is punishable by law.

"Athenians, Elpinike is a good woman, known for her patronage of the arts as well as her association with at least one of our finest and most beloved late artists. Let us hear how she discovered that Aspasia had committed this impious act."

Elpinike straightened her carriage. "Thank you, Hermippus, for acknowledging my status in the artistic community. I like to keep abreast of all that is going on, as any good patron should, and these two young gentlemen who are about to bear witness to Aspasia's crime brought to my attention the fact that she was positioning herself as the model for the colossal statue of the goddess, a statue paid for with public funds."

She went on to gloat some more about her insider status with young artists, how they came to her for advice, owing to her special relationship with Polygnotos. Now that the genius painter was no longer in this world, young men regarded her as the closest thing to him left on the earth and sought her company. Undoubtedly, she paid them for information, which was the way with meddling old women, but of course they would not admit to that in court. She went on and on about herself, and, frankly, I was delighted that she was taking the focus off of me and boring the jury with the details of her importance. She yapped until the device that measured speaking time ran out, and Hermippus had to remind her that her time was up. After she sat down, the apprentices took the witness stand and simply confirmed what Elpinike had said—that they saw me sit for Pheidias on several occasions during the time that he was trying to work out the details of Athena's face.

"We cannot ask Pheidias, now can we, because his accomplice, Perikles, sent him away to Olympia! Very clever, sir!" Hermippus pointed his long, crooked finger in Perikles' direction. "However, I have three witnesses who worked with the sculptor and who saw with their own eyes Aspasia seated before Pheidias as he drew her face. The last of those will speak now. I call to witness the sculptor Sokrates, son of the respected stonemason Sophroniscus. Sokrates has worked for three years with Pheidias on the Akropolis projects."

I thought I was going to vomit as I watched my friend stand up and prepare to speak. He had been privy to my innermost thoughts, owing to the easy intimacy we had established in the very beginning of our relationship. Would I hear all of my words used against me now?

Sokrates took the stand and gave the same testimony as the two apprentices—he had seen me on several occasions sitting for Pheidias at the very time that the sculptor was working on Athena's face. I could not believe that he stood there, testifying against me. I stared at him incredulously, but he did not look my way. Had he come under some threat against himself or his family? Witnesses were sometimes bullied into testifying, but Sokrates was not the sort that would succumb. I was certain that he was here of his own volition.

"May I add a bit of testimony that may help you to uncover the truth?" he asked Hermippus.

I froze, waiting for the ultimate betrayal, my insides turning against me with such vehemence that I worried for my unborn child, who was bathing in that noxious environment.

"I am known on the Akropolis for my love of conversation. Ask anyone, and they will tell you that Pheidias spent many hours in dialogue with me, if only to get me to do my work."

For the first time, some of the toothless men of the jury smiled. I wanted to smile too, but I was afraid that this humorous introduction was soon to be turned against me.

"In our many hours of talking, Pheidias spent much time extolling the virtues and qualities not only of Aspasia, but of her face. He often declared that Aspasia's face was the only one he ever saw that embodied the same beauty, courage, and wisdom that we attribute to the goddess. Pheidias did ask Aspasia to pose for him, and Aspasia agreed to sit, yes. But if he intended to use her image for the goddess, she was unaware of it."

Now the old men began to talk loudly among themselves, and the presiding magistrates had to call for quiet.

"I have spent many hours in dialogue with Aspasia as well. You see, my friends, I live up to my reputation as a talker. I know Aspasia to be a generous woman—agreeable, and of the sort easily absorbed into the plans of powerful men. Of course, she did not wish to model for Pheidias. She did not even think it was a decent thing to do, and she worried over what Perikles would think of such a thing. But she is an obedient woman, loyal to Pheidias, who is a friend and associate of Perikles."

The jurors began to mumble again among themselves. Alkibiades jumped out of his seat and shook an angry fist at Sokrates. "That is an outright lie! Aspasia is as obedient as a newborn buck. She is known throughout Athens as an outspoken woman who cannot keep her mouth shut under any circumstances!"

"She is keeping her mouth shut now," Sokrates said calmly.

The jurors laughed out loud at this, but the magistrates pounded the gavels until everyone was silent.

Sokrates continued: "Aspasia is an intelligent woman, yes, but the fact remains that she is but a woman, subject to the higher will of men. When asked to pose by someone as illustrious and important as Pheidias, famed throughout the Greek world for his talents, what was she to do? She could not say no. Everyone knows that an artist of the caliber of Pheidias must be ruthless in pursuit of beauty. I am sure that the good Elpinike, familiar as she is with the mind of genius, would bear witness to that fact."

Elpinike nodded in agreement, but without abandoning her look of contempt. Sokrates, paying her no attention, turned to the jurors.

"If the face of Aspasia haunted the sculptor's chisel while he formed the face of the goddess, the lady was not aware of it, and therefore should bear no culpability."

Hermippus was pacing impatiently, irritated with this turn of events. He looked jittery, wanting to get rid of Sokrates before he caused further harm to the prosecution. Sokrates, on the other hand, was beaming at the jury, stopping just short of taking a bow for his performance. He clearly loved being the fly in the prosecution's ointment.

"How can you be certain that Aspasia had no idea of Pheidias' intentions?" Hermippus asked gruffly.

"I have enjoyed the confidence of both Aspasia and Pheidias, and I assure you that this is one of the very few things of which I am absolutely *certain.*"

Hermippus opened his mouth to dismiss Sokrates, but the sculptor continued: "The men of Athens seek Aspasia's rational advice on irrational matters such as relations with women. She is known to be expert in logical and rational thinking. No rational person would intentionally commit an act of evil, for everyone knows that it would bring the wrath of the community upon him. Aspasia seeks no one's wrath, but everyone's goodwill." The theatrical setting brought out the actor in him.

"Thank you, Sokrates. Now please leave the stage," Hermippus said firmly.

Sokrates had done me a great favor by professing my innocence, but some rebellious part of me wanted to prove him wrong, which would give me a tiny iota of momentary satisfaction, but which would undoubtedly put me in worse stead with the jury. Did I want to be right, or happy? I wanted to be right; all my life, I had struggled against being an obedient woman. To save me, he proclaimed me thus before all of Athens, and though this was in my highest interest, still I wished to dispute it. The war was raging inside me, but it was one I knew I would lose. For the sake of my baby, if not my own freedom, I had to compromise. I hoped that when it was my turn to defend myself, my *daimon* would not betray my passions, but would guide my words to strike the appropriate balance.

The day was getting hotter, and my emotions started to run as high as the temperature. I had been lost in my thoughts, not realizing that we had moved on to the second part of the charges—that I had solicited decent women to become prostitutes.

Alkibiades rose to testify. He looked at me, gloating, and then turned to the jury with his prepared speech. "As shocking as it may seem to decent men, in the home of Perikles, the women's quarters are not separated from the men's quarters. Aspasia, an unmarried woman, a courtesan, has run of the entire household. I, of course, prevent my own wife from entering the premises, though this woman is her sister."

I wanted to jump up and ask if the freedom to move about one's own house was a crime when I realized that it might be so. I was not so familiar with the laws of Athens that I knew the minute detail of every statute. I was almost certain that the separation of men's and women's living quarters was based on custom rather than law, but I could not be sure. In any case, the revelation that Perikles kept no separate quarters for the women of the house hit the jurors' ears as scandalous, setting off a rumble of conversation among them.

"She must be a witch, with knowledge to make powerful potions," Alkibiades said. "How else would she be able to manipulate an Athenian man into this sort of chaotic arrangement? This sort of leniency? She is breaking all natural laws by her behavior."

True to character, Alkibiades was ranting just to hear his own words. I could see that Hermippus wanted to get his witness back to the topic of the charges against me.

"Alkibiades, you say that you witnessed Aspasia recruiting the wives of Athenian citizens for the purposes of prostitution. What did you see?"

"I entered the courtyard of the home as the wicked activities organized by Aspasia for the evening were reaching a climax. Fornication between men and women was taking place for all to see. Aspasia had invited the respectable women of Athens for the express purpose of corrupting them and seducing them into her own trade. She had tried to convince me to allow my own wife to attend the party but I wisely refused. I am pleased to say that my wife's piety remains intact.

"The women at Aspasia's party, however, had been plied with bowls of undiluted wine. I took it upon myself to sample the offerings. I could not believe what my tongue had discovered."

This was a complete lie. In fact, the opposite was true. I had ordered the slaves to dilute the women's wine. Whose wine had he tasted? I could not recall that he had stayed long enough to drink.

"Fellow Athenians, drunkenness could be the only explanation for what I saw. I witnessed the wives of Athenian citizens watching acts of open fornication as if they were at a theatrical performance."

Now the jurors really had something to talk about. Alkibiades had to raise his voice in order for the rest of his lies to be heard. "My fellow Athenians! Here is the most scandalous part: Under Aspasia's influence, the women were actually standing in line waiting for their turn with the men! Aspasia turned the home of Perikles into a brothel, and the women of Athens into its workers!"

"And was our own Olympian Perikles present as well?" Hermippus asked sardonically. "Or was he off chatting with the gods again?"

"No, he was upstairs in his bedchamber, waiting for the newly corrupted women to join him. I suppose he and Aspasia need the income from their brothel workers to pay for his extravagant building projects! That is what I believe."

"Well, that is certainly an outrage, Alkibiades. But why do you think the husbands of Athens agreed to allow their wives to enter this place of iniquity and fornication?"

"Because they were intimidated by Perikles, of course. Under him, Athens is no longer a democracy but a monarchy. He considers himself the city's ultimate authority. He behaves autocratically, as if he has modeled himself after the tyrant Kreon in Sophokles' play *Antigone.*"

"And the attending women? Do we know what has happened to them?"

"Their husbands may punish them in any way they see fit. There is no reason to drag them into the public sphere any more than has already been done by Aspasia. Women belong at home, in their own quarters. Making Aspasia pay for her crime will surely send that message. Athenians, we must restore order in our homes. The women of Athens used to shun courtesans. Now they are being drafted into behaving like them—attending parties, drinking to intoxication, and fornicating with strangers."

"Thank you for your eloquent testimony, Alkibiades," Hermippus said. "It is true, what you say. The world is turning upside down." He turned to the jury. "By convicting the accused, my fellow citizens, we may rid our city not only of Aspasia, but of her influence, which as we have seen is toxic to our wives. If Aspasia wishes to conduct business as a madam, then let her do it legally. We have invited the Board of Ten to the proceedings. If Aspasia is convicted, they will fine her an appropriate amount of money, and force her to pay the proper fees that all brothel owners must pay, including taxes on her income."

I did not want to turn around, but I could hear the jurors talking. I thought that Hermippus was merely trying to humiliate me by portraying me as a brothel owner, much as he would do if he were writing a farce with me as a character. But from what I could hear, the jurors were taking this seriously.

"True enough. If the woman wants to operate a brothel, then let her do so legally!" I heard a man behind me exclaim this, and I could not believe my ears when others in the vicinity shouted their agreement.

"Who can say what fury from Athena—virgin goddess, keeper of women's chastity and piety—Aspasia's actions will bring down upon the city of Athens?" Hermippus continued. "Does it matter if Aspasia set out to insult the goddess by posing for her visage, or even if she knew what she was doing? The fact is that a whore's face is on the statue of the goddess of the city. The fact is that respectable women were seduced into entering Aspasia's house and participating in dissolute activities. Only by conviction and punishment will Athena's wrath be assuaged. A vote to convict Aspasia is a vote to save Athens."

Hermippus' speech garnered thunderous applause from the jury. The swell of sentiment against me in the theater seemed very great. I wondered if I would be denied the right to speak in my defense after all. And if I did speak, would I be safe?

I looked at Perikles, who remained impassive. While his nonchalance normally contributed to my own feeling of serenity, this time it made me feel even more insecure. How could he remain so calm, considering what was being said against me, and the rousing approval it received from my judges, and the enormous consequences for us that might result? I did not wish to be carried away by insecurity at the very moment when I was to stand before these thousands of men and speak, but it did occur to me that Perikles might have been somewhat swayed against me by the testimony. Would his political life not be easier if he had a respectable Athenian wife who remained anonymous and in the home, instead of me, a constant target of public criticism? Surely he was sick to death of defending me when he had so many more important matters to attend to.

But now it was time to defend myself. I stood up, taking the stage.

"This is not the first time your comic imaginings have been presented on this stage, Hermippus," I began, putting my hand on my belly to emphasize my condition. I was not above using it to garner sympathy and to make them feel guilty for putting a pregnant woman through this nightmare. "But not to worry. Everyone admires your skill in staging a farce, and this trial is no exception."

I looked out over the entire landscape of spectators. The theater, said to have a capacity of fifteen thousand people, was about half full. I was not an actor trained in recitation and oratory, and I could only hope that my softer female voice would carry to those sitting farther away. I could not yell and scream with the thunder of Alkibiades, so I would have to find another tactic to utilize the theatrical setting to my advantage.

"I have been drawing up a mental list of the accusations made against me here today, many of which have nothing to do with the actual charges. But I will try to address them all, and put many of these ridiculous rumors to bed.

"As far as my being the instigator of the war with Samos, I won't address that preposterous idea, Hermippus. It cannot be proven, for one thing. No one knows the contents of Perikles' mind. He may have gone to war in Samos on my account. But that charge does not figure in this or any trial. You might think that it is immoral to go to war to appease a woman, but it is not illegal. You may go to where the laws of Athens are written for all to see. Nowhere is it written that starting a war at a woman's behest is a crime."

I could hear the snickers from the jury, and I must say that it gave me great satisfaction to use humor to make a comic poet look foolish.

"A good prosecutor sticks to the facts. The sun will be high in the sky and the citizens soaked with sweat by the time we finish. I wish your witnesses had known how to get on with it. As it is, everyone will have to go to the baths twice today."

This brought outright laughter.

"We have heard much talk today about the natural order of things. So I ask you, Athenians who so love your laws: Is it written on any stele anywhere in the agora that a woman must not upset the natural order? And is the natural order, when it concerns these issues, written for any eyes to see? I have not seen one Athenian law concerning women and the natural order, so whatever the natural order of things is, it will have to be clarified and in writing before you can prosecute me for upsetting it.

"I am on trial for impiety and—oh, it is so foolish that I can almost not utter the word—*procurement*. To refresh the memories of my esteemed jurors, I shall now recite the laws against impiety.

"There are four offenses that prescribe the charge impiety, according to the law—Athenian law, that is. The first such offense is wrongdoing in connection with a festival. As I have not taken part in any festival, except by invitation to march in the procession of the metic women at the Panathenaea—and my behavior at that event is not in question here—I cannot see how I can be prosecuted on this element of the law.

"The second offense is the theft of sacred money, a charge of which I am not accused."

"The statue of Athena was paid for with public funds, Aspasia," Hermippus interrupted. "Therefore, I submit that you did steal sacred money!"

"Hermippus, I invite you to come to my home and search for gold. Let us do it right now, or please stop this broad interpretation of the laws of Athens to include anything you wish them to encompass. One might say that you are absconding with sacred money today by staging this trial. I invite you to look upon the many jurors who will be paid today out of the public coffers."

A few of the old men of the jury beat their canes against the ground to signal approval of what I had just said, which gave me confidence to continue in this vein.

"The third category of criminal impiety is temple robbing, and again, if you believe that I have taken money or objects from any sacred place, let us search high and low so that I may be brought to justice."

"That is not the accusation, Aspasia, and you know it. You are the one who is going to keep us here until sunset, so please stop enjoying the sound of your own voice and say what you have to say."

"Hear, hear!" Many of the jurors shouted in support of this. Unfortunately, the approval for Hermippus was still outweighing any favor I was getting from them. Perhaps Sokrates was correct; I should try to wear the persona of a good and obedient girl. He had set the defense up for me. All I had to do was embellish it.

"The final category of criminal impiety involves a more general prohibition. One must not perform actions giving insult to the gods. Athenians, to address this aspect of the law, I ask you to listen to the testimony of Diotima, the High Priestess of Athena, who will speak in my defense."

It was so quiet as Diotima rose that one could have heard the fluttering of a tiny moth's wings. She pushed the long white scarf that was protecting her skin from the sun away from her face and spoke. "I have prayed to the goddess and opened the belly of a sheep. The entrails were clear. Mortals may claim that Aspasia of Miletus has given offense to Athena, but the goddess does not concur. That is all that I have to say on the matter."

Unlike other witnesses, she did not return to her seat, but covered her head and departed the theater, leaving a wake of concerned mumbling from the jurors.

I stood, striking quickly while I felt the tide turning in my favor. "The letter of the law is clear. Actions insulting to the gods may be punished as impiety. But as you have just heard, while you may be offended by me, the goddess Athena is not."

Hermippus did not seem either upset or surprised by Diotima's words. "I'll thank you to remember, Aspasia, that there are many gods, and Diotima speaks for only one deity. If you wanted to prove that you had immunity, you should have consulted with the clergy of all the Olympians, for I fear that while Athena is showing you mercy, many of her peers are not."

He seemed quite prepared to answer what she had said. I wondered if someone—perhaps Diotima herself—had tipped him off as to her testimony. The jury was happy to be relieved of the proof of my innocence, and began shouting approval for what Hermippus had said.

I could feel my confidence begin to slip away. I had lost control of the crowd, and of myself, truth be told. "Athenians, please hear me! I have no tribe, no family, no household, no father to care for me, no brothers to protect me, no place in your society outside of the home of Perikles. I am no threat to you! You have heard the words of the priestess. I am innocent!"

But I saw no sympathy in their faces. These were the cantankerous old men of Athens, who no longer had a place in civic or military life. Their hard work and good deeds, including any heroism they might once have displayed in battle, were long forgotten by the young, who were running the city now. They were beyond the years of drinking and sexual pleasure, no longer vulnerable to the charms of a young woman. Who knew how many of them were friends of the late Kimon, brother of Elpinike? In truth, they were much closer to Alkibiades' age than to Perikles'. They were a different generation, too—the generation that thought that Perikles' grand building projects cost too much and were ostentatious. It seemed to me at this moment that they were out for my blood. I could easily come up with more clever arguments, going word for word with Hermippus, challenging him, perhaps even mocking him and making a fool out of him. But I realized that the more I did that, the more I would prove that I was a dangerous woman, and one who had to be silenced, exiled, or made to live as a brothel worker.

I wanted to lie down on the altar and die.

Suddenly Perikles stood up, motioning for me to take my seat. I had no idea what he was about to do.

"Athenians, I would like to exercise my right as a citizen to speak. Will you hear me?"

A resounding cry of approval rang out from the jurors. A speech by Perikles was an unexpected bonus to the trial, a bit of theater they did not expect. Of course they wanted to hear what he had to say.

"I know that some of you here do not approve of me, but let me remind you that it was I who instituted pay for those who serve on juries. Before I pushed for that piece of legislation, which has proven very lucrative for our elder citizens, jurors had to give their time in court for free. I hope all of you will enjoy the money you have made today and put it to good use in our economy."

It was brilliant of him to remind the lot of them of their debt to him. No one could begin a speech like Perikles—that was one of the few facts upon which all Athenians agreed. Once he started speaking, no one could resist listening. He continued: "I must also censure you, Alkibiades, for invoking the name of Sophokles to criticize me. General Sophokles fought side by side with me in Samos, so don't think you can turn his words or characters against me. His plays portray the human condition in all its tragic beauty, whereas you are a mere murderer of character. And may I remind you that I hold no office *other* than general, to which I am elected every year. The people of Athens can rid themselves of me anytime they like. But they choose not to. So much for my being an autocrat. Please, brush up on your political terminology and your knowledge of the theater before you throw such language around. Now, to the business of this trial.

"I have but one argument to make in the defense of Aspasia of Miletus. All of you are familiar with our relationship. It seems to me that you are putting this woman on trial not for any crime she has committed, but because her status as a concubine makes her vulnerable. Notice that none of the legally married women who you say were behaving like prostitutes has been charged with a crime. No, you dare not attack a married woman for fear of reprisal from the men of her tribe.

"I would like to make Aspasia my lawful wife, but I cannot. She is kept in the concubine status against my will and against her will by the law I myself enacted that forbids marriage between a citizen and an alien.

"Why did I make that law? I made it to protect the wealth, as well as the women, of Athens. Do you remember, Athenians, how citizens were marrying foreign women, even Syrian streetwalkers they met at the docks? Individuals who were half Athenian, half foreign—the issue of those unions—were legitimate and were inheriting Athenian wealth and Athenian land. The law was designed to retain all Athenian resources for Athens, to keep our money and our land among our people. Citizens! I was protecting the freeborn women of Athens by making that law. I would never do anything to harm or corrupt our citizen women. They are our great treasure."

Hermippus interrupted him. "Perikles, thank you for your impromptu oration, but you are not on trial here. Aspasia is on trial for trying to gain your favor by bringing you women."

"Here is where you are completely mistaken, Hermippus. You are confusing real personages with the farcical characters you create for Athens's amusement. You portray me upon the stage as a carouser, but my fellow Athenians know that I have always said that a general's hands and his eyes must be pure. Aspasia of Miletus is privy to the inner workings of my heart and mind. She knows that the actions she is accused of would displease me greatly and violate my code of ethics.

"She is a wife of the heart, if not in the eyes of the law. Our child, whom she carries, I will love as I love my two sons from my first wife. It is my fault that my child will be born a bastard, but it is a responsibility that I will bear. I made the law and I will live with its consequences, though it breaks my heart."

"We didn't know you had a heart, Perikles!" one man yelled. It was not a criticism, but said with humor. Everyone who had heard it erupted into laughter. Though many had come today to punish Perikles indirectly by punishing and shaming me, true to form, he had won the old men over.

"Laws are not made for individuals. A law cannot be changed for me, or for Aspasia, or for our child, or for any man or woman. The laws are for the good of the citizen body of Athens as a whole. The laws serve the community and the community must serve the laws."

Now the canes thumped wildly in support of Perikles and what he was saying. He had complete command of the crowd. He did not stop.

"Athenians! Why did we fight the Persian king? So that we might preserve the right to govern ourselves according to our own laws, the laws we have set forth and agreed upon. My fellow Athenians, I serve the law, as you must too. It is our laws that have made a courtesan out of a respectable woman. You heard the testimony of the holy priestess Diotima. You have heard me swear that Aspasia did not bring women into our home for any purpose other than their own curiosity about what men do at parties. I ask you now to respect our laws, the sacred and holy laws that keep our society together and make it great, and not twist them to punish an innocent and helpless woman."

To the astonishment of every person present, and especially me, Perikles allowed one large tear to roll down his cheek as he uttered his last words. He let it slide almost to his mouth, and then he wiped it away dramatically before sitting down again. Later everyone who was present at the trial, and many people who weren't, would say that the departed Aeschylus, the gifted tragedian whom Perikles had sponsored in the Dionysian theatrical competition so many years ago, must have inspired his impassioned speech in defense of his lover. Even his enemies were amazed to see him so moved.

It did not matter what Hermippus said after that, for no one was listening. When the vote was taken, almost every juror was in favor of acquittal on all charges.

"Are you happy, Aspasia?" Perikles asked as he put his arm around me and we walked into the crowd of well-wishers who had gathered at the entrance of the theater.

"Of course I am," I said. "I am the happiest woman in the world because I have the love of the greatest man in the world."

I was relieved and delighted that I was acquitted of the charges and could continue with my life as it was. But I was disquieted too. The only reason I was set free was not because I was in the right, or because I had defended myself with skill, or even because I was innocent, but because two male Athenian citizens had vouched for my virtue. It was a victory, but one that did not leave me feeling completely victorious.

In the cities of London and Edinburgh,

Winter 1807–1808

THE LAWYERS EXPLAINED EVERYTHING to her—not once, not twice, but thrice, because, each time, she could hardly believe her ears. Elgin had sworn to stop at nothing to ensure that Mary was punished, by law and by God, and dragged through as much public humiliation and private pain as possible. Despite that, Mr. Nisbet, and everyone who knew Elgin, tried to persuade him against this sort of public drama, he stampeded ahead, with no thought to the consequences. "I will not stop until an Act of Parliament is on record, demonstrating for this and all future generations that Mary is an adulteress," he said.

There were to be two trials, the first of which was already under way. Elgin was suing Robert in a London court for criminal conversation, that is, for seducing his wife. Mary was waiting for Robert to return from the ordeal, but they already knew what the outcome would be, and what Elgin's prime motivation was in this particular instance—money. Elgin claimed, in this trial, that Mary had been a perfect wife and that the two of them had lived happily and harmoniously until Robert entered their lives and seduced innocent

Mary away. For this tribulation, Elgin was demanding twenty thousand pounds in damages. The outcome was quite certain because Robert was not issuing any defense. He merely allowed his lawyer to read a statement, saying that in a rush of emotion, he had written love letters to Mary, to which she had not responded. Robert was not about to fuel Elgin's argument that Mary was an adulteress.

But Elgin was not going to stop at one trial, no matter the outcome. Under Scottish law, he was allowed to sue for divorce based on adultery, which he would have to prove in court. He could not be dissuaded from pursuing this avenue of retribution, though it would mean dragging the mother of his children through the most disgraceful of proceedings. He did not care.

"Can I not sue Lord Elgin for custody of my own children?" Mary asked the lawyer her parents had hired to defend her in the latter prosecution.

"Actually, no, Lady Elgin. A married woman has no legal status."

"What does that mean, exactly?" Mary asked.

"Why, it means that the married female has no legal existence acknowledged by the courts. If a woman is married, her husband must execute any legal or business transactions on her behalf. All that a woman has belongs to her husband, and that certainly includes the offspring. I'm afraid that it would be impossible to initiate a suit in your name. There is no precedent."

Mary felt her heart begin to beat violently in her chest. "Surely there is a way to have my children returned to me? They are my children! They came out of my own body; they are my flesh and blood."

"But in the eyes of the law, they belong to the father," the lawyer said dispassionately. He would have been accustomed to dealing with a woman's hysterics when presenting this news.

"But they need their mother. They are little children!" Mary's eyes darted frantically from her mother to her father, but neither offered any suggestion or consolation. Apparently they were already aware of her helplessness before the law.

"Since I do not legally exist—which is what you are telling

me—if I marry Mr. Ferguson, might *he* sue Lord Elgin for custody of my children?"

"He might, but if he is not the children's natural father, then he has no legal grounds on which to do so. The courts will uphold the rights of the father in every case. A suit would be futile indeed."

"The only way for a woman to achieve satisfaction in an English court is to be a man. That is what you are saying, correct?" Mary's fury rose up. She was trembling inside, but she did not want to give this scrawny, black-clad vulture of the law the satisfaction of knowing how badly she was shaken. Let him think she was simply mad. "Apparently nothing—neither money nor titles nor social connections—can cure one of the condition of being female!"

"Lady Elgin, I understand your consternation, but surely you understand that children must belong to someone, and English law says that that person must be their father."

She might have pulled off his spectacles and clawed his beady eyes out of his head. But he was merely the messenger. It was not he, or even Elgin, who deserved her fury at this moment. It was the way of the world, *the way things were,* that infuriated her.

"It isn't fair," she managed to say. She felt that she had to say something.

"Perhaps in some instances the law is not fair, but laws must exist to prevent society from descending into chaos."

He said this as if he meant it to be comforting. He was that sort of man, she thought, the sort who was alternately meek and coldly rational. Did he actually approve of the way things were? Would he rip his own children from the bosom of his wife?

When the lawyer left, Mary turned to her parents, those two who had always been able to repair any harm that befell her. "What is going to happen to my children? Who is going to make sure that Bruce finishes his dinner? You know that he won't eat a single vegetable unless I coax and threaten him. Who will fix up Mary's hair the way she likes it, to match her dolly's? Who will sing to my babies when they are afraid?" She put her arms around her belly as she had when she was carrying each one of them, to hold them, protect them, and feel their presence. But they were not there. She could protect them no longer. "At least William was taken from me in a natural way. At least it was God who wanted my most precious one, and not Elgin."

Mr. Nisbet poured his daughter a brandy and encouraged her to drink it up. She let the stinging liquid slide down her throat, feeling all the passion go out of her body, until she was just a limp, defeated thing sitting by the fire.

ROBERT THREW THE PAMPHLETS and newspapers on the table. "Read all about it," he said, imitating a London newsboy. "Read about Lady Elgin's refusal to honor the commitments of the marriage bed. Read how her wicked seducer conspired to ruin a fine and pious lady."

There it was, under her nose, where she could no longer avoid it: "The Trial of R. J. Ferguson, Esquire, for Adultery with the Countess of Elgin, Wife of the Earl of Elgin."

"Read all about it, Mary, how you, a poor innocent female and the model of Christian behavior, were wickedly seduced away from your loving husband and made to commit all manner of evil. You know why Elgin painted the story this way, do you not?"

"To make you look as dastardly as possible so that he might collect the damages?"

"Yes, which he did, though not as much as the bastard originally demanded."

"Well, what did the court award him?"

"Ten thousand pounds! That is what the loss of you is worth, my dear. I hope you are happy with your value!"

Robert tore off his greatcoat. Mary could not tell if he was angry or relieved. " 'Tis a filthy society we live in, Mary, that wants to learn the private details of others' lives. Filthy and wicked are the ones who tell these stories in purple language and exaggerated lies, and wicked and filthy are the ones who consume it all daily, along with their breakfasts."

"I should think you would have wanted to protect me from this sort of thing," she said, tossing the horrible pamphlet aside, only to reveal the article in the London *Times*, detailing the proceedings.

Messrs. Hamilton and Morier and others who were in the service of Lord and Lady Elgin at the Mohammedan Court, where Lady Elgin was a social favorite of the Turkish Luminaries, and where, in her more pious days, she insisted upon services of the Christian religion being performed daily, testified as to the affectionate marriage between the Elgins before the appearance of Mr. Ferguson—

"Oh, it's all horrible. I cannot look at it. One does not want to see one's name and one's habits bandied about like this! It's intolerable."

"The greatest protection is a solid armor, which you must build against public opinion, Mary. We will be criticized all our lives for having the courage of our convictions—you for not allowing yourself to be Elgin's miserable slave, using your fortune to bail him out of his spending habits and risking your life to bear him more children; and me for seducing a vulnerable woman and subsequently for marrying a woman who allowed herself to be seen as scandalous. Hypocritical, ironical, and paradoxical, but mark my words, that will be society's judgment upon us."

Mary allowed her eyes to glance at the demeaning words on the pages. "I remember gloating over the published details of Emma Hamilton's life and the satirical cartoons of her exploits. Everyone loved seeing her in compromised positions. Now it seems that I've ended no better than she."

"You haven't ended, Mary. You are not even thirty years old."

"I have ended up in Mrs. Hamilton's position, which I scorned terribly. I did not dream that I would suffer the same insults. Elgin made a point once that I was just like her. Do you think he saw something in me, Robert? Some piece of me that was willing to be compromised? Other women are better than I. They take their suffering silently. I could not be made to do so."

"Mr. Swift put it well and succinctly when he said that satire is a glass where beholders generally discover everyone's face but their own," Robert said. "We are all vulnerable to public scrutiny and opinion. But here is what I think of public opinion. I give it less notice in my life than I give to the ass of the rat who eats the cheese in my cupboard. I suggest that you do the same. I am going to resign from the House of Commons immediately."

Mary started to protest. "But, Robert, the reforms you've been working for! All lost!"

"I no longer care a fig for society's structures, or the good opinion of its sanctimonious prigs. I only care for you. I brought this filth home so that you could begin to develop your armor, Mary. This is nothing compared to what will come out in the divorce trial."

"What? He is going to pursue that?" She had prayed every day that Elgin would be satisfied with ruining her reputation in the civil trial against Robert, and with whatever damages he might recover. The judgment against Robert was enough for Elgin to receive the Act of Parliament granting a divorce. He would only pursue a trial for divorce in Edinburgh, on their home soil, to punish her. She shared these ideas with Robert.

"Lass, be warned, and be ready. He would not be bringing this to trial unless he had convinced some of your closest associates— friends, servants, staff, perhaps even relatives—to give damning testimony. And you will have to be there, listening to every word of it."

"I don't understand. In doing this to me, he is bringing equal amounts of shame upon himself and his children. What sort of monster lives inside of him?" She was terrified to think that all the years of their marriage, this beast was lurking, waiting to attack.

"I have known Elgin for a long time. I never liked him, but I did not dream that he was capable of going this far. He's mad! Public opinion is already turning against him for what he is doing. Did you know that he sent another request for a British peerage based on his contribution to the British arts, and was flatly turned down? Most people are disgusted by his public pursuit of your ruin. No one is going to offer him a diplomatic appointment after this."

Elgin did seem on the road to personal ruin. A list of his enormous debts was published in the *Times* for the entire world to see. Mary had heard that Elgin's private letters to the General Paymaster and the Prime Minister, begging yet again to be reimbursed for his ambassadorial expenses including the excavation and shipment of the marbles, totaled his debts at ninety thousand pounds, including the accumulated interest. She did not doubt the figure, having paid for a goodly portion of it out of her own pocket. If anyone should be reimbursed it was she, but of course that would never happen. It would be remarkable if Elgin ever saw a cent himself.

"He's bankrupted himself, ruined himself," she said. "He will blame the marbles, and force anyone within earshot to listen to how his great devotion to the English arts has taken all of his money. He will never admit that it's his own habits that have gotten him into trouble."

Robert had been pacing, mulling something over in his mind. He snapped his fingers, looking every bit the cat that has just swallowed the sparrow. "That is the way to stop him, Mary. Lay claim to his precious marbles. You are the one who funded the excavations, the removal, and the shipping. Why, they are yours as much as his. If you threaten to take them away, he will capitulate."

Why had she never thought of that? Indeed, they were as much hers as anything accumulated in the marriage. She had the receipts and invoices to prove it. "They are his only possessions left that are worth anything," she said. "Broomhall is leveraged, and all of his stocks were sold long ago. Do you think it's possible?"

"I think we should investigate whether it is possible."

"Mind you, I do not want custody of those things! I have seen the last of them, I hope. They are beautiful, Robert, but that sort of beauty is, oh, I don't know, too much for us mortals to possess." There was something too disquieting about the marbles. She remembered the frightening vision of Nemesis.

"Such fanciful thinking from a solid Scottish girl," Robert said, teasing her.

"You have not seen them. They are mystical, perhaps even possessed."

He was smiling at her, and she could not blame him. She must have sounded ridiculous. It was nothing she could explain to him. The story would be too long.

"Even if they are not enchanted things, which I believe they are," she said, "I still do not want to be mistress of one hundred twenty tons of marble. But if I threaten to take them away from him, perhaps Elgin will settle things with me quietly. Perhaps if he thought he was going to lose them with no credit for collecting them, and not a cent made in profit, he would not be so quick to try to keep me from seeing my own children."

MY ENTIRE LIFE WITH Elgin has been disassembled!"

Robert had just walked in and was handing his coat and hat to the footman when Mary greeted him in the foyer at Archerfield. The Nisbets had stopped worrying over Mary and Robert's relationship, and had started to accept that he would be the son-in-law with whom they would grow into old age. They had come to depend on him to assist Mary and her lawyers in strategizing against Elgin. Truth be told, they had ceased to disapprove of him at all, welcoming him fully into their family as the single bulwark against the insanity they feared would befall their daughter over the loss of her reputation and her children.

"What are you talking about?" Robert asked, his demeanor immediately switching to one of concern. "Surely he has not imagined some new means of tormenting you?"

"There has been a revolt in Constantinople! Do you recall that, last year, it was my old friend Count Sébastiani who persuaded the Sultan to break his alliance with Russia in favor of France?"

"Yes, of course. I don't hold it against him. He's a good chap, and he really did use all his efforts to assist you when Elgin was in prison."

"Oh yes, I know," Mary said. She had nothing but fondness for the count, whom she would always remember as a friend. "But that forced England to side with Russia, wiping out all of our hard-won diplomatic gains with the Ottomans. Now it's even worse.

The Janissaries, who used to escort me all over town, have staged a revolt! They confined the Sultan to the seraglio, and the poor man was assassinated there by the Chief Black Eunuch!" Mary remembered that very man, the one who tried to sabotage her meeting with the Valida by refusing to send the state barge that the Valida had ordered to transport Mary. He had carelessly endangered her life by forcing her to ride in a tiny boat in tempestuous waters. All of that seemed so very long ago. Little Mary had just been born and Bruce was but a babe.

Mary's heart bled for the Valida, and for Hanum, who had been the Sultan's favorite. What was happening to her old friends now? Undoubtedly, both women were now confined in the same tower in which the Valida had lived for so long, waiting for her son to take power. With the change in regime, it would be nearly impossible for Mary to get a letter through. "I shall have to go to chapel later today to pray for the safety of my friends. Though who knows? The Capitan Pasha himself could have been behind it all. I suppose we shall never know. For all the intimacy I shared with them, I must say that the Ottomans remained inscrutable."

"While we are turning the corner on the past, I have received new information that may shock you even more."

"I do not think I can tolerate another shock, Robert." What now? Was someone else dead?

"Some powerful people are claiming that Elgin's precious marbles may be utterly worthless."

"What?"

Robert waved a pamphlet in the air. "Elgin has many detractors, Mary, the most formidable of which is the Society of Dilettanti. They are upholding the opinion of Payne Knight that Elgin's statues are Roman copies. The charge is outrageous, of course. Sir Joseph Banks consulted with the world's leading antiquarian scholars. The statues are not copies."

"I, above all, know that," Mary said. "I and the Learned Men found numerous references to what we saw in the ancient texts, which proved their authenticity. I do not know why Mr. Knight persists in his opinion."

"Undoubtedly because the arrival of the works of Pheidias on British shores automatically devalues everything he and his cohorts managed to steal out of Italy! That is why."

Robert had engaged all of his London contacts to try to find out Elgin's present strategy concerning the marbles. At great expense, Elgin had bought—with what, Mary could not imagine; it could only be more credit—a town home at Piccadilly and Park Lane to display them.

"Elgin's great fixation has been transformed into one of those circus spectacles, Mary, where the ring is full of trick riders, rope dancers, and acrobats!"

Robert had amassed a number of articles from London newspapers detailing the goings on at the house where the marbles were displayed. He spread these on the table, Mary ordered tea, and the two of them pored over the papers greedily.

Mary was not certain what to make of the spectacles that had been staged at the Park Lane address. Surely these were not the noble pursuits of Elgin's imagination. Boxing matches—events at which Lord Elgin disgraced himself by appearing—were staged in front of the sculptures so that the gentlemen present, for a ticket price of five shillings each, could compare the physiques of the boxers to the statues. "They greatly admired the form of the pugilist known as Dutch Sam." Robert was obviously enjoying himself.

"There is something terribly crass in it, is there not?"

"Oh, they are all standing about, drunk, imagining themselves ancient Greeks," Robert said. "A pitiful pastime for men grown past the university phase. Look at this article. Mr. Gregson, a popular prizefighter, posed in the nude for two hours in front of the 'masterpiece that is believed to be the god Dionysus.' "

"And here is a piece about Mrs. Siddons coming to see the marbles and swooning—swooning—for the sight of them! Oh, these actresses should confine their performances to the stage."

"I imagine your Emma Hamilton will be performing her dances there soon," Robert said.

"She is not 'my' Mrs. Hamilton, thank you. And I do not think she is performing anywhere these days, poor dear. I have been invited to a dinner in London given by her friends, at which time they intend to ask the guests to contribute to her welfare. The poor thing is quite broke, in the wake of the deaths of Lord Nelson and Sir William."

"And will you attend?"

"As likely as you attending one of Elgin's boxing matches. I am invited only because I am the scandalous woman du jour," Mary said.

"Yes, a scandalous woman with the rare distinction of having money."

Mary did not say so, but she wished she might help Emma Hamilton, who seemed perennially in need of funds. But Mary had her own misfortunes to occupy her these days.

"Oh, this is rich. Some swooning artist took one of his peers, a Swede, to see the marbles. The man lost control of himself on the drive back, shouting, 'The Greeks were de gods,' " Robert said, laughing so hard that he had to blow his nose on his handkerchief before he could finish the reading the piece aloud. " 'The overly excited artists drove headlong along the Strand, upsetting an oncoming coal cart and a flock of sheep.'

"It appears, however, that the government is siding with the Society of Dilettanti, rather than the swooning artists," Robert continued. "They've made Elgin an offer for the statues of thirty thousand pounds."

"Why, that's an insult!' Mary said. True, she despised Elgin and all of his endeavors, but her own sweat and money were in those pieces of marble. She had seen to them from the very beginning of Elgin's desire to copy and mold them all the way through the acquisition of the actual pieces, and then through the effort to raise them from the bottom of the sea. She was incensed, on Elgin's behalf and on her own—and on behalf of the magnificent treasures themselves, the unwitting immigrants to Great Britain, standing silently while the government that now might lord it over them served up this kind of insult.

"I am sure that the government's agents are using the words of the Society of Dilettanti to push Elgin to accept the low offer."

"Has he accepted?" Mary asked.

"Apparently he turned them down. Parliament has another scheme, though. Some members are questioning whether or not he actually owns the sculptures, whether he obtained them legally."

Again, Mary felt a confusion of emotions rise up inside her. "I obtained that firman myself from the Sultan! Of course he obtained them legally. Does our government think that the British ambassador to the Porte would run about the territory stealing?"

"Apparently they do, or at least they are raising the point. Certain Grecian scholars have published letters against the acquisitions. Surely you are aware of that?"

"Yes, yes," she said wearily, not even sure anymore whose side she was on in the matter.

"I'm afraid that this puts to rest our scheme for laying claim to the marbles, Mary. At this point, Elgin is out of funds, completely bankrupt and in debilitating debt. He would probably be eternally grateful to you if you took custody of the statues."

Mary felt her body go limp. She had rallied her spirits, thinking that she'd finally found a way to outsmart him and to reclaim her rights to her children. She was once again defeated, knowing that she had to gather her energy for the horrible, public fight ahead. "Elgin has nothing to lose now. He is like those pugilists boxing at Park Lane. I do not know if I have the skill to duck the punches thrown by a wild and desperate man."

Robert was instantly at her side. "We shall get through all of this, Mary. I am here with you, and soon you will be free of the tyrant, and we shall be married. That is when life is going to begin."

"My only consolation now is his pain and his disgrace. He cannot pay for that house on Park Lane. He cannot even pay for his own house, which he once thought to make into the height of baronial grandeur. Whoever acquires the marbles will have to pay for the transport because Elgin cannot do it. Oh, I can just hear his evil scheming mind roiling and toiling to find a solution to his many problems. The marbles are now his grand albatross. My hope is that he puts one end of a rope around his neck and the other around the enormous horse's head from the pediment, and both sink together into the sea."

In the city of Edinburgh,

March 11, 1808

I T WO U L D H A V E B E E N their ninth wedding anniversary. Instead, it was the day that Thomas Bruce, Lord Elgin, was suing his wife, Lady Mary Elgin, for divorce in an Edinburgh court of law on grounds of adultery, intending to prove—her lawyers had discovered—that she was so immoral, so loose, so lacking in judgment, so immature, and so suggestible where handsome men were concerned that she was unfit, not only to care for her four children, but to care for the vast sums of money and many acres of land she was to inherit from her family.

When Elgin's true motivation came to light, Mary could only slap herself on the forehead and mutter, "Of course!" It was money— the one thing Elgin had always sought from his alliance with Mary Nisbet. People didn't change. It was a cliché, but it was true. Elgin could find other women to bear more children carrying his name, but he would need Mary's fortune to transform himself from a disfigured and disgraced fallen aristocrat into a desirable catch.

"Do not forget that he needs your money to be able to hang on to those marbles until the British government finally admits what they are worth," Robert said. "Without the funds, he'll be forced into giving them away, which is what Parliament wants, don't you know?"

Mary knew it would be a grim day, but she felt a small sense of satisfaction when she awoke and saw that the weather was inclement. Rain poured down, embittering an already unseasonably cold spring. She remembered how Elgin suffered in the damp weather, and she smiled.

The rain did not stop the crowds. She arrived with her parents at the courthouse, where urchins selling newspapers stood under umbrellas, hawking out the headlines. "Lord Elgin sues Adulterous Lady for Divorce. Details of Her Affairs Chronicled Inside!"

Inside the courtroom, twenty-one grim-faced male jurors, each old enough to be her grandfather, were seated. Their white wigs sat atop undoubtedly bald heads, their pinched faces stared ahead solemnly at nothing. She tried to meet their eyes, careful not to smile at them for fear of being proclaimed a tart who tried to use her sexual powers to sway them.

She almost gasped when Elgin entered the courtroom. He looked older, much older. He had taken to wearing a new mask, the other one perhaps become too small for his widening face. His once-taut body had turned soft at the middle, and his quite correct posture had turned into a resigned slump. She almost felt sorry for him. No, she reminded herself, this is the man who is trying to destroy you. Pity will not do. And yet she was torn between gloating over his much-diminished appearance and her memory of how handsome he had once been.

It was one thing to prepare to hear vicious and untrue things said about oneself; it was another entirely to go through the experience of hearing them said. As Mary watched witness after witness called by the prosecution, she felt as if she were attending a tableau of her past, some macabre theatrical production in which she was the unwitting main character who had yet to appear onstage. They were all assembled, all the servants who had worked for the Elgins during their marriage—Duff, Mary Ruper, and Thomas Willey, the footman Mary had fired in London for drunken misconduct, among others. The whole cast was lined up, ready to breach all manner of trust. Elgin's attorney had even managed to drag a deposition out of poor Miss Gosling in the last days before that good lady died. Numerous employees who had gone to Constantinople with the newlyweds were on hand to give witness to the disintegration of Lady Elgin's feelings for her husband.

The opening statement by one of Elgin's lawyers was an endless recap of the marriage, focusing on the ardor and warmth the noble personage Lord Elgin brought to the union, recounting their days in Turkey, and taking their story all the way through Elgin's imprisonment in France. The lawyer presented such a delightful picture of blissful marriage that Mary wondered when, if ever, he would begin to address the charges against her. She needn't have worried. The trial against Robert and the conviction for criminal conversation was soon enough invoked.

Elgin's lawyer began his case by reading the testimonies given by Hamilton, Morier, and others at the trial in London. Mary wished she had read the pamphlets that Robert had brought home. He'd been right; if she had already read these horrible things, she would have been immune to the unique feeling of sitting through the awful impressions that others were made to give about her marriage and her behavior within it.

To her astonishment, most of it centered on the disappearance of Elgin's nose.

Everyone in their employ had assumed—incorrectly so—that once Elgin's nose had been removed by the doctor, surely Lady Elgin had become repulsed by him.

"It has already been proven in an English court of law that Mr. Robert Ferguson in fact seduced by degrees and in such a way as to especially suit the innocent and naïve character of Lady Elgin. The noble plaintiff was misrepresented to his wife by Mr. Ferguson, who attacked his public and private conduct and made him, in his wife's eyes, a victim of scorn and disgust. Oh, unhappy woman!" he said, as if reciting a monologue from one of Mr. Shakespeare's tragedies. "How little she must have foreseen that she would be making her children orphans and entailing upon them such miserable consequences!"

At that point, Mary's lawyer came forward. "Sir, please contain your theatrics, which may be appropriate for the London theater, but not for a courtroom in the fair city of Edinburgh." This brought a wave of snickers from the audience, but soon everyone was silenced by the reading of the testimony of Mr. William Hamilton, former secretary to Lord Elgin. Mr. Hamilton attested to the happy marriage between the Elgins, until "Lord Elgin contracted a severe ague which consequently resulted in the loss of his nose. At that point, the lady's interest in His Lordship began to wane. Even prior to this, Lord Elgin had complained of his wife's adolescent predilection for flirtation with handsome men." Hamilton went on to list the names of General O'Hara at Gibraltar, Count Sébastiani, and even Mr. Lusieri, the painter. And, of course, Mr. Ferguson. The testimony detailed how Elgin had sent Hamilton to London to spy on Mary, observing who went in and out of the house, and what letters were delivered. "Lord Elgin always harbored suspicions of his wife's conduct where men were concerned."

Mary wanted to rise to her feet and defend herself. In London she had been suffering terribly before and after Lucy's birth, but still working to free Elgin from prison. Robert was often present, but he too was using all of his connections to aid Elgin's cause.

But she could not speak out in her own defense. She had been told that it was unthinkable that a lady should stand up in a court of law and defend herself. Better leave that to the gentlemen lawyers. It would be unseemly for her to speak. The more she was seen as reserved and demure, the better off she would be when the jury was debating the outcome. "Better to be silent and regal, Lady Elgin. That way, no criticism can be leveled against you. Whereas if you speak, they will all find fault in something that you say, no matter what it is that you have said or how you have said it."

Servant after servant from the days in London was called, and Mary wondered who had paid for all of them to travel to Edinburgh for the trial. What expense Elgin was going through to do this to her! But none had much to say except that Miss Gosling, poor dead lady's maid to Mary, had disapproved of a married lady receiving a gentleman not her husband late into the evening. Thus far, no one had seen anything that would damn Mary for adultery.

Then a gossipy chambermaid, along with the waiter from Fortune and Blackwell's Hotel in Edinburgh, whom Mary recognized as the man who'd served her and Robert on the evening they were there, testified that Mary and Robert had taken rooms in the hotel at the same time. The chambermaid said that it had appeared that Robert's bed had not been slept in, whereas both pillows in Mary's bed had been utilized. The waiter confirmed that the girl had shared this scandalous news with him at the time.

During a recess, Mary's lawyer tried to console her. "I realize that it must be mortifying for Your Ladyship to have to listen to this tripe. But I wonder if his lawyer will ever be able to substantiate the charges. A thing so serious as adultery does not hinge on the condition of a pillow!"

As their last witness, Elgin's lawyer called Thomas Willey, the former footman discharged by the Elgins for his unreliable behavior when he was at the drink. Mary barely remembered anything about him save that he was lazy and indifferent toward his job, and always had red eyes and a runny nose.

"Oh yes, Mr. Ferguson was in the habit of frequently calling on Her Ladyship, both day and night, while she resided at Baker Street, often coming very late in the evening and staying until two or three in the morning. Lady Elgin was always happier in his company than in the company of any other. On one of these occasions, at about noon, I went into the drawing room about six weeks after Lady Elgin had delivered the little girl, and opened the door without knocking. I saw Lady Elgin lying at full length on the sofa, and upon my coming in, both Lady Elgin and Mr. Ferguson got hold of a shawl and threw it over Lady Elgin's legs."

"Were Her Ladyship's petticoats up?" asked Elgin's lawyer in a thunderous voice so that no one could miss his words.

Willey stammered, clearly embarrassed. Or was that part of his act? "I could not positively say. A little writing table stood in front of the sofa, which prevented me from seeing whether or not Her Ladyship's legs were covered. However, from the confused way that the shawl was thrown over her, I would have to say that, indeed, her petticoats must have been up!"

That was all that the jury needed to hear. Mary could feel the mood in the room begin to change. The jurors, who had occasionally sent curious glances Mary's way, would no longer look at her at all, so sullied a woman was she. It was as if she had suddenly disappeared. This was how life was going to be now. In the eyes of the society of which she had been a member all the days of her life, she was now a ghost to be looked through if encountered in public. Yet she would not be afforded any of the respect that one generally gave to the dead. Her living body would be flesh for the vultures of the world to feed upon as they liked, food for cruel gossip, both in print and around dinner tables and card tables in the cities that she had loved to frequent. She knew this as surely as she knew that she was sitting in the courtroom, and she felt herself die inside.

Only Elgin had the audacity to look her way. He was calm and smug, letting a tiny smile show on his lips to demonstrate how much he was enjoying burying her in the eyes of respectable society. She stared back at him, mortified at her own gall, until he turned away.

Satisfied that he had indelibly stained Mary's reputation, the lawyer turned to his true goal—listing the properties that Mary would inherit from her family and elaborating on how a woman so irresponsible must not be allowed to control such vast assets.

Though Mary remained silent, her attorneys argued well in her stead.

"Here is a list of Lord Elgin's debts compiled throughout the length of the marriage, and here is the evidence of Lady Elgin's payment of those expenditures," one of them said. He went on to read lengthy descriptions of Elgin's extravagant purchases intended to decorate his home, or "merely purchased out of boredom, or to improve his mood on that particular day."

The bankers, called in Mary's defense, did not disappoint, making it clear that on several occasions she'd had to take control of his finances rather than see him flee the country or be summoned to debtors' prison.

Finally, the list of assets controlled by Mary was to be presented to the court.

"You may approach the bench with your papers," the judge said.

"But there is no paper to present, Your Honor," said her counsel.

"What games are you playing here, sir? I demand that you submit the documents verifying the defendant's assets."

"But, sir, if I may, the defendant has no assets. She is under the age of thirty. She has not inherited a penny. Much to Lord Elgin's dismay, I am sure, you may see for yourself that Mr. Nisbet is alive and well and seated in the courtroom next to his daughter. I'm afraid that while this is true, Lady Elgin has no control over any aspect of her projected inheritance. The law states that a husband may have control over his wife's assets. Nowhere does the law state that the husband's rights extend to control over his father-in-law's estate!"

It took the jury no time at all to deliberate. Lord Elgin was granted his divorce on grounds of adultery. Lady Elgin was to forfeit all rights and privileges associated with the marriage, now terminated, including the custody of her children. No financial remuneration was awarded to Lord Elgin, since under the law, Lady Elgin had no fortune to give.

Mr. Nisbet tried to shield his daughter under his arm as he escorted her out of the courthouse. No one spoke to them. They walked toward their carriage in muffled silence. Mary knew that around her, people were talking. Newsmen who had attended the trial hurried away to file their lurid stories. She heard footsteps, and the slight patter of rain, as her father hurried her away from the building. Suddenly she threw his arm off her shoulder and stood erect. She stopped walking and turned her face up toward the sky. Her father had walked ahead of her, but he turned when he realized that Mary had stopped. He waved his hand to hurry her, rush her along so that she would not have to speak to anyone who dared utter a word in her direction.

She stood still, looking around. Everyone stood back from her, watching in astonishment as the shamed woman remained, against all reason, in the light of day, refusing to hide herself away as she should. Elgin walked out of the courtyard, talking to his lawyer and someone who looked like a journalist, some scruffy man with stained fingers and old spectacles. Elgin stopped when he saw Mary, and she looked at him and refused to turn away. She would let him gaze upon her for the last time, knowing that he had done the very worst to her now, and she would never have to look at him again, especially not on top of her, where he'd had the most power to do her harm. With that thought, she actually smiled at him.

Elgin made a move toward her. He looked as if he were having an automatic reaction to her smile; as if all the events of the past two years had dropped away, and he was responding to the pleasant look that he had seen so many times on his wife's face. But before he could advance, his lawyer hooked his arm through Elgin's to stop him. Mary continued to stare until it dawned on Elgin that her smile was one of triumph over his domination. He had tried to vanquish her, but the worst had happened and here she was, still standing, with a gentle spring rain falling on her face. When he realized that she was not going to stop smiling, he turned away.

Though her heart was broken, a small voice inside of her spoke, urging her to taste that part of the ordeal from which she had emerged victorious. Elgin had wounded her to the core by taking away her children. He had won that battle, but surely that arrangement could not last. She would continue to besiege him with requests to restore them to her. He had tried to deliver a mortal wound, but though he almost succeeded, he did not take away the one thing that she had left, which was almost as precious as her children, and that was her ultimate authority over her own body. Of that vessel, which enclosed the heart that she would now give to Robert, and of the fortune she would inherit that Elgin wanted so desperately, she would remain in control.

In the city of Athens,
in the first year of the
war with Sparta

WHEN OUR BOY WAS born, Perikles insisted upon
having the traditional ceremony to celebrate his birth.
In the agora, in front of a goodly number of the influential
citizens of Athens, Perikles held the child up, high above his
head, for all to see—the acknowledgment that he accepted
him as his son. It was a stunning gesture for the father of a bastard to make. The boy was irresistible, with his big hazel eyes
and full head of curly hair, head coming to a point just like his
father's to emphasize paternity. He looked more like Perikles
than did his two legitimate sons, so the father had an automatic
and instantaneous affection for the infant. At the ceremony,
much to my surprise, he announced that he was naming the
child after himself.

"His name shall be Perikles. He is the son of a general, and a
grandson of Xanthippus, hero of the Battle of Mykale against
the Persians."

Giving the boy his own name was more than a signal to

Athens that Perikles acknowledged the child; it was a challenge to the Athenians to accept the boy too.

We had had no time to celebrate my acquittal. Soon after the trial, the Spartans started to express displeasure over an alliance that Perikles had made with Korkyra, that island on the eastern side of Greece named after a beautiful sea nymph. Korkyra was a colony belonging to Korinth, a longtime ally of Sparta. The Spartans found the alliance unacceptable and sent a delegation to tell the Athenians to leave Korkyra. But Perikles would not back down, and eventually Sparta launched a military incursion, breaking the so-called Thirty-Year Truce long before its term expired.

On our son's first birthday, the first of the heroes who had perished in the war were brought back to the city. Instead of rejoicing over the fact that our son had survived the year free of the feared diseases of infancy, we were spending our days working on the oration that Perikles would deliver at the funeral for the war dead, a speech that would have to both properly commemorate the fallen men and garner support for the undoubtedly long war ahead. Athens and Sparta each considered itself, its military capacities, and its way of life supreme, and neither showed a sign of backing down.

The speech for the war dead was actually required by law. A vote was taken as to who would deliver it, and this time Perikles won unanimously. Over time, the speech had become a conventional litany of praise. But Perikles was determined that this speech would not be another predictable review of the valorous Athenians of the past, followed by praise for recent casualties of war.

"Their glory should not be dependent on my eloquence," Perikles had said to me as he was composing it. "Instead of employing the usual eulogistic conventions, I want this speech to reflect Athenian values, the highest of which is moderation. I will not succumb to the temptation to give excessive praise, yet heroes cannot be shortchanged."

"Then you must have a specific strategy," I said. "What is

it that you wish the speech to convey, besides honoring the dead?"

He thought about this for a long time, retreating into his private room and not coming out for hours. Finally, he surfaced. "I want the people of Athens to look upon the city we have built, and know what these men have died for."

With that in mind, he easily composed his address, reading it aloud to me, while I made suggestions for its improvement. When he had a final version, he read it to me, with a look of complete self-satisfaction. I shrugged.

"Does it not please you, Aspasia?" he asked incredulously.

"Oh, it pleases me," I replied. He could tell that I was taunting him.

"Do you find it just another oration in praise of a city that is bloated with praise? Is that how it hits the ear of the resident alien?"

"I have lived here long enough to call it my home, Perikles. No, I do not feel that you have overpraised your city. I wonder, though, if the audience will include the widows and mothers of the dead. Do you not want to say anything to them? You end your speech by advising the men to continue on and seek glory. What would you say to the women of the fallen heroes?"

"The women?" He paced about, thinking, swatting a fly away from his head. "Why must I address the women?"

"If I had lost my husband or son in battle, I would like to hear words of advice and consolation too," I answered. Our baby was asleep in a basket in the corner of the room. "Do we not deserve a kind word?"

"Yes, yes, of course," he said hastily, though I could tell that he wished I had not brought up this bothersome subject. He had finished with his speech and was pleased.

"I have it," he said. "I shall say the following: And now, if I must speak of female excellence to those of you who are widows, great will be your glory in living up to your natural character, and greatest of all shall be she who is least talked of among men, whether for good or for bad."

I frowned. "So that is it? You are exhorting the men to seek honor and the women to seek anonymity? That is hardly inspiring, Perikles. Do the women not deserve something more to guide them through the years of suffering ahead?"

"Have not your own experiences made you long for anonymity?" he replied. "I might have lost my mind thinking that I could not protect you from the harm that was coming your way, Aspasia. Do you not see? Women must be protected. You are the vessels of the future."

"But must we also be silent?"

"I am not arguing for silence. I am merely asking the women of Athens, in these troubling times, to refrain from behavior that might earn them infamy."

"Why is infamy ruinous to a woman, whereas it seems to enhance the reputation of a man?"

"Why did I have to fall in love with a philosopher?" he retorted. "There is no answer to your question, Aspasia. It's the way things are. Perhaps you could take up a deeper inquiry with your friend Sokrates. He seems overly eager to spill words on matters of this sort."

THE ATHENIANS BUILT A grand tent, a pavilion to compete with the Odeion, on the hillside beneath the Akropolis for the funeral ceremony. For three days, the bones of the dead had been laid out in cypress coffins—one for each tribe—so that friends and relatives could bring offerings. After so many days, the tent was piled with donations, which the families of the fallen could either bury with them or keep in homage to their memories. After the eulogy, a military escort would lead the procession to the cemetery. This torch-lit pageant would take place at sunset, a sacred time for returning a body to rest in the earth.

Perikles stepped up to a podium built high above the crowd so that the thousands of Athenians who had gathered to honor the slain soldiers might hear him. Women wearing long veils—undoubtedly the widows, mothers, and sisters of the dead—held hands, softly wailing against the louder cater-wauling of the professional mourners. Men beat drums, and military pipers played their mournful songs. A long phalanx of foot soldiers stood guard around the tent, their bright shields resting at their sides. The scene felt like something from the ancient days, the Age of the Heroes, as if the gods were still walking the earth, mingling with men, and at any moment Athena would appear on the hillside in her armor and bellow her stunning war cry.

As soon as Perikles raised his hands, all were brought to silence.

Out of respect and as a concession to tradition, he began his speech with a tribute to the ancestors. "For it was they who handed from generation to generation this society, kept free for us by their valor. I am speaking of our remote ancestors as much as of our own fathers, who spared no pains to be able to leave it to the present generation. But, Athenians, that part of our history that dwells on our military achievements is too familiar for me to elaborate on here today, and I shall therefore pass over it. Our form of government and the national habits and national character out of which it sprang are the subject I wish to dwell upon, so that you citizens, or any foreigners, may listen and learn.

"Athenians! Our constitution does not copy laws of other states. We are the innovators, not imitators. Our administration favors the many, not the privileged few, and that is why it is called a democracy. Unlike in other societies, in Athens no one is held back from government for lack of wealth. The poorest and most humble citizen is free to speak his mind at the Assembly, or to hold office, or to vote. Athenians are free and generous and live in an open society, where class does not interfere with merit, and where a man may do what he likes and not fear the anger of his neighbor, because he is free. And yet we are not lawless. We are safeguarded by the laws—written and unwritten—and the magistrates who protect the injured."

I remembered our discussion when he wrote these words. "How do you feel about Athenian law, having been prosecuted before the entire city?" he had asked.

"Another society might have murdered a woman who aroused suspicions or who others had deemed to have insulted the gods. It is commonly heard of in other places," I'd said. "I spoke in my defense, as did you, and I was acquitted. I could have suffered a worse fate."

But here I was, a free woman, the mother of a beautiful boy and the lover of the leader of this civilization whose virtues were being extolled. As I looked at Perikles standing in the shadows of the great monuments that he and Pheidias had dreamed up and convinced the citizens to allow them to build, I was struck with awe for all that had been accomplished in the years since I had landed on these shores.

"Athenians," Perikles was saying now, "think on our uniqueness among men. We have created thriving businesses, but we provide plenty of means to refresh ourselves from our labors. We have recreation and games and contests for all to enjoy. We live great and harmonious lives of pleasure in private splendor. We cultivate refinement and knowledge. The magnitude of our city draws the luxuries of the world into our harbor. We throw our city open to the world, and never do we exclude foreigners from learning or observing here. Contrast this with Sparta, which drives foreigners out, values only military prowess, and lives in suspicion of others. Athens is a lesson for all of Greece, indeed all the world, both today and in the future. As a city, we are a school for others.

"This is what these brave men have died for. Those of you who are still among the living must go on to seek honor, for it is honor rather than gain that gives one comfort in old age. Only love of honor never grows old."

Perikles was now reaching the crescendo of his speech.

"Look upon your city, Athenians, and become lovers of Athens."

He raised his right arm to the sky and then dramatically flung it in the direction of the Parthenon, whose growing shadow seemed to creep toward him. "The admiration of the present and succeeding ages will be ours because we have not left our power without witness. Here are the mighty proofs. Far from needing a Homer or others whose verses might charm for the moment, we have left behind us these imperishable monuments, purchased for us with these very lives.

"Such is the Athens for which these men, in their resolve not to lose her and all that she stands for, nobly fought and died. May their survivors too be ready in her cause."

As he finished his speech, I remembered what Diotima had said to me the night of our party, words that I had not apprehended until this moment. A man's greatest incentive is the love of glory. For that he will risk all. In the monuments, Perikles had earned the eternal glory that his soul had longed for. Sokrates had said that Diotima was the master of the Philosophy of Love, which, as she dissected it, was vastly different from the Philosophy of Domestic Relations, which I had been developing. The former appeared to be rooted in earthly life, but was a mere gesture toward what men were truly seeking: immortality. The latter was firmly fixed in daily life, which seemed to be women's domain. Should women also seek the sort of glory that men pursue? I desired to live free of restrictions, but I did not concern myself with whoever would remember me after my life was over. What did it matter to me who would evoke the name of Aspasia once I was mingling with the shades? I did not fathom how the echo of my name upon the earth would improve the quality of the life I was in the throes of leading.

Yet it seemed a pity that my name would die with me, unattached as it was to glorious monuments, but only to the man who built them. I looked up. The fading sun cast a reddish glow over the white marble of the Parthenon, momentarily breaking its aura of Olympian calm. It was true, what Diotima had said. The monument would long outlast us, our son, and everyone else who at this moment stood in its shadow. The Parthenon belonged to eternity, much like the souls of the men who had died to save her and all that she represented.

Perikles had finished his speech and was bowing his head in appreciation of the crowd's applause. The soldiers were lighting the torches to escort their fallen comrades to their final resting place. Families of the dead surrounded the tent, pouring libations into the earth. It seemed that the very skies were now ignited and the encroaching night air carried with it the smell of death. Rather than rejoin his people, Perikles turned away from ceremony and walked up the pathway to the Parthenon, where he alone would pray to Athena to guide his hand as we faced the troubled times ahead.

In the city of London,

in the year 1816

SHE TOOK A HACKNEY into Bloomsbury rather than rely on her private carriage. She wore plain clothes and went alone, during regular museum hours, hoping that no one would recognize her. Whom she might run into on Great Russell Street, she could not imagine, but London society was small indeed, and one had to be careful. Ironically, she had not visited the museum since she'd gone there with Elgin in the first days of their marriage— those few days together in London as happy newlyweds before they departed for Constantinople—to see the exotic objects collected by Captain James Cook in the South Sea Islands. Cook had explored the islands with Sir Joseph Banks, who many years later would help free Elgin from French captivity. The only indulgence she had allowed herself while dressing today was that she had dabbed some of the rose cologne the Capitan Pasha had given her so many years before on her wrists. She inhaled the sweet smell now, remembering how delighted she had been to receive his gifts.

The driver stopped in front of the museum, and she asked him wait for her. "I shan't be long, I assure you," she said.

The museum had been expanded since she'd last seen it, to accommodate the many treasures that had come pouring in from the corners of the earth. She had made it a point to discover in advance where the marbles were located. She did not want to attract any attention to herself during the visit.

Elgin, crushed by his ever-mounting debts, had sold them, finally, for a pittance. She still despised him, certainly, for keeping her beloved children away from her all these years, but each time she remembered his original sentiments, she felt a tinge of—what was it? Irony?—considering what had been his fate. Rather than being the hero of British arts, he was a man reviled. Lord Byron, the lame poet who wandered through Greece using, of all people, an unsuspecting Lusieri as his guide, had excoriated Elgin in his recently published epic poem *Childe Harold's Pilgrimage* as the bandit who delivered the final insult to an already enslaved Greek population by his rape of Athena and her temple.

Patience! and ye shall hear what he beheld
In other lands, where he was doom'd to go:
Lands that contain the monuments of Eld,
Ere Greece and Grecian arts by barbarous hands were quell'd.

Of the thousands of readers who eagerly consumed Byron's poem, none questioned to whom those barbarous hands belonged. For long stanzas, Byron bemoaned the fate of the Golden Age of Athens, reviling those British hands that had desecrated the monuments. Many had taken up Byron's point of view, making a demon of Elgin for what he'd done. Parliament had put Elgin through excruciating hearings to determine whether he had procured the marbles legally, and then paid him a fraction of what they had cost Elgin—and Mary—to collect. Mary had also heard that Elgin's appearance had grown so horrible that he lived a life of seclusion—and a bitter one too, she guessed. Let no one say that Mary Ferguson did not have presentiments, she thought. Nemesis' curse upon Elgin had proved to be more than fantasy.

But here she was, thirty-eight years old, married to her heart's companion, in control of her lands and her money, considered still very beautiful, and beloved by many for both her skill in entertaining and her acts of philanthropy. She pined for her children every day, but the grief was somewhat palliated by her loving relationship with Robert's son, Henry, by his former mistress. She and Robert had decided that Henry would not be hidden away like some embarrassment, but brought fully into their lives. He was a delightful boy, and a great comfort to a mother who'd lost her own dear ones.

Mary made her way to the room that housed the marbles. She thought that she would be able to see them on her own—somehow, she wanted privacy with them, these statues that had made such an impact on her life—but several young artists were there with sketchbooks, transfixed before the great statues, drawing furiously.

The statues were scattered about, with the two pediment configurations loosely pieced together as they might have appeared on the Parthenon. The frieze was partially reconstructed, though not in the order in which Mary had seen it before it was taken down, and the metopes had been hung on the walls, propped on heavy wooden stands. She walked up to the statue of the reclining Dionysus and touched it.

"Strange how and where we have all ended our days," she said aloud, touching the cool, gray marble.

"Excuse me?" One of the young men sketching had apparently thought that Mary was speaking to him.

She looked down at his sketchbook. He had been standing in front of the great headless female figure with drapery clinging to her lovely form, sketchbook in hand. "May I ask what you are doing?" she said.

"I am trying to learn from the techniques of Pheidias," he said. "Though with mixed results. I cannot capture the way in which he was able to demonstrate the subtleties of the female form beneath her drapery, and in stone, no less. I cannot do it with charcoal."

"Don't be discouraged," Mary said. "You are very young. An artist needs time to develop. I am sure that Pheidias required some time too. I believe these sculptures were made in the prime of his life, after he had created many opulent things."

"Thank you, madam. I shall think of your encouraging words when I return to my studio to try to improve this rendering of his Athena."

"Oh no, that is not Athena. That is undoubtedly the messenger goddess Iris, announcing Athena's birth from the head of her father. That was the subject of the eastern pediment of the Parthenon, from which this particular statue came."

"Madam, you are familiar with the pieces?"

"Oh yes, I saw them in their place of origin. I must say that they look lonely and out of place here in this dark, musty room rather than under the splendid Greek sunlight. Though they do retain their grandeur. I suppose nothing can ultimately diminish them."

"We are privileged to be in their company," the artist said. "Though Lord Elgin, who is responsible for their appearance on these shores, has been much criticized for his actions. Lord Byron has done him great harm."

"Yes, he has, and it is not entirely just," she said, amazed to find herself all these years later jumping to Elgin's defense. But she had played her own part in the story, and she was defending herself too, though the young man would never know that. "Perhaps Socrates was correct in his assessment of the poets—that they are verbose flatterers who move only women, children, and slaves. In any case, we should not wholly take the word of a drunken, opium-smoking poet as the ultimate truth."

"I, for one, though it may seem selfish, am delighted to be able to sit before these masterpieces," he said.

He spoke with the reverence and earnestness of youth. Mary longed for the days when she too had had such leanings.

"Lord Elgin is criticized, but I assure you that if he had not rescued them, they would by now be ground to bits for ammunition by the Turkish soldiers occupying the Acropolis, or hacked off and sold in pieces to travelers with money to spend. Or used to build newer, rude housing. I saw those degradations with my own eyes." Mary saw that she was growing in the young man's esteem.

"I hear the Scottish lilt in your voice," he said. "Are you acquainted with Lord Elgin?"

"No, just a once-curious traveler with a taste for history. I'll tell you something. If Lord Elgin had not salvaged these treasures, Napoleon might have gotten them, and Lord Byron might be writing accusatory poems about the French!"

"I am John Fitzwilliam, madam. It has been a privilege to make your acquaintance, Mrs. . . ." The young man leaned forward, waiting for Mary to introduce herself.

"It has been lovely to talk to you," she said. "My sincerest wishes for the success of your artistic endeavors." And she walked away.

Better to remain anonymous, she thought. After her brush with infamy, she was happy to have retired into a quieter life. Perhaps Pericles had been correct in the end, advising the women of Athens to live in a manner that guaranteed anonymity. Though she had played a crucial role in helping her husband remove these ancient treasures, she had never sought any credit for what she had done, or any of the glory that Elgin had futilely chased for his contribution to the British arts. And thanks to that, no one was writing nasty poems indicting her.

Yet the marbles were not only a touchstone to a glorious past, they were also a touchstone to her personal past. She was indelibly a part of their history now, though she would be just as happy if no recognition for her deeds ever came her way. In years to come, after she was gone and all those who knew her had also ceased to exist, would anyone think to wonder what had become of her? It was highly unlikely. Perhaps she, like Pericles' mistress, Aspasia, who had not heeded his advice to the women of Athens, would simply disappear from the record.

She laughed at her morose thoughts. Was it any use pondering those who were long dead? Or even what would become of her own reputation after she was gone? How it could suffer more than when she was alive, she did not know.

The still air in the room had become oppressive. It was unseasonably warm for a September day, and Mary longed to get back out into the fresh air. Enough truck with the past. What was it that her old nanny used to say? *Life is fer tha living.* She took one last look at the marbles, those symbols of the world upon which her own world had been built. The reclining nude seemed to be saying goodbye to her. Was it the god Dionysus? Or the personification of a river? She could not remember, though she would never forget the marbles themselves. She straightened her hat, nodded again to the young artist who was still staring at her, and went outside to find her waiting coach.

THE FATES OF OUR CHARACTERS

Mary Nisbet, Countess of Elgin, married **Robert Ferguson** in 1808. They inherited enormous estates and turned Raith House into one of the great salons of the day, entertaining scientists, artists, aristocrats, and other luminaries. Mary's children grew up despising her, but after fourteen years she reunited with Lord Bruce, who was in terrible health, suffering from epilepsy and other illnesses. He died in 1840. Mary's daughters did not see her for thirty years, but managed to reconcile with her in 1835. Robert continued as a respected scientist and a reformer, discovering a mineral that was named for him, fergusonite. He died in 1840 at the age of seventy-one. Mary retained her high spirits all of her life. She hosted a huge party on June 30, 1855, and died nine days later at the age of seventy-seven. Still embarrassed by the charges of adultery against their mother, Mary's heirs buried her in an unmarked grave, anonymous until a sympathetic descendant inscribed it in 1916.

In 1810, **Lord Elgin** married Elizabeth Oswald, a young woman half his age, who bore him eight more children. His debts continued to mount, and he and Elizabeth fled to France to avoid the creditors. His children by Mary remained in the care of his mother.

Elgin died in Paris in 1841, leaving his family encumbered with his debts, which they were not able to pay in full for another thirty-four years. Despite his miserable health, he lived to be seventy-five years old.

Emma Hamilton never recovered from Lord Nelson's death. Nelson's legal wife outwitted Emma for his fortune, and Emma bankrupted herself trying to maintain the home she and Nelson had shared. William Hamilton's male relations inherited his money, and Emma, accustomed to the high life, overspent until she had to flee to France to avoid her creditors. She died in Calais of cirrhosis of the liver in 1815.

Within one year of delivering his famous funeral oration, **Pericles** died in a plague that swept through Athens. Before he died, he legitimized his son by Aspasia, known as **Pericles the Younger,** who rose to the rank of general but was executed in 406 BCE, along with six other generals, for his part in the loss of twenty-five Athenian ships to Sparta.

After Pericles died, **Aspasia** was said to have married or taken up with the shepherd Lysicles. The comic poets continued to abuse her as a prostitute and a dog-eyed whore for many decades to follow. Yet, according to Plutarch, under her wise counsel Lysicles became one of the first men of Athens. Though after this she drops from the historical record, we must wonder, along with Plutarch, "What art or charming faculty had she that enabled her to captivate the most powerful men of the state and gave philosophers occasion to speak of her at length and in terms that were exalted?"

According to Pausanias *(Description of Greece* 1.22.8), **Socrates,** the renowned philosopher, sculpted the figures of the Graces at the entrance to the Acropolis, following in the footsteps of his father, a stonemason. Later in life, Socrates was tried, like Aspasia, for impiety. The charges included ruining the morals of the young and believing in gods of his own making—his *daimon*—rather than state-ordained gods. He was convicted, and subsequently executed by willingly drinking hemlock. He died in 399 BCE, shy of his seventieth birthday.

Alcibiades, I should note, is not the handsome character of

Plato's dialogues, but that figure's grandfather. Our Alcibiades was ostracized from Athens in 460 BCE. On the basis of a newly discovered tomb inscription, Peter J. Bicknell has plausibly theorized that Alcibiades spent his exile in Miletus and returned to Athens with his bride, who was Aspasia's sister, and his sister-in-law in tow.

Our most prominent characters, **The Elgin Marbles,** or **The Parthenon Sculptures,** reside in the Duveen Gallery of the British Museum. The marbles remain at the center of an international controversy, argued freshly every year as the debate over who owns the world's ancient treasures rages on.

The Greek government has built a new Acropolis Museum, scheduled to open in 2008, with the express purpose of housing the marbles, should Greece succeed in recovering them.

AUTHOR'S NOTE

I have tried to remain as true to the historical facts as possible. Small variations were introduced in order to serve the narrative; for instance, though the other incidents of Lady Elgin's Greek tours are true, she was not actually present when the great cornice fell from the Parthenon, though fall it did. Otherwise, I have tried to place the characters in this book are, in fact, where the historical sources, or their own personal letters, declare them to have been.

Some ancient sources assert that Hermippus prosecuted Aspasia for impiety and procurement, and only Pericles' tears saved her. Contemporary scholars have argued over whether she was brought to trial or merely prosecuted in his plays. Pheidias, however, was accused of painting the faces of himself and Pericles into the shield of Athena, and of embezzling. Some sources say that he was acquitted, and some that he was convicted and died in prison. This is unlikely because he went on from Athens to sculpt the colossal statue of Zeus at Olympia. The idea that Aspasia posed for the face of Athena is my own invention.

As far as the spelling of names and places is concerned, I chose to use the more authentic Greek spellings of certain names when the story shifts to ancient times, and the Latinized spellings in the more recent story.

My apologies to the spirit of Aristophanes, master of Old Comedy, for adapting his play *The Acharnians,* in which he lampooned Aspasia, to suit my own purposes.

Thanks to my beloved stepfather, Clarence Machado, for his motto that life is for the living, and for his unyielding support.

I would like to acknowledge herewith the unprecedented research into Mary's life and her role in the story of the marbles presented by Susan Nagel in her beautifully written book, *Mistress of the Elgin Marbles: A Biography of Mary Nisbet, Countess of Elgin.*

Suggestions for further reading and an extensive bibliography can be found at my Web site: www.karenessex.com.